ELIZABETH PARKER
The mother, watching her daughters bear their heartbreak, dreading the telegram about her sons she knows must come . . .

ORIANA
The "good girl," working in a factory to do her part in the war that claimed her man . . .

LOUISE
The wild one, sending one husband off to war, and herself into the arms of a hundred other men . . .

RON and RANDY
The twins they all loved, the sensitive one and the "manly" one, surprised to discover their true natures in the fires of war . . .

SINCE YOU'VE BEEN GONE
An unforgettable novel of America at war by
Allison Kerry

Since You've Been Gone

ALLISON KERRY

A JOVE BOOK

SINCE YOU'VE BEEN GONE

A Jove book/published by arrangement with
the author

PRINTING HISTORY
Jove edition/June 1982

ISBN: 0-515-05493-3

PRINTED IN THE UNITED STATES OF AMERICA

My previous books have been dedicated to ladies, with cause and gratitude. But I also owe this one to a good friend, a good soldier:

Sergeant First Class Richard H. (Swami) Shriver, Combat medic, Americal Division, WW II; Combat infantry, Second Infantry Division, Korea

1921–1980

chapter 1

The White House announced today it had not softened its stand on the Japanese oil embargo, and repeated it would not be lifted until "the Japanese Empire renounces further aggression." Government spokesmen said Japanese oil reserves have been depleted by as much as 30 percent over the past few months. . . .

—*Coshocton Tribune*, December 6, 1941

The year slipped by so fast. Oriana hadn't gotten over Thanksgiving, and here were cardboard Santas bright along Main Street. It was a letdown time of year, no longer smoked and dreamy autumn, but snow still hoarded its clean covers. It should be a nice, snug time on the farm, with harvest, canning, and storing out of the way. But coming winter meant being housebound with her father-in-law, and that wasn't good.

She jiggled the windshield-wiper knob and the old GMC pickup rattled its bed in echo. Air tasted wet upon her lips, and she made a face at the dashboard's slicky feel. Sparing a look behind at the sacks, Oriana saw them still wrapped dry, and turned off on Elm to follow it out of Coshocton.

Mom would be glad for this surplus from the farm, although this long-past harvest, it wasn't much: potatoes, dry corn, and onions. And a little sack of pinto beans put by before Steve Canfield saw them, pumpkins he hadn't fed to the hogs, and gourds for next year's bee-martin nests. Mom really liked to have little birds around.

Sunday traffic was thin but for jalopies circling or parked at Torrance's, where all the kids hung out. Although several other drugstores served the town, generations of high-schoolers passed reverently through Torrance's. Back down the street, her father's hardware store was locked and her sister gone from its counters. Dad didn't need a clerk with business so bad, but Joyce needed a hand and Dad was glad to give it.

Jitterbugging kids bounced out onto Torrance's sidewalk, doing the Suzy-Q and trucking like crazy as they broke, laughing, for beat-up cars. Oriana caught a bright shard of jukebox music and a twinge of nostalgia. She could almost breathe the wondrous smells of Coke and malt, almost hear bubble-sucking straws. It had been a long time since she danced and acted crazy or slurped a soda.

Maybe it was longer for her sister. Joyce had always dreamed harder and longer. That was why she'd married a football star; cheerleaders were supposed to, according to the dream. But Joe Dayton didn't stick to the script and go to college, just into an alley garage.

Beeping the horn, Oriana waved at the widow Donovan in her church dress. It was greenish black and beaded, and Mrs. Donovan had been wearing it every Sunday as long as Oriana could remember.

Her brother-in-law might have made money with the shop his pa left, if he could forget being Coshocton High's best-ever fullback. Any fall afternoon you could find him at the school, giving the coach advice while work piled up at the garage. His drinking buddies took their jalopies to his house, where he fixed them for nothing.

Joyce hated all those clunkers around her place, and the house as well. Oriana didn't blame her. It was sagging, sad-windowed, and peeling, stuck off between a spur of the Penn Central Railroad and Oak Ridge Cemetery. Who wouldn't be depressed there, with freight trains shaking the house at all hours, layering everything with cinders and soot? And on the other side, grave grass and tombstones. Poor Joyce —she was always so pretty, with sparrow hair brownblack and glossy, that proud cheerleader body she was about to let slump. When her dreams broke against harsh reality, when she discovered that Joe Dayton's princely trappings were left forever in the gym and happy-ever-after was a lie, Joyce Parker Dayton came down hard.

Stopping at a red light, Oriana listened to the truck motor clank and strain, and smelled fried oil. Her father-in-law was too cheap to fix machinery until almost too late. He'd probably run this in to Joe Dayton before too long, leaning on family ties for a better deal.

Joe would give it to him, and Joyce would stay on at the store because of a hundred deals like it. The last time she'd coffeed with her sister, Joyce told her about that old cafe on Main, where an Italian family had failed to make a go of it. I swear, Joyce said, I looked through the window where gold letters are peeling off, and saw her, identified with her just like that.

With her? Oriana had asked. Who?

The mama spider in her web. She hung there by the NRA sticker, that old blue eagle thing, what you call it?

National Relief Administration; President Roosevelt's first idea to beat the Depression, Oriana said.

Yeah. Anyhow, it didn't help the spider. She didn't move when I hit the window, and I saw she was dead. She trapped all the flies trying to get out the window and she just kept waiting —for things that never flew, never came like they were supposed to—until she shriveled up. She did it all just right: built a pretty web, worked hard, did everything by the spider book. But no more flies came, and she hung there so damned *sad*. I bet she was glad she didn't lay any eggs.

Behind her a horn blasted, and Oriana jumped, let out the clutch, and took off on the green light. Kids in a topless Model A roared by, yelling at her. She knew a little of what Joyce felt, but not that bitterness. Clay Canfield was no Prince Charming, but she hadn't counted on one. He was a pretty nice guy and a good father and she was glad for him. If she knew a little about making webs, she'd throw one around Steve Canfield and haul the old man off somewhere and leave him. If not princely, Clay might be considerably more charming out of his father's shadow.

There was no real hurry getting to Mom's, she thought.

With luck, the truck would break down and she wouldn't have to hurry back to cook dinner at the farm. Steve Canfield didn't believe in days off for women. Across the bridge, she turned right along the river.

Idling the motor so the heater would run, Oriana parked on the bank of the Tuscarawas and lighted up. She still didn't smoke around Mom and Dad, and took this chance to kind of stock up. Because Steve smoked Wings, everybody in his house did; they were all he brought home and Oriana couldn't tell much difference, Lucky Strike, Twenty Grand, or whatever. Except for Spuds; they tasted all mediciney, like Mom smearing her chest with Vicks, which always rose into her eyes.

Joyce and Randy were careful about smoking around the folks, too, and Louise better not, she was so young. Ron was the only kid who did, and Oriana figured it was his way of irritating Dad; one other way, that was. She turned on the radio. Clayton had put it in before they were married. His father never would have. Tommy Dorsey's orchestra played "I'll Never Smile Again . . . Until I Smile at You."

Joyce's unhappy marriage had made her once-bright smile go rusty, unused, but she wasn't looking around for somebody else to smile at—not yet. Oriana smoked and hummed along with that new singer. He was good, but she didn't see why high-school girls acted so crazy over skinny Frank Sinatra. She'd take Crosby or Ray Eberly any time.

She meant to talk to Ron about bothering Dad. Gossip said that Ron had had a hand in setting that fire behind Sacred Heart, the night before Coshocton High's big game with the Crusaders. If Dad found out, there'd be another scene to make Mom upset and worried. She didn't want Ron leaving home, but that would be better all around.

Her brother could be such a bastard because he worked at it. He was a troublemaker and downright vicious, so that all the young men in town were scared of him. That included the fiancés and brothers of girls he seduced, so he kept getting away with that.

But Ron's twin—Oriana drew deeply upon the cigarette and sighed. Too gentle, he was kind and quiet and all the things his brother wasn't. The whole family was proud of Randy's scholarship to Kent State; he'd be the first Parker to go to college. So patient he was, long-suffering because he wasn't rowdy and didn't play football or try to go all the way with every girl in town. But he wasn't what they said; he wasn't perverted, only too gentle for his own good.

She twisted the cigarette into a damp metal ashtray and pushed the butt out through a barely lowered window. Shifting into reverse, she backed around to the road. So long as she was covering Parker problems, she couldn't skip little Louise. The girl had always been sassy, being the baby of the family and taking full advantage of it. But lately there was an undercurrent to her smartness, and her clothes were too tight, especially the sweaters. Oriana wondered if the kid was about to get into trouble. There was that feeling about her.

On the radio, Wayne King played it slow and sweet: "We Could Make Such Beautiful Music Together." So long as little Louise didn't think that meant everything the boys were after, or that schoolgirl-crush music would play on forever. Oriana frowned; Mom probably had told the kid no more about sex than she'd passed to Oriana and Joyce, which was just about nothing. But could Oriana *really* talk to her? She doubted it. These days, kids were too flip and wild to listen to good sense.

It wasn't that far to the house now, but suddenly Oriana turned off on the road to Six Mile Dam. She'd been here plenty of times with Clayton when they were only going together, not engaged yet. She wondered if kids still used the area as a lovers' lane, if they still cut off through the brush when a police car sneaked up.

She could understand what was happening to Lousie because it hadn't been that long ago for herself. The hot juices rising, his touch magic and crazy on her bare skin; the desperate flavor of his mouth and the ache of her breasts, the languorous tickle spreading along her thighs—*hey*! She wasn't hard up for loving, so maybe it was the day, the trip home—her *old* home —that kicked off a whole string of thoughts. Maybe she was just happy to be out of her own house and away from Steve Canfield. Dammit, she liked being with her husband and daughter. The problem was with her father-in-law, but Clayton would never move out, couldn't move out. He loved being a farmer, and his pa owned the land.

She said to the gray day, "If you scare up a little sunshine, I'll grow up and go on home." And although the weather didn't respond, she turned across overlapping circles of tire marks this side of the dam and started back.

The cab rattled with that new music, boogie-woogie, and she only recognized Tommy Dorsey's version because she'd heard it so much. It was too quick and strange for her, and everyone said it was just an offshoot of swing and would soon die out. But the kids worshipped it and turned their jitterbugging into something more primitive and sensual.

That kind of music was dangerous for kids like Louise, Oriana thought, and laughed at herself for thinking just like Mom had, a few years back. That horrible Big Apple dance, Mom lectured, and the Lindy Hop—goodness! You all look like so many monkeys jumping around, and (with a defiant chin lift) in heat, too!

She caught a glimpse of gold through a rift in bruised clouds and continued to smile while she changed radio stations. There, that was better: "A Nightingale Sang in Berkely Square," a lilting but sad melody geared to the war in Europe, and Glenn Miller's band did it justice; Ray Eberly's deep voice sang it just right: "I may be right, I may be wrong . . . but I'm perfectly willing to swear . . ."

The only good of any war was its music. That song and others, like "The White Cliffs of Dover," layered the war in Europe with a lonely beauty it didn't deserve. And there was leftover marching music from the last war, Daddy's war: "Over there, over there, the Yanks are coming, the Yanks are coming . . ."

Daddy's had been the big one, the war to end all wars, but the world was at it again, and only borderline madmen like Steve Canfield wanted the U.S. to get into it. For years she'd listened to him yelling about the rotten Nazis and stinking Japs, but she also saw RKO Pathé newsreels at the Bijou.

Horrified, she'd watched German dive-bombers strike London, and recoiled at the flames and falling buildings, feeling some tiny part of the people's suffering. All her instincts shrieked warning at the very thought of *her* loved ones, *her* home, being sucked into that ugly, murderous vortex. Yet she'd learned early not to argue with her father-in-law. It made him worse and put Clay in the middle, and Oriana feared that as her daughter grew, Scooter would also get drawn into the fights. More than anything, she didn't want that.

Marching songs—she eased the truck along the highway and wondered if some secret band wrote music to lure other men into war, while others made flags and drums and speeches. If by some chance war did involve America—and President Roosevelt had promised that no American boy would ever fight on foreign soil—Steve Canfield wouldn't go overseas. He would send Clayton as his surrogate, for young men fought the wars old men started.

Was she unpatriotic? Oriana slowed for the last curve before the house and shook her head. She loved her country as well as anyone, loved Ohio and Coshocton and the farm, the green hills and rivers. But as mother and wife, perhaps she loved her family more. If that was treason, they could make the most of it.

Coasting to a stop before the Parker gate, which, as usual, needed a touch of paint, Oriana turned off the motor and looked at her old house. Suppose Nazi planes came screaming down and bombed the house? Mom and Dad, her brothers and sisters, gone in an awful roar of flame? Closing her eyes for a moment, she said a quick, Sunday kind of prayer that war would stay far from Coshocton, and felt guilty for missing church three weeks running.

The radio crackled and she remembered that it didn't go off unless you turned the knob. If it was left on, the truck wouldn't start and Steve Canfield would stomp around and yell that batteries didn't grow on trees, dammit.

". . . navy facilities at Pearl Harbor," the announcer said, hurrying the words. ". . . police report no looting . . . Hickman Field burning . . . military casualties are high, and reports of civilian deaths and injuries are filtering in . . . the Japanese planes circled back for another run on the harbor and Schofield Barracks, machine guns blazing . . ."

Where was Pearl Harbor, somewhere off China? It couldn't be in Europe, since Jap planes were doing the damage, but the other names were so English—so American.

"Honolulu is in a state of shock . . . martial law has been declared and we'll have more on that as soon as details are available. Meanwhile, civilians have been warned to stay off the streets . . . all hospitals are filled to capacity . . . Japanese planes . . ."

Honolulu, Hawaii. The news sank home and Oriana said, "Oh, my God! That's part of *America*! How—why—?"

She looked to the house and back, and reached for the radio knob, but it seemed threatening and she pulled back her hand to pile from the truck. Running for the house, she stumbled along the porch and rattled the doorknob, trying to get in. The door couldn't be locked, but she couldn't make it work.

Her brother Ron pulled it back from inside. "You always had trouble with machinery. What's the matter, old Steve after you?"

"The—the radio—"

Grinning, rubbing his broken nose, he stepped back. "We already have a radio, miss; got it at store discount. Now if you were sellin' *Liberty* magazine—"

"Dammit, Ron!" She darted by him to the big floor-model Sparton and snapped on the power.

Mom said, wiping her hands on an apron, "Not time for 'One Man's Family,' dear. Or was it some other program you wanted? Dear me, where's little Scooter?"

Oriana whirled to her father, sitting with his slippered feet up on the hassock, the rotogravure section of the Sunday paper across his lap. "Dad—the Japs—they bombed Pearl Harbor —Honolulu—*Hawaii*, Dad!"

Papers scattered from his knees as he leaped erect, and the warmed-up radio blared a jumbled repetition of all she'd heard before. She stared around at her family: Mom reaching for Dad's hand, Ron frowning, little Louise blank and uncaring. Randy and Joyce were missing. Randy was off at Kent State and Joyce was probably home with her husband. Oriana thought of her own husband and moved for the door again.

"Oriana! Where are you going?" Dad looked old and worried.

"Home, to be with Clayton and Scooter. Ron, will you get the stuff off the truck?"

Listening hard to every radio word, she fretted while Ron unloaded the farm produce. She held in the clutch and raced the motor until he came around and stuck his head in her window.

"Hey," he said, "the Japs aren't homing in on Coshocton, and they sure as hell don't have bombs marked for Canfield farm. Whyn't you bring Clay and your kid back for dinner?"

"I—" Oriana was surprised by threatening tears. "Steve probably wants to, so he can say 'I told you so' to Dad."

"Didn't mention Steve," her brother said, "but I'll go grind some glass."

The noise she made was between a laugh and a sob. "Ron, dammit—"

His lips brushed her cheek. "Take care, Sis."

She stared after him as he carried food up the walk. Ron Parker hadn't kissed her since he was a baby. Letting out the clutch, she wheeled the GMC for the farm, trying to listen to stunned, disbelieving reports from network announcers while her own disjointed thoughts hammered at her.

Had she been praying against war at the very second that Jap bombs were exploding on American ships and men? Maybe prayers didn't really matter.

chapter 2

British armored columns launched "Operation Crusader" today on the heels of a fierce storm. Aimed at relieving the battered garrison at Tobruk, the attack stunned troops of Field Marshal Erwin Rommel, the legendary "Desert Fox."

It is led by American "Stuart" tanks, newly arrived in Africa on Lend-Lease. . . .

—*Coshocton Tribune*, December 7, 1941, The Western Desert, Libya (Associated Press)

In Akron, farther from home than he'd ever been, Randy Parker sipped warmish punch and nodded because Martha seemed to want him to. The hall was hung with tired pink streamers.

"I'm sorry you missed the dance, Randall—oh, all right, *Randy*." She sat across from him in a party dress too young for her. "I did so want the pastor to meet you. We're not so strict, you know. We have parties like this."

"But no wine, for the stomach's sake."

Martha made her small, tight smile. "The Book also says, 'Look not upon the wine when it is red.' A small pleasure so easily turns into evil passion."

Randy was careful with his glass cup on a doily. "I couldn't get here sooner. The fraternity called at the last minute and I waited tables until eleven."

Her hand was cool and light upon his own. "I knew you'd come if you could. That's why I volunteered to clean up. Still, Holiness Church doesn't often accept unbelievers; they made an exception."

He wanted a cigarette, but the echoing old hall didn't seem the place, and there were no ashtrays. Randy said, "No outsiders, even at a dance?"

"Rarely. Usually boys or girls close to a member join the church before they're welcome. It keeps the young from being corrupted."

To keep his hands busy, Randy lifted his cup. Church made him edgy. Down home, Dad saw to it that the family went every Sunday, but Randy was never comfortable, especially in the knickers he was forced to wear because he wasn't old enough for long pants. His twin brother had ripped his own hated knickers so often that Mom gave up and made him long pants on her Singer. Randy couldn't tear his again after the first whipping.

"We hold young people's get-togethers every month," Martha said. "Of course, we're chaperoned."

"Sure," Randy said.

"It's terrible of me, but I'm glad you were late. I'd rather be alone with you."

"I like it better too." The deep breath he took brought echoes of any church: smells of furniture polish, face powder, and shoe polish—in winter, damp wool and rubber galoshes with snow still on them. Even now, in his first year of college freedom, if he got trapped at home over a weekend, he went obediently to services.

"Do you think I'm forward?" Martha asked.

"No, no, never that. You're so intelligent and old-fashioned, but kind of modern too. I guess I like all of you, Martha."

Lowering thick-lashed eyes, Martha Swensen fiddled with her black watchband. Heightened pink in her cheeks made her close to beautiful. Funny, he thought; he couldn't remember going with a blonde; the few girls he'd known were dark. But Martha was golden, her long hair braided and primly coiled about a sculptured head, translucent skin, eyes of morning-sky blue. She didn't use lipstick, and her fineboned face was what first attracted him—that and the erect, no-nonsense way she walked. In this whole year at Kent State, she was the only girl he'd dated. But there was always somebody else around.

Other girls here scared him: some busybusy proving severed umbilical cords, others hep jitterbugs, sorority queens, or sturdy, ambitious, small-town girls who still wore bobby sox. It had taken him this long to know he could handle his schedule, with all its heavy business and agriculture courses. If he flunked anything, it would mean betraying his family, his old teachers at Coshocton High, and this scholarship, so he didn't really have much time for dating. As far as anyone knew, Randy was the first Parker to attend college.

Also, the more college he had behind him, the better his chance to become an officer if something changed and the draft caught him. Nobody really expected war, and it was rumored that President Roosevelt was using America's first peacetime draft as another way to pull the country completely out of the Depression. This way, a lot of young guys got paid government money and were kept from being unemployed. The draft could also be a big mixup that just pulled men from business and good jobs. Maybe that wasn't bad, either. It was time big shots found what it was like, down among ordinary folks. He grinned, because that was how his brother would think.

He said, "Can I smoke?" and knew it was a mistake. Maybe Ron brought that on, too.

"We'd rather you didn't. Our bodies are temples for the soul, not sooty chimneys."

"Okay." He didn't exactly want to pull out his blue pack of Bugler tobacco and roll his own. Only a nickel, Bugler saved money, but it was embarrassing to roll a smoke in front of strangers and girls. He could never make one look like a tailor-made, anyhow, but someday he'd get one of the new rolling machines. Then he could make up ten or twelve cigarettes and stuff them into a Camel pack.

Martha said, "About our last talk—"

"I have to think it over."

Holiness Church was against war and warlike organizations. Martha said some men stood up for God and refused to register for the draft. Their cases were being considered in court.

She said, "It shouldn't be so difficult to make a statement for your Holy Maker."

"But I registered last month and took my physical. It can't be changed."

Martha's eyes were clear and blue, but right now they weren't soft. "You didn't tell me."

"I've only seen you twice since my birthday trip home, and what with the new semester—"

Small white teeth showed against her lower lip. "Will you go?"

"I—they classified me 4-F." It was the first time he'd said it aloud, and it didn't lie easy on his tongue.

"Is something wrong with you? What is it, Randall?"

"Nothing. The draft board didn't say why. Old Steve Canfield just classified me and told me I could appeal. He's head of the board, and the others just go along."

Jesus—4-F. It was nothing to brag about. Already, Jack Benny and Fred Allen joked about it on the radio: the last category, the bottom. Nobody classified 4-F would ever be called to service; they were cripples and crazy men and homosexuals.

He hadn't wanted to be called up right away because his scholarship might run out after he'd served his year in the army or navy. It might be even longer, because Congress had taken no action to drop the selective-service law, as it was supposed to. Newspapers reported that the OHIO—Over the Hill in October—threat never materialized. The original draftees had sworn they'd go over the hill—desert—en masse in the month their service should have ended, last October. Congress let the law stand, and the rebellion died muttering. But it didn't matter now. The war was on.

Martha's lower teeth slipped behind her lip, and he thought her mouth could look stern or surprisingly tempting as she said, "You won't appeal, of course."

"I won't appeal."

That would only haul it into the open, the dirty cracks and sniggers and sly winks he'd known through all his years of growing up. Ron tried to beat up every kid who said it aloud, but even he couldn't whip the world. Randy figured it would either slide off on its own, or he might start believing it himself.

Appeal his 4-F? Hell, no—not after the draft board sat fat and smug behind their long table, only Steve Canfield looking directly at him. Mr. Torrance, from the drugstore, and Mayor James Lee Mildon stared around the room. You get to stay in your college, boy, Canfield had said. He frowned, as if Randy shouldn't do this to him because they were sort of related.

"You're sensible," Martha said. "From the minute we met, I knew you were mature, sensitive, and thoughtful. Those fraternity boys are so coarse and wild."

"The Alpha Omega guys talk rough, but it's mostly just talk."

Her chin firmed. "But I've seen how they treat you."

"Because I'm not one of them. Alpha Omega pledges are too rich for drudge work, and I'm glad. That opens table-waiter jobs to guys who need them."

"Well, I think fraternities and sororities are snobs, and sinful to boot, and even though your draft board—"

Randy took out his tobacco, and put it back. Ron had showed up the same day, of course; same birthday and all that. Hung over and sullen, he eased off after the physical, saying it might be good to get the hell out of town, and they'd go together. When he got 4-F stamped on his papers, too, he blew up and spat dirty names at the board until Mayor Mildon rubbed his thinning red hair and threatened to call the cops.

Outside, Ron said shit, those bastards used a technicality to get back at him. Old mealymouthed Canfield had never gotten over the ass-kicking Ron gave Clayton that time. Felony conviction, bullshit! He'd sat in their jail ten days because he wouldn't let Dad bail him out.

They marked me 4-F, too, Randy said, and Ron put a hand on his shoulder. More of Canfield's red ass, his brother said. He's mad at the whole family, and maybe Oriana will have the guts to bust him with a skillet someday.

"Would you walk me home now?" Martha asked. "It's very late."

When he helped her with her coat, she turned within the circle of his arms, close and warm and smelling of soap. "Do you really care about me, Randall Parker?"

"Yes," he said. "I think you're beautiful."

Going tiptoe, she reached for his mouth. Her kiss was chaste, as always. Martha Swensen never French-kissed with her mouth open, but the trembling of her full lips stirred him. He edged back a little in case he got an erection.

"Fine," she breathed, voice shaky as her fingertips Brailled his face. "That's just fine, darling. God is so good to us. Let us thank Him on our knees." She hit the switches, and only a night bulb glowed dimly in the entrance hall.

"Wait a minute, Martha. Look, I can't even think about getting engaged. I have to get my diploma and find some kind of job. Dad's store is picking up a little, but not enough to hire me right off. And I don't think I want to go back to Coshocton. I can't think about another—well, family. Not right now."

He could just make out the shining of her face as she kept stroking his cheekbones, her quick, soft hands dipping to butterfly along his throat. Her body pressed against him, firm and warm. "God will provide for His own, Randall. Pray with me."

Prayer and her hands sliding over his chest didn't fit together, and he caught her fingers at his belt, embarrassed that his penis was strong against her belly, but shaken by it too.

"Martha—"

"Oh, do, darling—do!"

The slab floor chilled his knees. Martha's nails spasmed against his palm as she swayed back and forth. Crooning, she ran words together, her voice slowly rising. Although her thigh pressed his, and she held his hand to the marvelous roundness of her breast, Randy lost his hard-on.

"Glory, glory," she chanted. "Glory!"

chapter 3

German probes were halted today, 20 miles short of
Moscow. After two weeks of bloody fighting in
mud and snow, Wehrmacht troops dug in to consol-
idate their positions. . . .

—The Russian Front, December 7, 1941 (United
Press)

Across town, Ron Parker opened a beer for himself and
another for his father, the first Sunday in history they'd had a
drink under the same roof. "Too bad there's no recruiting
station here. Wouldn't be open today, anyhow."

"Akron, maybe," his father said. "Columbus for sure.
There'll be a line, but we can get there early."

Ron saw his mother's lips tremble as she said, "George
Parker, you'll do no such thing. You're a family man, and too
old for playing soldier."

Ron took a deep drink of cold beer. It helped wipe away
Saturday night. His father drank too. "Elizabeth, this isn't a
game. The country's at war. *War*, Elizabeth, and maybe it can
use me for—for training or something. I'm experienced."

A few months in uniform a lifetime ago, Ron thought. A
self-conscious young guy in the family album, the old pictures
faded. Could that count? Still, Ron looked at his old man

differently. At least he'd been somewhere, seen something, even if he never got overseas.

"Black Jack Pershing," George said. "By all that's holy, *he* can give 'em fits. He took the AEF and whipped the Kaiser all to hell and back. He's still alive, and—"

Ron watched his mother. He'd never seen fear in her eyes before, and it grew as she stared at him. She's thinking mostly of Randy, he figured. She ought to know he can take care of himself, and then some. But wait a minute. Why stick his neck out for those assholes on the draft board? They wouldn't take him before, because of his felony record.

"Glad you brought the beer," George said. "I'll buy a whole case, if the saloon's open."

"The Happy Hour's open," Ron said. "Everybody jammed around the radio. Chief Browning too. This is a different kind of Sunday."

He saw Louise darting through the kitchen. The back door closed softly. She was ducking out while the house was in an uproar. Sunday afternoon was family time, and not for dates, but the rule wasn't so important now that Randy was gone and Oriana and Joyce were married. He wondered if she was still running with the Deacon kid. He was a better shot than farmers or factory hands. She'd been smart so far, and he hoped she didn't get herself knocked up.

"All that beer," Elizabeth said. "This isn't a celebration."

"More like a farewell party," George answered. "Good bye to the Depression and one way of life, hello to another. Things will never be the same again."

"Just so nothing hurts my family."

Ron saw his father clam up, so as not to worry her more. Later on, she wouldn't be able to avoid the worry, but now she reached out for all of them, even through the walls to the rest of her children, a mama bird spreading protective wings. Mom, he thought, you can't keep us safe and warm forever; the nest has holes in it.

He turned when Joyce banged in through the front door, her cheeks wind-polished, much shinier than her brooding eyes. Before she got her coat off, Elizabeth was hugging her. Ron heard the half-questions and half-answers that only women sharing a problem understand. Another fight with Joe, he thought. He'd seen Joe boozing it up pretty good last night with that dippy broad from the Kit Kat Kafe. Without a team to use his bigness and dumbness, Joe Dayton wasn't much, and maybe Joyce expected more than he had to give. Their headache, not his.

When truck brakes squealed outside, he thought Joe had come to apologize, but it was the Canfields. The old bastard had come to crow how right he was about the war, and Clay to mumble yes-yes to everything his pa said. Ron doubted he'd have married Oriana if his pa said no.

Drifting toward the kitchen because things were always tense between him and Steve Canfield, Ron watched them troop in, little Scooter bouncing straight toward him. He picked her up and swung her around, grinning because it gave Steve the red ass. She was a good kid. Clay didn't mind; he'd gotten over that whipping long ago, but not his pa.

Oriana looked terrific, younger than Joyce. He didn't know how she managed with Steve nagging her for another baby, like she was his wife. Scooter had come close to killing Oriana, partly because the old bastard wanted her born where he and Clay had come into the world.

"Can I have a sip, Uncle Ron?"

He put her down. "It ain't Coke, Scooter."

Steve Canfield stopped bragging to crook a finger at his granddaughter. "Over here, Mary Joann."

Oriana met Ron's glance, and shrugged. She followed him into the kitchen and stole a gulp of his beer, looking over her shoulder.

"Hell with him," Ron said. "How you doin'?"

"Okay, I guess. Pa's probably the only man in the country in such good humor."

Popping another bottle cap, Ron said, "Sure, he's too old to fight. Too young last time, too old now."

His sister's dark eyes probed him. "Are you going?"

"Ain't you heard? Me and Randy are 4-F."

"That won't stop you. Maybe Randy, but not you."

He frowned. "Everybody thinks they know just what he'll do. Randy ain't all that easy to figure out."

Oriana looked back into the parlor. "You know what I mean. Listen to Daddy and Pa, running the whole war between them."

"Look at Mom," he said. "I wish they'd shut up."

Joyce came into the kitchen. "Got a smoke?"

Ron gave her his Camels and snapped his lighter. Joyce pulled smoke deep, and he thought she really needed it. "Hang on to the pack," he said. "I got more."

She nodded thanks. "Anybody heard from Randy?"

Oriana said, "Oh, he won't come, and won't call. You know Randy."

"Goddammit," Ron said, "he don't have money to call long distance, and he'll be here when he can. He's not a high-school kid, he's in *college*."

"It's a scary day," Joyce said. "Walking here, I realized *how* scary. People running around, radios blaring all over, kids hollering—if I was away from home, I'd call."

"You didn't say if you're going." Oriana took the bottle for another gulp.

He took it back. "Get your own, unless you're afraid Steve'll spank. How about your husband? Is he about to sign up?"

"God," Oriana breathed, "I haven't had time to think of that. Clay gone off to war, God."

"You and Scooter alone with Steve on the farm," Joyce said. "I don't envy you.

"Ron, got a beer for me?" Joyce said. "My loving husband may not wait for a Jap. He said something about getting that German out in the country."

"Hindeman?" Ron asked. "Gunter Hindeman? He ain't some kind of Nazi. He was born right here. You went to school with him, Oriana."

"Two years ahead of me," she said, "and he wasn't there much. His dad needed him on the farm a lot. He talks funny because they didn't speak English at home. And who knows? Maybe Hitler sent them here a long time ago."

"What the hell would Gunter Hindeman be doing for Hitler, spying on potato bugs? Joe and his bunch of half-ass, has-been football players—" Ron balled his fists.

Joyce said, "When you think about it, there's a bunch of industries not far away: tires at Akron and trucks in Detroit and I don't know what all; we've got enough stuff right here to put Coshocton high up on a bombing list."

"You're out of your fu—out of your head," Ron said.

Then Steve Canfield was in the kitchen as though he

belonged there, saying, "Every man's bound to do his duty. Even you, boy. I expect we can find *something* for you, bridge guard or air raid watcher, something like that."

Ron put down his beer bottle. "You can't find your own ass with both hands, you old fart."

His sisters gasped. Canfield's face turned mottled red as he took a quick step forward.

Ron's lips peeled back. "You got better sense than that."

Canfield stopped. "You, you damned, you—"

Casually, Ron put his back to the man, daring him to take advantage, hoping he would. If Canfield even touched him, he meant to kick in the bastard's ribs, him and his fucking draft board.

Oriana's *please* quivered in the taut silence. Moving slow and easy, Ron took his jacket off a peg and put one hand on the doorknob. "Tell the old man I'll get that beer later. After I see if Gunter Hindeman needs any help, but I don't think he will." He turned to look at Canfield. "Big difference between runnin' your mouth and standin' up to a man."

When Canfield only made a choking noise, Ron went out across the back porch and climbed into his Model A. He sat there a minute while the house got louder. Maybe he'd made things rougher for Oriana, and if it came down to breaking Joe Dayton's balls, Joyce would suffer too. Shit—for maybe the thousandth time in his life, he wished he were a little more like Randy.

Not *just* like him, not *just* like anybody. That was always the trouble. They put Randy and him into those cute fucking suits exactly alike. Their hair got cut the same day and even the barber made jokes like he'd have to cut the tip off somebody's ear, so folks could tell them apart. Wouldn't want to give the same twin two haircuts.

He got dirty as quick as he could, or tore up clothes so he wouldn't be part of anybody, so he'd only be Ron. It got him more whippings than he could remember, but finally they backed off some, Mom and the old man.

It went on through school, with snotty little bastards hollering, "Yah-yah! Two for a nickel!" Randy never paid attention, but Ron took after his tormentors, and didn't they learn.

Grinding the starter, Ron muttered under his breath until the

engine caught and he could pull out of the driveway. He'd
played football in high school, not because he liked it, but
because Randy wouldn't. He got left back three times and had
to go to summer school; Randy was the straight-A student.

Ron cruised up Main Street and stayed away from the
excitement there, although some guys yelled and waved him
over. He didn't see Joe Dayton anywhere, so he didn't stop.
Touching his bent nose, he grinned. Hell, he wouldn't let
anybody fix it, and was grateful to the Sacred Hearter who did
it to him. Not that he didn't wipe out the guy next quarter, but
he was glad anybody could tell him from Randy.

No need to go on collecting lumps, but the pattern was set.
Randy didn't talk about Ron's fighting because he knew why
he was doing it. They *felt* so damned many things about each
other. The twin-thing got spooky. Like the time Randy came
home from Ohio State wearing a new shirt and pants exactly
like those Ron had bought the week before. He couldn't afford
to destroy them, didn't really want to, but put them away when
Randy was around.

And was it his brother's shyness that turned Ron into the
cocksman of the school yard? But most girls he had dated in
school either got married or moved away. The new broads
made him feel old, somehow. Not that he turned any down. If
any girl *really* graduated, she had taken a course in screwing
from Ron. Maybe the school board would make it required,
like Home Ec.

He was away out to Clow Lane before he realized it.
Slowing, he turned onto gravel and looked for the Hindeman
place. A while back, he'd made deliveries there for Torrance's
drugstore. That was before Gunter's parents died, only a few
days apart. Pneumonia, Doc Shaw said, brought on by
stubbornness and too much hard work at the wrong time.

Gunter had lived alone out here for two years or more, never
marrying. Imagine, Coshocton ladies said, a bachelor in his
thirties; must be something wrong with him, and he don't
speak American good, either.

Ron had come upon Gunter Hindeman in a Sandusky
whorehouse, far from home and drunker than seven hundred
dollars. Every month or two, Gunter drove clear up there to get
his ashes hauled and tie one on. By the time they'd parted, Ron

knew him for an all-right guy. It took Gunter months to decide the same about him.

A couple of times they went to Sandusky together, and Ron discovered the answer to another question that bothered Banker Deacon. Gunter Hindeman kept just a few bucks in his account because he was suspicious of banks that might fail again, but more because he was a big spender in Sandusky.

It ain't I don't vant to talk vith nobody, Gunter had said there; it's *mein* tongue don't vork *sehr gut*. Not much to school I vent.

Ron had laughed, and the whores with him. He said, All the time to school *I* vent, and *I* don't talk better'n a billygoat. *Blaat!* he went, and Gunter went *blaat!* too, and the girls kept laughing.

Now he stopped the car at the closed gate and cattle guard. In gathering dusk, Gunter came out, a big, clumsy kind of man who never bothered anybody. Ron said, "Now I wish I'd'a stopped for some beer."

"I keep noddings *mein* farm on," Gunter said. "Too easy it is to drink and who der vork does?"

Ron took the outstretched, callused hand. "You heard the radio today? About the Japs?"

Gunter nodded.

Ron said, "Some jerks in town, they're beerin' up and talking crazy. I just—well, I came out to see you're okay." He couldn't see Gunter's eyes. "Probably just beer talk, I figure. Maybe you could go up to Sandusky for a few days."

"I am no Jap," Gunter said.

"You ain't Hitler, either, but some people . . ."

After a while, Gunter said, "I stay. *Danke, mein* friend."

"Yeah. Take care of yourself. The Sandusky girls couldn't stay in business without you."

Gunter didn't laugh. He bobbed his head under the old flop hat that had been sweated out of shape years ago. Ron got back in the car as Gunter Hindeman turned and plodded for his dark house.

Halfway back to town, Ron switched on the radio. It only buzzed and he heeled the dash. Dad had been so sure Ron would go with him to join the army, and that fuckin' Canfield was so sure Ron couldn't.

The radio belched words.

". . . the President will address Congress and the nation tomorrow. Meanwhile, reports from Hawaii are meager, and officials there cannot comment because of national security (*crackle, crackle, pop*) . . . military in San Francisco asking for a blackout . . . no panic . . . (*pop, pop*) . . ."

Turning the dial, Ron found music: "When the lights go on again . . . all over the world." For the first time he listened closely to the lyrics.

chapter 4

A thousand people gathered across from the Executive Mansion in Lafayette Square to watch a stream of cabinet officers and congressmen come and go. The crowd began gathering this afternoon, after announcement of the Japanese raid on Pearl Harbor. They sang "The Star-Spangled Banner" and "God Bless America."

A sidewalk peanut vendor summed up the optimistic mood: "Just three months, we finish them. . . ."

—Washington, D.C., December 7, 1941 (Associated Press)

Everything seemed brighter and speeded up, but not necessarily better. The war put an edge on everything, sharpened the senses, and made a needle point of frustration. It didn't seem right to go on preparing for Christmas when the country was backed against the wall. But Main Street was decorated as always, and store windows blinked come-ons to buyers.

George Parker eyed the tempting swing of the girl's tail, snug and attractive in its tight coat. She had good legs, too, and walked like a young girl should, free and easy and graceful, not stomping along clumsy as any plowboy.

He slowed along the sidewalk to enjoy the sight, just as she got into an old pickup and exposed a tempting length of leg. Good Lord—it was Oriana! He caught the briefest flash of her profile, but enough to recognize his own daughter. And here he was, lusting after her.

Not that he'd ever do anything about this new and troubling lust, and if he'd even suspected it was *Oriana*—

Turning blindly into a storefront, he stood there until the truck pulled off. Then he walked back up the street, shaking his head.

It was past time to do something about this—this roving eye. But what? He couldn't go to Pastor Montgomery and say, I've just developed an overwhelming desire for young girls, and what can I do about it? If I pray hard, will it go away, or should I have some grisly kind of operation?

Maybe Catholics had the right idea. He'd heard that priests gave sinners a certain number of prayers to recite and the slate was wiped clean. But a Methodist couldn't do that.

Old Doc Shaw would laugh and ask if George wanted his tallywhacker clipped or what. Saltpeter? Hell, George—it don't do no more for not diddling than Spanish fly does *for* it. Along about your age, seems you should be damned glad you still got the interest. George could just about recite Doc's advice word for word. Anytime Doc had a few drinks, the story would be all over the Masonic lodge, a big joke on poor George, trying to kick over the traces this late in life.

He continued to walk, head down and not looking at passersby unless they spoke to him. When he remembered the delivery out on Pleasant Valley Drive, he was clear down to Ohio Bell Telephone. Turning back, he hurried left on Walnut and along the tracks, staying on Hickory Street until he was back to Main.

Exercise and cold baths wouldn't do it either. He'd tried that until he was sore all over and damned near frozen blue in the bathtub. What in the world's gotten into you? Elizabeth asked. Raking and trimming trees and I don't know what-all. You're not a young man, George.

Didn't he *know* that? Hadn't he watched his hair turn splotchy and his belly get tighter against his belt? All those wrinkles, and his nose looked bigger. Good Lord, he watched the world running by and knew he couldn't keep up; he didn't have to be reminded.

Guiltily, he chanced a look at the kid walking ahead. She wore pants, and he couldn't decide if that was better. It showed the contours of her sweet little tail, and outlined her thighs, but sometimes half-hidden, mysterious movements beneath a skirt were better.

Gnawing his lip, he turned into his own store and found Joyce busy at the plumbing counter, and a woman waiting where he'd set up the lamp display. Gratefully, he moved to her with his salesman's smile. She had marvelous breasts.

When Joyce went into the storeroom to fix coffee, George was mildly surprised that he'd stayed so busy she had to reheat his cup. Business took his mind off things, usually, but it seemed that an inordinate number of his customers were young and pretty.

"Maybe I've earned my keep today," Joyce said.

"You always do. Even if nobody comes in, I'm easy in my mind when I have to leave the store, knowing my daughter's taking care of it. I couldn't trust just anybody."

"Sure," she said, "like you trust Joe to help with a delivery."

"Well—he got busy and forgot, I guess. It'll wait until tomorrow, and he'll have my old truck put back together by then." It bothered him to think his daughter's eyes were misting up. "It's all right, really."

Moving away and busying himself at the paint counter, he noticed gaps where the brushes hung. A good sign, folks buying brushes and the like before spring. By the wall, a number-four shovel was gone too. It took a war to make the Depression really over.

It hadn't hurt Coshocton as much as it had other little towns that depended solely on agriculture or one manufacturer for survival. The rubber housewares plant, Pretty Products, had only laid off a few men, as had Edmont Work Gloves. Carnation Milk's condensary had kept going through the worst times with just about a full crew.

But small businesses along Main and Walnut had struggled to hang on. When money was so tight, folks made do until they *had* to buy a pipe fitting or replace a worn-out tool. They sure didn't paint and pretty up the house, and used kerosene lamps because they were cheaper than electricity. George sold them lamps and shades, but damned few, and now that things were looking up, some old-timers were still running scared and pinching every nickel. Maybe they thought the U.S. would lose. He stood by the window and watched girls go by.

Louise Parker cut her last class. It was only Study Hall anyway, and she wanted to take a ride with Deke. She liked the classy '40 Studebaker Champion; it wasn't noisy and painted all over with goofy signs. It was black because Deke's old man was a banker and didn't want his boy to be a show off.

"When I take this baby to Kent State," Deke said, "I'll get a new paint job. What you think about red?"

She slid over and put her thigh next to his. "Red? You better wait and see what the other guys are driving."

"Yeah." He patted her knee. "You're a smart kid. Wish you were goin' with me."

"You haven't left yet." Louise eased back when his hand moved up from her knee. "My old man's no banker, and even if he was, he wouldn't put me through college. My brother Randy went on a scholarship, but he's a *boy*. Girls don't need college. They just need to get married and have babies."

Billy Deacon cut off the Muskingum River bridge and took Route 16, the sleek car purring along. "I don't know about your brother bein' a *boy*—"

"Hey. Lay off my brother."

"Watch this," he said, and kicked the gas. "Up to sixty real quick. I was just a freshman when your brothers went to Coshocton, but some guys still talk about 'em. I mean, it's funny they're so different, bein' twins and all. Ron is one tough guy, but Randy—"

"Okay, drop it, will you? Where we goin'?"

"Just around. You in a hurry?"

"Uh-uh, long as I'm back by five."

He slowed the car and glanced around at her. He was good-looking and practically a college man, and rich. She wished she were a lot older. Jeepers, guys her age were so young, and only a couple had cars, anyway. She sat up when Deke drove off the road and into a clump of soft maples. He put one arm around her shoulders and drew her close. She liked the scent of his shaving lotion. Most guys in her class smelled like bubble gum.

Melting to Deke, she let her breasts push against his sweater and opened her mouth for his tongue. He kissed good, and she allowed his hands to slide over her hips. When he cupped one breast, she let him and moaned against his straight white teeth. She walked her fingers through his wavy hair.

But when he tried to get a hand between her legs, she held them tightly together and caught his wrist. "Don't—no, Deke."

"What the hell? Every time I take you out, you act hot at first, then back off. You some kind of cherry?"

Louise said, "If I wasn't, you'd know all about it. Boys have to brag. They just can't keep their mouths shut."

More gently this time, he kissed her again, but she didn't part her lips. "Come on," he said. "I'll never say anything. It ain't right, teasin' me all the time. A man can take just so much. It don't bother girls near as bad. And I may have to go get killed."

The car heater had gone off with the motor, and tree shadow was quickly cooling the Studebaker. "Look, Deke—I want it as bad as you, I swear. But jeepers, I'm the one catches hell if something goes wrong." Would they really draft a college guy?

He used the dash lighter to start two cigarettes. She marked the smooth way he did that, holding her cigarette between his lips a little longer, making it intimate like. She rolled the window on her side down about an inch to let smoke out.

River odors came in, chilly and muddy smelling. She shivered. She wasn't kidding Deke. Every date with him got a little harder to handle because she *did* want it. She was scared about three different things: that her old man and mom would find out; that she would get pregnant; that word would get around that she was round-heeled.

And everybody said that once you gave in to a guy, he didn't respect you any more. If she went all the way with anybody, Deke would be it, but what would that do to her plans? He wouldn't marry her if she was easy, and she'd been thinking about that since their first date.

But what if he started getting it from some college girl and forgot all about the kid he'd left back home? It wasn't fair. Deke was the best chance for her to *be* somebody, Mrs. Banker driving a fancy Packard, going to big parties and having a maid. The Deacons had one, a colored woman.

"You won't get caught," Deke murmured, his forefinger moving from one of her hard nipples to the other. "I swear you won't, honey. We may not get another chance, the war and all."

She swallowed the lump in her throat. "Those things don't always work. My mom would just *kill* me, and Daddy too. But Ron scares me most. You know how crazy he can get. Ron and me, we're closer than anybody else in the family. Oh, man, if Ron even *thought* I was caught—"

That was a lie. Ron wouldn't give a good goddamn. He was only close to his twin, but he'd jump at a chance to beat up a boy over his sister.

"How come this is gettin' so complicated? I mean, we haven't even done it yet, and you're talkin' about that crazy man coming after me. Hell, how'd he even know *who*—"

"There!" she said. "There, dammit! Right off, you think if I do it with you, when you're gone I'll do it with somebody else and you won't be responsible."

"I didn't—"

"Take me back to town. It's too far to walk, carrying these books."

Mouth set, he keyed the ignition and goosed the accelerator so the wheels spun hard. Jerking the wheel, he got the car back on the road, and saw the state cop in time to slow down.

"All I said was—I meant if you didn't tell your brother, who—?"

Staring out her window, she made believe she didn't hear him. He would feel confused and guilty now, but she shouldn't carry it too far. After a few pouty minutes, she turned back and put her head on his shoulder.

"I can't stay mad at you for long. I just don't want to think about you going away. College is bad enough, but the army?" She clicked on the radio and fiddled with the dial until the strong Cleveland station came in. Judy Garland was singing "Nobody's Baby," and Louise hummed along.

"Nobody's baby, that's me. I could really, *really* belong to a man, heart and body and soul, give him everything, do everything in bed. My man won't have to ask for it, I'll ask

him, and make him so happy he won't know there's another
woman in the world. But right now I'm nobody's baby."

Watching his face now, she saw him glance up at the
courthouse clock. He said, "Almost an hour before you have to
be home. Would you really do *anything* with a guy you love?"

"All there is," she purred, acting like she knew it all. What
more was there? She didn't half believe the stuff in that *Maggie
& Jiggs* comic book she found in Ron's room that time, all that
dirty stuff. Those were only cartoons, not real people. "Let's
go by Sacred Heart and see where the fire was. Everybody at
school was talking about it. After, we could park at the
fairgrounds for a while."

When they stopped for a light, two senior girls waved and
said hi to Deke. Louise smiled big and sweet at them, knowing
they were burned up at a sophomore riding around with such a
popular guy.

"You've got so much waiting for you," she said after they
pulled away. "Big football games and frat parties, dances and
all that. Away from home, nobody to say what time you have
to be in, staying out all night if you want."

He stopped the car just inside the fairgrounds gate. "And
getting a hotel room?"

"You're mean, Deke. But I won't try to hold you back. I
—oh, gee, I'll miss you so."

She put her cheek against his chest; he stroked her hair.
"Come on, Louise; I'm not leaving tomorrow, you know. My
Dad means me to go to Kent State, so he might pull strings on
the draft board."

She'd be lucky if she could hold him without going all the
way. She had to think hard about that. Maybe he'd be anxious
to come home for more, maybe not. And there was always the
gangly boy in home room, the shy one whose old man was a
big shot in the Shaw-Barton Company. He didn't have a car
—yet.

Kissing Deke hard, she broke away and bit his ear, squirming on the seat like he was driving her batty. After a while she
didn't have to pretend. Louise Parker was no cold fish. She
was plenty passionate, but that didn't mean she'd lose her
head. One little corner of her mind always knew exactly what
she was doing.

chapter 5

Flag-waving soldiers of the Imperial Japanese
Army occupied Suchow today, driving remnants of
a Chinese guerrilla band before them. Observers
could see smoke columns rising over the village as
low-flying Japanese planes continued to bomb the
mountains. . . .

—Northern Provinces, China, December 19, 1941
  (International News Service)

Elizabeth Parker blinked into the round, oak-framed bathroom
mirror and toyed with the idea of coloring her hair. But that
was nonsense; graying was part of life's pattern, like wrinkles
and grandchildren. Once you tried to deny age, the pretense
went on and on.

Besides, now she would probably get old much faster. The
unthinkable had happened: America was at war, and had been
since the President called the sneak attack on Pearl Harbor a
"day of infamy" and officially declared war on Japan and the
other Axis Powers, Germany and Italy. But maybe it would be
over quickly, before her own family was torn apart.

Turning from the sink, she felt guilty for hoping other
women's sons would go first, but didn't take back the thought.
Fingering her tummy, Elizabeth pulled it in. She wasn't bad

for fifty-one years, and if she really dieted, maybe she could be another Lana Turner.

The war cloud hung just behind her shoulder, but she tried to move it away, picturing George with dyed hair and a cute little Ronald Colman mustache. He'd look silly because he'd still be George. He couldn't be a silver-screen lover, no more than she could be a vamp.

He wouldn't have to go. He was too old. Surely they wouldn't take her husband. She moved briskly about the bath, trying to enjoy housework routine, but it wasn't the same. Although she was wife and mother and grandmother, now the placid years had all been jerked from under her. Nothing would ever be calm and flowing again.

She used the dustrag on the banisters going down, although they weren't often sticky since Oriana, Joyce, and Randall were gone. She still had Ronald and little Louise, and that was a blessing. Girls married younger every day, and the draft took so many boys.

High-up government had lied to her on the radio. Ohio's own Senator Taft said he questioned all the money Congress appropriated and didn't see any need for a big army. Roosevelt promised that American boys would not die on foreign soil. A hard band tightened around her heart as she imagined her boys in uniform, being taught to kill other mothers' sons.

Dusting the brass hall tree, Elizabeth made a face. When it came around again, she'd drop her *Saturday Evening Post* subscription. The magazine ran scary articles and gory pictures of the fighting. *Ranch Romances* ignored the war, and that was much better.

"Mom?"

"Oriana? I'm in the kitchen."

She'd named her oldest child after a Tennyson character. In her senior year at Coshocton High, she had been deep into romances, classical and poetic. When her other babies came along, she was more sensible.

"Hi." Oriana pecked her cheek, and Elizabeth smelled the farm in her daughter's dark, glossy hair—shiny apples and piney winds. Oriana looked fresh, clean, and capable as she swung a basket of potatoes and a gallon jar of milk onto the faded wooden drainboard.

Elizabeth looked closely at her, as if she might need to

remember everything about the girl, the way her crowfeather hair curled above close-laid ears. Oriana wasn't exactly beautiful, not like Dolores del Rio or Merle Oberon, although she had some of their angular facial bones and slightly slanted eyes. Her mouth was generous, her coloring healthy, her chin kind of square and stubborn. Oriana's eyes were almost black, a very dark brown. When she was small, Elizabeth had sometimes seen gold flecks in them.

"Where's my grandchild?"

"In school. She tried to rebel this morning; said school wouldn't be open because there's a war. I almost agreed with her. It seems funny *anything* should go along as it was."

Elizabeth turned gas on beneath the coffeepot, then brought out cups and saucers and a single spoon. Oriana was watching her weight, though heaven knew she didn't have to. "Thanks for the produce, but if it's any trouble—"

As always, Oriana said, "It's just what we have too much of, stuff that might go bad. If you can't use it, maybe Joyce—"

"How's she doing?"

"Okay." Oriana went to turn off the gas and bring the white enamel pot to the table. "You know, I'm glad you don't call *my* child anything but Scooter. At least I picked her nickname."

It was still touchy for Oriana, Elizabeth knew. Steve Canfield had named her baby, and her husband went along. Names don't mean anything, Clay Canfield said; one is good as another, and Pa had named the kid after his dead mother and Elizabeth's dead mother together—Mary Joann.

"Half a cup," Elizabeth said. "It's close after breakfast." She sugared her coffee, hesitated, then dipped a spoon of heavy canned cream. "How early do you get up on the farm?"

"Whenever Steve Canfield does. He officially begins and ends each day."

"You look very pretty, dear. Work makes you glow."

Touching her hair, Oriana said, "Thanks. About Christmas: I'll bring everything the night before. Got a fat tom turkey penned up and Indian corn to decorate the table. Everybody coming?"

Oriana meant would her brother Ron stay for dinner. That awful fight between him and Clay still hung between them. Steve could never admit that a slip of a boy had beat up his burly, grown son.

"Randy wrote he'd be home from college. There'll be Joyce and little Louise, your daddy and me—" She glanced at Oriana. "I never know Ron's plans."

Oriana took an Old Gold cigarette from her purse. "You mind? I still don't like to smoke in front of Daddy."

"No, of course not. I might start smoking myself, but I can't stand the taste and it makes me cough."

Smiling, Oriana said, "Modern mom. What's the *Saturday Evening Post* say about women smoking in public?"

"I'm giving up the *Post*."

"But not Ron? Mom, he should be out on his own, not hanging around the house, worrying you when he stays out all night. Why can't he—"

"Now, dear. I'm thankful your brother's not off in the army or clear across country like the Harris boys. Thelma Harris hardly ever hears from them. They work in some airplane factory."

"Defense plant workers won't get drafted. Maybe they can get Ron a job out there, something besides part-time soda jerk or delivery boy. The farmers here won't hire him to drive a truck at harvest or a tractor at planting. They hear about his fights and speeding tickets—"

"Whatever he does," Elizabeth said, "he's your brother, and may get sent off to war." Once she'd said it, the chance became real. She wanted to bite her tongue.

"But if he was only a *little* like Randy— Sorry. I'm taking it out on somebody else again. It's not bad living with Clay, but his pa—never mind; you've heard it all before."

"Is he still telling you to get pregnant?"

"Now he's blaming Clay too. You think he'd be happy about Scooter, so pretty and no trouble at all, but oh, no. He just has to have a grand*son* to carry on the name. What in hell is so great about being a Canfield?"

"Now, Oriana—"

"I wish *he* could have a baby. A breach birth would serve him right. My God, I wake up in the middle of the night scared to death I might be caught—"

Elizabeth got up to pour more coffee, to hide a quick flush of embarrassment. She was uneasy talking about pregnancies and such. The idea of that man! The way he tormented Oriana was worse than his crowing about how right he'd been about the

SINCE YOU'VE BEEN GONE

war. A year ago he said Senator Taft was a traitor, and Hamilton Fish too; he called the President dumb for not sending our whole navy to England with the Lend-Lease destroyers. Now that he was proven right, Steve Canfield was insufferable.

She said, rubbing her palm across oilcloth marked by a thousand meals and more, "He just doesn't know. He didn't serve in the World War. You were only a baby then and your daddy didn't get sent overseas, but he was in uniform."

Tapping another, unlit, cigarette on the tabletop, Oriana said, "Wonder why Steve Canfield didn't serve. He never talks about that."

"Daddy doesn't talk about his service, either. I was so scared when the boys at Camp Upton were dying of influenza—awful, awful. I had you, and Joyce was on the way—or was she here?" Elizabeth chuckled. "It's better to think on the good things, my wonderful children and the good times in this house."

It had been good, with George getting started in business and working so hard to buy out old man Chestnut. He'd never turned to bootlegging for money during Prohibition, like many others. She could name Coshocton families that had gotten their start by breaking the law, and some who'd gone to jail for it.

The Depression had hurt about everybody. Nobody actually went hungry in Coshocton because farmers were generous, sharing food they couldn't sell. Some lost their land when times got harder and they couldn't keep up their mortgages. But most farms had been settled way back, and somehow the taxes got paid.

"All we have to fix Christmas Eve will be pies and cranberries. We can bake bread in the morning, and—Mom?"

"Yes, dear? I was remembering the other war and how your daddy got started, after. It took a while for the world to settle back, it seemed like."

Oriana sighed. "Clay shouldn't have to go. Being a farmer ought to keep him out of the draft. I don't know what I'd do, living out there with just Steve."

Elizabeth clenched her coffee cup. "He hasn't—I mean, you're his daughter-in-law and—has he ever—you know?"

"Why, Mom!" Oriana laughed. "I didn't know the Ladies'

Club discussed things like that." Sobering, she went on, "No, he hasn't. He *looks* at me, but I guess he isn't that crazy. It's just being around him, his business, the way he pushes Clay around, how he ignores Scooter because she isn't a boy—"

"He'd d-damn well better not make that child suffer," Elizabeth said.

Oriana laughed again. "Mom, you're priceless."

"I'm not just trying to be modern, you know. I've cursed before."

Mostly when she was alone, she admitted. She had never thrown mean, hateful words at George, though they yelled at each other plenty of times. You could say you took back the words, but that didn't mean they'd never be forgotten.

Oriana rose and carried their cups to the sink, where she rinsed and placed them upside down on the drainboard. "Joe's supposed to have a rebuilt carburetor for us, and I hope so. Steve means to take his trade to the Shell place if Joe gets behind again."

"I don't think it'll matter," Elizabeth said. "He signed up in the army."

"Jesus! Without consulting Joyce? What does she—I'd better stop by and see her."

"Ask her about Christmas?" Elizabeth kissed her daughter's cheek and watched her through the gate and into Steve Canfield's rattly old truck. She felt somehow naked and threatened, as if something huge and ponderous loomed over her house and family, a monstrous power nobody could stop. Shivering, she ducked back inside and closed the front door, resisting an urge to slide the bolt.

Leaving a trail of blue smoke, the GMC almost turned corners in town by itself. Oriana thought she could drive around Coshocton in her sleep without bumping a fender. She should be able to; she'd never been out of the county. Clay said everything was right here, and there was no sense running off to look somewhere else. It was like that song, "Back in Your Own Backyard."

Maybe so, she thought, but just once she'd like to see for herself. Zanzibar, Rangoon, Tripoli—wonderous names that rang with magic, places for adventure and romance on moon-silver beaches.

But Main Street was real, and she parked down from the Buckeye Men's and Boy's Store, serving Coshocton since 1909. She couldn't remember ever looking in the window herself, but every so often Steve Canfield made a point of saying what new things were in, for *boys*.

Even if Joe had enlisted, Joyce was still a better example for little Louise to follow, growing up. Joyce had no kids and no in-laws, for both of Joe's parents were dead. But would Louise pattern herself after anybody? The girl was about to become a handful. She was already sassy and hard to reach.

Oriana didn't think she'd been so smart-mouthed and uppity, nor had Joyce. Mom would've slapped them silly back then. But little Louise was the baby—probably came as a big surprise—and got away with just about everything. Hands in coat pockets, Oriana hipped open the hardware store door. She'd done it for so long that there was a shiny place on the brass.

"Hi, Joyce. Daddy here?"

Her sister leaned against a counter, a pretty girl with a sad mouth and angry eyes. "Down to Jacobs Insurance, probably trying to cut back on his premiums. Underwood might have a better deal, he figures. I think they're about the same."

Hopping up on the back counter, Oriana sat bumping heels against familiar, scarred oak. "Did Joe really sign up?"

"He did."

Oriana waited, but Joyce did not go on. Her sister looked tired and needed to do something with her deep brown hair.

Joyce said, "I sold a toilet and tub today; new folks in town. Farmers are buying early for next year, after that good crop. But Daddy sure doesn't need me here. I keep trying to get on at the paper company, but the steno jobs are taken and my typing's rusty anyhow. Any other job goes to a *man* with a family to support."

"It'll pick up. The war—"

"The goddamn war! Sure—it solves everything for men. They can run off to God knows where, but here we are, we lucky women, doing the same damn thing."

"Joe didn't ask you?"

"Ask me?" Joyce's mouth twisted. "He didn't even *tell* me until I heard it from half the bums he drove down to Columbus with. They got drunk and had a party."

Oriana offered a cigarette and Joyce took it. Oriana said, "You can come home now, get out of the house you hate. Soon you'll have a good job, and with no kids to care for, you can save—"

Joyce hissed a knife blade of smoke. "Maybe I'll divorce him. I've wanted to, a hundred times."

Sharing some of her sister's pain, Oriana dropped from the counter and around back of it to Daddy's stool. So pretty, her sister, voted Most Popular at Coshocton High; cheerleader, despite Mom's embarrassment over such short skirts and tight sweaters; good student, everything breaking right for her. Until she got married and it all stopped. So bitter now, her sister.

The door clinged warning from the little bell overhead, and she saw Joe Dayton slouch in. Once, high-school girls had palpitated when he ran the ball or just walked big-chested in his letter sweater, but no more. It had taken Joe about a year to look seedy and start a beer belly.

He said, "Joyce—"

Oriana said, "Excuse me. I'll be in the storeroom if—"

"Stay," Joyce said, now erect and stiff at the counter.

"Sure," Joe said. "Your whole damn family will hear every word, anyhow. Stay, big sister, and watch a soldier tell his old lady good-bye."

"If you're a soldier, the country's in trouble." Joyce pointed at the cardboard suitcase by his feet. "Did you pack your Sacred Heart game ball and senior sweater? In the army, nobody knows who you *were*."

"Goddammit, woman. I came here to—to do it right before I go off to war, and you jump right in bad-mouthin'. Can't you say a goddamn thing without naggin' at me?"

Oriana slipped from the high stool and ducked into the storeroom. The dividing wall was thin and she couldn't help hearing them, but she didn't have to watch them cut each other into agonized ribbons.

"You're happy," Joyce accused. "You're so damned happy to get away from me and from Coshocton that you couldn't wait."

His voice rumbled. "Look, it was the patriotic thing to do. I mean, me and the fellas had a few beers and kind of got caught up in it. A man don't have to ask his old lady about a thing like that."

"How many of your friends actually signed up with you?"

"Ah—just Tommy Appleton. Jerry and Mason got too drunk and sick, and they turned down Blackie."

There was a stretch of quiet, and Joyce said, "You might have discussed it with me. It's my life too."

"They'd of got me anyhow, woman. Everybody says it's better to enlist first. I mean, I ain't in a defense plant, and no kids, and in good shape, so—but I didn't expect to leave so quick."

Oriana's eyes ranged the shadowy storeroom, seeing the sagging couch where Daddy sometimes sneaked a nap; boxes and barrels and stuffing she used to play in as a child. The curly wood shavings, thin and twisted, used to get down her neck and itch her.

In the store proper, Joyce said, "I might go to Daddy's; I don't know."

"I figured you'd run to Daddy, all right. I'll be sendin' you allotments anyway. Fifty a month, the sergeant said."

"I might move somewhere else, but use Daddy's address. I mean to get a real job. Hell, I'll have to."

Joe grunted and Oriana could hear his feet scrape the cement floor. "You won't be doin' no more than any patriotic wife. I —you goin' to kiss me good-bye?—I got to catch the noon bus."

Oriana moved away from the wall and into shadows. She didn't really have to go, but she used the toilet, set into its tiny closet, and made noise when the old pull-chain roared water down the pipe. What a farewell between husband and wife; what a sadness between two people. She wanted to cry for her sister, for the cheerleader's lost cheers.

When she went back into the store, Joyce was wiping her eyes with a fingertip. Oriana said, "I'm sorry."

"Me too." Joyce's full lips looked bruised, as if she had bitten them. "Doesn't even let me know he's leaving until the last minute. I may never see the son of a bitch again, and he'd rather spend his last days with his *buddies*. I need a cigarette. I need a drink, too, but I don't suppose there's a bottle in your purse."

"Can I do anything?"

Joyce shook her head. "Not unless you can go back about

five years, and when the pastor says, 'Is there anyone here knows why this man and this woman—' "

Oriana put her arms around her sister and pulled her close, holding Joyce until all tenseness went out of the slim, fine body. "You can do anything you want—stay, leave, work, sleep in, whatever. Maybe this is what you need, Sis."

She stepped back then. "I have to go by the library before I head home. I want to pile books on the table before Steve come in. It irritates him for a woman to waste time and get wild ideas that ain't good for her, bigod. You should hear him."

Joyce rubbed her face with a plain hankie. "Are they all like that?"

"Not Daddy—I don't think. I really have to run, Joyce."

"What if Clay signs up? What will you do then, you *and* Scooter?"

Oriana's stomach tightened. "He wouldn't, and probably won't get drafted, either. Somebody has to produce food for the army, and farmers will be exempt. If—if somehow he gets called up, I'll handle it."

"And Steve Canfield?"

"Him too. But it won't happen. Look—do you want to come out to the farm for a few days? Scooter will be tickled and you can sort of clear your head, walk by the river, sit under the trees."

Her sister brushed a kiss along her cheek and worked up a smile. "Thanks anyhow. I belong in town, and I'll be swell, so don't worry."

In the truck and headed for the library on Fourth and Locust, Oriana knew she would never trade places with Joyce, despite her father-in-law. She had a husband who cared for her, and she had her child. She wouldn't allow a war to interfere with her family. Oriana smiled; she was beginning to understand Mom.

chapter 6

England's Prime Minister, Winston Churchill, spending Christmas Eve with President Roosevelt, claimed a "blood right" to be in the United States. "Beyond the fact that my mother was American and another ancestor fought in Washington's army, I might have made it here on my own," he said.

The Prime Minister shared in the traditional Christmas tree-lighting ceremony on the South Portico. . . .

—Washington, D.C., December 25, 1941 (UP)

Oriana brought a platter of pancakes from the kitchen and heaped her daughter's plate first. It didn't have the desired effect, because Steve was wrapped up in the news. When Clay finished with the syrup, he poured some atop Scooter's lavishly buttered stack.

"Bastard Japs," Steve Canfield snorted. "They jumped into Hong Kong the same time they were bombing Pearl Harbor. Couple days later, they're all over the Philippines like a bunch of yellow snakes. But we got at least a bigod fighting man out there. If General MacArthur had his say a year ago, those slant-eyed little bastards wouldn't have caught the fleet napping."

He shoveled food into his mouth without taking his eyes from the newspaper. Oriana smiled at something Scooter said about school and warned the girl to finish her sausage.

"Be quiet," Steve said, "and listen to the radio. The British are still gettin' hell kicked out of them in Burma, but it'll take the Japs longer'n they count on, bigod. Same way in Singapore."

"*All* your meat, Scooter. You know what I said about Santa Claus."

Clay held out his cup. Oriana poured coffee, and Clay said, "I still don't know all those places; they're just a bunch of names."

"Liable to see them up close," Steve said, and pointed to his cup. Oriana filled it and sat down. He frowned at her. "Always pour too damn much. How'm I going to get the milk in?"

"Sorry," she said. Then, "Clay's married and a father *and* a farmer. He won't get drafted."

"Man don't have to wait for the draft." Steve cocked his head until the radio announcer gave way to the soft strains of Wayne King's orchestra playing " 'Till Reveille." "And they better get to writing better songs, bigod. Something *strong*, like 'Over There.' "

"And 'My Buddy'?" Oriana asked sweetly.

Steve snorted again. "That ain't no war song. Bunch of pacifists and so-called conscientious objectors want us to think so. None of them's showed up at our board, and they better bigod not. So many red-blooded American boys enlisting—"

"You said you wouldn't." Oriana looked at her husband. She watched his fork worry the last of the pancakes.

"Didn't exactly enlist."

"Volunteered to get drafted," Steve said.

She stiffened. "Without talking to me?"

Steve said, "A man don't *ask* his wife."

"Scooter," she said, "you can go play now. Be sure to wear your mittens."

"Leaving for Fort Dix, New Jersey, end of next week." Steve grinned at her. "Guess Clay meant to surprise you."

If a shark smiled, Oriana thought, it would look like that. "I'm surprised, all right. God*damn* you, Clay!"

"Now, honey—I didn't want to upset the holidays."

Christmas cold slid under the door and wrapped an icy coil

around her middle. Atop the table, her hands fisted and opened like someone else's fingers gone arthritic and clawed. Quavery and brittel, shards of a voice pushed up from her throat.

"How do you expect me—our baby—"

Reaching, he covered her hand with his capable one, with its fine scattering of pale gold hairs. "You'll be all right. Pa'll hire two or three handymen, sure-enough rejects and not criminals or conscientious objectors. He means to put in as much corn as he can, then hold back the hogs and cows until the price goes—"

"You belong right here," she said. "With Scooter and me, producing extra food for the Allies, working your own land like nobody else can."

Steve grunted. "Ain't exactly his land yet. Wouldn't look right, would it? My own boy stayin' home while I'm drafting other boys. Clay ain't one of your—well, he just ain't. He's American clear through, and not about to shirk his duty."

"Clay," she said, "just once, can't you talk for yourself?"

Clearing his throat, he said, "Now, hon. I figure we'll knock out the Japs in three, four months, no more'n six. They can't shoot worth a dime, account of those slant eyes. Then we'll go after ol' Hitler. Oriana, I didn't come right out and tell you before, because here it is next to Christmas—"

"Whole lot of boys ain't spending Christmas to home," Steve said. "Lot signed up right off, and there's MacArthur in the Philippines—"

"None of them are *my* husband or Scooter's father! I— we—"

"That little girl's apt to forget her rightful name, you keep callin' her that. We *all* have to make sacrifices, woman. Roosevelt said so. Now be quiet, more news coming on the radio."

When Oriana jumped up, her chair crashed over. She aimed a finger at her father-in-law. "You, dammit! Why don't *you* go? You wanted this war, why don't you jump in the middle of it and let Clay be?"

"Now, hon," Clay said. "Now, Oriana—"

Steve's muddy eyes sharpened and a flicker of light from cold sun slid through the kitchen window and glinted along his unshaven cheek. She saw a drop of syrup hanging at the corner of his mouth. "Canfields ain't run-of-the-mill," he said. "Ain't convicts or sissies, neither—like some I could name. I got an important job right here. Who better'n me to know which Coshocton boys are shirkers and which ain't?"

She didn't look at her husband when he said, "Pa—hon, come on now."

"They told me in Columbus that I'm old and not fit for the front, and needed more here. Said I was to be Civil Defense chief too, maybe head up a scrap drive." Steve leaned back. "Clay gets to represent the Canfields, and it's only right."

When Clay reached for her arm, she twisted back and stormed out of the house. No jacket, no hat, she walked fast, not noticing the cold, not sorting out the frosty smells of winter, not hearing its special crisp sounds. Tears blinded her and she angrily dashed them away.

"Mama, mama, wait!"

Her daughter came panting, breath trailing little hurried clouds.

"Mama, where you going? You don't even have your galoshes on."

Folding her arms across her belly, Oriana hunched over Scooter as snowy wind flailed her hair and struck down her spine. She was colder than she'd ever been, icicled deep into her soul.

Through teeth clamped so hard they hurt, Oriana said, "All right, dear. Want to go back to the house with me?"

Randy Parker sat in the coffee shop with Martha Swensen. "But this may be the last frat party until the war's over. The guys are making it a big one, and I have to be there. I can't turn down sixty cents an hour. It'll buy presents for my family." And you, he thought, but didn't say it.

Martha said, "You're brighter than any of them and they know it. That's why they torment you, use you for a drudge."

"It doesn't bother me, and when I've cleaned up after, I'll be free to catch the bus to Coshocton." He touched her hand. "Will you come with me and meet my folks?"

She was quiet. A jukebox played something sentimental, and another couple laughed together, down the room. The counterman turned a sizzling hamburger. Martha said, "You've asked me before, and I said Holiness Church duties were more important, that we spend the night and day in quiet prayer."

"Well," Randy said, "I really wanted you to—"

"I'll go with you."

"What? Hey, that's terrific, that's just great! I'll let the folks know you're coming. It won't be as if you're a stranger. I've written letters. Gee, Martha, this is really swell."

"Maybe they can help me change your mind. It's only logical that—"

"I can't be a minister. First, there's no money for changing schools, you know that. And"—he looked down the cafe to the laughing people in the far booth—"I just can't deal with theology and human souls. Right now it's hard enough to keep my grades up, but divinity school—"

Martha tented her fingers and closed her eyes, murmuring. Randy glanced around the cafe and back. "Please, Martha, not here."

She opened clear eyes. "Anywhere, anytime is right for prayer. God will answer mine and guide your path for doing good in His name. He will keep you out of the army."

Her voice was rising. Randy caught her hands. "Martha, people are staring at us. Please, I—I'll think about it."

George Parker said, "We'll close up early, Joyce. Nobody buys hardware on Christmas Eve. But if we put in other items, those new blackout lights, different lamps, air-raid whistles and such—never mind. That's for later on. Say, you *are* coming home with me?"

His daughter shrugged. "I guess. Joe's supposed to call, if he can get through. The lines are apt to be tied up for days."

Turning the toilet light out and the night light on, George locked the alley door. "I still say you'd be better off with us. Your old room's ready."

"Mine and Oriana's room, you mean. Louise has it now, doesn't she? I don't know. I'm kind of used to being alone —even when Joe was here."

George stooped to close the little safe and twiddle its dial. These days there was money in it. The war wasn't a month old, and it seemed everybody was buying whatever they thought might be in short supply, anything that had even a slight chance of being rationed: wire, glass, lightbulbs, anything.

He said, "While Joe's away, you could save on rent by coming home. I'd feel better, knowing you're safe."

Joyce cleared the register. "I'm a grown woman, Daddy. My husband's supposed to take care of me."

"He can't, honey. Not while he's off in the service."

"He's got a good excuse now. He could have stayed with me for Christmas, and signed up after. I'll dust those shelves tomorrow, Daddy."

"Tomorrow's Christmas, Joyce. It'll be fun roasting chestnuts and making eggnog and singing carols like we used to. And Randy's bringing his girlfriend for the holidays."

He helped her on with her coat, wanting to squeeze her and pat her hair, to say everything was all right. But Joyce didn't like that. She was determined to be strong and independent, somehow.

She said, "Oriana's not coming?"

"Later tomorrow. We won't open presents until Scooter gets there. Steve insisted on having Christmas at the farm, since Clay'll be leaving soon after."

On the sidewalk, he swung the old padlock into place and shook it. She said then, "Joe could have waited like Clay."

"Have to give him credit, honey. First thing December eighth, there was Joe and all his buddies in line."

"They were drunk," Joyce said, opening the truck door before he could and hiking up on the seat. He glanced quickly at two bobby-soxers who jiggled by.

George drove slowly beneath Santa Claus faces and big stars strung across Main. The Chamber of Commerce wouldn't light them this year because of the war. Who'd bomb Coshocton?

"Hear how San Francisco went crazy?" He glanced over at the courthouse. Not a single light there, but a fine-looking girl waited on the corner. When Joyce didn't answer, he went on, "Three times that Sunday night they thought they were getting bombed. Some mixed-up general kept saying Jap carrier planes were making passes over the city, even though our pursuit planes couldn't find them and all those big searchlights didn't pick them up. He acted mad when folks doubted him, and said it would've been better if the Japs *had* dropped some bombs to wake up the city. I'm glad we don't live out there."

Joyce asked softly, "How long will it take, Daddy? The war?"

"Don't know, honey. Might be a whole lot longer than we think. Even though the radio and newspapers seem to be downplaying the news or skipping some, I think we're just finding out what bad shape our army and navy's in. Does Joe know anything about when he'll go over, or where?"

Joyce shook her head. "He sent me one postcard, telling me he meant to call tonight. One lousy card."

Again, George had the urge to pet her, comfort her. "He's probably real busy. The army keeps 'em hopping. You'll see. Soon as Joe gets time, he'll tell you all about it." He paused and said, "I don't know if he'll say exactly *where* or *when* he gets shipped over. They might start censoring mail so it won't be easy for enemy submarines to find our troop ships. A slip of the lip can sink a ship, they say."

Pulling to the curb, George stopped the truck. It ran for a few seconds after he turned off the ignition. "Wish he was here to tinker with this old truck."

"Better get a new one," Joyce said. "They won't be making any more until after the war. If this one breaks down completely, you can't make deliveries. Torrance has a new Chevy and old man Canfield grabbed a new tractor and *two* trucks."

"Doc Shaw's making do with his old Hudson; says defense people might need new cars more. Says if he has to, he'll drag out his old buggy and buy a horse. I guess I'm with Doc, but I admit it's kind of ironic, first time I can afford a brand-new truck, and it's not patriotic."

Joyce got out and looked at the bay window. "No lights on the tree."

"Just tinsel and popcorn strings, and those funny old decorations you kids made in school, long ago. Your mom will never throw them out."

"Before we go in," she said, "did you and Ron really try to sign up?"

He sighed. "Just me, and the sergeant almost laughed at me. At least I got a free medical checkup out of it."

"Mr. Cassingham got accepted, and he's older than you. Did they find something wrong, something you haven't told us?"

He took her elbow and walked her to the front steps. "Nothing to worry about. Blood pressure a little high and a jiggle in the doctor's stethoscope. Sometimes my heart goes

boom-bumpity-boom instead of boom-boom-bumpity—
something like that. Don't say anything to your mother."

She turned to him on the porch. "I thought Ron was going with you."

"I thought so too." He sighed again. "He never showed up."

chapter 7

Herd the Japs up and pack them off. Let them be pinched, hurt, hungry, and dead up against it. . . .

—*San Francisco Examiner*, January 6, 1942, columnist Henry McLemore

---

Louise Parker stretched her legs under the Studebaker's dash. "You know, I wish somebody'd get smart and put a record player in a car. Then we could play our favorite bands over and over. There's so much dumb old war news on now."

Deke caressed her thigh. "Music's good, but loving is better."

"Honestly! Is that all guys think about?"

"It's all I can think about around *you*, little Louise."

"Don't call me that! You know damn well I don't like it. Little Louise, baby Louise. That's crap."

Deke kissed her ear. "But your *are* little. Like a diamond, a beautiful doll, a tiny Venus de Milo."

She moved around to kiss him, but kept her thighs together. "I'm not that fat. Deke, you're not signing up, are you?"

"Not me, baby. My old man would throw a fit. I have to graduate first, and he knows somebody in Washington. Guess I'll be an officer, if I have to go at all."

Louise nibbled the side of his throat. "Air Corps, huh? They look so spiffy with their silver wings and all. If I was a man, that's what I'd do—fly."

He didn't say anything. Deke's breath turned ragged and his hand slipped under her sweater. She wiggled so he could unsnap her bra, and gasped as her freed breast fitted his hand.

"Man, man. Stiff nipple, warm and round. Louise baby, please. I may be dead this time next year. Don't keep teasin'."

Stroking his hair, she let him burrow beneath her sweater and kiss her breast. It felt crazy good, his mouth and tongue working. Before she realized it, Deke's other hand slipped between her legs. As long as he went slow and easy, she didn't fight him. But when he tried to pull her over on top of him, she jerked back, panting and shaky.

"N-no, Deke—"

He yanked her back over him and she felt his thing push against her, long and thick, outside his pants. He said, "Dammit, baby, what the hell are you—"

Daringly, she reached down and closed her fingers over it. When he shuddered, she squeezed it gently and moved her hand up and down, up and down. Deke's hungry mouth dipped back to her breasts. Moaning, he chewed at her, sucked at her, and she could feel dampness in her mound. Suddenly he arched and hissed, holding her waist so tight she had trouble breathing. His juice flowed hot over her hand. That's how it is, she thought. The books and cloakroom giggles didn't prepare her for this. Jeepers, what would it be like to go all the way?

He wasn't pushy now, only embarrassed as he fumbled out a handkerchief and rolled away from her to clean himself. Louise didn't mind all that much, but she rubbed her hand under the seat edge.

"Deke, have you gone all the way with girls?"

He lit smokes for both of them and passed her one. When he drew hard on his cigarette, its brightened glow outlined his mouth for a second. "Sure, plenty of times."

"Who with?"

"I—hey, I don't tell."

Pulling the bra out of her sweater, she crammed it into her purse. "I'm not ashamed to be a virgin; you shouldn't be, either."

"Dammit, I said I've had plenty. Guys are different. They start early. I never heard a guy called a virgin."

"They had to be, with some girl. Was it Melanie De Hart? Kate Stewart? I bet it was that peroxide blonde cheerleader, what's-her-name."

He said, "Open the glove compartment and get the bottle."

"I won't drink any. I have to be around my family, and somebody's sure to smell my breath."

"It's for me. After *that*, I need a drink. How many guys have you done it to?"

"This was the first time. I thought it'd be a good idea. You were getting rough."

Deke drank again and coughed. "Wish I'd brought a chaser. Look, I'll be honest because I like you more than any girl I ever knew. If you won't tell it around."

"Me?" she said.

"Prostitutes," he mumbled. "Whores. That's all I've been with, in Youngstown and Akron. Once in Sandusky."

"Don't you catch something awful from women like that?"

Deke rolled down his window and flipped the cigarette butt. "Not if you're careful. A guy's got to learn sometime."

"Whores," she breathed. "Paying money to do it. Jeepers. Were they pretty? Old?"

He started the car. "I'm taking you home. See you tomorrow?"

"Call me up. I probably can't get away until after dinner." She clicked on the radio, feeling kind of good, feeling older.

". . . from Ryukyu Islands, a Japanese force estimated at ten thousand men has landed on Lamon Bay, close to Manila . . . General MacArthur has withdrawn his troops to the Bataan Peninsula . . ."

"Find some music," Deke said.

chapter 8

The Office of War Information announced today
that the carrier *Lexington* went down in the battle of
the Coral Sea on May 8. Casualties were heavy. .
. .

—Washington, D.C., May 30, 1942 (INS)

When she peeled off her garden gloves, Elizabeth felt that good
kind of tired from a job well done. Her Victory Garden was the
best on the street. Putting the kettle on, she took down the can
where used tea leaves were kept. These were good for at least
another two cups. Tea wasn't that hard to come by, but like the
government said, everything had to be used to the limit.

She did the same thing with family coffee, boiling and
straining it repeatedly. Coffee wasn't rationed yet, like sugar,
but would certainly be before long. When the kettle whistled,
Elizabeth began her tea routine, and sweetened the liquid with
a dab of honey. It just didn't taste the same, but molasses or
honey was something people had to get used to. Down at the
Busy Bee Cafe, they had a sign: *Use Less Sugar and Stir Like
Hell*.

Radio announcements told her she was in the front line,
doing a job almost important as the country's servicemen. One

pound of fat, she was told, had enough glycerin to make powder for fifty .30-caliber bullets. If every family in America stopped buying just one can of something for a week, thirty-eight Liberty Ships could be made from the saved metal. Make do, use it up, wear it out, or do without, the government said.

And of course, Elizabeth dutifully peeled labels, washed and flattened every can so collectors could salvage them. She felt good about all this, not moaning and fussing like some women—that Patricia Alexander for one. A body would think the whole war was started just to harass her. Pat Alexander made the sewing meetings miserable, always complaining. But so long as she contributed something to the war effort, they couldn't very well chase her home. So much to do: Red Cross and Salvation Army sewing; Bundles for Britain. Elizabeth was so busy nowadays, she had little time for her family. But there was no forgetting them, though they seemed farther from her, not so close knit any more. Joyce had moved back home after Joe was shipped out, but she often stayed late at the store, and little Louise was hardly home at all, between school and dates.

George—Elizabeth sipped tea and frowned—she wasn't so sure George's wartime responsibilities weren't too much for him. It wasn't enough that he built a big scrap-metal bin in front of the store, but he took it upon himself to make rounds through the county, using up his A-Card gasoline, four gallons a week.

He had a seat on the Office of Price Administration board too, but as president, Steve Canfield ran that to suit himself, coming down hard on certain hoarders and tending to look the other way when some friend or big businessman became entangled in government regulations. It was all confusing to Elizabeth, who had trouble coping with red points and blue points.

She took off her stained smock and slipped out of the old pair of George's pants she wore for garden work. They were so baggy and knee-grimed she didn't want to be seen in them. Stuffing them into the laundry tub, she swished a onetime coffee can through the water. It was half-filled with bits of soap that would normally be thrown away. She'd poked holes all around the can with an icepick, and it made perfectly good bubbles.

Washing up, Elizabeth thought ahead to the canning yet to do. There wasn't much ready to put up in May, just some early English peas and shallots, but she would make time in her schedule for it. She'd never canned much, only jellies and jams, after Oriana got married and brought so much fresh stuff from the farm. But now it was important to put everything by. She felt a little guilty about getting so much butter from Oriana. So she gave her ration stamps to Hansen's Bakery, trading them for bread or sweet rolls.

Donning a house dress, she dug out the carpet sweeper and went to work, thankful that her own boys were still safe from harm. She supposed she ought to feel guilty for that too. But she was glad they were home and not fighting for their lives in some far off country.

They didn't see Ron much, since he now worked night shift at the glove factory. The plant was running day and night, turning out equipment for the army, but it might have to shut down if the rubber shortage got worse. The Japanese had grabbed those countries that grew rubber. Elizabeth hadn't thought about it before. Rubber was something always around, like gasoline or tires or sugar. Goodness, who ever thought of shortages in America?

Vigorously, she swept the parlor. Ron had never worked so long at any job before, and she was proud of him. Randy was still in school, quieter and more studious since meeting Martha Swensen. A fine, strong girl, Elizabeth thought, but pushy about her religion. She acted as if she owned Randy, more like *she* was his mother. Still, she was the first girl Randy had showed real interest in.

Elizabeth put away the Bissel. She hated the thing, but it was better than a regular broom. She really wanted the Hoover vacuum that George had on display at the store, because it'd probably be the last available for a while. She'd say something to George. No woman deserved the machine more, and it wouldn't hurt the war effort.

Ron Parker found his way around campus to the frat house where his brother waited tables. Dusk was gathering. When he slowed the Ford to smile at a college girl, she smiled back. He felt pretty good. Randy didn't know he was coming, and he hadn't told anybody at home, either. He was running a little early, since it hadn't taken near as long at Youngstown as he'd figured.

He might have gone to Sandusky, but it wouldn't be the same. Why the hell did Gunter Hindeman do it? He ought to have told the whole fucking county to kiss his rosy ass. But no, the dumb farmer went and signed up for the marines, to show he was as good an American as any. Hell, he had an exemption because he was a farmer, and a damned good one.

Drawing the Model A curbside under a big elm tree, Ron shut it off. Of course, Gunter didn't enlist right off. He waited for that bunch of bastards from town, so they wouldn't think he was running. They came all right, eight of them in two pickups, hollering and beating on Gunter's gate with tire irons.

Ron gripped the steering wheel and smiled. That bunch of assholes sure didn't expect to be hit from behind. Ron had three on the ground before the other drunks noticed, two squealing like stuck hogs because his jack handle broke their collarbones. It was funny how Joe Dayton tried to act brave and back down at the same time. Big fullback Joe Dayton, high-school wonder and pack leader.

"Ain't none of your business, boy. We come after this goddamn Nazi, and you got no right bustin' nobody with that jack handle."

Ron looked where Gunter was coming from his house with a lantern. "You got the right to gang up on a guy who's a better American than all you shitheels put together?"

"Goddamn," one of the Britt cousins said. "Willie's head is laid wide open. It might be fractured."

"You and that jack handle," Joe Dayton said. "If you didn't—"

"You can have it," Ron said, and threw it into Joe's belly. He followed with a hook to Joe's head, banging his other hand to the throat. When the big man reeled back, Ron kicked him neatly and solidly in the groin.

Everybody got scarce, loading their wounded into the trucks and hauling ass before Gunter Hindeman even reached the gate. All the big clod carried was his lantern. He lifted it and said, "Vell, now. Not your fight this is."

"Anybody comes sneakin' around at night again, carry a

shotgun or a double-bitted axe, you dumb Dutchman. I wasn't buttin' in on your fight, I needed the exercise."

"*Danke*," Gunter said. "A liar you are."

"Sure," Ron said. "Everybody knows that."

That was months ago, and he hadn't known then that Gunter was waiting for his uncle's family from Pittsburgh to come run the farm. After they got there, Gunter signed up and left without a word to anyone.

Ron pocketed the car keys and walked around the old building, all worn brick and ivy, looking for the kitchen door. Gunter Hindeman shouldn't have gone off that way, damn it. He oughtn't let a bunch of drunks chase him off his own land. Joe Dayton and four of the gang took off and volunteered out of town so they didn't have to face the laughs for getting whipped. The others stayed quiet in the hospital, so nobody really knew much about that night at Gunter Hindeman's.

The smell of food reached Ron as he climbed the steps to the back door of the frat house. Two black cooks paid him no mind, so he stood just inside the swinging door to the dining room. When somebody came in or went out, he caught glimpses of tables and guys eating. Waiters in white jackets hurried around, bringing trays of food or taking away dirty dishes. He saw Randy among them.

Guys in letter sweaters at one table were giving Randy trouble. When he came close, somebody patted him on the ass or whistled at him, or some such bullshit. They had the whole dining room laughing. When he'd start away, they'd say *oh, come on, dearie* in falsetto voices.

Randy finally came into the kitchen and Ron said, "What the hell's wrong with you, man?"

Slipping out of his white jacket, Randy said, "Hi. I didn't know you were coming. It's good to see you."

Ron jerked his head at the door. "You ain't answered me."

"That?" Randy shrugged. "Just horseplay. I'm through for the night. Want to come up to my room? It's just down the street. What are you doing here, anyway? Mom wrote that you're working nights on a steady job. That's great."

Ron stared at his brother. "You let those bastards call you queer?"

"What's the difference? They get tired of it after a while."

Ron shook his head. "The difference is you and pride. I know you got the guts."

"I have the job too," Randy answered. "And there's only another year after this. Come on, let's go catch up on everything."

"You still got your girl? What's she think about this grab-ass crap?"

Randy hung up the white jacket and took down his windbreaker. "Martha understands."

Out on the back steps, Ron said, "You screwed her yet?"

Randy looked away. "I—she's a very religious girl."

"You ever tried? Never mind, just give me your address and I'll see you later. Somethin' I got to do first."

"You won't make trouble?"

"Got to see about my car; left it parked too far away."

Randy waited for hours in his room, but Ron didn't show. Puzzled, he fell asleep in his clothes, and when he woke, still no brother. Worried now, he downed coffee warmed on the hotplate and reached for the doorknob. Then he saw the folded paper slipped under the door and bent for it. A set of car keys fell out.

In scribbled pencil, the note said: *Came to give you my car. Take your girl out in it, and maybe you'll get lucky. Joined the army yesterday and you're the only one knows. Up here nobody cares about my "record" in Coshocton, so I don't need my old jalopy now. Oh—your school's football team may be fucked up some this year. Don't answer questions, don't deny anything. Okay? And say my good-byes at home.*

He found the Model A parked in front of his rooming house and drove it gingerly to the campus. Ron thought a lot of this car. He'd also been scornful about fighting a war for those fat-asses on the draft board. Something had changed Ron's mind.

That day, in almost every class, Randy was conscious of whispers and stares that broke away from him when he stared back. He couldn't understand it. When he checked in to wait tables at Alpha Omega that evening, he found the reason.

"Jesus," somebody said as he carried his tray past, "look at him, not a mark on the bastard. Now how in hell—"

". . . ruined the backfield . . . two of 'em could be out for the season . . . would you believe a guy like him could . . . ?"

". . . just called 'em out and damned near crippled Bart Jolson . . . looked like a train hit him . . ."

"Look at that jacket . . . not a smudge on it . . . how you figure he . . . oh, hello, Randy. No hurry with the potatoes, no hurry with anything . . . take your time, buddy."

In the kitchen the black cook said, "He come in here and put on a white jacket. Everybody thought it was you, but I seen that crooked nose. Anyhow, he throwed a pitcher of water on 'em at the table and dared 'em out. Whooie, but that man's a flat-out *he-dog*! Like to eat 'em up, bustin' heads and stompin' ribs, time they went down. Never seen nothin' like it. All these frat boys got it in their heads *you* ain't to be messed with, and I ain't about to tell 'em no different. Best you don't, neither."

So like his brother, Randy thought; so damned like Ron to do a thing like that, if for no other cause than to show he was different, not a look-alike, act-alike twin. But he'd mauled those lettermen for another reason: for love, although he'd never say that. And it was a going-away gift only he could give. But why join the army?

Randy didn't find out until he drove home the next weekend, without Martha Swensen. His dad asked if he knew Gunter Hindeman had been killed on Guadalcanal—the German who farmed that place out Route 541?

Funny, George said, before Hindeman went into the marines, some town kids had been bothering him, acting up because he talked like a movie Nazi. Funny a boy like that should be the first Coshocton serviceman killed in action.

"You'd think Ron would tell his mother, at least," George said. "Going off like that, when we thought he finally settled down. He was working steady and keeping out of trouble. He could have gone to Detroit or somewhere and made more money, but he stayed home. I started to think he was growing up and considering marriage. Still, I don't feel bad that he's in the service, but I wish he'd told your mother." George looked at Randy.

Randy said, "They didn't care about his police record where he enlisted, and he told them, too."

George said, "No cause for you to think about going, not until you finish school. I mean—Steve Canfield might have it in for you, but you could go off like your brother did. I hear they're taking convicts right out of prison and putting them in uniform."

"Did the telegram say how Gunter Hindeman was killed?"

"No. Just the War Department facts. His uncle got it. They're putting Gunter's name on the honor roll down at the courthouse."

"And leaving room for plenty of others," Randy said.

George looked sharply at his son. It wasn't like Randy to be sarcastic or bitter. "Yes," he said. "Other Coshocton boys might have to make the supreme sacrifice."

"For God and country."

Jaws tightening, George said, "That's nothing to get smart about, boy."

"I'm not. I was thinking of another religion, one that doesn't believe in any kind of war. Martha Swensen can't see any reason for war, and her church worships the same God."

"Then she's pretty mixed up. Can't she see Hitler as the embodiment of evil, as Satan himself? And the sneaky, dirty Japs—"

Randy just stood there blanked out, looking ready to agree with anything said. This temporary flare up was the only one George could remember. Even as a baby, Randy had gone along without making trouble, giving up when his brother snatched a favorite toy. College didn't seem to be changing the boy very much, and he only had a year to go.

"Well," George said, "I have to get back to the store. Randy, do you know I had to hire another clerk? Your sister's mostly the bookkeeper now. Store's doing real well, a runaway business, even if sudden shortages catch us. One week it's batteries, the next, alarm clocks. You wouldn't believe my back orders."

George left the house and walked all the way to the store. It made him feel good to swing along in the early autumn air, and he was saving gas too. He hadn't been all that casual about Ron. Why had his son suddenly run off to enlist? Things were tough overseas, worse than the news let on; he could sense it. The Solomon's campaign, and Guadalcanal? Where the hell was it? A chunk of island jungle nobody had heard of, only a place for Gunter Hindeman to die.

Japs were sinking American warships all over the South

Pacific, and there were rumors of terrible losses on America's East Coast, merchant ships exploding within sight of land. In Florida, people drove down to the beaches to watch U.S. ships torpedoed and sunk by German U-boats. Coastguardsmen kept the crowds back far as they could, but word kept getting out about hurt, oil-blackened, and shocked survivors crawling ashore. Near Miami, the playground for the rich, cemetery for ships and seamen.

But he shouldn't dwell on that. Ron would make it through the war okay. Surely the Allies would begin to roll back the enemy before long.

Pausing before his store, he looked through the big window and saw Holly Melborne waiting on a customer. Just watching her move stirred his blood. He'd been lucky to hire her. So many kids had gone off to war plants, dropping out of school to make more money than their parents ever imagined. Boys not due for the draft were working after school and weekends. More than a few caught the bus to a big town, lied about their age, and worked in a defense plant until the leaderman caught up with them. Even then, not all were kicked out.

But Holly—George moved to the side of the show window so he wouldn't be easily seen. He'd have hired her even if he didn't need her. It wasn't that she was beautiful; she wasn't. But she was young and vital, and a pure, animal sexuality oozed from her every pore. Each move she made seemed to be calculated to strike deep into a man's vitals, from rhythmic swing of honeyed hair to damply parted lips. Holly didn't walk, she undulated, all sleek muscle and unconcerned grace as her skirt pulled tightly across hips and firm buttocks. When she stood arrogantly lazy and slack, high melon breasts pointed their rounded tips hard into sweaters she always wore, as if struggling to break through.

Her perfume was musky, too heavy for a young girl. Her graygreen eyes were always half-lidded, as if she had just climbed from between warm, tangled sheets and was thinking of going back.

Joyce hated her, and it was true that Holly sometimes let a sale go sour because she didn't really care whether she made it. But that was happening all over town. Every business had its share of suddenly-in-demand workers who could quit and find another job the same day.

Deep breath steadying him, George entered his store, nodding to the people he knew, smiling welcome at strangers who spoke twangily or with slow and syrupy accents, come for work at Pretty Products, now gearing up with a big defense contract. The strangers were from Kentucky, West Virginia, and Indiana. Some had never worked at anything but struggling hillside farms. They were here for the big money, and would work overtime at every chance. But beyond shopping, they were clannish and tight-mouthed, walking lightly and warily. Already there'd been bad cutting scrapes out at the new, rowdy roadhouses that had sprung up like toadstools. Ohio boys fought with fists. The newcomers tried to kill.

"Daddy," Joyce said, "that girl keeps ringing up wrong prices on the register and—"

"Now, hon, she just needs a little time."

Joyce sniffed. "I don't think she tries; or she's not bright enough."

"Help her some, when you're caught up on those orders. Anything new on that number-four wire?"

"Nothing. They don't even bother to answer now."

He watched Holly Melborne stretch and yawn. She wasn't looking at customers, but straight at him. George swallowed. "Joyce, why don't you knock off? Randy's home for a few hours. He came to tell us Ron enlisted."

She frowned. "Without saying anything to—oh, that mean, selfish son of a—I hope he gets so lonesome he hurts. Okay, I'll go see Randy, if you can keep things going here, especially with that lazy girl."

"I'll handle her," George said, and was conscious of his palms turning damp.

chapter 9

The Office of Price Administration announced today that all processed foods will be rationed. These include soups, vegetables, canned juices, and all soft drinks containing sugar. . . .

—Washington, D.C., August 8, 1942 (INS)

Joyce recognized him immediately. No woman could forget Franco Butera's swarthy good looks. She'd just turned from the onetime restaurant window when there he was, smiling down at her with those perfect white teeth, those sultry black eyes.

"Joyce? Joyce Parker?"

Stunned, she murmured, "The spider—someone swept her away."

"Spider?"

"I—I stop here sometimes to watch this spider, dead and lonely in her web because the restaurant closed and there were no more flies for her to catch. Now she's gone. I guess somebody'll open the store again."

His chuckle lifted from a corded throat exposed by an extra button left open. "You used to do good in English, in poetry. Old lady Miller still teaching it?"

"No, no, she's been gone a long time." Joyce wished she'd taken time to straighten her hair, put on lipstick. She must look terrible. "And where—where have you been? It must be years—"

When he shrugged, curly little black hairs peeped from his open collar. "I was the star in art class, remember? Well, Pop scraped together every dime he'd been saving to bring his sister from the old country, and blew it on me. Wanted me to study in Italy, sure I was another Leonardo or at least Botticelli. It didn't take long to find out I wasn't, and my aunt in Sicily kept trying to sell a little hunk of rocky land with a few olive trees, but there was this *Fascisti* mayor, and she never made it here." His smile was wide and white. "And since Pop isn't exactly a Rockefeller, I had to walk and damned near swim and beg a way to Portugal. From there I worked my way home on a Brazilian freighter."

That's the difference, she thought. He's so European now, easy and sure of himself. In school he'd been sullen, a loner despite being so handsome. Maybe because he was the only Italian. She couldn't remember seeing him at parties.

"And you?" he said, taking her elbow. "What happened to the prettiest girl in class—except she got prettier? No, beautiful."

Why was her mouth dry? "I—I got married, you know. After that, well—"

"To Coshocton's star fullback, right? Then to college and the pros. Right again?"

They were passing Torrance's drugstore. With only the suggestion of his lean body against hers, he stopped them at the door. "The school hangout. I wasn't here much. Pop kept me sweating at the shop. Maybe I should have studied shoemaking in Italy. What say we have a big malt and stop blocking traffic on the sidewalk? Unless your husband might—"

"Joe's somewhere in England," she said. "It's the first time he got away from Coshocton. No college and certainly no professional football." Joyce paused. "I'm supposed to hurry home and see my kid brother and—oh, well, sure. Only let's make it the biggest, most fattening and goopy banana split they can put together."

"You got it," he said, and opened the door for her. For one

crazy instant she felt he might bow her inside. His laugh was nice, silky and easy. His mustache was glossy black and thin, setting off lips women would give a year's ration of nylons for. But there was nothing womanish about them in Frankie's face. His heavy-lidded eyes gave warning that here walked a man not to be trifled with.

Heads turned when they sat at a round table, on chairs with twisty wire backs, but swung as quickly away, school-kids only lazily curious. Only the soda jerk stared a bit; he was older. From behind the marble counter he said, "Yeah? What'll you have?"

Franco Butera raised his hand and crooked one finger. The soda jerk came reluctantly from his counter, rubbing both hands on his apron.

"Now," Frankie said, "you build the biggest, damnedest banana split you can create. When you think it's perfect, think again and make it better."

The counterman—Johnny-something, she recalled—said, "You want two of 'em?"

"*Marone!* You think one of us is going to watch, *stupido?*"

Joyce saw something move across the soda jerk's face, uneasiness, a touch of fear. More than confidence had come back from Europe with Franco. He wasn't the kid who'd walled himself off except in art class, the frowning boy in shabby clothes trotting home after school to work in his father's little shoe-repair shop.

She said, "You didn't just get back from Italy? I mean, with the war going—"

"I touched home base for a little while, working on my Pop. Not *for* him, *on* him. Then I went to Washington, and that town's crazier than Rome. It took months, but I got it done. *Paisans* are everywhere, and the country's not scared of us. Japs and Germans, sure, but jolly wop cooks and fat opera tenors? So we ate scampi and pasta and drank Chianti by the gallon. And what do you know? Those wops in Washington gave the Butera Corporation a big fat government contract to supply half the army with shoes and paratrooper boots, millions of them."

"That's terrific," Joyce said. "The Butera Corporation?"

"Sounded better than Butera's Shoe Repair." Franco laughed, a deep, silken music that caused bobby-soxers at the counter to turn for another look. "We bought that old dairy out toward Plainfield. The milking barn was a good start, with those cooler sheds. Brought in all the newest machinery, and imported talent. We'll be turning out the first shipments within the month."

Joyce couldn't relate Butera's darkish, leather-smelling shop with Frankie's grandiose talk. In her mind she saw the old man hunched over his shoemaker's bench, nails sticking from a corner of his mouth, gnarled fingers caressing each shoe as if it were alive and beautiful.

Franco murmured, "I know—pretty big dream for the old dago's kid. But what people here haven't yet realized is that a mountain of government money is begging somebody to shovel it away. And money doesn't give a damn who uses it, or how long your family's been in the country, or if you have a funny name—"

He stopped talking when the soda jerk placed giant splits before them. Joyce spooned whipped cream and a cherry.

"Our fat, sleepy country got bombed awake at Pearl Harbor. The bigwigs realized we needed *everything* to fight a war, and needed it *fast*. They're putting out defense contracts on a cost-plus basis, and you know what that means? It means they don't give a damn *what* it costs Butera's to make a pair of jump boots. We get paid ten-percent profit, no matter what. If the boots cost a hundred bucks apiece, we get back a hundred ten. *Marone*. Anybody can't make it rain money with that kind of setup is too dumb to count his own fingers."

She watched his eyes gleam, the excitement lighting his face. Here was a man going somewhere fast, a man who'd already knocked around the world on his own. "But where does the money come from first? I mean, to buy the old dairy and build on it, the machinery and wages—"

He looked at her over a spoonful of vanilla ice cream. "You're really interested? Business talk bores most women."

"Right now I'm not most women, but until today I guess I was." She felt his eyes reach into hers and slide deeper, way down inside.

"Good. A woman without brains is just a piece of meat. To take the analogy a little further, a fat government contract is like a great big filet mignon on the grill, and when a banker gets a whiff, he wants a bite. He can get it by furnishing the onions or baked potato. Our illustrious First Ohio National president's mouth is still watering, and he's already tasting some gravy. Mr. Horace Deacon is always ready to throw hundred-dollar bills at me, if I just walk in the door."

Seeing his face change subtly, Joyce watched him spoon a gap in his banana split. He said, "It was only a few years ago that he wouldn't hire me as janitor, like Torrance's here wouldn't put me on as delivery boy. And my Pop—he was good enough to make their shoes last longer than any other cobbler, but not good enough to use their silverware. Nobody ever invited Pop and Mama to dinner. Not one goddamned time in twenty years."

Joyce said, "I didn't know—"

"Hell," he said. "Can't blame the pillars of local society. Everybody knows all us dagos are criminals. Look at Al Capone, Lucky Luciano."

She touched his hand. "I never realized—when you weren't at school dances, I thought you were working hard. Kids don't see much beyond their own little worlds." She covered her embarrassment by concentrating on her dish. The split was losing its flavor.

Softly he said, "I knew you. I watched you a lot. But you were dating the football hero, in a crowd that didn't know I was breathing. Know what I used to call you in my head? *La principessa*, the princess. You walked like you were wearing a crown."

Joyce swallowed. "Me, a princess? *Me*? Good Lord, I was probably wearing my sister's cut-down clothes and worrying about—I didn't feel like a princess. Joe was—well, the fairy tales lied. There's nothing at the end of the rainbow."

"*Mangiare*—eat. Your cup runneth over with whippeth cream."

She had to laugh with him. Such a fascinating man, mercurial in mood, with that challenging hint of danger just beneath his Latin charm. "I'm full up," she said. "It's sinful to waste a concoction like this, but—"

His eyes probed hers again, direct and admiring and something else—promise? Franco said, "Waste not, want not? Did you get that stuff about cleaning your plate because people in Italy were starving?"

"With my mom, it was more general, just Europeans. When

I was real little, I took this half-eaten bowl of mush—Christ, how I hated mush—and I wrapped this gunk in a package and stuffed it through the post-office mail slot. It was addressed to *Starving Europeans*. In red crayon, as I recall."

Throwing back his head, Franco Butera laughed. She watched the play of his throat and saw a hint of blue around his closely shaven chin. His hair was rich and curly, trimmed just so, and no rim of dirt marked his polished fingernails, the first she'd ever seen on a man. He sobered quickly, one of those lightning mood changes she was coming to expect of him.

"They weren't kidding about hungry kids in Sicily. What they eat is a hell of a long way from spaghetti and meatballs. They brown garlic in olive oil, and pour it over plain pasta. If they're lucky, a little goat cheese, hard bread, sour wine. That's why so many believed in Mussolini with his Black-shirts. *Il Duce* promised them a full belly and the return of Rome's ancient glories, Rome's ancient empire. The *paisans* don't give a damn about glory and empires, but that full belly —ahh."

Some kid put a nickel in the jukebox, and the Andrews Sisters filled the drugstore with "Apple Blossom Time." Leaning closer so she could hear, Franco said, "I guess I ought to ask about your husband, the glamorous fullback, but I won't. I'm glad he isn't here."

"I'll be with you in Apple Blossom Time . . . I'll be with you . . ."

Was it betrayal to feel like this, unpatriotic because her husband was giving his big-mouthed all in some English pub and she was sitting across from a handsome man, glad her husband was in England?

"I—I'd like to see the Butera Corporation," she said. Let the gossips gloat over juicy new scandal. She was gut-sick, soul-sick, of her life as it was.

"That's great," Franco said, helping her on with her coat. He paused to drop a bill on the marble counter, a Continental flip of his hand signaling *keep the change*. Three bobby-soxers stopped giggling and followed him with their eyes.

Oriana Canfield was striding down Locust Street, aimed for the public library, when she saw the maroon car with its top down. Joyce was in it, next to a dangerously handsome stranger, her hair wind-flagging, riding a peal of laughter. At least Oriana thought it was her sister. Joyce hadn't looked so carefree in years, and the flashy car was gone so quickly, she couldn't be positive.

On the library steps she paused to sniff the odors of autumn, leafsmoke, and that odd premonition of chill that waits in certain shadows, harbingers of true winter. But that was a good way off.

Inside, she returned books to Mrs. Kiplinger, smiling and agreeing with the librarian's thumbnail reviews of each novel. Mrs. Kiplinger no doubt read every new title as it arrived, and could rattle off characters and plots like a runaway typewriter.

This building was Oriana's retreat. With Scooter at Mom's, and Steve Canfield out of sight in his OPA office, Oriana could find peace in this solid, quiet old building. Here she found aloneness without being alone, for a thousand lovers, a thousand adventurers peopled her reading corner, undying Juliets by other names, duchesses and serving maids, Anne Bonney pillaging across pirate seas.

Searching out a slim volume Mrs. Kiplinger had deliberately misfiled on a technical reference shelf, where any racy book was banished, Oriana took it to the comfy-shaped chair in the corner. She settled there to glance through *The Grapes of Wrath*. It would be a classic, despite its lurid reputation, and she meant to read it again, if only to confound Mrs. Kiplinger.

There'd been three V-Mail letters from Clay on flimsy, pale blue paper that folded over itself to make an envelope. Sometimes they arrived like that, in bunches; sometimes several weeks went by without a letter.

This morning, when she'd discovered that Steve Canfield had opened each letter before she even saw them, she hurled a skillet of pan-fries into the sink and stormed out of the house with Scooter. His hired hands could damned well cook for themselves, and as for her father-in-law, he could just—just go *screw* himself.

Before taking Scooter over to Mom, she drove the new pickup straight to the post office and gave Mr. Fulton hell. From now on, she warned, he was to hold her personal mail at General Delivery, and if he so much as allowed Steve Canfield to *sniff* at her letters, damned if she wasn't going to call the Postmaster General in Washington about it.

Then she read Clay's letters at Mom's house. They were about the same, somewhere in the Pacific, an occasional word inked out by a censor. He always asked about Scooter, and when Oriana answered, she filled him in on everything their daughter was up to. He sounded cheerful enough, and had made sergeant in a very short time. Clay said he liked the responsibilities and trust, that he had some close friends.

It seemed the war was doing something for Clay, getting him from under Steve's domination and showing him belief in himself. He'd be a different man when he came home, one she could respect. Maybe then they'd discuss another child, and it would be *their* decision.

Her letters to him were as newsy as she could make them, much detail about the farm and crops, and how all the county was pulling together so the war could be shortened. Everyone who wanted a job had it. If the work was connected with defense, and ninety percent seemed to be, people put in overtime previously unheard of, working sixteen, eighteen hours a day. And it wasn't for the money.

So many people bought War Bonds, and school kids cut into their lunch money for War Stamps. There was always some kind of drive under way: scrap metal, which her father worked very hard at collecting; aluminum donations that caused housewives to reduce family cookpots to bare necessities. And kids searched roadsides for tinfoil to turn in, making a game of who could put together the biggest ball.

There was no defeatist talk, Oriana wrote. Everybody knew in their hearts it would be only a matter of time before our boys crushed the enemy on both sides of the world. She hadn't written Clay about a man who'd tried to sell gas-ration stamps and was savagely mauled by a crowd before police could rescue him.

She didn't know of any draft dodgers in Coshocton, and men with deferments were checked every so often. If one quit his vital defense job, he could be expected to ride the next train to an induction center. The 4-Fs, she wrote, were kind of hangdog, embarrassed about their status. Some had gone to other centers and covered up weaknesses, to be accepted. Mr. Lidell—did Clay remember him?—had learned that a salt-free diet and certain medication could lower his blood pressure. He fooled the doctors and was in a tank unit somewhere, happy as could be. Blue Star flags hung proudly in so many windows, signifying a family member in service.

Oriana wrote that Ron joined up, but said nothing about the Gold Star flag for Gunter Hindeman. Gunter's uncle hadn't accepted it, but turned his back and left Pastor Montgomery and the mayor standing there in the farmyard, not knowing what to do or say.

And Oriana didn't mention Randy. He didn't come home often from school. The last time, there'd been some name-calling in Torrance's. *Slacker, lousy 4-Fs, why the hell ain't you in some kind of war work, dearie?* Oriana wondered how she'd react if she had a son called to war, and thanked God she had only a daughter.

There was no honor in Pacific jungles, battling an enemy something less than human: creeping, sadistic animals who gloated at the killing of helpless wounded, butchers who tortured captive American soldiers the night long, so that their screams of pain might lure their buddies to the rescue—and a death trap.

Oh, God, she thought; she should have cared more for Clay. There had been so many ways she could have been a better wife—even to giving him a son. At the thought, she pressed both fists against her belly. The pain, the drawn-out, gut-ripping agony of Scooter's difficult birth. Swallowing hard, Oriana sat erect in the old chair. She could have been more loving, more attentive, more cheerful. If only Clay didn't bend to every wind his pa stirred up. If only they'd lived alone, without Steve Canfield's cold shadow always across them.

The Grapes of Wrath hit the floor and startled her. She slid from the chair and leaned to recover it. When Oriana stood up, she was looking into gray eyes on a level with her own. She knew them, knew the slim face, but couldn't put a name to him. He was in uniform, but not one she recognized.

"Hello," she said.

"Hello back, Oriana Parker."

"Canfield," she corrected, "Oriana Parker Canfield."

His smile was lopsided, and she tried not to stare at the cause—a thin, pinkwhite scar reaching from his temple to the left corner of his mouth.

"David Shepsel," he said. "My father is Sam Shepherd."

"Of course! The drygoods store on Main, close to my dad's

place. But Shepherd, Shepsel—I don't understand." He'd been a year ahead of her in school, she remembered; no athlete, nothing outstanding about him, not even a semi-serious romance. "You've been gone awhile. I thought you were off to school somewhere."

"In a way," he said. "If we can find a place to have tea—ah, coffee—I'd like to tell you about it."

She saw Mrs. Kiplinger's glasses glint around a shelf. "How about my house? The Parker house, I mean."

That half-smile might be permanent, the scar always holding up one corner of his mouth. But his eyes smiled too. How odd, she thought, he's only about twenty-six, but he wears the eyes of an old man, tired and wise and filled with many hurts.

Turning his uniform cap slowly in his hands, David Shepherd—Shepsel—followed her to the library desk. Oriana placed *The Grapes of Wrath* upon it, smiled at Mrs. Kiplinger, and said, "I found this in the wrong section. I'm sure you'll want to correct it, Mrs. Kiplinger—and thank you."

When they were outside, David said, "She's still doing that. I found *God's Little Acre* secreted under Agriculture."

Oriana laughed free and clear, her first real laugh in days. "She's consistent. That's where Steinbeck was. My truck's right around the corner, but if you have a car—"

"No car. Will your husband, your family mind if I—"

She dug car keys from her purse. "My husband's overseas, my mother wants to be surrogate to any serviceman far from home, and my daughter is dazzled by uniforms. That *is* a uniform?"

"The RAF," he said. "Flight officer in the Royal Air Force. At the moment I'm sort of sailing under false colors. I'm on convalescent leave, before being transferred into the U.S. Army Air Corps. It's an option they gave us, after America got into the war."

"After America—you mean you've been over there and back already?"

"Since 1939," he said. "It seems longer."

Now Oriana understood ancient eyes in a young, scarred face. David Shepsel had seen things others had not, and they had marked him for all time.

chapter 10

In an attempt to clear up confusion about proliferating government agencies here, the administration released this rundown: WPB (War Production Board); WLB (War Labor Board); WMC (War Manpower Commission); WRA (War Relocation Authority); OPA (Office of Price Administration); OWI (Office of War Information); WSA (War Shipping Administration); OWM (Office of War Mobilization). . . .

—Washington, D.C., August 9, 1942 (AP)

Randy could almost see her body vibrate beneath the plain flannel robe. He was just as nervous as she, although he still had on his pants. He might have felt more naked in a robe, but he'd never owned one, or pajamas, either.

"I have a bottle of wine," he said. "It's not very cold. That old ice box—"

"Don't," Martha said, almost inaudibly, "don't make it more s-sinful." Her face was drawn, ashen, and her normally pink lips seemed bloodless. She stood in the center of his shabby room, and for a moment Randy had the scary impression she was about to spread her arms for martyrdom on a cross.

"Look," he said, "you don't have to do anything you don't—"

"But I do. I gave my word, and if I can bring you into the fold somehow, *any*how, I will be forgiven."

"Damn it, Martha! That whole evening's a blur to me. I drank two whole pitchers of beer at the frat house, and still don't—"

"You're not backing out? Randy, Randy—that's the only barrier between us, the true word, the true light. When you accept them, we will be as one."

He'd promised to join Holiness Church, but only to get her off his back, maybe so she would allow him to go on fondling her body. Damn it, he *had* to find out, and Martha was the only girl he knew, the only girl he was comfortable with.

"I'll put out the light," he said. "There's no bed lamp, and the switch is over here." He brushed her shoulder in passing and she drew back. In sudden darkness, he approached her carefully from behind and put his hands lightly upon her waist. She trembled, and he thought of the young mare out on his grandpa's farm; when anybody came up on her suddenly and touched her, it was as though she turned into tightly wound springs, shaky all over.

Moving up against her, Randy felt the taut curves of Martha's buttocks, the flaring of her hips. Arms around her waist, he pressed harder. She gasped when his risen maleness strained against her. It felt good, warm, wonderful, and he'd never known such a rush of blood throughout his tensed body.

She was a statue he could feel but not see, rigid as his penis, but cloaked with such marvelous softness. He raised his hands to the bounty of her full breasts, cupping them gently and finding resilient nipples to roll between forefingers and thumbs. Her haunches backed to him, rolled against him, and he kissed the scented nape of her neck.

Tenderly he urged her toward the waiting bed, a savage drum pounding in his throat. Martha's hair drifted over his face and he breathed deeply of its incense. She was murmuring something and dragging her feet.

". . . *the lips of a strange woman drop as a honeycomb, and her mouth is smoother than oil . . . but her end is bitter as wormwood, sharp as a two-edged sword. Her feet go down to earth; her steps take hold on hell . . .*"

"Don't, Martha—don't, darling. You're not a strange woman, but my love—Martha—"

Her knees touched the bed and she stood braced there until he reached down for the hem of her nightgown to lift it up and away, her limp arms unresisting. The heat of her naked flesh seared him. With something between a sob and an exultant cry hanging in his throat, Randy pushed her down.

". . . *rejoice with the wife of thy youth . . . let her be as the loving hind and pleasant roe . . . let her breasts satisfy thee at all times . . .*"

Randy lay beside her, kissing her throat, her chin, finding her parted and quivering lips. Rolling half atop Martha, he kissed her long and deep, daring to slide his tongue into her panting mouth. She tasted of forbidden fruits, and the flavors of her answering tongue were exotic.

". . . *let her breasts satisfy thee at all times . . .*" she breathed against his teeth.

He kissed down her arched throat to the valley of frankincense and myrrh, nuzzling between the living hills while his hands roamed the length of her body. Her nipples were large and vibrant. He bit each lightly and laved them with his tongue.

Smooth, so very smooth and warm was her belly, heaving gently, reaching up at him and falling away. He circled the dimple of her navel with his tongue, and her moans grew louder.

". . . *how fair and how pleasant art thou, O love, for delights . . .*"

Randy's whole body strained to her, needing so desperately to be taken into the flaming core of her, to bury himself in the enchanted cave of her belly. God, God—her mound was swollen and aquake, quicksmall ripples pulsing it, haired deeply and springy, throbbing against his palm.

But when he started up, when he meant to mount her, Martha's hands locked into his hair and held him at her belly. ". . . *I would cause thee to drink of spiced wine of the fruit of my pomegranate . . .*"

Did she mean—? He'd never had a woman, and now—did she mean—? The musk of her was tantalizing, rich, and somehow feral, as if some great, sleek she-animal had been roused in her den, and wakened to full heat.

Her pubic hairs curled fluffed and springy as he tasted flowered juices, and suddenly he spread his mouth wide to cover all of her, to thrust his tongue into the secret place and grip the flexing mound with his teeth. His hands slid under her buttocks as she lifted to him, squirmed and hammered at him. He was animal with her, dominating, subjugating, and her wild cry of ecstasy was the paean of his triumph.

She was gasping something else from the Song of Solomon —" . . . *and his right hand embrace me* . . ."—but he stopped listening, or could no longer hear for the staccato frenzy of his heart. Martha may have tried to hold him off with weak palms against his chest, but he threw his length over her, and spread her sweated thighs with powerful hands.

Plunging into her, he demanded her core, and slippery velvet satins clung to him, caressing and contracting as he drove and drove. It was too quick, and the fiery explosion wracked his very soul. He may have cried out, or only called her name over and over in the haven of her breasts.

Joyce Dayton had no idea something this big was going on in Coshocton—a little way outside town, anyway. She realized then how she'd cut herself off from everything but the store and home—not even her own home, but Daddy's. Franco Butera still held her elbow, and that was something else; no man had hurried around from his side of the car to open her door in a long, long time.

"Wouldn't know the place, eh, *Principessa*? Somewhere in that center building is the old milk barn; beyond that, we bulldozed the hay barn and put in an assembly line. See over there, that wing with the step roof? Norfolk and Western Railroad will have a new spur there within another week, right up to one of the loading docks."

"You must be turning out a lot of boots," she said, conscious of his thigh brushing hers as they walked. "Your father's old shop—"

He released her arm. "My old man, right now, he's at that hole-in-the-wall on Mulberry Street, repairing other people's dirty, worn-out shoes. And not charging a dime more, although all his materials have gone up, when he can find them. You know it's impossible to get rubber heels? Not for the Butera Corporation, of course, but for Butera's Shoe Repair. I brought him a case of heels, and soles too. He wouldn't accept them; said they're for the soldiers. There he sits, cutting heels and soles from cowhides and layering them by hand."

They stopped for a short convoy of trucks to go by, and now Joyce could hear the growl and whine of machinery, smell leather and dye. Franco opened a frosted glass door and guided her through.

"Down the hall," he said. "A modern office, secretary if he wants one, big leather chair—he won't even use it. Says all his brains are in his hands. Damn! You have that kind of trouble with your father?"

Joyce shook her head. "Not really, but I guess they all need to keep us where they can touch us, close enough to say, 'Hey, what time did you get in last night? Hey, you want to help your mother in the kitchen?' They don't want us to really grow up."

They turned into an office, all deep-pile carpet, glass, and chrome. It was imposing, even to a bright little bar off in a niche of paneled wood. In here she could barely feel the rumble of machinery. Franco steered her to a barstool that could have rocketed from a Buck Rogers book. He didn't ask what she wanted to drink, *if* she wanted a drink. He mixed two and saluted her with his glass.

"To you, *Principessa*."

The drink was dark pink and flowery, bitingly cold. She didn't want to ask what it was; she felt smalltownish already. "Delicious," she said. "Do you treat all visitors so royally?"

He smiled. "Only important ones."

"Okay, so I'll be important. Let's see, Mr. Chairman of the Board—I'll need about umpteen thousand loafers, a milli-bushel of two-tone bucks, and—oh, by the way, do you deliver?"

God, the way his dark, dark eyes could reach into her and find the tender places, those special nerve ends she thought long scarred over. When she put down her glass, surprised it was empty, the room seemed to contract, bringing Franco ever nearer, nearer, until his eyes filled the world.

The spell was broken when the office door banged open. Joyce flinched.

"Hey, boy." The man was shaped like a Parker Hardware nail keg, with only streaks of gray in otherwise black and curly hair—like Franco's. "Hey, *figlio*—what the hell you do—" He caught sight of Joyce and said, "*Scusa*, lady. I got to talk to this—"

"Pop," Franco said, moving from behind the bar, "I'd like you to meet Mrs. Dayton. You know her father, George Parker."

Guiseppe Butera bobbed his head and looked over the old-fashioned wire-rimmed glasses he wore. "*Si*—you the little girl come my shop all you life. How'sa you papa?"

"We were just going to—" Franco said.

Butera made a cupping, grabbing motion with the spread fingers of his right hand, palm up. "Go nowhere, hey? Not until I talka' to you. What's this no more inspect, hey? No *stivale*, not one *scarpa*, leave this shop until it'sa inspect; *capish*? What you want, American soldier to lose the sole, bust off the heel, when he'sa fight?"

"Now, Pop—"

"No 'pop' me, boy. You speak respect, and you respect Butera boots, hear me, *capish*?"

Franco said, "Half the factory hears you, Father. We can discuss this in your own office. Mrs. Dayton—"

"I should go," she murmured, and remembered she couldn't, not until Franco drove her back to town.

"Please," he said, "please, *Principessa*. I'll settle this in a few minutes. Wait here. Have another drink." He took his father by the arm and urged him to the door.

Before it closed behind them, Joyce heard the old man say, "*Principessa, principessa*? What the hell you think, boy? She'sa married woman, and her husband gone to fight, *si*? What the hell—"

Uncomfortable, Joyce moved about the plush office, looking at sketches of the plant and seeing it was meant to expand even more. If the war lasted long enough, Fanco Butera would be a rich man. She shook off that thought as dumb and unpatriotic, and wandered back to the bar. Finding the bottle Franco used to mix their drinks, she poured reddish stuff over ice. It didn't taste the same.

Why should she feel guilty about being with an attractive man while Joe was overseas? He rarely took time to write, and when he got around to it, his letters were like some third-grader's English assignment: *How are you? I'm fine. How's the old town? It's good over here. Did you get the allotment checks* yet?

She had the checks, fifty whole dollars a month, twenty out of Joe's pay, thirty from the government. It was supposed to support a GI's dependent. If he had kids, the check would be bigger, but far from enough to keep a family in food, housing, and clothes.

And Joe had the guts to ask for stuff from home. They didn't get enough cigarettes, he said, so she sent him two cartons of Luckies bought from her carefully hoarded account. His next V-Mail was a little different; the guys all wanted to know where he got the "white Luckies." She told him what the ads said, that Lucky Strike green had gone to war, something about the metallic content of the dye being important to the war effort.

She wanted to be more important, to *do* something vital, build ships or planes or tanks. Detroit's last cars were turned out in '41, and now the giant plants were rolling out tanks. Of course, Dodge was producing trucks for the military, and some other plant made those little jeeps, or peeps, as they were sometimes called. She'd also seen those open-sided, two-seater vehicles with a big canvas top, command cars. She'd rather work on tanks or airplanes, or maybe navy ships. That would put her closer to the fighting, the real war. *Life* magazine had already run picture features about women in war plants, in dangerous ammunition factories, how well they were doing, how much they were needed.

The itch was in Joyce, urging her to get out of the house and stay out, at least until the war was won. It wasn't as though she had a child to care for, like Oriana, and business was so good at the store that Daddy could hire another clerk-bookkeeper to replace her.

She drank off the reddish, sweet stuff and treated herself to another round. It wouldn't be like after her marriage, when she'd moved out of Daddy's house and into her own. Her very own house—it took her maybe six months to hate it. Every day the same loneliness, the same lousy, paint-peeling walls, Penn Central freights passing in the middle of the night to rattle every dish in the cabinet and jar pictures off the walls.

This time would be different. There'd be only herself to cook and clean for, with no eye on the clock, waiting for a man to come home, when and if he decided. This time the house or apartment would be truly hers.

"A penny's too cheap for your thoughts," Fanco said. "How about twenty red points and a dozen blues?"

"How about three or four pairs of black-market shoes?"

"I don't think you'd look good in our boondockers or boots. Pretty soon we'll drop those hightop shoes and go to all combat boots with buckles—but they'd hide too much lovely leg."

Joyce's face felt warm. She said, "I'm sure the ladies in uniform will get used to them, the WAACS and such." She sensed that Franco was about to say something else complimentary, and changed the subject: "Did you and your father come to an agreement?" The three drinks of sloe gin had made her fuzzy.

"Pop's full of old country ideas about quality and can't see that the government needs our boots right *now*. They're spot checked, but if we stopped to look over every pair, half the assembly line would be idled. Pop wants to run his own hands over every shoe, every boot. So I told him I'd put on a bunch of new inspectors; that calmed him some."

"Will you hire more people? I've been thinking of doing war work."

Franco laughed. "No more inspectors; I lied to him. But if *you* want a job anywhere in this plant, just name it."

She hesitated. "Do you mean that?" It wasn't Cleveland, Toledo, or Columbus, but it was a job, different and challenging.

He leaned across the bar and touched her hand. "Sure. What can you do?"

"Type a little. I'd have to practice to get back any speed, but I've kept books and done filing for Daddy."

"You're hired, *Principessa*. Private secretary to the boss —that's me. I'll transfer old Mrs. Green to the president of the board—that's Pop. She can really catch up on her knitting, and you—well, you won't stare disapprovingly at me over the top of your glasses, will you?"

"I don't wear glasses," Joyce said.

chapter 11

The First Panzer Army was stopped just beyond the Manych River today by desperate Russians who blew up a big dam here. German tanks were not able to ford the flooded valley, giving men who wear the Red Star a breathing spell. . . .

—Stalingrad, August 14, 1942 (Reuters)

Elizabeth prowled her purse for ration books, while eying the meat counter. It was her habit to look for bargains, although there were none these days. There were ham slices with fat and bone, fifty-one cents a pound and eight red points; fairly lean pork chops, thirty-seven cents a pound and seven points; tough, small steaks beaten by the butcher's tenderizer, forty-three cents and eight points.

Well, she had to spend her red points anyway; new ration books would be arriving within two days, canceling out any unspent coupons. Each family member received forty-eight blue and sixty-four red points a month; with Joyce moved back home, and doing George's books too, Elizabeth made do very well. She *did* miss all those fresh farm vegetables Oriana used to bring in, and it almost broke her heart to pay twelve blue stamps and sixteen cents for a can of applesauce. She just *wouldn't*, and felt righteous when she put back the can.

She understood that the boys in service needed canned foods, and tin was dearer than whatever it held. But every month a wife had to start juggling accounts all over again, because the OPA was always changing values on everything, usually for the worse. A pound of roast beef might be one stamp this week and four the next; and every cut of meat had a different point value. And every month, up went these big, complicated charts on the latest changes.

It was frustrating, a headache to Mr. Herbig too. She'd been buying from Mr. Herbig ever since she could remember. He said he spent so much time running around remarking cans and whatnot, that he'd hired those girl clerks; he had young men before, but they were gone with the draft. Ha-ha; not Gone With the Wind, but the draft, and a different war, right?

Early on, Mr. Herbig had hinted that old and valued customers like Elizabeth could have steaks, fish, or butter, whatever they might need, without ration stamps.

She couldn't possibly do that, she said with a snap in her voice; why, the Parkers would not accept fresh produce even from a farm in their own family. If the rest of America had to struggle with rationing, so would the Parkers.

Mr. Herbig had apologized, and shamefacedly admitted that he'd only been *thinking* about holding back for his best customers. A lot of stores did it, he said. Why, he could name two or three places right close by. But Mrs. Parker was right, and he was glad she'd helped him make up his mind. No kind of black market for him, no siree.

Piling purchases into the stripped down baby carriage that it no longer embarrassed her to push to and from the grocery, Elizabeth thought proudly of her husband. George worked very hard at volunteer jobs, riding a bicycle or walking to conserve gas. He might have gotten a prestigious "E" windshield sticker like policemen and clergy, doctors, people like that. Steve Canfield had one because he was a farmer, but claimed it took so much paperwork he ought to hire an accountant. As if he hadn't already pushed it off on Oriana, without paying her a dime.

Thinking of one child led to another, for they were all linked to each other, and to her—to George also, of course. But a mother had a special chain to her own, an umbilical cord that had never been severed, and never should be.

Oriana—she worried about her oldest, and Mary Joann with her. Oriana came to town often these days, and it was always a joy to baby-sit little Scooter. But for Oriana to be seen with that young Shepherd boy—Donald, David?—that was bound to cause gossip, what with Clay Canfield overseas and all. Not that she didn't trust Oriana; it was only the looks of it. Tongues must already be wagging.

And Joyce just up and leaving her father's store to go work for that foreign family. It paid better, and Joyce had never looked happier, but still—

Ronald. A terse V-Mail from him only once in a blue moon. Ron had never been close to anyone, even as a baby. To Randall, yes—she saw that where others didn't—but the boy was always a trial and tribulation. She worried about him now, and hung the Blue Star service flag proudly in the parlor window. If only he'd write something meaningful; if he'd say *I love you, Mom*. She would never quite forgive him for joining up without telling her good-bye.

Randy. He'd be coming home soon to be reclassified by the draft board, and she hoped with all her heart that he wouldn't be called up. One boy in the service was enough, although some poor mothers had already lost more than one to the enemy. Her heart ached for them, but still she prayed Randy wouldn't have to go.

Louise. She was hardly ever home, and her school marks were slipping. What's the difference? Louise asked. If you'd let me, I'd be working up in Detroit, making big money. I'm plenty big enough, but you treat me like some teensy kid. If you'd just sign my work papers—

Possibly she was too hard on the child. Louise *was* right in the middle of aluminum drives, and a good used-paper collector. She'd even pitched in on one fats drive, but only that once; she claimed the stink of lard and old cooking oils made her sick.

Louise stayed out too late, and rode around with boys too often. It seemed children were growing up so fast now. She'd ask George to speak to Louise—if he got in early. He was always off somewhere doing volunteer work, or trying to line up stock in short supply. It was unbelievable, but nobody could find an alarm clock to buy, or lawn mowers, bicycles, or ice skates.

She reached the house and pushed the old carriage up its walk. It was so peaceful here. When the door shut behind her, it usually closed out trouble, because this was the solid place, the dependable place built upon the rock of her family. But after she'd hauled the grocery filled carriage around back to the kitchen, she thought of the children again.

She'd never liked making them; at first she'd even hated it, and George, for making her carry them in her swollen, always sickish body. That was a wife's duty, the sex thing that led to pregnancy. But after the twins—a few years after, really—she began to like having George inside her. And that first marvelous night, that historic night when she had to bury her face in the pillow so the kids wouldn't hear her cries of joy, had changed everything for her. She liked to think it was better for George too, but of course she never carried on more than that irrepressible moaning, or made the first advances. Things like that weren't ladylike, and were best left to prostitutes.

Inside her warm kitchen, putting perishables into her prized refrigerator, she admitted she wanted George home more often, and *that* way more often. Elizabeth smiled. She'd blamed George for the other kids, but little Louise was as much her fault as his. They just got too excited to stop, and the memory of that craziness heated her face even now. When the groceries were safely put away, she called up the stairs for Louise, but the girl wasn't home. George must certainly speak to his daughter, and firmly.

Louise Parker felt whorish, waiting in the Studebaker, its top up, her body slumped down. Maybe the tourist-cabin manager was suspicious and ready to call the cops. Deke looked much older wearing a hat and eyeglasses bought in the dime store, and he'd been growing that mustache long enough that nobody would think it was false. She liked it, even if it got scratchy sometimes.

Again she felt whorish, and wondered what it would be like to do it for money. Jeepers, to wait all naked for some guy she'd never seen, maybe even some old guy with a fat, hairy belly—yuk. But suppose he offered ten dollars, maybe even twenty? It wouldn't take long to buy real silk stockings, or nylons. When she used leg makeup, and that cute trick of drawing a line down the backs of her calves with an eyebrow pencil to imitate seams, Mom didn't like it. But Mom wanted to keep her in bobby sox forever.

Daddy wasn't quite as bad, but he raised a ruckus when he saw her jitterbugging at that school dance. All the girls wear skirts that sort of swirl way out when they spin, she told him, and our panties are kind of like bathing suit bottoms; nobody can really *see* anything.

Deke came sauntering back to the car as though he signed into tourist camps every day. Maybe he had, she thought, off at Kent State. Not *every* day, natch; men were supposed to tire out kind of quick. They couldn't just keep on going, like women—something about all that gooey stuff. Every time that stuff let go, it weakened them. That's what the girls said, anyway.

One thing was for certain, and that was to make damned sure the guy wore a rubber. If he didn't, you'd swell up like a balloon and have a baby. Oh man, the very idea scared goosebumps all over Louise. It was one thing to play with a guy's thing while he fingered you, but getting knocked up—

Deke slid behind the wheel. "Last cabin from the road. Told the old guy we just got married and don't want to be bothered. He kind of grinned, but that was all."

"What name did you give him?"

"Not Smith or Jones, you can bet. Mr. and Mrs. Caleb Montgomery."

Louise giggled. "The preacher? Oh, man!" For a second or two she was afraid she wouldn't stop laughing and it would go on, higher and louder. But hell, women lost their cherries every day, and she'd never heard of one dropping dead from it.

He parked the car behind the cabin and carried the big, near empty suitcases they thought would be good faking. Deke fumbled awhile with the key before he got the door open. She whipped inside quick.

The room was bare and dingy: a double bed, chair at a little table, bathroom door open to show a shower, a basin, and a toilet. It had one tacky picture on a wall: a slumped Indian and a tired horse on a mountaintop, the sun setting behind them.

She wished there was a radio; some good jump music would help right now—the Merry Macs doing "Jingle, Jangle, Jingle," or the Modernaires and "Elmer's Tune"; even Billie Holiday belting out "Lover Man," especially "Lover Man."

"You want a drink?" Deke held out a flat pint bottle. "Nothing but water for a chaser." He looked about as nervous as she felt.

"I guess," Louise said, and took a big swallow that nearly choked her. Sputtering, she reached for the water glass.

"Not very smooth," he said. "The war's taking all the good alcohol, and about all you can buy is made out of potatoes." He took a long pull at the bottle and shuddered.

He looked pretty good in his new Victory suit, she decided. In Coshocton, Sam Shepherd Drygoods had been the first to display them. The suits came with only one pair of pants and no cuffs, and had narrow lapels and no vests. The one Deke wore was charcoal, with neat pinstripes.

Slipping from her coat, Louise sat gingerly upon the edge of the bed. It creaked. She kicked off high-heeled shoes borrowed from Joyce's new wardrobe and, without looking up at Deke, pulled the sweater over her head. She couldn't reach the chair from the bed, and got up kind of bent over to put the sweater on it.

"It—" Deke said, "it ain't like you're doing it with just anybody. I mean, this may be the last chance we'll ever get. You know I'm getting drafted and—"

"We don't have to go through all that again." She stepped out of her skirt and half-slip. Her panties and bra were plain. Her back to him, she reached around and unhooked the bra, dropping it atop her other clothes.

The light went out and she thought, Holy moley! I'm going to be struck by lightning or something. When she heard Deke grunting out of his clothes, she peeled down her panties and whirled for the bed. It would be easier in the dark, but she hadn't *asked* him to turn out the light.

Scrambling, she was between the sheets and under a thin blanket. The gas wall heater didn't hiss much warmth, so she had some excuse for shivering. The bed dipped under Deke's weight, and she rolled to him, glad for the heat of his body, for his arms around her. Already it felt different from the heavy petting they'd done before. They were completely naked against each other, with nothing between their bodies. When he pulled her tighter, her breasts flattened to his chest, and her hard nipples seemed to burn into his flesh.

Their teeth clashed, and his tongue was wet fire inside her

mouth. Deke's hands cupped her cheeks, and his stiff thing, trapped between their bellies, seemed to be trying to push clear through her. She gasped away from his mouth when he got a hand between her thighs and used his finger. Wiggling, she bit him on the throat, on the shoulder, until he winced.

But when he started to roll over on top of her, Louise got her own hand loose and felt over his thing. She closed her thighs and rammed him with one hip. "Damn you, Billy Deacon! You promised to use a rubber."

"Baby—listen, sweetheart—I got one right here, feel it? But first I want to—to feel you inside, all shaky and juicy like you get around my finger. I'll put on the rubber before anything happens, I swear, baby—oh, baby—"

"Bullshit! You put on that rubber first or I'll be outa here so damn fast you'll think the Penn Central just went by."

Even after he'd fumbled and squiggled around, she checked to be sure he was wearing the rubber, and hoped it was a good one, expensive. If she got caught, she'd go see his father so damn quick—

The head of it was already spreading her, pushing inside, and she tried to make herself go limp. Everybody said it hurt the first time, and there'd be blood. It *did* feel bigger and harder and longer than when she used her hand on it. Deke's upper body weight was on his elbows, and he kept shoving, prodding.

"Damn!" She flinched and tried to back off his thing, but Deke held her down and rammed harder. It hurt and he was deeper inside her, but when she struggled, something gave way and his pelvis came right up against hers. He was all the way inside her and moving, kind of rolling his twat around, and all of a sudden it didn't hurt anymore.

Hiking her tail, lifting her belly up at him, she got her legs wrapped around his and moved with him, matched his stroking. He groaned and went stiff all over and his weight came down harder on her. He was all sweaty and panting into her ear.

Was this *it*? Was this what all the stories and lies and warnings were about? Oh, man, oh, man. It felt kind of good, and kind of powerful, because she could stop any guy by locking her legs, or she could spread them and get about anything she might want, and Louise Parker wanted one hell of a lot. Imagine all this bullshit about something over so quick and meaning so little.

She lay beneath him, staring up through the dark at a ceiling she couldn't see, but knew was faded and water stained. When Deke rolled off her, she heard the rubber snap as he took it off.

He bumbled around in the dark and found the bathroom. She watched the crack of light under the door and heard the toilet flush. It took a long time for the tank to fill up again.

Back at the bed, he said, "Want another drink? I got water to chase it."

She felt around and took the bottle, propping herself on one elbow to drink. She didn't cough when it burned down into her belly, but damn near upchucked when the water slid down her throat. It tasted of chemicals and rust and was sort of greasy.

"Couple more of these," Deke said, "and we'll be all ready to go again. Did I hurt you much? I mean, I know it tears up a woman, the first time. But if you're not too sore, it'll be better next time. I swear it'll be better for you."

"Sure," she murmured. "Why not?"

But if they did it again, Louise didn't remember. All she remembered was drinking that lousy whiskey and missing the toilet to puke on the bathroom floor. Deke stuck her head under the cold shower and rubbed her hair almost dry, the motion damn near making her sick again.

He got her into the car and kept the windows down so cold air would help sober her up. She promised herself no more whiskey—at least not so much. Oh man, he might have screwed her again, without a rubber. Next time around, she meant to keep a clear head.

Next time? Deke wasn't kidding about the draft. All his old man's connections couldn't keep him out of the service. It was true this might have been the first and last chance they had with each other. He was leaving in two days, and said it would be tough to break away from his family. She was doing it with a man going off to serve their country, maybe to die on some faraway battlefield.

They were into town, passing lights that told her it was still early in the night. Shepherd's Drygoods was open, and so was the drugstore. She felt as though it ought to be dawn, or next week.

She had lost a part of her life that couldn't be called back.

chapter *12*

> Pete Gray, the St. Louis Browns' one-armed out-
> fielder, is unquestionably Rookie of the Year.
> Using a masterful drag bunt to compensate for
> being an otherwise weak hitter, he so far has 38 hits
> —all singles. Gray is outstanding proof that cour-
> age and determination pay off, and an example to
> returning disabled veterans. . . .
>
> —St. Louis, August 14, 1942 (INS)

David Shepsel hugged part of Oriana back into town with him.
She had made his homecoming easier, for there were flowing
depths to her, and a wondrous kindness that smoothed jagged
edges of memory and warmed the cold, hurting places.

The very belly of the sun could do no more, nor a thousand
more fiery crashes of Heinkel 111s or Dornier 17s, or whatever
dark Condors come by night over England. His cold would
always be with him.

He walked slowly down Main Street, not quite believing that
anyplace on earth lived tranquilly, without piled-high sandbags
and boarded windows, arrows pointing the way to air-raid
shelters. He stopped to breathe the air, untainted by burned
homes and things that had lived in them. He stopped to listen to
the silences of peace.

Here he was no warrior returned, but a stranger to his homeland. Or Joseph in his coat of many colors. But this son now wore bluegray clothes that did not reveal tatters and wounds, nor the blood in which they had been dipped.

The sign swung above him; the window stickers and little signs signaled great Americanisms—Lions, Chamber of Commerce, Kiwanis, Coshocton Boosters, Elks—all stones in the battlements Samuel Shepherd threw up for protection. People were inside the fortress, and David slipped in among them, waiting unseen by the old notions showcase until the tide ebbed and his father looked up.

"David—oh, my God, *Davida!*" Sam Shepherd swung around the counter and rushed to fling his arms around his son, to kiss him on the cheek. "David, my son—my son."

How small his father had grown, David thought, how much older and going gray. "Do you know," he said, "that's the first time you called me 'little David' in Yiddish?"

Sam moved back a step, but clung to his son's arms. "No it's not. Last time, you were two years old."

The door opened and closed, a bell over it tinkling both ways. David said, "Customers."

"Wait," Sam said. "Please wait. I'll lock the store."

David put his back to the people and looked at the shelves, at the display window where a man's suit was on display, at bolts of material and racks of thread. He knew without looking that the living quarters in back would be the same: gas stove with a small oven, old oaken icebox, a table and two chairs, single beds in curtained alcoves. Yes, and a cramped bathroom next to canned foods bought as bargains in case lots.

Beyond that, a storeroom for bulk goods picked up at bankrupt and mill end sales. And the two old trunks. Ah, yes, the trunks.

"David. I've shut the door and put up the sign. Come, come in back and we'll have tea, like the old days. David—an act of God, to bring you home."

"A *mitzvah*, you mean?"

"Don't; I am your father, David."

"Yes." David followed him beyond the curtain and watched his father put on the kettle, bring cups from the cupboard, canned milk from the icebox, the sugar bowl, spoons, one of them bent.

"So many years, David, and without a word. Always, I was afraid the Western Union boy would come; then I was afraid you hadn't given them your home address or our name. Why, David—for God's sake, why? Three years—three *years*."

"I enlisted as Shepsel," David said. "The little sheep. Is that why you chose Shepherd, the shepherd and his little lamb? I've never been ashamed of my real name."

Sam's hands shook as he poured boiling water through a metal strainer bottomed with black tea leaves. "Ashamed? That's no word to go with terror, boy; terror and horror and your heart torn from your body. You talk of shame. Shame? I tell you of *pogrom*, and there are no words for that—in any language—no words that can wrap it all into a package to fit in a man's hands and say, Here—this is how it was, how it is, and how it will always be."

He splashed water on the oilcloth when he filled his own cup, then took the strainer to the sink. The tea leaves would not be washed down the sink, David knew, but saved and mixed half and half with fresh ones, for next time.

Sam sat in his chair, eyes on the steaming cup. "I admit I am afraid, that I lied."

"You didn't have to be afraid here," David said, "or lie about who you are. You didn't have to deny our religion, our God."

His father caught fistfuls of his own hair and shook his head with his hands. A strangely biblical action, David thought.

Sam's voice rose strained through a taut throat where tendons stood out. "You accuse me, your father. *You* accuse, and in all your child's wisdom, you tell me there will be no pogrom here. The wise ones—they said that in Russia, in Poland, in Germany, in Hungary: There can be no pogrom here, because we will it, and we are the rabbis, the wise men."

David said, "And so you ran. Not only to New York, where there are many Jews, but farther, where there are none. If I hadn't found the *yarmulke*, the prayer books, in the old trunk, and the prayer shawl—"

"I curse myself for keeping them," Sam said, "and I should curse you for finding them, for running from your father. I—I can't do that; you are my own, foolish and rebellious, but my own."

"I missed a lot," David said, warming his hands with the hot cup. "No church, no prayers of my own, because you took Sundays in all churches here—Trinity Episcopal, Grace United Methodist, even Sacred Heart. You offended no one; you've been more American than anybody in town—Mr. Red, White, and Blue. Any hometown organization needed money? There's good old Sam, right up front, even if he had to squeeze old tea leaves. The Masons, Knights of Columbus—call good old Sam first. Any amount, anytime, just so nobody discovers Sam Shepherd is really Samuel Shepsel, the Jew."

His father shook. "You—you—my own son, my own blood! You run away to fight in a war that wasn't even yours, and come home to fight your father. All right, all right! Your grandfather was killed in a pogrom. May God rest his soul, he hid me before the cossacks rode him down and chopped him into pieces to carry on their swords. Your mother, your *mother*, boy. Ah, she died in a grand pogrom, meant to cleanse the land of all Jews. She rolled you under the bed when they beat down the door, and tried to fight them as they hit me with rifle butts and tied me up."

David said quietly, "Father—"

"No, you'll hear it all. You see, they got more pleasure by forcing me to watch them rape her over and over, man after man. They cut her throat, and set fire to the house and left me to burn with her."

David said, "I'm sorry, but—"

His father's eyes were fixed upon some far and haunted place. Sam said, "You were a baby, else I wouldn't have fought to get loose. To die with her—*that* would have been a *mitzvah*, God's own blessing so I would never hear her screams again, so I would never again look upon Shuah's blood.

"But you *were* her blood, and my son, and only a suckling small enough to carry inside my shirt and keep you warm. I begged goat's milk to feed you, and stole oats to make gruel. Once when it was very bad and only a smoking ruin where a village once stood, I bled my arm and mixed water with it, so you could feed."

"Papa," David said, his eyes misting over, "please—"

"I walked away my shoes, and walked through rags wrapped around my feet. I stole, I begged and prayed; I even robbed the poor of my own kind, so you might live. And once I killed a man for his coat and the black bread he carried. And once, when we were far from our village, I whored for a rich man, for then I was young, and my wife had called me handsome."

David took his father's hand across the table, and knew this tale, this chant not unlike a cantor's, had been kept a lifetime in Samuel's belly.

"I got you to America," Sam went on, "but it was not the Promised Land. Some said 'Jew boy,' and some said 'kike,' or 'yid,' or 'sheenie,' or just 'goddamn Jew.' So I worked day and night in sweatshops, and paid women to feed and clean you. I kept my tongue within my mouth and did more things that will never be forgiven me. Finally there was money to bring you here, to open this store.

"I said *kaddish* for the soul of my wife, Shuah, for the last time, and called you Davila for the last time. You were two years old. Then we were no longer Jews."

David got up and went around the table to bend and draw his father's head to his chest. "Papa," he said, as if he were a child again, that child carried a thousand miles against a man's thin belly and fed that man's blood. "Papa, I love you."

Sam stood up too. He held to David. "You understand, my son? When we became no longer Jews, there would be no pogrom for us."

Stroking his father's head, holding him as if Samuel were the child and David the parent, David said, "I blamed you for robbing me of my heritage, of a belief that cried out in my heart. It told me *why* I wasn't like them, and made me proud. I could hold onto something, Papa. But no Jew can stop being a Jew. When I read what Hitler was doing, the *Kristalnacht*, when German mobs smashed windows of Jewish stores, looted and killed, when the swastika was smeared on synagogues even over here, I had to fight it. *Fight* it, Papa. I became one of the new Jews, those who won't allow others to humiliate them, who will not turn the other cheek, who refuse to die quietly. They kill us, we kill them. Eye for eye, tooth for tooth. The new Jews have drawn a line, Papa. We will not be pushed beyond it."

Still holding his father close, David said, "And someday we will go home, to our own land."

Sam lifted his head. "But this is your home."

"No, Papa. Home is where Moses led us."

"*Nu*," Sam murmured, "you are the old Jews reborn, the sons of Joshua."

chapter 13

Authorities here admitted to the loss of four Allied heavy cruisers and one badly damaged off Guadalcanal, where United States Marines are battling entrenched Japanese. Officials surmise that the Imperial Navy force slipped through narrow waters between two chains of the Solomon Islands—a strait called "the Slot" by American sailors. American flattops had been withdrawn in light of fuel and fighter shortages, and the task force off Savo Island was caught. . . .

—Washington, D.C., August 14, 1942, War Department press release

Down the street, George Parker saw the man in uniform enter Sam Shepherd's store. So many uniforms these days, he had trouble keeping them straight, although he envied all who wore them. He'd know army olive drab or suntans, of course; he would recognize Ron a mile away, in winter or summer uniform. If the damned kid would only write and put his mother's mind at ease. And pretty soon, there'd be Randy; draft boards were reclassifying everybody. If the war got any tougher, maybe George himself would get called up. Truck driver, road guide, anything—he'd do any job.

He went into his store, said good afternoon to this woman, hi to that man, and sorry, that shipment isn't here yet. It seemed folks were buying anything, everything; each new rumor of a shortage brought them out in swarms.

Holly Melborne lolled hipshot behind the counter, languidly ringing up sales brought her by the other employees, Betsy and Annie; Harry was out delivering small purchases on his bike. Holly turned smiling to George when he headed for the storeroom, those sleepy lights moving in her eyes, her lips damp. When he passed close to her, his skin felt her heat.

She wore too much makeup, and made mistakes at the register, and never hurried. But she had that way of looking at a man that went straight to his crotch. George went on into the back, followed by the aftershock of her musky perfume.

What the hell was he thinking? He was old and married all his life and had kids older than Holly Melborne. He was a grandpa. He thought of Ron. That kid took it all, lived hard and fast, and didn't give a damn who knew it. George would bet Ron had screwed half the girls in town. Made a lot of trouble too, more than all of George's other kids put together. If Ron wanted Holly, he'd whisper to the girl and she'd trail after him like a well-trained hound puppy. But Ronald Parker had no gray hairs, no little potbelly, and no young girl would back away from him in disgust at being propositioned by an old lecher.

George wandered aimlessly around the storeroom, finally sitting on an old sofa shoved back against the far wall. Could he really ask Holly to—to what? Not go out on a date with him, not even to a movie; they'd be recognized anywhere.

What, then? Come right out and say it: You're driving me crazy, young lady. How about sleeping with me? If she didn't slap him, where would they go—one of those tourist-camp places? George wished he had a drink. His palms were sweaty, and he wiped them on his knees.

Where he sat was shadowed by crates and boxes, and when Holly came back to use the bathroom, she didn't see him. George closed his eyes, doing his damnedest not to picture the girl lifting her skirt and dropping her panties.But he couldn't shut out toilet-flush noises. He was sweating and his groin ached. When she was gone, he sat in the shadows until his erection had gone down.

Private Ronald Parker, 32742677, stayed where he was when the rest of the second platoon broke ranks. He waited for Sergeant Santee to say where and when. The other GIs moved slowly into barracks, some glancing back, buzzing among themselves like excited bees.

Santee said, "Around back, smartmouth, so the orderly room can't see."

Grinning, Ron slouched around the building. For damned near two months he'd put up with the sergeant's bullshit and the corporal's bullshit and even crap from some PFCs. Now it was coming to a head. Hell, he'd joined up to fight a war, not to be screwed over by a bunch of hillbilly noncoms. It seemed like any asshole wearing stripes talked through a mouthful of grits.

This Santee was a big bastard, but slow and clumsy. Ron's grin widened. Santee probably had just as many muscles between his ears. Behind the raw pine barracks, he turned, noting the upstairs windows crowded with faces. Okay, he'd give them something to watch.

Santee took his time peeling out of his fatigue jacket, and from behind the first platoon barracks came half a dozen more NCOs.

"That's it," Ron said. "Got you a lot of help, you bastard."

Santee rolled thick shoulders, opened and closed big, scarred hands. "Just me, hotshot. Them men come to see what you might call an object lesson."

"Well, now," Ron said, and slipped in snake-quick to pop the sergeant over the left eye. Catch the spot just right, where bone was tight up to the skin, and it just *had* to cut deep. Usually scared the shit out of a guy, when his own blood flooded his eye.

It had been a good punch. Santee was bleeding like a stuck hog when he came plodding toward him. Ron circled him, bobbing in and out, slamming in a gut shot, double-hooking with his left to the head. He cut Santee under the left eye and split his lips. Santee kept coming. If they were in an alley, he would stomp the man and bust him with anything handy, but not here, with so many watching.

Stupid son of a bitch, Ron thought, rolling away from a wild overhand right, he'd make hamburger out of this hillbilly.

When Santee pawed with his left and dropped it, Ron counter-punched with a straight right that jarred his arm clear to the shoulder. Santee stumbled back two or three steps and went down on his ass.

Ron had barely worked up a sweat. He felt good, oiled and ticking like a fine motor. He was untouched, unmarked. Dropping his hands, he watched Santee climb to one knee, then the other. The sergeant's face was a bloody mess. He pawed at the blood and came at Ron, unsteady on his feet.

All right, you asshole, Ron thought, let's see how you take a busted nose and maybe a broken jaw to go with it.

One of Santee's fists brushed his shoulder, and Ron heard the big man grunt when he pumped both hands viciously to the body. Lucking out, Santee caught him high on the head as Ron slid away. Ron shook it off and feinted low, leaned in, and whipped a hook to Santee's nose when the man dropped his hands in reflex protection to his gut.

The sergeant rocked, snorting blood and grunting, damn near blind. He came slowly, doggedly, at Ron again. Ron stuck him with three quick jabs and rolled under a wild swing. Backing off, he said, "Shit, ain't you guys goin' to make him quit? You want me to *kill* this dumb bastard?"

Nobody said anything. Six noncoms stood quietly watching.

Ron set his feet and, when Santee reeled to him again, pulled the string on probably the best straight right he'd ever thrown. When his fist exploded against Santee's jaw, the big man dropped as if somebody had kicked his legs from under him. Santee landed on his butchered face.

That's it, Ron thought. Guys who go down like that never get up. Panting some, he stepped back and rubbed the knuckles of his right, flexed the fingers, lucky he hadn't broken it.

Ron sneered at the half-circle of NCOs. "Haul your buddy off. Maybe the medics can put him back together." He bent for his own fatigue jacket, but when he straightened up, a little sergeant said, "Wait, soldier, you ain't through."

"You?" Ron laughed. "Where's your M-1, Bickston? I'll wait while you fix bayonet." A slim but solid little man who wore the only mustache in the company, Sergeant Bickston had been on field problems with the first platoon, but that was a different family; he didn't know much about the man.

"Ready?" Bickston asked, hands casually in his pockets. "Got your breath back? Hands all right?"

This one didn't talk mush-mouthed, Ron thought, but he didn't have good sense, either. Ron had ten pounds on him. "Yeah, I'm ready."

"Good," Bickston said, and jumped about eight feet through the air. Two GI shoes slammed into Ron's belly. He stumbled back into the barracks wall, gasping hard for air.

Bickston kicked him on the left kneecap, and when Ron went off balance with the sudden pain, the sergent punched him twice in the throat, not with fists, but with extended and folded knuckles that reached under the chin. Ron couldn't breathe, and the pain stabbed clear through to his asshole. How the hell did he get on his knees, and why couldn't he drag enough air? His lungs fought desperately, and if they didn't get oxygen quick, Ron would pass out—and might not wake up.

A rough hand dug into hair that Ron had refused to get crewcut, and he was pulled upright, braced against the wall. The red haze cleared and he sucked air noisily, gratefully. Jesus, was his Adam's apple crushed?

"I can break your neck right now," Bickston said, "or crack some ribs, or mangle your balls. You got no say-so about it."

Ron's throat tortured the rasped words: "G-go ahead and do it."

Bickston stepped back. Ron stayed propped against the wooden wall. On the scuffed and sandy ground, Sergeant Santee sat up.

"No," Bickston said. "You just *might* make a soldier one day, soon as you learn to go *with* the army, not against it. You got to know you're part of a team, just one little fuckin' part. You do what the coach says, because when this outfit goes into combat, a single fuckup like you can get good soldiers killed."

The sergeant pointed at the other NCOs as they helped Santee to his feet. "Santee couldn't take you. If I can't, there's Corporal Culowicz—thirty-eight pro fights as a light-heavy, and only six losses. If somehow you luck by him, check on that short ugly sergeant. Chief comes in so fast and low you don't even know it until he's got you by the throat—with his teeth. He's one crazy Apache, and might forget he ain't supposed to use that butcher knife he keeps on him somewheres."

It still hurt Ron to breathe. He said, "So?"

"So if you take one NCO, there's another one, and another behind him, because we can't let smartass recruits run things. This is the *army*, man; it stretches farther than you can see, and you're just one small cunt hair curled up in it. That's the object lesson Santee told you about. Take it to heart, Parker; it'll save you a lot of trouble."

"No rule against it, far as I know," Steve Canfield said. "You can sit on that bench, young lady, but keep quiet unless somebody asks you a question."

"Thank you," Martha Swensen said.

From the middle chair behind the long table, Canfield said, "We'll get right to it, then. You, Randall Parker, stand up and tell us why you oughtn't be called up—though I guess everybody knows." He grinned to the right at Mayor Mildon, and to the left at Torrance.

Randy said, "I'm part of the Holiness Church now, and it doesn't believe in war and killing."

Canfield's brows went up. "Well, I'll be damned. Didn't figure *you'd* pull that conscientious-objector stuff. How long you been an angel or whatever in this church?"

"About two months."

"Handy, ain't it?" Canfield asked. "Along comes this order from Washington to reclassify everybody, and suddenly you got religion."

From her bench, Martha said, "That's not so."

Canfield aimed a finger at her. "Stay quiet, miss, or out you go. Parker, was it up to me, you'd never been called back. About all the army'd use you for would be a nurse, and the army likes their nurses to be real females."

Randy said, "I wouldn't mind the medics, the guys who go along with the fighters and fix them up when they get shot."

"Randall!" Martha said.

He didn't turn to look at her, but kept his eyes on Canfield. "I'd like being a medic. Just so I don't have to carry a gun."

Shaking his head, Canfield said, "I don't believe this. Maybe you don't want to be showed up by your outlaw brother, but more likely you're just puttin' on a show. You know damned well we ain't about to mix the likes of you in with our boys."

"Hold up, Steve," Mayor Mildon said. "We're not here to judge nobody, just see if they're fit to do their duty."

Canfield's mouth curled. "Be like turnin' a fox loose in the henhouse. And as for this objector crap—'scuse me, miss—"

Mr. Torrance said, "I don't remember how come we classified him 4-F in the first place."

"Habits and traits," Canfield snapped. "Men of low moral character, and if that don't fit cute little Randy here to a tee—"

Randy took two long steps forward, so he was standing right over them. He said, "You're hinting at what this whole damned town's been saying for years. Come on and say it out loud—call me a fruit, call me a queer. Then, by damn, I mean to make you *prove* it, you sanctimonious son of a bitch! And if you *can't* prove it in a court of law, I'll take you for every dime you have and every inch of ground you own, to boot."

"I'll just be damned," Mayor Mildon said, and Mr. Torrance said, "Amen, boy. Any name calling will be Steve's, and nobody else here."

Canfield's fists drummed the tabletop, and a muscle twitched in his jaw. Randy waited, feeling good in one way and anticipating trouble in another. Behind him, he knew Martha's eyes were icepicking his back, but he couldn't help that.

"You got it, boy," Canfield gritted. "You sure bigod got it." He banged an inked stamp on one paper, then another. He thrust a paper at Randy. "You're 1-A, boy, and I sure hope some Jap shoots your head off, or some Nazi runs a tank over you."

"Gee, thanks," Randy said, and turned to walk out. Martha was waiting for him in the corridor, face blanched and eyes blazing.

"Why did you do it—*why*?"

"It's been building for most of my life, I guess. Today it sort of blew up."

"But you made him angry, and up until then he wasn't going to take you. But now—now—" Her eyes filled with tears. When he tried to put an arm around her shoulders, she pushed it away.

"You've not only betrayed me, Randall Parker, you've also betrayed the church. You took the oaths and promised me —and oh, my God! What if I'm pregnant? What if I'm carrying your baby, your illegitimate child? Oh, dear God, that I allowed myself to be seduced—"

"Now wait," Randy said, "it seems to me there were two of us involved in that. I sure didn't rape you."

Tears streaked her cheeks. "Y-you traded on my virginity, my purity, by swearing to join Holiness Church."

"Shhh! They can hear you in there."

"I don't care! I just don't care anymore! Oh, Lord God of Hosts—"

Taking her by the elbow, Randy hauled her outside. She sobbed convulsively. "Look, Martha—if it makes you feel better, I—we'll get married before I have to report to the induction station. I'll make you beneficiary for my insurance. The government gives everybody ten thousand dollars' insurance, so if anything happens to me—"

"Money. You offer me pieces of silver. Am I a Judas, selling my faith for—"

"Damn it, Martha! What the hell do you want from me? Marriage, insurance, an allotment—"

"You'll wear a uniform, be an Antichrist. You'll be with the rest of them, maiming and murdering."

He shook her arm, his fingers biting deep. "I thought the whole idea of religion—any civilized religion—was to help your fellow man. I can do that; I can learn first aid and save wounded men. What's more Christian than that?"

She went quiet with a suddenness that bothered him, crying silently as he led her along the street. Would she stay quiet after he got her home to his folks? He hoped so. Mom was worried because Ron didn't write, and Dad looked drawn and nervous lately.

His sisters would take the news calmly; both had husbands already in the service. Maybe Dad would be sort of proud. It still bothered him that he couldn't go out and fight.

A new pickup screeched to a stop at the curb, and Oriana piled out. "Randy! Is he—is my goddamned father-in-law in there?"

"What's the trouble?" Randy asked. "You know my—my fiancée, don't you?" His sister wore a look he'd never seen, her full mouth stretched tight, eyes kind of flat.

"Damn him," she said, and Randy noticed the yellow paper crushed in her hand. "Goddamn Steve Canfield to hell!"

Martha Swensen said, "I can't stand here and listen to such blasphemy."

"Then get the hell away!" Oriana snarled. "Steve Canfield is a son of a bitch who—who—" She slumped into Randy's arms, face turned into his chest. "Clay's been killed in action," she sobbed. "I guess that makes his pa happy. He was so damned eager for Clay to sign up. But I'll be damned if I let him hang a gold star in *my* window."

chapter 14

The Japs who are petted and pampered in Wyoming's Relocation Camp are the same kind of Japs that American boys are fighting in the Pacific. They are the same breed of rats as those over in Japan who have murdered American prisoners. . . .

—*The Denver Post*, August 16, 1941

She didn't care that they were the only customers in the Poplar Cocktail Lounge. And Oriana didn't give a damn that word would wildfire through town that the widow of Clayton Canfield was playing around with the Shepherd boy—Shepsel, he called himself now. She could just hear the gossips sniff: *And with her soldier husband, a hero fighting for his country, barely cold in his grave in foreign soil.*

"Never drank wine this early," she said. "Anything this early else, either; I mean else this early. Oh, what the hell."

"I know what you mean," David said.

"I don't, damn it. It's just—I have to talk with somebody, not *to* or *at* somebody, *with*. You know what I mean there too?"

"Yes," David said, and she wished to hell that damned jukebox would break down. "Good-bye, Mama, I'm off to

Yokohama"—oh, sure. And "Fighting Doug MacArthur."
Better "This Is the Army, Mister Jones"; if you wanted,
you could dance to that one—"No private rooms or telephones . . ."

She didn't realize she was humming aloud until David said,
"I used to do the same thing with 'The White Cliffs of Dover';
hated the damn song, but I was always humming the thing,
especially on a mission."

"You never say anything about flying. I mean, Clay seemed
to like what he was doing, or maybe the censors wouldn't let
him say anything else." Closing one eye and focusing on her
wineglass, she said, "I think he really, really liked it. I mean,
why not? His pa kept telling him it was the greatest adventure
of a man's lifetime. You think that, David? You fly around on
your great adventure?"

"It's not like that, Oriana. It's mean and dirty and filled with
so much black hate, you never get it out of your system. And
that's from my nice, clean viewpoint at three thousand feet. On
the ground it's a hell of a lot worse. Civilians in London know
that; mothers digging dead children from the ruins of their
homes know it, and lads manning antiaircraft guns know it,
when they go off duty and find they no longer have homes, or
anyone who lived in them."

"My God," Oriana murmured. "Let's get out of here. I need
to walk somewhere, walk and walk. Will you come with me?"

"Of course," he said.

He was at her side as she turned onto Seventh Street and kept
walking. She was silent, and he didn't intrude upon her new
kind of aloneness. When they reached the fairgrounds, she
said, "All the kids used to sneak cars in there and pitch woo.
Maybe they still do, if they can get gas. Maybe my husband
did too; I can't remember being here with him, though."

She led him a block to the right, and right again on Sixth,
heading back to the truck parked at the lounge. Moving slowly
now, Oriana said, "I loved him, I guess. He was a nice guy,
and kind. He was tender too. And—and he loved Scooter,
loved our daughter so much—yes, I must have loved him. His
pa was always in the way, and Clay never stood up to him. It
was getting so I was mixing my husband up with his father,
and maybe I didn't love Clay so much then."

Brushing at her eyes, she said, "Damn, oh, damn! Now I can't even tell him I'm sorry."

"It's like that," David said. "Four or five of us go up in Spitfires to try and knock down Jerry bombers before they get to London. Two of us return and start thinking how much nicer we might have been, how we shouldn't have snapped at Roge or Smithers, or bought them another round or something. Sometimes you don't want to get close to another flying mate. That way you won't miss him so much when his Spit flames in or goes into the Channel before he can bail out."

She walked slowly beside him and took his hand. He said, "But you miss him even though you barely knew his name, because we're all up there doing the same job."

Oriana murmured, "Winston Churchill said it: 'Never have so few done so much for so many.' All the newspapers here run pictures of RAF planes and pilots. They've really been marvelous."

"But you're wondering why I transferred out?"

She squeezed his hand. "Oh, now, I—"

"I love the British," David said. "I love their tough, carry-on attitude, and I came to know them well. But I'm American, and would rather fight in my own country's uniform, under my own flag."

Letting go his hand as they stopped under Poplar Street's corner lamp, she said, "I understand that. Clay's letters home showed a kind of pride, but I—it might have been his father's indoctrination coming through. It makes no difference now; dead is dead, and it doesn't matter what or who killed him. God—why do men fight wars?"

"English women are fighting this one as well—from mothers working nights in munitions plants targeted by the Luftwaffe, to service girls working barrage balloons and ack-ack guns, and others—ambulance drivers and NAAFI volunteers. That last is like your—our—Red Cross canteens."

Oriana nodded, keeping hers beneath the street light, loath to walk closer to her truck. Was that because of David and his understanding, or because she didn't want to go home to the sullen, somehow accusing silence of Steve Canfield? It was easier when Scooter wasn't in school, although her grandfather ignored the child more now than he had when her daddy was alive. But with Scooter nearby, Oriana could avoid the man and his brooding stare, and pretend she was all wrapped up in her daughter. She was feeling Scooter's pain with her own, seeing the child brave and chin-up, but seeing too that slight quiver of Scooter's lips.

"I want to do something like that," Oriana said. "The Women's Army Auxiliary Corps won't take volunteers who have small children. I want to—to—oh, hell!—make tanks or bullets and shells to kill *them* back. Cooking for hired-on farm workers and housecleaning isn't enough. Maybe nothing will ever be enough, but I want to try."

He took her elbow and moved them from the vague circle of the corner light back toward her pickup. Beyond it she saw the road to the farm she didn't want to take alone. God! Was she skirting around more with David, needing more than her child and family could give? Oriana was glad for the darkness that hid her face.

"You could do defense work, I suppose," he said. "The war will go on far longer than anyone here expects. There's the tire plant using that new synthetic rubber—"

"Not here!" she said, too violently. "But someplace where my hands can *feel* iron, where I can hear great motors roaring and know I'm helping them on their way, all the goddamned way to Tokyo. Detroit's good for that. They're turning out tanks instead of cars, big steel monsters with guns on them." It was the first time she'd put it into words, firmed it up—war work in Detroit. Mom would be glad to care for Scooter, and Oriana could come back every weekend or so to spend time with her child. She just *had* to get out of Coshocton.

At the truck, David said, "I'm glad we met again, and I wish you well when you go."

Clutching his arm, Oriana said, "Not right away. I mean, *you* don't have to go back right away?"

"Soon," he said.

"I'll see you again, then?"

"If you wish. If it doesn't make trouble for you."

She tried to laugh, and it came out all jerky. "You didn't forget Coshocton's way of life, how it feeds on gossip."

David took off his cap. "I didn't remember it like that. All I remembered was its peace, the slow, soft, flowing peace of Coshocton, where tomorrow always comes."

He opened the pickup's door for her, and the overhead light

went on. She stood on the curb, unwilling to climb into the cab. Could David have felt like this below the wing of his fighter plane, not really wanting to lose touch with the earth and life, even for a little while?

"I—I'll call the store," she said, and an outlaw thrill raced through her body as he leaned toward her. The touch of his lips was brief and light upon her forehead.

"The pain wears down after a while," he said. "It's always hanging there, but the edges grow blunt and it doesn't cut. Thank you, Oriana."

"I thank *you*. Oh, God, how I thank you. You came along at just the right time."

When the cab imprisoned her and she flicked on the headlights, he stood back, a slim, lean shadow. She drove away, losing him to the night.

At the farm, the porch light was on, and the upstairs windows showed that hired hands were still awake. Marching from point to contemplated point inside her head, Oriana didn't notice the thing in the front door glass until she reached for the knob. It was church satin white and oblong, bottom fringed with gold tassels, centered by a big gold star.

Something turned in her stomach. Maybe it was right to show that this house and family had forever given a son to the war. What sickened Oriana was *why* it hung there, and who had placed it. It was a banner not of sacrifice, but of pride—*his* damned, perverted pride.

"You son of a bitch!" she said, and slammed open the door.

He was in the kitchen, chair-back cocked against the wall, mug of coffee in one hand. She clamped her teeth hard together and went to the stove from habit, standing with her back to him.

"Had to bring in old lady Blackwell to cook supper for the hands," he said. "Where the hell you been, and how come you smell like a beer garden?"

Forcing words through her teeth, she said, "Where I go is none of your damned business, and it wasn't beer, but wine. I don't want to say more to you right now. You wouldn't like hearing it."

"Mom," Scooter said from the doorway, and Oriana went quickly to take her hand and walk with her now because Oriana needed life and warmth in the bed. Closing the door behind them, Oriana said, "How'd it go in school?"

"The kids kind of stay away and quit talking about the war if I walk up. I have to *ask* can I play with them, and before —before Daddy went off, everybody wanted to pick me."

Oriana sat on the bed and hugged her daughter. "Your friends don't know how to handle it, darling. They're afraid of hurting you, and maybe afraid *of* you—not that you *do* anything to them, but they're afraid what happened to Daddy might happen to their own fathers or older brothers."

Scooter was grave. "Everybody's daddy won't get killed, will they?"

"No, darling."

Why not? Who picked men to die and men who'd come home? If Clay hadn't been so quick to volunteer, maybe he'd be right here, right now, man sweat and earth smell; quick kiss held to a hard, enfolding body. Oriana shivered.

She shouldn't stay in this house a minute longer. Shades of Clay hung everywhere: his old shaving brush in the bathroom, his thin robe in the closet, work clothes, rubber boots in the barn, high school graduation picture framed on the dresser.

"We're moving, Scooter. I'll get the suitcases and you start gathering your stuff."

"Where are we going?"

"To Grandma's, dear. It's closer to school, so you won't have to ride the bus, and—"

"So we can stay away from Grandpa—*this* Grandpa, I mean?"

Oriana nodded. Kids caught on quick. Scooter didn't say much, but she was sensitive to happenings around her. And soon she'd have to be told Mother was leaving her behind, as Daddy had. Would she understand she wasn't being abandoned?

They filled suitcases swiftly, making them difficult for Oriana to carry. She looked around this room, peeped into Scooter's old bedroom, and realized she'd have to return. But not tonight—in the morning, when the house would be emptied and Steve Canfield gone to one of his officious duties in town —OPA, draft board, Civil Defense—anything that made him look important and patriotic.

He blocked the entry hall and she put down the luggage.

Scooter grabbed her skirt and hung on, staring big eyed at her grandfather. He said, "Where you think you're going?"

"We're going home."

His face was dark. "This is your home."

"Not any longer. It was while Clay was here, but not now. Please get out of our way."

Canfield reached for her, but stopped his hand in midair, turning claws into one accusing finger. "You! You get my son's ten thousand dollars' insurance money, his blood money, and right off, you run with it."

"You're talking blood money—*you*?"

Scooter made a scared little noise and Oriana picked up the suitcases. "Scooter—open the door for Mommy, please?"

"That truck—"

"In my name. The others are registered to Clay and you. You did that so you could grab more new trucks, remember? And as for Clay's GI insurance—that goes into the bank for Scooter's education."

For a tense moment she thought he would strike her, but he got his rage under control in time. "Go on, then," he gritted. "Leave your dead husband's house, take his kid off to God knows what. But you'll never get one inch of this land, not one board from this house; I'll see to that. I'll burn the goddamn house first, and sell off the land in so many little chunks it'll keep lawyers busy for years trying to straighten everything out."

She set the luggage on the porch and turned to say, "All I want is the rest of our things. I'll be back for them tomorrow."

"Go on, damn you! Get out, get out!"

When she keyed the truck's ignition, the roar of the motor blanketed the curses of Steve Canfield's sendoff. Oriana forced herself to relax neck muscles gone tight and aching, to let down hunched shoulders and breathe deeply. The truck headlights slashed the darkness ahead, and she came out on West Chestnut, and turned off before reaching Walhonding bridge. Oriana pulled into the familiar driveway of home, already fretting about the time she'd have to leave it again. But she meant everything she'd told David Shepsel; Oriana Parker Canfield was going off to a factory that made war tanks, and it would be enough if her work shortened the war by a single minute. It might be enough to save the life of some other husband, some other father.

Her dad was in his bathrobe, her mother hovering anxiously behind. "Oriana," he said, "what—why—?"

"Take the suitcases, George," Elizabeth said. "Come in, dear. Scooter, how you're growing."

Her mother acted as if it were normal for a daughter and child to show up in the middle of the night, and Oriana was glad for it, glad to turn Scooter over to her loving hands and soothing voice. It was another relief to drink coffee quietly with Dad. After the initial shock, he waited for her to tell him, if she wanted to, only if she wanted to.

"Dad," she said after her second cup, "I've decided to work in a Detroit war plant, if Mom will keep Scooter."

He glanced up at her, then down at the oilcloth covered table top. "You can do defense work right here."

"I don't want to stay in Coshocton, so long as Steve Canfield's here. I'm strong and not afraid of hard work; the farm did that much for me. I—I *need* to do something better, to help make tanks and guns that'll kill Japs."

She felt his hand comforting hers upon the table. He said, "I know how you feel. The store—well, that's not enough for me now. I wish I could go with you, do anything that'll pay back for Clay and all the others. I feel so—so left out, with Ron and Randy gone, and now you—but hell, I'm crying over my troubles when you're worse hurt. Tell me what to do, baby —anything you want."

Oriana moved her chair around the table so she could put her head on his shoulder, to be patted gently upon the back, as he'd done when she was a child who'd skinned her knee.

"There, there, baby. It's okay; it's going to be all right."

Murmuring against his shoulder, she told him about Clay's insurance money, how she meant to come home every weekend if she could get a B or C gas sticker for the truck. Then she cried a little.

chapter **15**

Three Jills in a Jeep was praised by critics today as a poignant reminder of what the Hollywood Victory Committee has done to help bond sales all across the country.

"Americans sometimes need to be reminded of sacrifices," the President's Coordinator of Motion Pictures, Lowell Mellet, said, "and ever since Pearl Harbor, Hollywood has had only one aim as it asks itself: Will this picture help win the war?"

—*Hollywood Reporter*, August 17, 1942

Joyce looked beyond the steel-mesh fence to where trees carried only a hint of coming color changes. It was only the first breath of fall, but later each leaf would flutter a little while, then find a resting place on the ground. She had never liked that time of year.

Turning from the office window, she stopped at the water cooler before returning to her desk. Although the plant, the town itself, buzzed with activity around the clock, underlying the hectic pace, Coshocton seemed to be holding its breath, waiting for something dire.

There had been that inspiring, star-spangled air raid on Tokyo, sixteen B-25 bombers that showed the Japs it could happen to them, too. Nobody knew where the planes came from, and when newsmen asked President Roosevelt, he told them "Shangri-la."

That was from the old Ronald Coleman movie; Shangri-la was a magic place in the Tibetan mountains where nobody ever got old, a fairy-tale place. But the papers did print the name of the man who'd planned and led the startling raid—Major James Doolittle.

And Coshocton celebrated the big naval whipping the Japs took at Midway: four aircraft carriers, one heavy cruiser, more than two hundred planes and 3,500 men. Our own casualties were "light," the communiques said.

It wasn't long afterwards that newsreels showed U.S. Marines landing at Guadalcanal, some weird jungle island nobody had heard of. Then the casualty reports started coming in. "The War Department deeply regrets to inform you that your son . . ." Eight dead from their own county, telegrams going out to mothers all over Ohio.

Or "your husband," she thought. Angrily, she shook off the idea. She had no intention of carrying guilt for Joe Dayton. When he'd joined up, her first feeling was relief, and the longer he stayed away, the better she felt. Still, if he *did* manage to get his fool self killed—

Joyce gripped her desk, then forced herself to go through bills of lading. There were times when the whole world seemed made up of shoes and boots, carbon copies and inky ribbon changes. It was then that the world made its only sound —the hum and clatter of busy machinery.

But there was Franco Butera to make up for it all. His being there, sometimes to stroke her hair or touch her hand in passing —those intimate little things made monotonous work worth-while. Joyce had expected more, immediately. But unexpected and vital business kept snatching Franco out of town, so there'd been no more than a rare, lingering kiss in the stock room or his private office, the urgent pressure of his hardness against her body, so fleeting, so sharply remembered.

When, dammit, where and *when*?

She hadn't heard the door open, and she jumped when warm breath tickled her ear. He whispered, "*Principessa.*"

Guiltily, she looked toward the hallway that was a bridge to other offices, and found it empty. Half turning, she smiled up at him, delighted by his nearness, the strong beauty of him. Then, back a respectable distance, smile in no way diminished, he said, "Just so happens a short trip just came up—no longer than the weekend, say. I have to sign some papers on a new plant in Findlay. That'll take no more than an hour or so, so that leaves us from Friday night until Sunday afternoon or evening. I've taken the liberty of booking a hotel suite—for two."

Hand fluttering to her throat, Joyce said, "I—I—well, that's wonderful. But how—we can't leave town together. It'd cause too much talk."

Walking around the desk, he picked up a sheaf of shipping orders and pretended to scan them. "You can drive?"

"Y-yes, but—"

"You'll take a company car. I'll leave early in my own and meet you at the Carleton. Your key will be at the desk."

"Franco, this is—"

He laughed, that rich, male chuckle; those lips, whose lightest touch could weaken her, smiled over bright white teeth. "Don't say 'this is so sudden,' please. I'm very sorry business and the war have kept us apart so long. I promise I'll make it up to you."

She felt the pulse running wild in her throat, and her lips turned dusty dry. "The C-Carleton?" Under what name, she wondered. She'd never done this before, and was certain to mess up something.

"As Mrs. Franco Butera," he said, as if he'd been living inside her head as well as in her blood.

Joyce's hands shook as she tried to arrange carbons. "I—I'll be there."

"I suggest you leave early," he said, low voiced. "Here's a requisition slip for our motor pool. If anybody gets nosy, you're being sent to Columbus on hush-hush business for the company, and that's *all* you can tell them. The car's tank is full, and it carries a C stamp."

She could only nod, caught up in this conspiracy. It would be so damned simple, if it weren't for Joe. Simple even if her husband were here, but since he was overseas—

"Oh, hell," Joyce murmured as she watched Franco down the hall, saw his swift, certain, arrogant stride.

Looking up at the clock, she figured she ought to start

putting things together. First, cover the typewriter and arrange papers for the in and out boxes. Good lord! There'd be no time to go home for fresh undies and a nightgown. She clicked upen her purse—not enough money there for a whole new outfit, either. Maybe she could get by on makeup and perfume.

Purse strap on her shoulder, requisition firmly in hand, Joyce stopped only for another drink of water. Her throat was so dry. While she waited at the motor pool for her company car, she wondered if Franco would remember to buy some of those—some rubbers, damn it! What was she, some frightened virgin dreading the final, irrevocable step? No, but a wife who sure as hell didn't want to get knocked up.

What to tell her mom? Damn, she should have called from the office. Now she had to drive home and pick up undies and the one keen nightie she owned, and a pair—no, both pairs —of nylons. Another dress—oh, Lord, she hoped she wouldn't be late. Maybe Franco would think she'd lost her nerve and was standing him up.

Hurrying up the walk, Joyce clutched her purse like a shield against arrows of curiosity. She was lucky; her mother didn't seem to be home. Up the stairs and into the bedroom, *her* bedroom ever since she could remember, shared with Oriana. Teddy bears and petticoated dollies, those first forbidden, hidden lipsticks. With a deep breath, Joyce felt under the bed for an overnight bag. Closet door open, she held one dress to her body and discarded it, put another aside as a maybe.

"Rummage sale or what?"

Joyce spun to see Louise leaning against the doorframe, munching an apple. "I'm going out of town—being sent out of town on company business."

"I'll bet. Your marvy boss goin' too?"

"Louise, I'm in a hurry." Toothpaste and brush, how could she forget them? Mouthwash and—oh, lord!—how far was she from her period?

"What'll I tell Mom and Dad?" Louise asked.

"Just what I told you: I'm gone on company business for the weekend. I should be back Sunday night."

"You better be. Dad won't believe your story longer than that."

Joyce crammed things into the bag and latched it. "Damn it, Louise, I'm a responsible adult."

Around a crunch of apple, Louise said, "And married."

Holding back an urge to slap her sister, Joyce pushed by her and was almost down the stairs when she heard Louise laughing. "Little" Louise was well on the way to becoming a first-class bitch.

And was there a name for Joyce? None, she yelled at herself, *nothing*! Because whatever might happen, Joe Dayton had already done it a hundred times over, and was probably at it this moment, trying to get into some native girl's pants.

Besides, everything was changing. She was making more money every two weeks than her husband ever made in six. For the first time she had her own bank account and War Bonds. If she really wanted to, she could up and cash in the bonds for what she paid for them, seventeen dollars and fifty cents, withdraw her account, and take off. And if she hung around Coshocton long enough, those bonds would mature at twenty-five dollars each. She'd have a big savings account and another for checks. Joe Dayton could whistle for any part of it —and that included his fifty dollar a month allotment, too. That was for *her* support, wasn't it?

She maneuvered the Butera company car carefully through light Coshocton traffic, but when she hit the highway, she fed gas to the official looking, dark blue Chevy. It felt good to be whipping along for a change, free and independent. She wasn't running *from* anything, but *to* something, someone.

Hanging withered in a patterned web built identical to her mother's, with the exact, unchangeable specifications of a thousand webs gone before was not for her. No, Joyce Parker was on the move and it was exhilarating.

Turning left on Route 30, she zipped along well over the national speed limit of thirty-five miles per hour, but kept an eye out for motorcycle cops. She felt daring and eager, but a little bubble of unpatriotic guilt lifted her foot from the gas pedal. Although the Butera company drew all the gas it needed, she'd be stupid to get a ticket.

Eyes on the nearly deserted road, Joyce probed her purse for cigarettes and thumbed the dash lighter. Her purse clinked, a sound made by those goofy white pennies, zinc or something, that replaced copper needed for the war. Now their tinny rattle made her realize how little money she carried: two or three dollars and some change. If something went wrong—

She laughed, touched the glowing lighter to her Chesterfield and put it back into its little cave. She turned on the radio and fiddled with the dial until the rich music of Jimmie Lunceford's orchestra surrounded her like a mink coat, warm and intimate . . . "Blues in the Night."

A warning, the lyrics moaned: *"My mama done told me, when I was in pigtails . . ."* Mama had told her exactly nothing, only hinted about good girls and bad. *"A man's gonna' sweet talk, and give you the glad eye, but when the sweet talkin's done . . ."*

How could anybody know, without trying? She wasn't asking for more than today, for no more than gentleness and caring. It had been so long.

. . . *"A man is a two-faced, a worrisome thing, who'll leave you to sing . . . the Blues in the night . . ."*

If he walked away, it wouldn't matter; not that much. Was she, could she be, in love with Franco Butera? He was so handsome and forceful, always driving, reaching for more. He meant to taste it all, she thought, to wring every drop of pleasure. Franco was in love with life itself.

And in some remote, dreamy way, with her?

Franco Butera would probably never say *I love you*. And she wasn't the kind of woman who needed to hear it to clear her conscience. She would have her great love, the grand passion, discovered late but with such beautiful truth.

Dick Haymes had gotten lost a mile back, and Glenn Miller's instrumental, "In the Mood," rocked the Chevy. Joyce's fingers followed its swift beat on the steering wheel. She'd bet Franco was no jitterbug. His sinuous grace would be better with a slow fox trot or waltz, like Andy Russell doing "Amor" in that tingly voice, or "I Don't Want to Walk Without You," sung by Helen Forrest.

Had so many years raced by from saddle shoes and dimes saved up to buy song sheets, yellow, green or pink, with all the lyrics of "Hit Parade" songs? Once she could have sung half the night, sardined into some boy's car; if you didn't know the words, you were kind of square. It was better to swing and be jivey, to do the Lindy Hop, to shag and truck and really cut a rug. Slow, sweet music was okay once in a while, if you wanted to snuggle and sing into your partner's ear.

Now she was aboard a carousel, and nobody had pushed her

onto it. If love happened to get mixed into what she was about to have with Franco, okay. If she missed the brass ring, she could still enjoy the ride, and not regret for the rest of her life that she hadn't had the courage. Better to be sorry for something she'd done, than for something she didn't do.

Through Mansfield, she turned right onto 23 and looked at the gas gauge; it had barely moved, and yet she felt she'd come a thousand miles. Was that because she was traveling in time, not distance?

When she found the Carleton, she parked in its lot and used the rearview mirror to apply fresh lipstick and check her makeup. Then she made herself get out with her bag and lock the car door. Head up, she strode into the hotel as if she had stock in it.

"Mrs. Butera," she said to the desk clerk. "My key, please."

His smile wasn't a leer. "Yes ma'am, suite two. Mister Butera hasn't arrived yet. Bellboy!"

"Never mind," she said. "I'll find it myself. We're traveling light."

Maybe that was a mistake. She thought his eyes flickered, although his smile didn't slip. "Of course, ma'am; to your right on the second floor, and the elevator is—"

She nodded cool thanks and marched to the elevator. Nobody was there to operate it, and she stood uncomfortably until she realized it was that new, self-service kind.

Thankful to be out of the damned thing, Joyce moved down a silent, deeply carpeted corridor to suite two, where the key turned noiselessly. Inside, she wobbled to the bed and sighed down upon it. It was a strain, acting like another man's wife. She lit another Chesterfield and recalled how embarrassed she'd felt the first night of her marriage to Joe, registering at that Detroit hotel, how she'd tried to make her new wedding ring conspicuous.

To be doing something, she unpacked the small bag and put toothbrush, paste, hairbrush, and comb in the bathroom. After consideration, she changed to the nightie, wishing it were really slinky.

What if Franco didn't like her, wasn't satisfied with her in bed? She'd had so damned little experience, and he'd been around—Washington, New York, everywhere.

The door opened and she uncoiled from the bed, every nerve

humming. Franco carried flowers, and a bellhop struggled with a heavy valise and an ice bucket.

"Hi, *Principessa*," Franco said, and to the boy: "Atop the dresser is fine, thank you." Whatever the tip was, the bellhop bowed over it and backed respectfully from the room.

"Roses," Franco said, "red as fine wine, and white carnations, for—"

"Not virginity," she said. "Not even purity."

He smiled at her. "Virginity is highly overrated, and purity is in the mind. You—you're a study in browns, sienna and umber; your hair, eyes, skin, each a different shading, all beautiful."

She felt the touch of his eyes through her thin nightie and cursed herself for instinctively crossing her legs.

Coat off, he spun bottles in the big silver bucket, and held two glasses in one hand. "Just a good sparkling burgundy; a little early for champagne, I think."

She stood to take her glass, hand shaky. He smelled wonderful, of shaving lotion and man musk. Joyce clinked glasses with him. "To what?"

"To here and now, you and me, and bubbles in the wine."

"Agreed." She drank quickly and held out her glass.

"You don't have to be afraid of me," Franco said, those heated lights moving in deep, soft eyes, "or of yourself." He refilled their glasses and moved back a step.

Draining her glass, she set it upon the bedside table and lifted the nightgown over her head, letting it fall into a puddle at her feet. She stood proudly, showing him her body, glad that her breasts were high and firm, that her waist was slim, that her belly was flat and her legs good.

For the first time, she didn't want the lights out. She wanted to revel in his appreciation, to see him undress without one awkward movement, quick and graceful. His curly chest hair narrowed to a thin line down to his navel, then spread again, thicker and deeper, a springy black forest from which his manhood rose, thick and powerful.

Joyce moved to meet him, gasping as she flattened her nipples to him, as his staff throbbed between their bellies. She opened her mouth to him, raced her tongue over his, let their teeth clash as his hands found and crushed her buttocks to pull her impossibly closer.

Panting, lashing his tongue with her own, she tried to climb him like a tree, hugging him fiercely to her, going tiptoe to coil one leg about him, then the other, and he helped by lifting. He was at her mound, and she twisted to settle upon him, to have him suddenly and strongly within her depths.

She moaned into his mouth, and moaned again as he carried her to the bed and lowered her gently.

Was there fierce tenderness, or tender fierceness? Something of both overlapped in the way he moved inside her, how he kissed her breasts, the way he sometimes drove violently, then backed off to stroke easily. It was maddening, and she bit his shoulder as she crested, as white hot lava burst within her.

Still he moved, using his hands to turn her this way and that, keeping only so much weight upon her, supporting the rest upon knees or elbows. She drifted only a moment before rising to meet him again, this time with a rhythmic attack of pelvis and groin as she clung to his shoulders and rolled back to try for more of him.

When the new orgasm thundered through her, Joyce felt his own eruption, and ground wantonly upon him, dug her nails into his back, groaned and hissed words she'd never said out loud.

Resting beside him, empty without him locked into her body, Joyce tasted his sweat with the tip of her tongue. He was so damned beautiful, so powerful, and hers, *hers*.

Blissfully, eyes closed and enchanted lassitude bathing her body, she listened as he talked with her, *really* talked with her. She heard how he'd been moving, dealing, picking up any company that could somehow be considered a defense industry, incorporating and spreading the Butera network into businesses that would last far beyond the war's end.

"And your father?" she asked, stroking his chest with a fingertip.

Franco didn't answer right away, then said, "He's too occupied with the shoe factory, happy enough if I let him run a close check on production quality, signing papers when he has to. All this old-country crap. He hasn't really gotten it through his head that Sicily is our enemy now. He acts like it's not part of Italy and has nothing to do with Mussolini."

"He's lucky to have you running things." She tilted her head so she could nuzzle behind his ear.

He chuckled. "I keep telling him that. Like I ask myself if you're happy in the Coshocton office, if you'd rather be somewhere else—here, Bowling Green, Marion."

She snuggled closer. "I just want to be where you are."

Stroking her back, he said, "My executive secretary can travel with me, everywhere I go. Would you like that?"

"Sure."

"The gossip wouldn't bother you?"

"Gossip? What gossip?"

"Okay, *Principessa*." He eased her onto her back again and kissed a path down her throat, making exciting detours from nipple to nipple, then wandered down her tummy. She fingered his hair, trembling at the deft caresses of his tongue and tender nipping of his teeth.

When his tongue twirled into her navel, she arched and tried to draw him back up her body, but down he went, and down, and when he pulled her into his mouth, Joyce went dizzy. Nobody ever—not even her husband, surely not her schoolboy lover—nobody had done this to her. Was it right, was it—

Moaning, she gave herself up to him, opened to him for whatever he desired of her. Room lights seemed to brighten and dim, the bed to leap and spin, and her thighs closed upon him in repeated spasms. Blinded by the explosions of a rainbow, Joyce rode a magic fountain that carried her higher and higher, then tore her into a million ecstatic bits that sang into the stars.

chapter 16

Emily Post told the Office of War Information today that it is all right for female plant workers to hitch a ride to their jobs. "But," Miss Post said, "the hitchhiker should display her ID card; waving the thumb is still vulgar. . . ."

—New York, N.Y., August 18, 1942

Randy Parker worked at becoming a corpsman. While other draftees bitched and grumbled and screwed off in class, he bore down hard, trying to absorb it all. When barracks lights went out at 2200 hours, he sat on a toilet in the latrine, one in a long and open line, studying. A sign on the raw pine wall warned: *Do Not Flush While Seated*. It seemed that hurry-up plumbers had somehow crossed pipes that sometimes erupted boiling water. Not always, just often enough to scald somebody's balls.

The whole damned camp was slapped together ticky tacky: putty flaking off windowpanes; green lumber warping to let in dust; furnaces that hadn't been used yet, and nobody around to know how to work them; splinters worked up from morning-mopped and Friday night scrubbed floors; resin seeping from raw two by fours.

Hey, man, they said to him as they stood at the piss trough, hey, Parker—you buckin' to be a real doctor? College boy, you got no more chance than a popcorn fart in a whirlwind. You just another goddamn pill roller, one more chancre mechanic for short arm inspections. Man, before this fuckin' war's over, you're goin' to tell 'em to skin it back five million times, and look up that many one-eyed cockheads to see if a rolled up rifle patch ain't holdin' back clap discharge.

I don't know, they'd say while he concentrated on his books, I don't know, Parker—maybe you'll really *like* that part of it, nursie. Then they'd give their cocks a last shake and laugh and go to bed.

In the beginning, a few loudmouthed him for being a conchie, of trying to duck out on the war. But several other COs came in for training, one a burly, drawling mountain man who nearly crippled a ring of hecklers. Because he didn't believe in killing, Private Billy Ray Chapman announced, that didn't stop him from chastising any damn fool who'd make fun of a man's religion, and he allowed that he didn't need no jawbone of an ass to do it, neither. From then on, he was known as Chastise Chapman, and the conchies weren't bothered much.

Basic training for medics was short on military and long on first aid. They could left face, right face, and salute, maybe even parade ground march a little, but there any resemblance to front line soldiers ended. They couldn't carry weapons because of the Geneva Convention, so no arms study or range firing was required. Harassed doctors lectured and gave demonstrations and, Randy thought, hoped enough training rubbed off on their pupils to save a life now and then.

Randy learned to feed plasma and morphine into a vein, learned pressure points and splinting, and took pride in his job. Horror stories were coming out of the Pacific, tales of Japs sniping medics as choice targets because of the red cross on a white background on their sleeves. They told of Japs sneaking into behind the lines aid stations and bayoneting wounded and medics alike, and the word was that combat medics over there carried weapons and used them.

And when his specialized training was at an end, Randy was called into the commanding officer's office. Major Tompkins was large, ruddy, and informal, much more doctor than military man. "Parker," he said, "oh, yes, Parker. An excellent record, young man, excellent. If I had grades like yours in medical school, I'd have finished in two years, two years."

Standing at attention, thumbs along the seams of his fatigue pants, Randy stared straight ahead and said, "No thank you, sir," when the major asked if he'd like to remain as cadre, an instructor when his training company was dissolved and its men shipped where they were most needed.

"Yes," Major Tompkins said then. "Yes, young man; I suspected that would be your answer. I could order you to remain, but I respect you too much for that, yes. It takes guts to —to thine own self be true, come hell or high water. You've been through the deluge here, and hell is waiting for you. A good combat medic is the toughest job in the army; even GI riflemen will admit to that; yes, even those poor, miserable front line fighters admire the doc who has to crawl out under fire and treat one of their wounded buddies, try to drag him to cover."

The major sighed, stood up, and came around his desk. "I wish I could do more than put a letter of commendation into your 201 file, but I can shake hands and wish you luck, son."

A little numb, Randy moved through the orderly room, to stop when the first sergeant said, "Well, you cadre now?"

"No," Randy said.

"Had two sets of orders cut." Sergeant Kilbride handed a sheaf of rough mimeo papers to Randy. "One if you stayed here, and these. At least you're not goin' to the Pacific, not right off, that is."

The first sergeant tilted back in his swivel chair, frowning. "Damned if I understand you guys. You won't tote an M-1, but you'll expose your precious ass to a bucketful of enemy bullets. I just can't read you guys."

Randy grinned. "That's okay, Sarge. Most of us can't read ourselves."

There was more: picking up his 201 file, that fat packet of his military history that would travel with him wherever he was shipped; saying a few good-byes, the hardest to Chastise Chapman; rechecking his basic clothing allowance and cramming everything, issue and personal, into one duffel bag. He was lucky to be able to lift the damned thing.

Martha Swensen had brought his—and Ron's—old Model A

up to store in a garage off base, complete with an A sticker and enough gas to get him back to Coshocton. Major Tompkins had given him three extra days before he had to report to the staging area at Indiantown Gap, Pennsylvania. He paid the storage bill, grunted his duffel bag into the back seat, and pointed for home.

Martha had called him at least once a week during basic, and when he couldn't be brought to the phone, she'd left messages —too often biblical quotes carefully chosen to play upon a guilt she wanted him to assume.

Damn it, it wasn't all his fault. She'd gone at it with just as much enthusiasm as he, maybe more. And ever since that night, she was the maiden seduced and betrayed, overpowered by the male beast and forced into mortal sin. She hadn't come right out with it, but in her letters he read marriage as the only possible atonement—if ever she could forgive him, even then.

Some miles down the road, he discovered that civilian air smelled different, tasted better. He grinned into it, realizing that the wind carried the flavor of freedom, that it was unregimented.

He'd talk it over with Martha, of course; whatever her faults and despite the inflexibility of Holiness Church, together they had helped him find unexpected strength in himself, and a clearer sense of direction. When the war was over and he went back to college, he'd change his major. Maybe he could go on to medical school, somehow.

It would be great to see Mom and Dad and his sisters, to drink a malt in Torrance's and just walk up and down Main Street, or just sit and look at the Tuscarawas River.

When they were young they did that, Ron and himself, just watched the river. Once in a while, puffs of sultry wind made them feel the lift of individual hairs standing along their forearms. Summer sun and the river's lazy whispering, emerald smell and green taste of the grass stems they chewed. The world was spun around them like a big ball of grocery string, and they had no need for words. When a hint of shadows lay upon the Tuscarawas, they'd start for home, arms around each other's shoulders.

When had they stopped doing that?

At home, Elizabeth Parker finished wiping the last dish and put it away. All day she'd had this nagging feeling, an expectancy she couldn't name. George hadn't come home for lunch again, so it wasn't to do with him. Joyce's new job took her out of town a lot, like now.

She was worried about Joyce and that Butera man. Not that she put stock in bits of gossip that floated back to her, because she knew her daughter, knew all her children had been raised properly. But if enough waggle-tongues kept at it, folks could start believing the worst, and that would hurt Joyce, and maybe reach Joe overseas.

Overseas, she thought, Ronald. Something might be happening to him, some terrible thing that came clear across the ocean to pick at a mother's nerves. A month had gone by since Ron's last short V-Mail note, and about all he'd said then was that "somewhere in England" was cold and the beer warm.

Elizabeth put on the kettle and got out her little perforated tea measure on its delicate dip chain. She always felt a twinge of guilt when she used it, because it was aluminum. But she'd given so many pots and pans to the scrap drive already, her cooking utensils were barely enough. Surely the country didn't need her little tea dipper.

Oriana. She'd been too quiet and withdrawn since Clay was killed. About the only time she showed her old self was with that Shepherd boy. Shepherd or Shepsel? How could that young man change his family name? That was mysterious and probably illegal.

It was just fine, having Oriana and Scooter here, although folks were beginning to talk some about Oriana seeing the Shepherd boy so much, what with her husband so recently killed.

Killed. Elizabeth stood beside the stove and thought how stark and mean that sounded. *Killed*. On purpose, somebody Clay had never seen had up and killed him, on some miserable little island nobody ever heard of—Tulagi, Gavutu, Tanambogu. Elizabeth read the war news faithfully and listened to the radio every night.

Impatiently she jiggled the teakettle over gas flame. Maybe she ought to be grateful for the Shep—Shepsel boy. Because of him, Oriana hadn't gone off to Detroit yet. The insurance

money for Clay's death had already come in, and it was fine for
Oriana to put every bit of that ten thousand dollars into a trust
fund for Scooter. But she might be a little more careful of her
reputation, although Oriana had never once stayed out all
night.

Steve Canfield had phoned many times, but Oriana wouldn't
speak to him. Elizabeth didn't fault her much for that, but still,
he was her father-in-law, with his son dead. To keep peace in
the family, Oriana ought to be civil to the man, at least.
Sighing, Elizabeth admitted she didn't like Steve, either. He
was always so bossy and know-it-all, and the way he talked
about Ron and Randy—

The kettle whistled and she poured boiling water over the tea
dipper. After she'd swished it a few times and darkened the
water to her satisfaction, Elizabeth placed the dipper in her
saucer. Randy. That was it. Her intuition was trying to tell her
about Randy.

Had he also been suddenly shipped overseas? The army
never allowed boys to tell when they were leaving, or for
where. That was for their own safety. *A Slip of the Lip Can
Sink a Ship*, and that other poster seen everywhere: *Enemy
Agents Are Always Here; If You Don't Talk, They Won't Hear*.
The poster that bothered Elizabeth most was all ominous black
and fiery reds, with Hitler's giant, sneering face dominating
the background, and up front, the contorted body of a young
mother, a bayonet centered in her chest. Beside her, an infant
cried fear and pain to the cruel sky. The lettering was: *This Is
the Enemy*.

The crying child upset Elizabeth most.

When the car pulled into the driveway, Elizabeth recognized
the sound of its motor and jumped up, bumping the table and
spilling tea across the oilcloth. That old car—she made a pass
at the tea puddle with her apron, then got tangled in the thing.
But she made it to the door when he crossed the porch.

"Hello, Mom," Randy said, and she gathered him into her
arms, crying some like any silly mother whose son has come
home, even for a little while.

Four thousand miles away from Coshocton, Ron Parker felt a
different and somehow bothersome warmth in the girl's arms.
Sweated and smooth, her naked body pressed closer, but he sat

up and reached for the bottle beside the bed. After a long pull at it, he made a face and lighted a cigarette as a chaser.

"Me too, luv," she said.

He passed her the Phillip Morris—why the hell didn't some decent brand come in the PX issue?—and took another for himself. Any American smoke was better than limey stuff —Player's, Capstans—they tasted like anemic calf shit, ground up.

"I've been listening," he said. "That noise like a spook howling away off. What the hell is it?"

She laughed. "Only the wind in the wires on our barrage balloons, Yank. You get used to it. Want some water for that whiskey?"

"Okay," he said, and watched her bare ass undulate across the room to a sink. That stuff about the English being cold and snobbish was all bullshit. These women screwed as good as any others, but quicker and without acting like only perfumed paper had ever touched their gold plated snatches. It made a difference, he thought, for a country to be years at war, and getting bombed pretty steady. Nobody knew if they'd still be around tomorrow, so they took what they could every night.

And the limey servicewomen—Flora here was a lance corporal in the ATS, the Auxiliary Territorial Service, which American GIs promptly renamed the Army Tail Service —these women were all right. A guy had to respect them for doing tough jobs, taking over for their men who were fighting all over, Africa, India, Burma. Ron grinned, picturing some Coshocton split tails working ack-ack guns and searchlights while kraut planes made bombing runs. Hell, he thought, after the first explosion, the girls he knew would be hauling ass in every direction.

She brought water in a thick tumbler, this soldier woman who outranked him, who'd already seen death up close and dirty. She had long, sleek legs and a pair of knockers Gypsy Rose Lee would be proud of. Flora's hair was regulation cut, curling just short of her uniform collar, a chocolate brown with red glints in it. The hair between her thighs was just a little darker.

He got a real kick out of hearing Lance Corporal Flora Harksinger talk. His outfit had been in England only two weeks —Flora called it a fortnight—when he met her in a pub; that was British for gin mill. Seven GIs and a lieutenant got picked to put on an American weapons show for limey civilians in Southampton. Ron figured he was chosen because the first sergeant wanted to get rid of him for a while, not only because he was the best goddamned gunner in the 16th Infantry.

When his special duty unit got to Southampton, it was right after payday: mortarmen from G and M Companies, to demonstrate the 60- and 81-millimeter tubes; a B Company light machine gunner who petted his air cooled weapon like it was a woman's ass; a corporal who was always oiling his .50-caliber MG; a BAR man who knew his weapon from bipod to butt plate, but had a rough time answering questions about it. The big bastard was bashful. Not Ron—he could talk all day about his beautiful, water cooled machine gun. Then there was the jeep driver and the lieutenant. The setup was a tent in the town's sports center, and polite Britishers asked knowledge-able questions about the guns, but liked the jeep demonstration better, when Kulongski bounded the four-wheeler all over a field that had ups and downs in it, grassed dirt walls. They'd never seen such a handy little vehicle.

Every evening, Kulongski drove the lieutenant to an officers club, and picked him up there early every afternoon. Between times, everybody got drunk and cemented relations with the limeys, mostly at this pub, The Brickmaker's Arms.

Ron met Flora there, all neat and tidy in her lady soldier's uniform, drinking warm, dark beer like a trooper. He'd been with her ever since. She was an ambulance driver whose unit had taken over a nearby schoolhouse, and she had pull with her sergeant major, so she could get off almost anytime she wanted. In fact, the bedroom Ron now thought of as theirs was a spare in the sergeant major's house.

The air raid siren screamed, so close it seemed to shake the bed. It went on howling, up and down, up and down. "What the hell?" Ron shouted.

Flora tilted her head. "Sounds like Jerry's after the docks again."

Ack-ack guns suddenly agreed with her, and chunks of their shrapnel hailed back onto the roof. There was another, much louder blast, and in its echoes, the thundering crashes of glass and roof tiles.

"Jesus," Ron said, fingers white around the whiskey bottle's neck. "That was close."

"I'll have to report in," she said, hurrying into her clothes. "Would you like to take shelter? There's one just down the street."

So calm, so damned calm. But she'd been through many air raids, and this was his first real one. Still, Ron thought, he'd *never* get used to bombs slamming blindly down anywhere and everywhere. He pulled at the bottle and rattled his teeth against the water glass.

Flora laughed. "It just takes time, luv; after a while, you can almost sleep through it."

Ron was sure the whole building wobbled when the next string of bombs marched across the town. He couldn't show fear, not while this unafraid girl adjusted her hat and brushed at her blouse. He couldn't remember being this scared. Before, he'd always fought back, but here he could only lie still and hope a kraut bomb didn't smash through the ceiling.

She stooped and brushed her lips across his. "Kiss-kiss," she said, "I shall come back, as soon as this is over." Her hazel eyes held his. "You're a lovely man, Yank. Wait for me."

"Sure," he said, grinning at her.

Antiaircraft guns stepped up their fire, whackwhacking steadily. More crashes, farther away now, German bombers, trying again to knock out docks and shipyards. Stubbornly the British rebuilt what must be kept running, and worked on bombed-out houses, blocks and entire squares of them, when they could. Ron had seen the limeys working—old men and women, and kids too old for shipping off to country villages.

The AA guns slowed and stopped. Ron took another drink and figured RAF fighters were on the big planes' asses. They'd splash some krauts in the Channel and follow the rest as far as the Spitfires' gas would allow, before swarms of Messerschmitts and Focke-Wulfs rose to escort their surviving bombers home.

He went to the window and peeped through the blackout curtain. Fires blazed in a dozen places he could see, redbright sparks spiraling high into a quietening night sky. Jesus, he felt left out of everything. Flora was somewhere out there in her ambulance, hauling hurt people, her crew trying to keep them alive until she could reach a field hospital. She'd told him that sometimes she couldn't get the vehicle through until rubble was cleared, and people died right behind her seat, while she had to wait.

Goddamn! You'd figure the goddamn U.S. Army at least to set up automatic weapons on barracks roofs at Tidworth, where his outfit was stationed. Or station BAR men and machine gunners in towns like this. So what if you probably couldn't hit high-level flights? Sometimes dive bombers came in low enough for .30 caliber tracers and armor piercing rounds. His own against regulations, juiced-up gun could rip off a full belt inside twenty seconds, 250 slugs that might not knock down a kraut pilot, but would sure as hell make him peel off not so close to the ground and his target.

He sat on the bed, listening. The raid was over, and the guns had gone silent. Fire trucks were at work. Ron could hear their motors, and now burned smells filtered through the blackout screens. He thought he heard a scream, just once and far off. He smoked more cigarettes and lowered the level in the bottle of black market Scotch. There was one more stashed under the bed; he'd work on that with Flora when she returned. Glancing at his watch, he saw that it was already Sunday. No weapon demos today, especially with Southampton digging out from under another raid. Maybe his special duty unit would pack up and go back to Tidworth Barracks. This gravy train couldn't go on forever; he'd have to play toy soldier again, waiting around for the Second Front everybody talked about, a landing in Europe to pull kraut pressure off the Russians.

Once he got up to refill the water tumbler, and once to go down the hall to the WC—the water closet; wasn't that a goofy thing to call it? And the army had its own term: latrine. The navy called it a head. As far as Ron was concerned, a shithouse was a shithouse.

He didn't remember falling asleep, but she must have pulled the covers up over him, because he was snuggled warm into them when she shook his shoulder.

"Yank—Yank?"

"Uh," he said. "Gimme a minute—yeah, baby—yeah, Flora?"

It wasn't Flora, but her sergeant major, a blocky, no-nonsense woman with short grayblack hair. She said again, "Yank—" and her mouth quivered.

"Jesus Christ! Not Flora—they didn't hurt *Flora*?"

Standing erect now, hands locked behind her back as if at parade rest, Sergeant Major Morgan said, "No; I'm certain they didn't hurt her. It must have been so quick—"

Bare-assed and not giving a damn, Ron leaped from bed and grabbed the woman's arms and shook her. "Quick—so quick! Goddamn it, what the hell do you mean?"

"Lance Corporal Flora Harksinger is carried officially as missing in action. In a fortnight her family will be notified her status is killed in action."

Ron shook her again. A tear spilled down her weathered cheek. Ron said, "What the hell you mean, KIA? You just can't find her, that's all. Maybe they're dragging her out of some wreckage right now, maybe she—"

"It was a direct hit on her ambulance," Sergeant Major Morgan said. "Five hundred pounder, we think. Only bits and scraps of the ambulance flung all about, mixed all in among downed building stones. Only bloody bits—"

He let her go and took a step back, fists lifting. "Bloody, *bloody*! Damn you, don't say *bloody*—"

Both the woman's cheeks were streaked now, but she held her shoulders square, military. "We don't use bloody like that, Yank. It's like you would say *fucking*; and that's how I mean it —a bloody fucking waste of a fine girl in a bloody fucking waste of war."

Ron sat on the edge of the bed. He could still smell the scent of her in its sheets, musky warm and flowery.

"She cared for you," Sergeant Major Morgan said. "So I came to tell you."

"Yeah," Ron said, staring at the floor. "Yeah, thanks."

When he looked up, she was gone. He put on his uniform and counted the crap game winnings in his wallet. Then he killed the one bottle of Scotch and brought the other from beneath the bed. Angled right, it just fit in the dumb gas-mask case that regulations said had to be carried at all times. Nobody ever carried the mask itself, just the case, filled with some kind of goodies the U.S. Army had and English girls hadn't.

They couldn't even find her body. He stood outside in the

smoky street and thought how they couldn't even find enough of Flora to bury her right.

You're a lovely man, Yank, she'd said. Shit, shit, *shit*! A lovely man.

chapter 17

A major Russian counter offensive pushed off today
in another effort to relieve the city of Stalingrad. It
follows closely the collapse of a Rumanian mountain division in the Terek Valley, which Moscow
claims has forever smashed German advances in the
Ural Mountains. . . .

—The Russian Front, August 14, 1942 (UP)

Oriana had just waved good-bye to David, driving off in his
father's pickup, when another truck pulled up behind her. She
glanced at it and turned quickly for the house.

"Wait!" Steve Canfield called. "Wait—please?"

She'd never before heard him say please. She walked to the
truck. He held something out the window. "A War Bond for
little Mary Joann—a thousand dollar bond, Oriana."

This was so unlike him that she was thrown off balance.
"Why—why, that's good of you." Her fingers brushed his as
she took the certificate, and his felt feverish, dry.

"She's my blood," he said. "I owe her, too. I—" Canfield's
tongue flicked over apparently dry lips. "Look, I know I ain't
been easy on you, but since Clay—since my son died, I been
doin' some thinking."

"I won't go back to the farm," Oriana said.

"Ain't asking you to; I know you got your mind made up and that's all there is to it."

Damn, she thought, he had really changed. "Well, I thank you for Scooter's bond, and—"

"His things," Canfield said. "All them things of his in the house, clothes and letters and pictures and the like. I thought —I thought you'd want them. If not for you, then for Clay's baby. She'll need stuff to remember her daddy by."

Oriana frowned. The day she left the farm for good, she wasn't thinking about mementos: the picture scrapbook, Scooter's baby records and crayon sketches, little things that meant nothing to anyone else; Clay's floppy old sweatshirt she liked to wear on cold winter nights.

"Thanks," she said, "I'll drive out tomorrow—"

"Plenty of today left," he said. "I—well, it bothers me to have his things around the house. I ain't been sleepin' much of late, and—" He passed a hand over his eyes. "I took down the Gold Star, Oriana."

She bit her lip. Maybe she'd been too hard on him; maybe Clay's death had affected Steve Canfield more than anybody knew. Impulsively she said, "All right. I'll tell Mom where I'm going and follow you to the farm."

He kept the hand over his eyes, his head bent. "I could bring you there and back."

"All right," she said, and went around to climb into the cab. "We won't be that long, and Mom won't start worrying until dinnertime."

"Thank you," Canfield said. "I appreciate this. I mean, seeing Clay's things wherever I turn, the twenty-two rifle for his twelfth birthday, the twelve-gauge pump I got him for Christmas. I kind of expect him to walk in the kitchen door and take down that twelve-gauge and whistle up the dogs to go quail hunting—"

"I can't take the guns," she said. "Please give them to somebody else."

He went quiet then, and she looked at the countryside, a creek and the landmark of an old, crooked birch, a small burst of wildflowers just off the road. Clay had loved the farm and never felt really comfortable away from it; if he'd lived

—Oriana pushed the thought back. Ifs and wishes and might-have-beens were best forgotten, and quickly.

"Home," Canfield said, stopping in the yard and setting the truck's emergency brake. "House feels real empty nowadays. See where I put in the bunkhouse? Takes a lot of cookin' to fill all those bellies. Keeps old lady Blackwell humping, just to stay even with 'em."

She climbed down and saw most of her flower borders gone, probably not watered since she'd left, only a few brown stems canted this way and that. She felt bad, as if she'd abandoned them to this fate.

Canfield opened the door for her, one more surprising move. Though she'd steeled herself for shock, the house embraced her, and Oriana was sorry she'd come back into it. Too much of Clay was here, the years of him and her and Scooter had soaked the walls, and she recoiled from them. She didn't belong here now.

"Know how you feel," Canfield said. "Like you run off and left somethin' behind, and now you've come back and can't remember what it was."

Once again startled, she looked at him. For some reason he looked sweaty around the eyes. He said, "Recalled you got a taste for white wine, so I put a bottle in the icebox. Not icebox, refrigerator; I can't get used to callin' it that."

"I—" she darted glances around the entry hall, parlor, toward the kitchen. "I don't see Mrs. Blackwell."

Canfield shrugged. "Gone off with the other hands; it's payday, and can't none of them wait to get to town. You want some of that wine?"

She shook her head. "Thanks, but—if I can just go to Clay's —to our old room, by myself—"

"Sure," he said. "Anything you want."

God, she thought, even odors left ghosts; Clay's shaving lotion, last winter's apples, the paste of newish wallpaper they'd hung together. Specters ganged up on her, but she was determined not to cry, and went through dresser drawers, bedside tables, putting off the closet until last. The take-home pile grew upon the bed: scrapbooks, photo albums, a carnival kewpie doll, Scooter's bronzed baby shoes.

Then she opened the closet, big, dark, and mothbally. Her fingers traveled along familiar things: Clay's robe that he'd

only worn twice, his blue serge suit, and the particular old
sweatshirt. Holding it against her body, she looked in the
dresser mirror. Clay never got to put in the full length mirror
he'd promised.

He used to say how cute she was when she wore his comfy
sweater to bed, like a little lost girl who needed warming. She
didn't look girlish now; there was some hint of antiquity about
her face. It made her think of David Shepsel's old, old eyes,
and guilt turned her from the glass.

She hadn't *done* anything with David. His good-night kiss
was always gentle and light upon her lips. Not exactly chaste,
more than friendly, but demanding nothing. His furlough
would end soon, and he'd return to war, three years of luck
already used up.

As she put aside Clay's sweatshirt, Canfield entered the
room. When she looked a question at him, he held out a big
glass of white wine. "Had a nip myself; thought you'd like this
about now. Don't it all seem so empty and forgotten?"

Oriana sipped the wine she didn't want, uncomfortable with
him in the room. "I have everything I want from here. Now for
Scooter's room—"

Canfield stayed between her and the door. "I got a business
offer for you."

"Business? I'm moving to Detroit. I've been holding off
leaving because—" She couldn't say David. "If it's anything
about the farm, I'm not interested, and Scooter is pretty well
set up already."

Canfield hadn't shaved that day. She could see wiry grayblack stubble on cheeks and chin, see that strange paleness
about his eyes. He said, "Fine piece of land. Be worth a lot of
money when I'm gone."

Oriana was uneasy. His eyes seemed to be peeling away her
clothing, layer by layer. "I—well, that's good of you, of
course, but Scooter and me—"

"Ain't talkin' about Mary Joann; just you. You and me. Got
the will all wrote out, and all I have to do is sign it."

She stared at him, belly going tight. "What do you—"

Taking a step toward her, Canfield said, "If that ain't
enough, I'll give you a bond like Mary Joann's, *two* of 'em.
That's a whole lot of money in hand and more to come if you'll
just, just—"

"Live here with you again? No—you never liked me, never liked Scooter. If you'll just get out of the way—"

He put a hand on her arm and she moved back, holding tightly to the wineglass because she had nothing else to cling to.

Canfield said, "You're wrong about me not likin' you. For years, it tore me up to hear you and him in the night, them bedsprings squeakin'—"

She started around him and this time he flung her back. She threw wine at him and he slapped the glass from her hand. "Goddamn you, woman! It ain't like you're pure. Whole damn town knows old man Shepherd's boy has been puttin' it to you. And I ain't askin' something for nothin'."

The wall was at her back, the bed against her left knee. "You evil, *evil* old man! Take your damned money to Cleveland and buy yourself a whore. I'm not for sale and never will be."

Inch by inch he moved in upon her, eyes glittering, tongue tip flicking his lips. Like a snake, she thought, like a huge, deadly snake.

"You still ain't got the idea, woman. *You're* the only piece of ass I want, but it's more than for the fuckin'. Clay couldn't do it, but *I* can. I can make a boy baby with you, a Canfield, dammit—a Canfield! So the name won't die out, so there'll always be a Canfield walkin' this land."

Oriana put out her hands, palms almost touching his heaving chest. "M-marry some young woman, then." Oh, God, she thought, stop him; please, please stop him. "You're not—not too old to start over, raise another family—"

"Been watchin' you shake it for years, jigglin' them high tits, shakin' that fine ass around. I mean to make another son with you, woman; ain't nobody else will do."

His hands clamped her shoulders, and when she tried to lift a knee to his groin, Canfield spun her onto the bed. His weight was across her, a hand tearing at her dress front. Oriana screamed, and he ripped her dress to its hem, and jerked the hem apart. She kept screaming, hoping for somebody, *anybody* to hear.

Canfield silenced her mouth by clamping his over it, his tongue thrusting deep. She bit him, slid off his tongue, but caught his lower lip. He cursed and lifted himself to slap her with great, sweeping blows with the flat of his hands.

Her head was a bell clapper, clanging a big hollowness, back and forth, and it hurt. The bell stopped ringing, and she knew her bra strap was broken, that her breasts were painful beneath callused hands.

A knee shoved between her legs and forced them apart. She heard her panties rip and struggled for air. Hard and careless, his fingers drove inside her, and as Canfield bit her breast, he whinnied like a stud horse mounting a mare.

Pawing blindly, Oriana's hands closed on the base of the bedside lamp. She swung it hard against the side of his head, and again as the shade fell away and the lightbulb exploded. He rolled half off her, fingers still buried within her mound. She got an elbow under herself for more leverage, and beat him harder with the lamp base. There was blood, and she pulled from his fingers, jerked away from him, and got to her knees upon the quaking bed. Both hands around the lamp now, she lifted it high to smash him for good.

But he wasn't moving and his eyes were only half open, his exposed penis going flabby. Blood oozed from his head and matted his hair, puddled the bedclothes.

Oriana dropped the lamp and crawled off the bed, her knees so weak they almost gave way. She gasped for air, steadying herself while her runaway heart thumped under her breast. Was he dead? She leaned against the wall, her clothing in tatters. Had she killed Clay's father, Scooter's grandfather?

Staring at him all the while, she creeped around the bed. He didn't move, obscene with his pants tangled around his knees, the shiny stain widening beneath his head, his mouth open. Oh, God, oh, God.

She pulled the sweatshirt over her head. She still wore shoes, high heels absurd with the old sweatshirt-nightgown. There was a conveyor belt inside her head, rolling her to collect scrapbooks, albums, the other things. But she shuddered to a stop before she could force herself to feel in Canfield's pocket for the truck keys.

Oriana went cold then, shuddering. She couldn't touch him, but she had to get back to town, had to *think*. He looked dead, but maybe he wasn't. She prayed he wasn't dead, backing from the room as she prayed for Steve Canfield and for herself.

Scooter—oh, God, what about Scooter if her mother went to prison? And Mom, Dad—

She had a difficult time finding the number in the phone book, and her voice was squeaky as she gave it to the operator. God, please let him be there.

"D-David? Oh, I'm so—so glad you answered—you're there, and—oh, David, please come get me right away. Right away, David. I'm—I'm out at the farm, the Canfield farm."

She was afraid to say more, afraid the operator might be listening. She hung up the phone and gathered the armful of memories.

Fifteen minutes later, a thousand years, she stood in the yard clutching them to her breast, and when David roared up, he had to pry her fingers free of them so she could get into the truck.

"You look bloody awful," he said. "Bits of clothes hanging from under that sweatshirt—and your mouth bleeding, one eye swollen—what in God's name happened?"

Her voice didn't tremble now. "He tried to rape me and I think I killed him. Please, David—may we go now?"

chapter 18

Charlie Chaplin, the "Little Tramp" of motion
picture fame, married Miss Oona O'Neill, 18,
today. The former Miss O'Neill is the daughter of
playwright Eugene O'Neill.

Mr. Chaplin, defendant in a paternity suit by
Hollywood starlet Joan Barry, has come under fire
lately for what officials consider inordinate demands that the U.S. open a second front to aid the
Russians. Chaplin is not a citizen of this country. . . .

—New York, N.Y., August 19, 1942

George Parker pretended to be shocked and sorry about what
happened to Steve Canfield. Secretly he was a little glad,
because Canfield ran the draft board to suit himself, as he did
Civil Defense, the local OPA, and Defense Housing. As soon
as he squeezed himself onto some committee, he started to
bulldoze it.

Served him right for working a tractor right up to dark, and it
was a wonder he didn't kill his fool self when he hit the stump.
The old John Deere really pitched him ass over teakettle.

In the storeroom, George grinned while unpacking a small

shipment of electrical parts that had been back ordered for months. Canfield would certainly have kept the accident to himself, if he didn't need Doc Shaw to stitch him up. As it was, he waited until the cuts started to fester and Doc Shaw said he carried on a lot, because the pain was worse than if he'd come straight in after the accident. George's grin widened; anybody else would have, but one thing Steve Canfield hated more than anything else was being made out a fool.

Now the whole town knew, and Steve was holed up at the farm until he healed. Somehow, Coshocton was getting along fine without him, and George would just as soon the healing took more than a few days.

Oriana had been out there just before the accident. She hadn't said so, but Scooter dragged out the picture album and scrapbook they'd brought back. George marked another item still on back order and thought about Oriana. He wasn't sure how he felt about the Shepherd boy squiring her most everywhere, but it seemed good for her. He'd bless anybody who would hold her in town so she wouldn't go off to work, but Coshocton was whispering that she was a *new* widow.

Hell with gossip, he decided. Oriana and David Shepherd didn't sneak and hide, and she came home every night, regular as punching a time clock. Clocks, he thought; damn it, somebody high up in Defense really screwed up on clocks. That dunce, whoever he was, just cut off all civilian distribution of clocks, since their metals were needed for the war. But how the hell did he expect war workers to wake up? Did everybody have to keep a rooster?

He laughed, picturing roosters crapping all over hotel rooms, crowing all at once. And if any was a bantam, that little devil would start hollering any time after midnight and keep it up for hours. George lifted a new, wartime clock from the shipping crate and hefted it. The thing was mostly compressed paper, even its hands, and glass didn't cover the face, but some kind of cloudy celluloid. Its tinny bell might do the job, though. George winced at the price; at three dollars wholesale, these things were no bargain, and wouldn't hold together long.

He stood up with the invoice clipboard and knuckled his lower back. How long did folks expect Oriana to stay in mourning? It was good to see her coming out of her depression and playing with Scooter again. When she talked to the

Shepherd boy on the phone, her face shone a little. *Shepherd*, not that other name. Maybe the boy was hiding a criminal record. No—more likely he'd changed it to get into the Royal Air Force, although George couldn't think why.

Still, the kid had been at war for years, one of the brave Spitfire pilots who went up after waves of German bombers. In the daytime they had to fight through Hitler's escort fighters to reach the bombers; at night they took off and tried to meet the Nazis before bombs could be dropped on London.

RKO Pathé newsreels showed those daytime dogfights all the time, and the movie crowd clapped whenever a German bomber blew up or went down in smoke. At night, all you saw were searchlights stabbing the black sky, antiaircraft shell explosions, and quick streaks of tracer bullets curving every which way.

The ground movies showed huge fires and buildings falling and the English working like hell to control the fires and dig out victims—women and little kids. You had to give England credit for hanging on, and for years before America got into the war. Damn, he thought; that should have been sooner, and maybe Pearl Harbor wouldn't have happened. The fleet would have been prepared, and those goddamn sneaky Japs would have run into a wall of antiaircraft fire.

But those Londoners—sleeping in subways every night, toughing it out in spite of everything thrown at them, even smiling and holding up two spread fingers in the V for Victory sign. You saw that every time the newsreels showed Churchill and that big cigar; hell of a man, old Churchill.

George made a point of catching Edward R. Murrow's nightly broadcasts from London; sometimes you could hear warning sirens and bomb explosions, but the announcer's rich voice never faltered. It all made George's own war effort seem so damned puny. Anybody, even a woman, could do as well: collecting scrap metal and old tires, asking folks to take change in War Bond stamps, drilling for Civil Defense. It wasn't much for a grown man.

Damn—if he were in construction instead of hardware, he'd be accepted by the SeaBees. That outfit was made up of older guys: heavy equipment operators, builders, anybody who could lay out a jungle airstrip in a hurry, or put up landing docks, anything that needed building, often right there in the front line.

What great stories and pictures about them were coming out of the Pacific. That SeaBee lifting a tractor blade high so Jap machine gun bullets bounced off it while he went ramming into a pillbox. Then he spun the heavy bulldozer around and around, burying the Jap bastards, so that later, no sneaky little son of a bitch could pop up and shoot somebody in the back.

When George opened *Life* magazine and saw that full page picture of a Jap on fire, running a little way before falling over dead, it made him sick. But hell, he found out the marine *behind* a flamethrower was in more danger than the slant-eyed shits in their spider holes and pillboxes; the flamethrower was heavy and clumsy and didn't reach far. A whole lot of brave marines died trying to get close enough to use the thing so their buddies could advance.

George rubbed the small of his back again, and made a final notation on the clipboard. If he *could* get into the service, if he *did* get sent overseas, would he have the guts when it came time to kill or be killed?

That was what every man had to find out for himself, and every man ought to get that chance. If not, he'd go on wondering for the rest of his life.

Heading for the coffeepot set over a low gas jet, George put his clipboard aside. He heard the cash register ring out front, and somebody laughing. Not Holly Melborne; if a hundred people were laughing at Abbott and Costello, her low, throaty chuckle would stand out.

The front door chime sounded again and again. The shop was as busy as could be, but he just didn't feel like going out there. He poured coffee and considered sugar and canned cream, but sipped it black. Patting his slowly flattening belly, George felt he was getting somewhere on his diet. He didn't make a point of it at home, because Elizabeth would fret and wonder and ask if he was sick. He just ate smaller portions and skipped lunch, and it was working. Already he felt younger and looked it, too. Too bad he couldn't try some of the stuff that touched up gray hair. Not that he had all that much, but everybody in town would be sure to notice.

The coffee was bitter, but he kept sipping it. Lately he didn't feel downright old, but got out of bed kind of frustrated and stayed like that most of the day. Seeing Holly Melborne come in every morning, so fresh and so *young*, had something to do with it. And the way Harry kidded around her, when the kid ought to be out making deliveries.

She'd looked hurt when he mentioned that the store phone should be kept open for business. For a while she didn't take calls, but pretty soon boys rang her up again, and George didn't have the heart to make her quit talking to them. Talking, hell—more like sultry whispering while her long, scarlet-tipped fingers caressed the old-fashioned upright receiver: up and down slowly, fingers curled around the length and sliding up and down.

Somebody touched George's shoulder and he said, "Jesus!" and slopped hot coffee over his hand.

"Gee, Mr. Parker," Holly said, "I didn't mean to scare you or nothing."

"You didn't scare me; I was surprised, that's all. I didn't expect anybody to come back here."

"It's about closin' time, you know. Gee, you work so hard back here, all those boxes and everything. Harry ought to come help you more."

Her perfume sneaked to him and he ducked his nose into the coffee cup to avoid it. "Oh, I can handle shipping by myself; been doing it all these years."

Were her eyes just a little tilted? She touched her full bottom lip with her tongue, dampening bright red lipstick. "Gee, it's hard to imagine you doin' this for so long. I mean, you just don't look that old."

George swallowed coffee before answering. "Well, I am."

"Can I have some of that?" She brushed him in passing, and the young animal heat of her seared him. "Harry and Betsy already went home. Annie's still hangin' around, though."

"I—I'll tell her to take off. No sense either of you staying past closing."

Her eyes slid over him. "Don't I get to finish my coffee?"

"Sure," he said. "I didn't mean you had to hurry. I'll go tell Annie. I didn't realize how late—"

"You just work *so* hard." Her voice stroked the back of his neck as he left the storeroom. George told Annie thanks for staying over, and he'd lock up—as soon as Holly was gone, of course. And Annie said, "Sure," and "Thanks, Mr. Parker."

Locking the door and pulling down the green shade that said *Closed* on the other side, he walked toward the storeroom, but veered in time and stood behind the register. He always went over the tape and cash on hand, this time of evening. Now he hesitated, listening for something, anything to signal what Holly was doing, getting her coat and purse, putting on makeup, whatever.

Most times, she only came through the back to use the toilet, or to eat lunch sandwiches with the others while George manned the counters. It made him feel kind of dirty, to think of her on the toilet, like his guilt after masturbating when he was a horny kid.

And it bothered him, men and women using the same rest room—fancy name for a toilet and sink jammed into a corner. It hadn't even had a mirror until Holly Melborne came to work. He had been meaning to have another rest room built, so he wouldn't embarrass himself and whoever was using this one by rattling the doorknob.

George set his jaw and clinged the cash register; somehow the *No Sale* tab was significant. Compartmented sheafs of paper money stared back at him, and change slots were full. If he ever caught up on his back orders, the store would finally make a real comfortable living for the family.

Right now he could forget the store and do something important for the war effort. He could get a job in Detroit, or right here, in the synthetic rubber company. The tires it made were pretty good, and had to be, since the Japs had grabbed all the islands where rubber trees grew. It sure made a man proud of a country where scientists could come up with something so indispensable, and do it so quick.

Going off to Detroit might sound better—being independent and acting a bachelor and all that—but George knew damned well he'd miss home. Except for that trip to camp during the other war, he'd never left Coshocton, or seen reason to, and maybe that was the problem.

Automatically, he flip-counted bills and rubber banded them into hundreds for stashing in the gray canvas bank bag. If he put in a lot of overtime at the wages the tire company was paying, all of it could be saved for—for a trip around the world, maybe.

Of course, Joyce couldn't take over the store, since she had that good job at Butera Corporation, but Elizabeth sure could. Between kids, she'd helped out, and she knew the business. Elizabeth might really like the idea.

So close that he quivered at warm breath in his ear, Holly said, "How come you forgot me?"

George knocked over a stack of quarters. Oh, Lord; her firm breast was against his upper arm and he felt the pressure of a hip. Her perfume attacked him and he tried to swallow it away. A wisp of hair left sparks along his cheek.

"S-sorry, Holly; I guess I'm just a creature of habit." He fiddled with the change, fingers gone clumsy, afraid to turn to her, she was that close. "I have this counting up habit—"

Holly said, "There's good habits and bad habits. Sometimes you can't say which is which, if you don't try 'em all." She stroked his upper arm from behind, the same way she stroked the telephone, only with the sharp ends of her nails.

"Damn!" he said. "Somebody might see and get the wrong—"

She laughed. "The shade's down; it always is. And nobody hardly looks in the show window, anyway."

Easing away from her, shoving change into the bank sack that rattled so loudly he was sure the whole town could hear, George turned and said, "Holly, I'm old enough to be—"

"Not interested in fathers; I got one, if you can call a dirty old drunk 'daddy.' Lays around in tore-up BVDs all summer and don't shave 'less he has to. Only reason he's got a job now is account of the war." She leaned against him in that strange, bone-melted kind of way a woman has when she's ready for a man.

Trying to find words he couldn't say because his throat was clogged up, George let her take his hand and lead him back into the storeroom. There was an old settee against one wall; he used to nap on it when afternoons were real slow, depending on the door chime to wake him for a customer. Holly led him right to it, and it seemed he'd made this trip before, in eager dreams forgotten in the sane light of day.

His lips were dry until she parted them with her quick, darting tongue of wet flame. She caught his hair in both hands while her tongue circled his, then she bit his lower lip so hard a sound escaped him.

At him like a sleek animal, Holly somehow shed most of her

clothes while undoing his shirt and loosening his belt. George gasped at the ring of teeth around his nipple, and caught at her shining hair, running it through fingers suddenly made sensitive, as if the skin had been peeled away to leave only nerve endings.

Then she was beside him on the settee, firm young flesh hotly demanding, kissing and biting him while her hand cupped his sack and played with his swollen rod. George had never known a woman who did that. He responded by cupping the pear shapes of her buttocks, so smooth and slick and, above all, young. They carried no fat and didn't sag, and their sculpture wasn't known to him. Neither was the lifting of her flat, silken belly, nor the flavor of nipples gone stiff and vibrant within his lips.

Squirming, she grasped his penis and guided it into her with an exotic, practiced flip of her pelvis. Slippery, pulling, all satin wet and elastic, she wrung him deep within her tight vagina. Holly's buttocks rolled beneath his hands, and her sweaty belly swept up and down his own, across and back. She hissed into his ear, "Fuck me, fuck me!" And the words knifed through him, stabbed in dark and wounding places, for no woman had ever said the words to him, not even the two whores—one black and one white—he'd bedded before he married Elizabeth.

Digging fingers into her buttocks, George reached deeper, withdrew, and hammered deeply again. She was liquid fires and moans of rapture, grinding voluptuously upon him, and he was never more powerful, never this intense. Though she tossed and squirmed, he could feel the individual downy hairs of her, and knew by her broken, rhythmed churning that she was near. He stayed with her, proud male conqueror timing his moves to hers until she strained against him, nails raking his back, and the climax was volcanic.

Tick-tock, her head went; tick-tock; parted, swollen lips murmured things he did not understand. The world contracted and so did his throat; George lowered his face to share her moanings, to breathe her labored breath. It took a long time before Holly's pelvis stopped all motion, and yet she locked him inside her, refusing to release him.

He was amazed to find himself still hard when at last she

eased from beneath him. With Elizabeth—and he flinched at the thought of her—with his wife, it was always just once.

He was more amazed when Holly Melborne teased her lips down his chest and belly, helpless as she nipped and licked. She overpowered him and took him in her mouth.

George Parker was shocked and ashamed, but they were weak emotions soon swept away. Even as he gasped and stared at the dusky ceiling, he knew his life would never be the same.

Not after this; not ever after this.

chapter 19

Josef Stalin himself pinned Russia's highest award
for valor on the bosom of Miss Katya Petrofsky
today during ceremonies at the Kremlin. Miss
Petrofsky, 18, is credited with killing 22 Nazi
soldiers as a sniper. . . .

—Moscow, August 19, 1942 (Reuters)

Louise Parker wished she hadn't listened to Deke. They could
have gone on just the same, but when she got a little drunk, she
agreed to do it. Deke had sounded so funny, bitching that
screwing with a rubber on was like taking a bath wearing
socks.

She looked out the car window. Columbus was a stupid hick
town just like Coshocton, only bigger. That goddamn doctor,
looking at her like she was some kind of crawly worm he'd
have to pick up with tweezers. He knew she wasn't twenty-
one, but Deke paid him for not asking questions, and for the
diaphragm too.

The son of a bitch had black hair clear down the backs of his
hands, and a few bristles on his fingers. He knuckled her hard,
fitting her for the damned thing, feeling around with those big,
stubby fingers like he wanted her to come so he could watch it.
Fat chance.

How the hell could any woman come, feet jammed wide in
stirrups and the table tilted back so she was spread wide open?

149

Looking up pussies with that mirror thing on his head and feeling around inside, stroking and rubbing. The old bastard probably jacked off in his pants while doing it, or hurried to the toilet while he was still hard.

"This goddamn cigarette lighter," she said, and banged it with the heel of her hand.

"Hey," Deke said, "take it easy, huh? Just push it in like this."

"Push it in, pull it out. That's all you bastards are interested in."

"Did he do something funny to you? The nurse wouldn't let me in, so—"

"Funny? Hell, no, it wasn't funny." Louise jammed her Pall Mall into the glowing lighter for a long drag. "Jesus, the things I do for you—"

"It'll be better, I swear. It'll be more fun."

"More fun," she said to the northeast edge of Columbus, as it slipped by the Studebaker. She tried letting cigarette smoke curl from one corner of her mouth, like Lana Turner in that scene with Clark Gable. It got up her nose so she coughed and sneezed at the same time. Dammit; Lana Turner hadn't just been fitted with a gadget that would keep her from having babies.

"You want to stop at a tourist camp in Mansfield?" Deke drummed on the steering wheel, his forefingers like drumsticks, ratatat, ratatat.

"No, dammit! And watch the road."

"But I thought—I mean, since I'll be leaving so quick and all. This whole trip—"

Louise dragged on her Pall Mall and lowered the window on her side to flip it out. "Sure, sure—and all the money you spent. I know." She turned to face him, knees sideways on the seat, saddle shoes drawn under her pleated skirt. Deke had given her three pairs of silk stockings—his daddy knew somebody—but she was saving them for parties. Besides, she couldn't wear her slave bracelet with them; they were too precious to chance a run, and they'd look better with strap high heels. Deke hadn't bought her a pair yet, but he would. And that wasn't being a whore, either; whores took money, and getting little presents wasn't the same.

"Our regular place," she said. "You can lift the back seat out of the car and we'll take our time, all the time you want. I don't have to be in early. Mom thinks I'm over at Julie Winthrop's."

"Doing some kind of war work, right?" he laughed.

She fiddled with the radio knob. Deke was one of the few guys with a radio in his car. And Roger, whose old man was a big wheel at the Barton-Shaw factory. She hadn't let Roger go all the way yet, mainly because Deke hung around so much. Roger wasn't going in the service, though; he had an exemption that said he was vital to defense work. Deke's old man had screwed up somehow, but Deke wouldn't be a common soldier. He was going to be a lieutenant. He'd look terrific in his uniform, she decided.

But Roger Barton would be here, and Deke wouldn't be. On the radio, Billie Holiday sang "Lover Man" low and haunting. Louise liked swing better, real fast jitterbug stuff, but the Blues weren't bad, once in a while.

"They say she's a drunk or something," Louise said. "You believe that?"

Deke swung the car past a poky Nash. "You still reading those song sheets and movie magazines? They wouldn't tell you she's a drunk, though. I heard she's a dope fiend."

"Dope?"

"Yeah, you know: morphine and cocaine and heroin—tea, too."

She bumped his thigh with her knee and the Studebaker swerved. "Now you're making fun of me. How can anybody get drunk on tea?"

He laughed again. "I forget you aren't hep to campus talk. Tea is marijuana, baby; I thought everybody knew that. It makes you crazy."

Louise switched radio stations. ". . . *my mama done tol' me . . . when I was in pigtails . . . my mama done tol' me, hon . . .*"

" 'Blues in the Night,' " she said. "Damn, ain't there any jump music on? You ever take any of that marijuana?"

"You don't *take* it," he said. "You smoke it. And no, old Deke Deacon doesn't need it. I'm already a sex maniac, right?"

She let his hand feel around her thigh, wondering if some tea would help. Maybe, but she wouldn't know where to get any, and the cops put you in jail if you got caught.

"You do swell," she said, unbuttoning his shirt and sliding her hand along his chest and the top of his belly. Cripes; boys made such a big thing out of doing it, and then they bragged. Deke swore he didn't, but she figured his college pals knew all about her. So long as people in Coshocton didn't get the idea she was screwing. They wouldn't come out and say it straight; she would be known as "easy," or a girl of "loose morals," or just "that Parker girl."

Damned hypocrites; men and women screwed, although she couldn't picture her mom doing it. All grownups acted like they never heard of such a thing. Bullshit.

"Hey," Deke said, "you wearing that new thing now?"

"Hell, no—that goddamn doctor would've figured I was going to screw right away."

"He showed you how to work it, though?"

"He *told* me, after feeling all around inside me. I know how to put it in, and use the jelly. Cripes, you think I'm stupid?"

Patting her thigh, he said, "I think you're great. I'll miss you like hell when I'm away. You could come up to Kent State and get a job. I'd pay your room rent."

"Sure, and what do you think my old man would do? I've kind of been thinking of it—goin' to work, I mean. Not in Coshocton, somewhere out of town. Maybe over at Willow Run in Michigan. They're always needin' help there; says so in the paper. I could make my own money."

Deke fed more gas to the car, peeling off on State 541. "Gee, I don't know; it's hard to get a place to sleep there. Not a whole room, either, just a place to sleep. And you have to finish school, and—"

She pinched the inside of his thigh. "School? I'm almost seventeen, and can quit anytime I want. Besides, I'd be helping the war effort. You gettin' jealous?"

On the left, the clump of maple and birch waited for them, quiet in this windless afternoon. Deke slowed for the turn, and moved along the dirt road that took the Studebaker out of sight. He got out and walked a little distance from her while she went through the contortions that got the damned diaphragm settled in place. Then it was her turn to walk into the trees. Deke wrestled out the back seat and hauled it after her. Funny, she thought, they'd only done it once in a bed and this would be the first time she'd done it in daylight.

Joyce Parker watched the same daylight filter through her office window at the Butera Corporation. Her responsibility had grown quickly in this new job, and she understood much of what Franco meant to do. He was always hurrying here and there, his phone calls piling up. But he managed to catch up, even if he had to stay well into the second shift. Franco was going to be rich, diversifying into many other businesses besides army boots and shoes. That wasn't why she didn't mind staying late with him, though; she just wanted to. If he didn't force overtime pay on her, she wouldn't take it.

Glancing at his oaken, name-plated office door, Joyce reminded herself that she was one lucky girl. He loved her for what she was, for the newness she felt bursting inside, and the way she responded to his teaching. What a lover he was, able to kindle flames in her that took days to fade. They were together often. When he drove her home after work, he never even followed to the gate, but stood at the car until she was safely inside and away from prying eyes.

They had another place, way out in Cressingham Hollow, a new building where apartments could also be entered from the garage below. Joyce truly lived there, every fiber of her being coming alive the moment she entered the door. Now she twitched upon the real leather chair behind her desk and listened to the hum of the factory. Outside and down at loading docks, steel doors clanged and voices of platform men and drivers floated up to her.

Her phone buzzed and she politely asked the caller's name, put him on hold, and pushed the intercom button for Franco's private office. The name was one on a special list her boss had prepared, or she'd have made the guy wait. She looked at the window again, then through her open office door; beyond she could see typists busy at their desks, the staccato rapping of their machines blending into the always living, vibrant, changing voice of the plant itself.

There'd been one change after another since the lucky day she came to work here. Each of them added to the plant, a constant spreading out that speeded up production with added machines and long belts that high, buckled combat boots and brown dress shoes rode to big crates in Shipping. Franco always drove for more and more production, and needed so many employees that they were coming in from Mansfield, Marion, and Zanesville, and from farms between.

Joyce opened the middle drawer of her desk and glanced at the V-Mail letter from Joe. It came two days ago, but she hadn't opened it. Not that she felt guilty; she didn't owe Joe Dayton a damned thing, fidelity included. Joe the football hero; Joe the sometime mechanic, the lover picking dates from barstools. Hell, Joe Dayton didn't know what loving—real, honest, and open loving—was.

She flicked open the letter with a shortened but carefully tended fingernail. It was different from his usual, labored *I'm fine how are you*? He was already a staff sergeant and would be sending more money home, since he couldn't spend any where he was. The censor had blocked out the next line. Then Joe said he was the best damn mechanic his outfit had, but he wasn't about to be a grease monkey forever. He could do more than fix tanks; he wanted to ride one into combat. It wasn't much trouble getting transferred *to* the front; asking for a rear echelon job was something else. She should say hello to all the gang for him.

Joyce refolded the letter. It made a funny kind of sense. Joe needed to be the star fullback again. He had to be out on the field with pompom girls and the cheering section yelling his name.

What did the Japs yell? *Banzai, banzai* . . .

For the first time Joyce realized Joe Dayton could be killed, and wondered about her reaction. He was an ass and boring and would never get anywhere, never grow up. But you couldn't live with a man for years and not feel something for him. But now there was Franco. Comparing Joe to him was putting a kindergarten kid beside a college graduate, they were so far apart in everything.

Clay Canfield was dead already, and what had happened to Oriana could happen to Joyce, leaving two widows in the Parker family. Oriana took it hard, but she had Scooter, and David Shepherd to lean on. Nobody ought to blame her for leaning on a man.

Joyce hadn't been close to anybody in the family of late, but she had a hunch Oriana was getting out, that her sister was only waiting until David had to leave.

If Franco was leaving, Joyce would go with him in two seconds flat. If he asked her, she thought; if he asked her. He hadn't even come close to mentioning marriage, but maybe that was because she wasn't a widow.

She closed the desk drawer on Joe and his letter, on Oriana and what ideas Franco Butera had or didn't have. What she should be thinking about was Ron overseas, and Randy. A couple of days and Randy would be headed for that "somewhere" that censors were so fond of, meaning anywhere, meaning the enemy wasn't to know where and when. Joyce wondered if that really mattered, since the government had moved all those Japs—Nisei, or whatever they were called —clear off the West Coast and penned them up somewhere.

Other aliens had been locked up, those goofy German Bund guys who used to strut around in swastikas and hold rallies. The FBI even ran a check on old man Butera because he'd come from Italy. Long before Mussolini's rise, Franco had told the agents, and his father had been an American citizen a long, long time.

Joyce remembered one agent sort of roaming around the plant and apologizing to Franco. Just our job, he said; everybody in Washington knows white folks are one thing, no matter where they come from. Japs are different; even if they're born here, they're still sons of heaven who have to obey Emperor Hirohito, that buck-toothed little son of a bitch —excuse my language, ma'am.

The phone rang and old man Butera came storming through the door at the same time, waving a combat boot. She barely had time to hit the warning buzzer before he crashed his son's door. She knew Franco wouldn't want people down the hall to hear whatever made his papa mad this time. Reaching to close the door, she was jarred back by the old man heeling it again. White hair in disarray, black eyes snapping, Giuseppe Butera spat a rapid stream of Italian at his son. He used the combat boot like a club, slamming it up and down on Franco's desk, scattering papers.

Once more, Joyce tried to close off the altercation, but the old man caught her movement from the corner of his eye. "No! Leave open the goddamn door, *capish*? This *figlio*—this son of mine, you shoulda know, whole goddamn factory shoulda know! United States to know!"

"Papa," Franco said. Joyce had never seen such hardness set upon his face. It had gone pale except for a crimson spot on each cheekbone.

"Papa, hell!" the old man shouted. "Papa, sonnabitch! You look this boot! Look this sonnabitch boot stitches—cheap thread, no wax, buckle comes off before leava goddamn factory. Look this sole, one good push, itsa pull loose. You not make enough money, you got to use *a buon mercato*—cheap sonnabitch thread?"

Joyce wanted to back away, to somehow close off the old man's yelling and protect Franco. But there was something so furious, so outraged in Giuseppe Butera's attack that it cannonaded about her, pinning her as it skewered Franco.

"Papa," Franco said between beautifully white and evenly set teeth, "I don't think business—"

"*Affari*, bullashit! Business—whatsa kind business get boy killed, eh?"

Franco flared back. "*Killed*? Did his little tootsies get wet? Killed—what the hell *you* know, old man? It's a crime to cut production costs? Mexican leather, not American: twenty thousand bucks less on my last run. Unwaxed thread: four grand. You don't know a damned thing about real production. You never outgrew that two-bit cobbler's bench. I gave you a job so you could feel important, and you come raving in here about me killing some kid."

The old man turned the boot in his hands, scarred and bent fingers moving over roughout leather, clinking buckles more tin than brass. The silence drew itself as tight as a drawn bow.

Then Giuseppe Butera said, "This lady, this Signora Lawrence, livsa right here, Coshocton." He had stopped yelling, and his voice was tired, but with a different edge to it. "This *ufficiale*, this captain of her son, writes letter to her. It'sa how her boy dies. A good *capitano*, I think; a man who wantsa for mother more than telegram says same thing everybody."

The boot in his hands turned slowly. Standing rigid behind his desk, Franco did not change expression, but Joyce saw the burning of his eyes. Why, she thought, he *hates* his father!

The old man said, "Thisa boy on night patrol; sole of boot comes off. When he'sa try fix, buckle makes noise and Jap blows him up, two more with him. Eh, big businessman—you go this mother and say *scusare, signora*, production cost. You say save four grand because no wax? Go, big businessman, I give address. I am *vergognoso*; you bring me shame."

One long stride, and Franco was around his desk, snatching the boot and hurling it against a wall. Joyce heard silence behind her and along the corridor, a breathless quiet sprinkled with quicksharp whispers.

"You old fool!" Franco shouted, swollen vein throbbing in his left temple. "*Stupido*! I'm not the only corporation making combat boots; there's fifteen, twenty more. A dumb kid screwed up and got knocked off. It happens every day, every night, and nobody can blame me or my corporation for every stupid bastard who stops a bullet. You're ashamed of *me*? You don't know what shame is. *Marone*!

"Did *I* go to parties? Was *I* invited to the rich homes, the fuckin' white Protestant homes? Hell, no; I was the wop shoemaker's kid, the one who had to run to the shop right after school and help out, cut that goddamn leather and hammer tacks and my fingers. When the fuckin' Protestants played football on Saturday, *I* had to haul ass all over town, delivering shoes—the shoes you made me shine up, goddamm it!"

Joyce watched the old man's back, straight and still. She didn't want to look at Franco's face, distorted and ugly.

Franco said, "So *I* made it—me! I got the contracts and swung the loans and made this corporation, *my* corporation. You'd still have split thumbnails and a mouthful of tacks, if it wasn't for me—*me*, dammit!"

"Your corporation," his father said.

"Goddamn right! You signed anything put in front of you, old man. *I* control this outfit. Oh, you won't run out of pasta and *bombarole*; I left you a few shares of stock, but you don't have anything to say about running the corporation, nothing —*capish*?"

The slap was a cannon crack across Franco's face that staggered him into Joyce. She tried to brace him, but he spun her away. Guiseppe Butera slapped his son again and again —full-armed, sweeping blows that sent Franco reeling across Joyce's office and into the typing pool, where all machines went mute.

"Papa," Franco said, shielding his face with crossed arms, "Papa, goddammit! Don't hit me again—don't make me—"

Giuseppe said, "Twenty thousand save on Mexican leather cured in piss; four grand—that'sa how you say, big shot? —four grand no-wax thread. Only you don't show this on paper to United States, eh?"

"Shut up!" Franco hissed as Joyce followed the men, helpless, sick, aching for Franco's humiliation, for the hate she'd seen in him.

Louder, for all to hear, Franco said, "You're wrong, old man; any audit will show me clean. Hell, look out there at the flagpole. What do you see under the flag? You were so damned proud of that blue pennant with the big white *E* for Excellence. That's what the government thinks of me and the corporation. Washington's proud of this factory and its workers, yeah—and everything else the conglomerate is doing."

Giuseppe lifted his arm to strike again, but let it fall.

"That's smart," Franco said, finger slashes fiery on both cheeks, a droplet of blood at the corner of his mouth, beading his mustache. "I'm not going to take any more from you, crazy old man. You're senile and stupid and holding up the war effort. Get out of here, out of my plant. The guards won't let you back in."

The old man was a head shorter than his son, but to Joyce he seemed much taller, standing upon two thousand years of civilization and the dignity of Caesars. His wrinkled face was a strange sculpting of mortal hurt and the hard marble of a centurion bust.

Giuseppe said then, "I go. You no longer my son. I go, but I come back."

Franco dabbed a neatly folded white handkerchief at his mouth. "Don't try it."

After the old man stalked off down the corridor, Joyce timidly touched Franco's arm. He put away the handkerchief and turned to face the room of typists and clerks, smooth-faced and handsome again, urbane. "My apologies, ladies. It seems my father aged quicker than I thought possible. I'm sorry he caused such a disturbance. Please go on with your work. He may not be proud of you, but I am. Each of you is doing an important job for the nation, and I thank you."

Fingers gentle but urgent upon Joyce's elbow, he maneuvered her away from the whispers that rose to become chatter, then turned into the machine gunning of typewriters.

Behind the closed door of his office, he poured a drink at the small bar and lifted an eyebrow at her. Joyce shook her head, afraid to trust her voice.

He tossed off one drink and refilled his glass. "Would you believe that? Jesus, after all I've done for him—new house and car, cleaning woman to help Mama, everything."

"Frankie," she said, "I don't remember anybody ignoring you in school. Was it really so bad for you?"

Sipping at his glass, he said, "Did *you* ever invite me to a party?"

"I would have, but you were older; and I never had a party. We couldn't afford one."

His grin was radiant again. "What the hell. We'll throw ourselves a party, a great big bastard of a party—and maybe we won't invite anybody."

Joyce said, "It wouldn't be a party, then."

He put the empty glass back on the bar. "You think I'm cruel, that I cheated my old man out of the factory."

"No, Franco."

"Yeah, baby. So I'll explain it to you just once. He couldn't swing government contracts and loans. Without me, there'd be about three hundred fewer Coshocton workers making boots for the army. He'd never have thought of using collateral of one company to borrow to start or buy another company. He has no idea how big the Butera Corporation is, all the things it does." Franco touched his swollen lip. "And it's growing; after the war, it'll be a diversified giant. When the cost plus contracts dry up, when all the new, one product companies fold or go desperate for financing, I'll still be around."

He smiled, but without charm. "Coshocton, hell—not the county, but the *state*, baby. Everybody who amounts to anything in Ohio will know who I am."

"Maybe you'll start painting again, when you have time. I never saw any of your paintings, Frankie."

"Told you I was no good at it. And you're calling me Frankie again. Why?"

Joyce looked away. "I—I don't know. Maybe you don't seem so—cosmopolitan, since the fight with your daddy, not so Italian now."

He nodded. "And that's what I am, just a good, clean American boy out to save his country and turn a million bucks doing it. Unless of course, I have to turn *paisan* to swing another deal."

She couldn't think of anything to say, and just stood there until he motioned her back to work.

chapter 20

This seacoast English city saw its first American casualty today. A United States B-24 bomber of the 8th Air Force, limping for its field after a raid on German shipping, didn't quite make it. The plane went into the sea just short of this heavily bomb-damaged city. . . .

—Southampton, England, August 20, 1942 (Reuters)

Oriana stopped hugging Scooter and came erect, into her mother's arms. "Don't cry, Mom. I have the truck, and maybe I can get home every weekend."

Elizabeth propped her glasses high to wipe her eyes. "But you didn't say proper good-byes to—to your father and Randy, and Joyce said—"

Oriana stepped back and felt Scooter's little hand slip into hers. "I stopped at the store and the factory first, and kissed Randy long before he left for the bus station. You know his girl's coming in today and he has so little time."

"I know, I know." Elizabeth fumbled with her apron. "It just seems everybody should be together like a real family for good-byes. Oh, this awful war."

Scooter said, "Don't worry, Grandma; I'll take care of you."

Anxiously she looked up at Oriana. "Every Saturday and Sunday? You'll come back then, promise?"

Patting her head, Oriana said, "If I can, darling. You know I'll see you every time I can."

"You could work in a defense plant here," Elizabeth accused.

"Mom, I told you it isn't the same, and so long as Steve Canfield's in Coshocton—"

"I know what you said. I just don't understand it." Elizabeth jerked her head at the door. "And driving off with another man—"

Oriana glanced through the screen door to the curb, where David Shepsel waited in her truck. "I'm only dropping him off at his camp. He has to report in. He's a soldier, Mom; he's been a fighter pilot since 1939. I owe him for that; everyone owes him."

"You don't owe him your reputation."

"Repu—" Oriana stared. "Okay, Mom, have it your way —Coshocton's way. It doesn't matter. Scooter, I'll write and call often, soon as I get settled. One more hug, baby?"

She drove miles without talking, and David didn't intrude. Once in a while he touched a kitchen match to his pipe. Fragrant smoke touched her before streaming out David's slightly lowered window.

Finally he said, "The first time is hard, leaving everyone you know and love. This time it was difficult for me because my father and I came to understand each other. Not completely, of course—that kind of understanding is left only to lovers."

She didn't say anything, and he went on, "My trip home made me remember how nobody understood a chap in my old squadron, Terrance Whitney. He was called Terry the Cherry because he'd never been with a woman. Some thought him a fag, but that wasn't so. He was one of my hut mates, and got squiffed one night when we were alone. He cried about it, being pulled by a starchy Church of England family upbringing and pushed by his flight mates."

Oriana waited, then asked, "What was his problem?"

He turned her way. Watching the road, she could see his face from one eye corner. "Oh," he said, "Terry simply believed—or had been made to believe—he should go chaste to his marriage bed, as should his wife."

She rummaged one-handed into her purse for cigarettes. David lighted one for her and passed it over. She said, "And did he hold out? Did he remain Terry the Cherry?"

Humming, David tamped his pipe bowl. She recognized the tune he said he hated, the one he caught himself humming on a mission: *"There'll be bluebirds over the white cliffs of Dover, tomorrow. . . ."*

"He did; splashed his Spit into the Channel and didn't come up. I've often wondered if, in his last moment, Terry prided himself for sticking to his convictions or damned himself for never bedding a woman."

"That's so damned sad," Oriana said.

"Sorry. That story seemed part of my reason for coming home, you see. I had to know if I was really so wonderfully holy, so completely right."

"And?"

She kept the truck headed for Detroit as David told her of his need to be part of something bigger than himself. Shy, quiet, and with no truly close friend, he was first elated at finding the hidden religious objects, then angry.

"My father couldn't completely sever *all* ties to the past; that's why he kept what he did—skullcap, shawl, other things. God, what wonderment and outrage I felt. I belonged to an ancient belief, to a God of my own people, to history. And my own father had denied me this. I was furious at him, this turncoat, this cowardly traitor who cowered behind a false name. This, while Nazis were beginning to round up Jews, while those with money fled their homelands, and those without money were penned behind barbed wire.

"Did *he* send money? Did *he* speak out? No, he remained in hiding, so that his Christian neighbors thought him one of them. He out-Americaned his fellows, joined every community organization, volunteered for everything civic, hooray for the flag, boys, hooray. Oh, I had a long list of grievances, and righteously put my father behind me."

David scratched another light for his pipe. "I came back, the blooded warrior, to accuse him. Damn, what agonies Samuel Shepherd underwent to keep his infant son alive, to bring *me* to America's haven. Did I tell you he fed me blood drawn from his own skinny arms? That kind of frantic struggle to keep a life, that terror repeated and growing ever more horrible, ever more threatening—it's worked into the marrow of my father's bones. Freedom can't dig it out; perhaps nothing can.

"Samuel Shepsel gave his blood and name and respect for me. He denied his God, and *I* called him coward."

Oriana felt for his hand. "But you're friends now."

He closed her fingers gently within his. A truck roared by; lights showed in some houses now. "My father kissed me when I left, held me to his chest as if he could protect me with his body again. He said: 'Go, son of Joshua and of Samuel, and when the walls have fallen, return to me. I am proud of you, Davida.' "

Oriana said, " 'Davida'?"

"The diminutive, a pet name."

"Davida," she said, the sound of it lying soft upon her tongue. "So much better than 'Davy.' "

"I've talked a lot," he said. "You're pulling up your own roots and I ran on and on about myself."

"I'm glad—Davida. You made me more certain, gave me strength."

He chuckled. "You were strong enough, walloping your father-in-law."

"That was desperation and—yes, *hate*. To think he'd try —that he would even *imagine* I'd let him—oh, Jesus. I get mad all over again."

Putting away his pipe, David said, "We're almost there. It's still odd, to see all these lights. The outskirts of Detroit would send any Londoner into shock."

Low-voiced, Oriana sang, *"When the lights go on again, all over the world . . ."*

"Better than bluebirds and the cliffs of Dover. You know, I have a theory that those birds, aided and abetted by numerous careless seagulls, had much to do with turning those cliffs white."

She laughed; David could do that to her, make her laugh, even at herself. "Light me another cigarette?"

When he passed it to her, she felt the second hand dampness of his lips, too quickly gone. "You know, I have no idea where I'm going—in Detroit, I mean. First I have to find a place to stay, then apply for a job, and I don't know what I *can* do. Defense companies have school programs—welders, machinists, riveters—I'll do anything but type. I'm not here to do inconsequential woman's work; I'm going to help kill Japs, Germans, or whoever.

"The Ford company's big aircraft plant is Willow Run, and word has it that living conditions there are impossible. There's a tank factory in town, and others that turn out army trucks, jeeps, and command cars. But you're going to fly again, so maybe I'll try Willow Run. I'd make certain every plane I work on is perfect, because it might carry you."

When Oriana stopped for the traffic light, David said, "I actually have two more days' leave; this is Monday, and I don't have to check in until 2400 hours Wednesday. Don't let it bother you; I lied a little because I knew how badly you wanted out of Coshocton."

She shifted gears when the light changed. "David—Davida, I don't know—"

"Don't fret; I don't mind reporting early. You can drop me anywhere in town, and I'll grab a taxi to the bus station."

"I won't," she said. "After I find a hotel, I'll drive you to the station or all the way. I have plenty of C stamps left; good thing I was a farm wife—woman."

At the Fairmont, the doorman looked askance at the truck, but touched his cap bill to David in uniform, and whistled up bellhops for the luggage. No reservations? The desk clerk frowned until David put on his broadest English accent and said things about vital defense inspections, staunch allies and all that, y'know. Oriana bit her lip to keep from laughing when David motioned the man closer over the desk and said, "A bit hush-hush, y'know; man in your position discreet, eh? Any suite would do temporarily for Royal Air Force Wing Commander *Sir* David and Lady Shepsel."

Bowing, on the verge of stuttering, the clerk apologized for having no suite available, but if Lord and Lady Shepsel would be content with a large double? Yes, your lordship; we'll be especially careful of the small musette bag—and the sealed one, oh, yes, sir.

When baggage was inside and bellhops tipped, Oriana threw her arms around David's neck and laughed and laughed. "Oh, you marvelous fool. He'd have turned me down flat, but not Lord and Lady Shepsel—oh, my ribs hurt, and I almost blew it. Secret luggage and Wing Commander—"

Still holding to his accent, David said, "Certain the bloke

couldn't tell leftenant from colonel, y'know; these foreign types, these ruddy colonials—"

Oriana was suddenly conscious of his body, of her breasts and belly and thighs against him. Lashes damp from laughter, she lifted her face and David kissed her ever so gently. When she let go and took a backward step, so did he.

"Sorry about that 'lord and lady' thing. I was only being sure you got a room. I'll just take my kit and slip off down the back stairs."

"No you won't. I promised to see you off, and—damn, we don't even have the makings of a farewell drink, and do you think we should call room service so quick, and what if *I* have to say something, they'll know right away and—"

"Oriana," he said; just that, and she came into his arms again. His lips were again softly upon hers, but slightly parted, so that she could drink his breath and find it sweet.

She felt his trembling, the pressure of his lifted penis. There was an urgency in him, held back until she probed his mouth; then his arms were hard as he strained against her, his hands sliding from her waist to her buttocks. She lifted to his pelvis, shuddering. It had been so long, so long.

Just fitting each cheek, David's spread hands rotated her groin against him as she broke the kiss to gasp for air. He said, "You—me—" the words trailing off when she would not allow him to release her buttocks, when she reached down and around to band his wrists. Tippytoe, ticktock; up and down and around, her body demanded to search his, to know the intimate feel and new shaping of him.

At the bed, David said, "It's so damned awkward about clothes," and Oriana replied, "Please, let me." But he said, "I want to undress you," and they got mixed up and laughed. Oriana felt she wasn't far from giggling hysterics.

It changed when they lay naked upon the bed, finger-skipping each other's body, touching, gliding, her heart soaring and swooping in this reawakened flesh and bone and fluid.

"You're so beautiful," he whispered into her mouth.

She murmured, "You too," against his lips and, urgency turned compulsive, clasped her fingers around his penis, lifting her pelvis so he could caress and explore her mound. A moment, a minute, a mini-eternity, and he was covering her, she was guiding him to her entrance. Softly yearning, she parted for him, and felt another maleness reach inside her. She had only known her husband's, only Clay. There was a difference, but mainly in this other body, this unfamiliar rhythm she followed so easily.

She came swiftly, wadded bedspread clutched in each hand, heels dug into the mattress and knees bent, back arched. A pulsebeat later he burst inside her, but they clung motionless only a moment. Then the rocking of their joined bodies began again.

This time it was slow and easy, a sweetly languid movement that Oriana had no desire to hurry. She tasted his throat, the lightly haired and faintly sweated expanse of his chest. David's whispers tingled her ear as she gradually eased from beneath him, holding him clasped within her depths so he wouldn't mistake her intent and withdraw.

Always she had wanted this for herself, to somewhat dominate even as she submitted, but Clay had resisted. Occasionally, when he did give in, he sulked afterward, as if she had stolen some part of his precious manhood.

When she rolled atop David and gave him her nipples one by one, it was very good to feel him far up, to hold him near motionless as she ground sensuously against his pelvis. For this wondrously bright moment, he belonged to her and she could do whatever she wished to him and with him. Never had Oriana been so free, so abandoned. She used her lover for her own erotic pleasures, instead of matching his desires and bending to his needs. It was marvelous to be selfish, to take in the giving.

Without hurry, she crested with him, head thrown back and hands braced against her thighs, leaning backward to capture each liquid vibration of David's release. A thought of pregnancy passed through her mind but did not linger, for all that mattered was David—tender, beautiful, and adoring David.

It was a time for celebrating, so he called for champagne in an iced bucket, delivered almost instantly by room service. No, she said, she wasn't hungry yet—not for food, anyway. She toasted him and wrinked her nose at bubbles tickling crisp and cold. They were so comfortable with each other, she thought; no half-ashamed covering up after the act, no secrets in darkness. They kept bed lamps on, and Oriana was glad for it, for she could examine him minutely, imprint him upon her mind as the memory of him would always be stamped upon her body.

He was slight, but not thin; tall, but not towering; gentle, but not girlish. He carried two flak wounds that she hated for marring his lovely skin. She kissed them at hip and haunch, and grew afraid because of them.

"Do you *have* to go back? To flying combat, I mean?"

"Yes, love, it's what I do best."

"But you've done so much already. Can't someone else take over now?" Her fingertips caressed the redblue scars. "You might be hurt, or—or—" She forced herself to say it: "Or be killed, like Clay."

Sitting upon the bed, he poured some wine for them. "Do you feel guilty about your husband?"

"No," she said. "I haven't soiled his memory. He was Clay and you are Davida."

"That's good, darling. There's no need to forget the dead, or perpetuate their memories, either. I learned that when messmates didn't come back. We never carried on that morbid tradition of the flyers of that other war. No empty chairs at table, no flinging toast glasses into the fireplace. 'Here's to the next man to die . . .' What bravado. Then there was knightly jousting among the elite, or so they liked to believe. They were far above the slogging brutality of the trenches, meeting a sporting enemy in heroic, individual clashes."

He lighted cigarettes and gave Oriana one. "Now we're all down in the muck and blood with women and children, where death isn't a damned bit selective."

Oriana drew on her cigarette. "You won't be sent to fight Japs?"

"I don't imagine; my experience is in Europe, and that's where I'll probably be used."

"One of my brothers is there; the other finished training but doesn't know where he'll be sent." It was so damned absurd, talking about war and death and guilt, when the most beautiful thing in her life had just happened to her, next to having Scooter. Scooter would love David too, given the chance.

Oriana said, "Tonight and tomorrow and tomorrow night too. It has to last me until I see you again."

Sometime during the night they had club sandwiches and

more champagne; half of the next bottle went flat while they made love, but they drank it anyway. Oriana was afraid to sleep, afraid to give up one precious second. Once in the dawn, when graypink marched threatening to the window, she awakened beneath the covers and snuggled against David's man-smell, so warm and wiggly.

She dreamed he asked her to follow him, and there was a rosy glow of military camps, a freighter to England, the crew not at all surprised to see them making love on deck. There were bluebirds over Dover, wheeling and darting to escape strikes of black killer airplanes.

chapter *21*

Psychologists claim the wartime rise in juvenile delinquency is dramatic: eight percent among boys, 31 percent among girls.

"Astonishing," said Dr. Adolfus Mennenger, "and attributable to teen-agers who hang around bus and train stations and other places where servicemen on leave congregate."

Local authorities claim no such rise among Coshocton teen-agers. . . .

—*Coshocton Tribune*, September 2, 1942 (UP)

Martha Swensen posed three steps down from the top of the stairs, like Joan Crawford making a grand entrance. Her grand entrance brought a concerted gasp from everybody in the front room, and a choked off giggle from Louise Parker.

Behind the bride-to-be was Randy's mom, her eyes swimmy, her face coral pink. *Jesus*! Randy exploded to himself, and glanced quickly at the preacher to see if he'd said it aloud. If so, Pastor Montgomery hadn't noticed; his mouth was hanging open like everyone else's.

Martha wore a bright red dress with fluffs and ribbons up top, except for the plunging vee neckline that showed the upper rims of her breasts. Jesus, Randy thought again. She wasn't even wearing a bra. Her skirt was sizes too small, and way too short.

Her bright hair was put up fancy atop her head, all ringlets and glitter, and her makeup—damn! If he didn't know better, Randy would swear she was a Sandusky whore, or maybe one of the V-girls who'd started hanging around USO clubs and train stations. V-girls weren't money charging whores, just patriotic kids doing their bit for the boys in uniform. Fucking for Old Glory, the GIs said, and at least you ain't *paying* for a dose of clap.

But Martha Swensen? Smile brittle and scarlet, she came downstairs one exaggerated step at a time, rolling her hips. Randy went stiff legged to meet her, and whispers blew soft and puzzled through the wedding party.

Randy's dad was there of course, with his four employees; Joyce with her boss (which Mom didn't like; Joyce was a married woman with her husband off fighting for his country); little Louise and her new boyfriend, Roger-something, kid of the tire company big wheel; and Scooter, solemn and big eyed.

Oriana had called, so sorry she couldn't make it on such short notice, especially since she'd just started the job, but her heart was with him. *All the best, Randy, the very best and I love you. She's a lucky girl.*

Ron; he really missed Ron. It was a different kind of missing he couldn't tell anyone else. His twin was somewhere in England at last word, and by now could be anywhere, anywhere but here. What would Ron think of his brother's bride, all got up like a hooker? He'd laugh, Randy knew. Ron would play it straight until the ceremony was over and then he'd laugh like crazy. Or maybe he'd look at Randy and cry. Nobody else had ever seen Ron cry.

Randy took Martha's extended hand, and when she stepped down to the new carpet, he shifted his hand to her elbow. They stood before Pastor Montgomery, not touching.

Martha hadn't been herself from the minute he met her at the Greyhound station. Right away she'd started talking marriage. I think I'm pregnant, she said; oh, dear God, Randy! What this will do to the church and my family. I—I just might commit

suicide, take pills or drink iodine or jump in front of a train.
Oh, Father in heaven, grant me absolution; I'm a scarlet
woman, seduced and sinful, a scarlet woman.

Hush, damn it! he'd said, because people turned to stare;
hush now, Martha. She sniffed into a hankie and said he just
had to go back to Columbus with her if he had a single grain of
goodness to him. Reverend Harding would marry them in the
Holiness Church and that might atone in some way for what
Randy did to her, for the bastard child she carried in her
dishonored body. But she didn't suppose a man who deflow-
ered innocent girls cared about that. Go on, abandon me, leave
me to my disgrace. Oh, I have become the great whore of the
Pharisees . . .

"*Do you, Randall Parker* . . ."

He just about had to drag her from the bus station and cram
her, with bag, into the Model A. Never said I wouldn't marry
you, he said, especially with a baby coming, but I can't go
clear to Columbus. I report to Indiantown Gap, Pennsylvania,
in two days.

Sniffing, Martha dabbed at red eyes and asked why. He told
her it was a staging area for Europe, and he didn't know how
long he'd be there—probably only days.

Her mouth thinned when she said if he'd stood up for his
rights and refused to go, if he *truly* believed in not killing
folks, he wouldn't be in uniform now. And they could *still* go
back to Columbus because the Holiness Church—

". . . *take this woman, Martha* . . ."

He'd whacked the steering wheel and almost driven up on
the sidewalk. Has to be Pastor Montgomery, damn it! As it is,
we'll be lucky to get it all done—license, blood tests, my
folks, the pastor. Martha said, Well, if you're going to be
stubborn, like you were about not serving God, but the army—

". . . *to be thy lawful wedded wife* . . ."

Redundancy, his English prof at Kent State would have said;
unlawful wedding?

And why was Randy Parker thinking of everybody but his
bride?

". . . *to have and to hold* . . ."

He was scared, dammit, afraid of taking responsibility for
anyone else. He thought he'd come of age when he left the
family and went off to school. Not so. Now his manhood had

to carry its weight in a war and, from a distance, shelter Martha and his unborn child. Ron—he wished he could talk to his brother, wished he could reach out and touch him.

". . . *forsaking all others, so long as ye both shall live*?"

What the hell happened to sickness and health, richer or poorer, death do part, cleaving and forsaking? Had he missed all that?

". . . do," Randy said, "I do."

Martha left a heavy smear of lipstick on his mouth, and he hadn't time to wipe it off before Mom kissed him, and Joyce, then Louise and Scooter. Dad hugged him and said something about luck; the girls from the store didn't kiss Randy, but shook hands.

Joyce's boss, Frank, or Frankie, had a grip like a weight-lifter; big, good-looking guy in expensive clothes, dazzling smile that fronted for hard eyes. Martha cooed over his present, a big, costly radio that had overseas bands; there were other things hastily wrapped, and a couple of champagne toasts, which Martha wouldn't even fake by just touching the glass to her shiny red lips. She made sure everybody knew it was against her religion.

And Randy heard a murmur he wasn't supposed to, when Joyce whispered, "She sure isn't dressed like Carrie Nation."

So he drank more wine than he ought to, and danced a little with the ladies; slow stuff from Mom's electric Victrola, which she was so proud of. Yeah, he said to small, sly jokes; uh-huh, he said to wishes for a long and happy marriage. And he remembered one girl who danced real close, so he felt a lot of her; she was Holly.

Then he was telling Martha to come on, dammit. He'd phoned the Luxor Hotel in Canton; pretty close to home, but the honeymoon wasn't going to be much anyway, with so little time. Martha wanted to eat some more, maybe dance some more with Frankie; but he said no, we have to get going.

In the car, he said, "You don't need any more lipstick."

She didn't put away the tube and kept staring into her compact mirror. "Oh, you noticed."

Randy's mouth was sticky inside; marshmallow fruit salad or sour wine. "And I finally understand why you got yourself up like that. You might as well have yelled it into their faces: sinner, whore, scarlet woman. Scarlet woman, scarlet dress and lipstick, all that goddamn red rouge. You picked one hell of a time to embarrass me, yourself, and everyone else."

"Randall, don't you dare use the Lord's name—"

"And don't you dare act up around my family again. They're good, honest, churchgoing people, and if their religion isn't yours, that's too damned bad. There's a bunch of trees up ahead, and a gravel road I know. I'm pulling in there so you can change."

"Out in the open, where—"

"Martha," he said softly, "if you don't want to be dropped off at the nearest bus station, do as you're told."

In Canton he bought a pint of Three Feathers while she waited sullenly in the car. He had room service bring Cokes and ice with the two small suitcases. There wasn't much to see from the hotel window, so he mixed a drink. He never drank much, and the brand was all he could remember at the time. It tasted awful, sort of rancid-buttery.

Martha flounced onto the bed to stare disapproval. Makeup peeled, she looked much better; an attractive woman, when she let herself be. He swallowed another cocktail and it tasted no better, but he was trying to feel like a bridegroom.

She went into the bathroom and made splashing noises. He looked at the whiskey and remembered that liquor production had been abruptly curtailed. Distilleries now made medical alcohol for the services and cut what regular stock they had on hand with inferior cane spirits. It kept them in touch with civilian trade and future consumers, even if bootleg stuff, green and raw, was run under their label. The war was barely under way and far from won, but businessmen looked ahead.

Nobody had tied old shoes and tin cans to his car; nobody threw rice. Old shoes were saved for re-repair in case ration stamps ran short, and it was unpatriotic to waste food. Even without a war, Ron wouldn't have gone that route.

Maybe he could look Ron up in Europe. Mom had given him the Army Post Office number, so it shouldn't be tough to find him—if his outfit was still there. There'd been so much talk about the Second Front, an invasion might come off any time. President Roosevelt had just about promised Josef Stalin that, to pull pressure off Russia.

Back at the window, Randy thought his was a hell of a wedding night; nothing to see in Canton, Ohio, and if the town had a nightlife, Martha wouldn't go celebrating, anyhow. Martha Swensen Parker. He blinked back at a cafe sign down the street. He didn't even know if his wife had a middle name.

That bullshit about wearing red—what kind of twisted satisfaction did that give her? Why was she flogging her own soul? A baby. If Randy made it through the war, by then the baby might be a big kid who wouldn't know his daddy. Could he put himself through medical school and support a family too? Not without help from his family, that was sure. If Martha had her degree and went to work, saved—

He smelled her before turning, a heavy perfume unlike Martha, unlike any girl he knew. She might have poured it on to kill his whiskey odor. He drew the shade and clicked off the overhead light. A single bed lamp showed her bare and beautiful, belly yet unswollen. Before, it had to be in the dark and shameful, but now she stood naked and bitchy, big breasts high and proud, the vee of her mound catching light and turning it bronze.

Martha wore shoes with the highest heels he'd ever seen, a strap glittering across foot top and around slim ankle. The shoes were red patent leather. . . .

Half a world away and not too sure whether it was day or night, Ron Parker looked at the empty shotglass beside his beer and picked up the mug. In another four, five years, he might get used to this piss-warm beer they called 'arf and 'arf. He didn't have five years; probably he didn't have five days, because the MPs would finally catch up to him.

He signaled the publican for another round and put down a ten-shilling note. He didn't even know how long he'd been over the hill, but he did know it had been easy staying ahead of the MPs. GIs gone AWOL usually showed it—unshaven, wrinkled uniforms, a hunted look about them. Ron kept himself sharp and supplied with an up to date phony pass. He'd swiped a whole pad of forms in a port battalion's orderly room, where the top kick turned his back for a fifth of uncut Scotch. He wore the Service Battalion's shoulder patch too, not the First Infantry Division's single red numeral.

The MPs had an AWOL infantryman on their checklist, not a rear echelon commando. They cruised London pubs for Private Ronald Parker, but the name on the pass was Steve

Canfield, its serial number that of some draftee from the Eighth Service Command, which took in about five states in the deep South and West.

Come to think of it, he hadn't seen Big Red One patches for a while. Maybe the outfit was on landing maneuvers or alert; it could be buttoned down for the real thing. If that was it, he was far up shit creek with a soup spoon for a paddle. A general court martial would hang his ass out to dry for avoiding hazardous duty, like the book said. That could buy him five or ten years' hard labor.

Tossing down whiskey, he chased it with warm beer. Maybe he'd turn himself in before long. It was just that after Flora's death— son of a bitch! There he went again, ready to knock the whole fucking world onto its miserable ass. He couldn't turn off her memory, or drown it. Ron didn't want to forget her; that was impossible. He just wanted it to stop tearing out his guts.

He hadn't meant to go over the hill, but when he came out of that first running drunk, he was in London, a long way from Southampton, with another woman—a nice chubby kid calling herself Peggy. Just Peggy, m'luv; no family name, my family'd have naught to do wiv me now, nor me wiv them, so fuck all.

He paid her until money ran low, and tried to tell her good-bye, but she'd have none of that. If he'd stay out of sight until trade dropped off, her bed was his, and he might send Yank trade her way. Not exactly her mac, not really a pimp, understand. She could give him some kind of signal if she thought the customer might be trouble; he could follow her home and wait. Ron could also keep away competing macs who tried to force girls into their own stables, like a bloody stallion with a herd of bloody mares, all passing him their money.

During daytime, he went out to hustle pub customers with a variety of slick bar top tricks and crooked little wagers. He wanted no money from Peg; if he accepted a single bob, he'd forever feel like a pimp.

"One thing," he said to Peggy, "just one thing. Don't ever say I'm a lovely man. Understand?"

She had apple cheeks and that clear English complexion, and said she was eighteen. "But you *are* a—all right, luv. Now kiss me; it's bleedin' strange that men will pay to mount me, and so bloody few kiss a whore, though I've had dates who went down on me and never fucked me a'tall. Passin' queer, I'd say."

So he kept on drinking and screwed Peggy a few times and didn't catch anything. Every day or so he'd promise to turn himself in and take whatever the army threw at him. And every day he saw inside his head the image of Flora's bombed ambulance, a crazy, chopped up sardine can with its wheels blown off, the dark, new-sticky blood. Then he'd get blind drunk all over again, and hope Peggy would knock off early for the night, so he could hold her warmth while she slept.

Since it got worse every day he was gone, Ron stayed away, uncertain what or who he was now. He worked the bars, never the same ones too often, where he might become recognized and familiar. Early evenings, if he was drunk enough, he'd wander back to a couple of pubs whose keepers thought he worked at some secret job that allowed him much time off. From these, he'd send GIs to Peggy's corner, or the room. Hell of a fine lady, he said, got a snatch that really eats up a man, not like other Piccadilly Circus whores who just lay there like a sack while you bang away. This Peggy girl—she was brown-haired and had meat on her bones, big tits—hung out down the block, on the corner. No thanks needed, buddy; just doing another GI a favor. Well, yeah, I'd appreciate another drink.

By now he was smoking lousy limey cigarettes when he couldn't hustle good ones, eating lousy limey food when he remembered to eat anything, and walking away from fights, damned near running if he had to, because a brawl brought American MPs or English "red caps," and it wouldn't matter which would haul him away. They'd soon know the 3124th Port Battalion carried no Steve Canfield on its roster. Steve Canfield; at first it was a joke, but now he hated the name almost as much as he hated the man. Shit—everything was dipped in it and flavored by it.

The sirens went off, sudden and piercing. Ron didn't flinch; he was used to them now. Far off, a string of Jerry's bombs marched explosions toward Piccadilly. " 'Ere now," the publican called. "Drink up, gentlemen; sounds like Jerry is serious this day."

"Fuck all old Jerry and his misbegotten bombs," another

Englishman said. "He'll not be making me lose my beer. You go down cellar, John; I'll see to the cashbox."

There was an Underground entrance where Peggy showed her wares. Another stick of explosions came closer while ack-acks chewed the sky. Peggy would go into the subway until the all clear, Ron was sure.

Boarded up and cross taped windows didn't stop the blast that blew them across the room and into the bar—splinters, glass, and bricks mixed together. Ron climbed off the floor and blinked, coughed in brick dust. The old guy who'd stayed to keep his beer was dead; it didn't need two looks to tell that.

A child was crying.

Ron wobbled out into the street, ears ringing and the left side of his face slippery. The street was burning and the kid was still crying. He thought it was only in his ears, and blew his nose to clear them, getting a mess of mortar and blood into his hand. Wiping it on his pants, he listened and heard it again —thin and scared and hopeless.

Clang, clang!—a firetruck at the end of the street. *Whee-ooh, whee-ooh!*—that funny kind of up-and-down siren on Limey emergency vehicles, on ambulances like Flora had driven. Somebody in a white helmet pulled at Ron, but he shoved the guy away, head tilted, listening.

"Come on, Yank—you're hurt rather—"

"You hear it? Hear that kid crying? She's in the house over there. *That* one!"

"I don't hear—Alf, do you—"

"Wouldn't do no good anyhow, Yank. That house is about to go, fall any minute. Come now, let us help—"

A patched hose was spitting water at the fire, and a wave of heat seared Ron. He took a deep breath and stuck his head and shoulders into the jet. Pressure knocked him spinning, right up to the house whose walls were crumbling, dropping chunks of stone and flaming brands onto the cobblestoned street.

He spun through a door and ducked a tongue of fire. "Hey, you! Hey, kid! Where are you?"

More bomb damage than fire, he thought—before a smoke cloud reached for him. When he bobbed under it, a falling beam just flicked his shoulder, enough to put him to his knees. Goddamm glass. "Kid—hey, girl! Damn it, I know you're here—"

"*Misterrr* . . ." fading, weak, giving up.

"Don't do it!" he shouted, coughing. "Goddamn it, don't you quit! Holler again—put your—face to—to the floor—and —and yell like hell!"

Shit. The fucking fire was after his personal ass, it and the fucking house, sawing at him, baking him, dropping stuff all around. But he heard her again, stronger this time, low and off to the right.

He crawled because he had to; something was wrong with his leg, and that goddamn glass raked him. But he could breathe because he had to, and when the slewed-around door wouldn't open and he couldn't get leverage to shove hard, Ron gulped hot air and dust. Then he came to both hands and one knee, and butted the son of a bitch.

They always said he was a hard-headed bastard, and a good thing too. He had to back off and ram the sagging door twice more before one hinge gave and he could reach inside. He didn't find her; she found his hand and hung on with all her might—poor little kid who could barely grip his fingers.

The smoke had turned black, or maybe it was stuff in his eyes, or the shit that kept falling on him. He dragged her as gently as he could, as quickly as he could, and cursed the broken glass.

A stream of water slapped his face and cooled him, but it was pushing them back into the house. He had her cupped against his body, turtled protectively over her, and somebody had sense enough to lift the hose over and behind them.

Oh, Christ—mouthful of water like the best, coldest beer. Now he could drag the fucking leg that wouldn't work, and thought he saw white helmets running at them, but staggering back. He was under the fire and blessed by water, cradling the kid under his chest and along his belly, knowing she was alive. It was all right, by God. They were making it—making it.

Heavy, so fucking heavy; son of a bitch never hit that hard in his life; chopped him across crawling hand and wrist. Couldn't pull out; tried and tried, but it wouldn't turn loose. White hats—fuckers yelling and splashing—white hats running up, falling back. Fire dropping lower, lower and he was so thank you God grateful for the water, but the bastard glass stabbed him, and the kid, the kid.

Funny as all hell, scooted around that way, one leg dead and the opposite hand trapped. Scoot, scoot . . . hey, little Scooter, where's your mom? Know damn well you don't play with matches, Scooter—scoot like a tied-up turtle, get her by the arm and suck in all the air, bunch together every fucking ounce of strength in the world and throw her, scoot her along the waterslick ground; sorry about those bumpy cobblestones, kid.

They feel cool and blessed Our Father wet against his face, but gritty water kept getting in his mouth. Some asshole had him by the ankle, stretching him, pulling him apart like a turkey wishbone. Short side wins, Randy, short side wins. No, long side wins, Ron.

Guess you're right, dammit; I always get the short end of the stick. You do it yourself, Ron, you always do it yourself.

Turn loose, you son of a bitch—tearing my leg off.

Can't pull him out, sir! Jammed under that stone and—look lively, men! The wall's about to go!

White hat running in low, staying this time. *Whee-ooh . . . whee-ooh!* Funny siren for ambulance . . . ambulance like Flora drove in Southampton . . . *whee-ooh!* . . . until the five-hundred-pounder made a direct hit.

You're a lovely man, Yank.

Jesus loving Christ.

Bloody fucking waste of bloody fucking war.

Sergeant Major, Sergeant Major on parade: Call slow step for Lance Corporal Flora Harksinger; muffle the drums.

One eye staring and water pushing dirt and glass over the other, Ron Parker could just make out a white helmet way up there, then the rubber boot, and something gleaming metallic echo to the fire.

His one ear heard the wall let go, and the shiny thing flashed down and he was free.

But he no longer gave a shit, and tried to smile into the blackness.

chapter 22

According to a release from the state convention of
sociologists here, the new independence of working
women will plague marriages already strained by
separation. For the first time, sociologists said,
about three million married women have experienced the glamor and independence of their own
generous paychecks. A recent study concluded that
a "goodly number" of war workers surveyed "did
not miss their husbands and were happy to be
free. . . ."

—New York, N.Y., September 7, 1942 (UP)

Beyond the storeroom wall, George Parker heard the delivery
boy being kidded, which meant the store was momentarily free
of customers. He listened for Holly's sultry, mocking purr and
didn't hear it. It wasn't near closing, but she might already be
gone.

Damn it. She'd started cutting corners: arriving a few
minutes late, stretching lunch hours, leaving a little early. He
hadn't said anything to her yet, and knew damned well the
others wondered why. He'd surprised a knowing wink from
Betsy, a smirk by Annie, pimpled Harry leering from the
delivery bicycle.

Maybe his own conscience was printing headlines across faces actually blank and unsuspicious. But he'd soon have to make a show of calling Holly on her work habits and attitude, or the other employees would start dragging it too; fair for one, fair for all. Or worse—a hundred times worse—they'd spread the tale that old George Parker—yeah, the church deacon, that's the one—well, he's messing around with the Melborne girl, and her not much older than his youngest daughter.

George wanted a drink, and he was no drinking man. A week ago he would have bristled at being called a womanizer —good Lord, an adulterer. There were moments yet when he couldn't believe it, times in the middle of the night as he lay sleepless beside Elizabeth's familiar warmth, in the solid, calm shelter of their bedroom. All the together years, the long closeness and understanding, were threatened now.

And for what? He paced between empty cartons and among emptied barrels overflowing with wood shavings; at least wood wasn't in short supply yet. Veering from the bathroom, he opened the alley door for fresh air. There was no back way out for him if this—this middle age stupidity became known.

Dammit all, he'd told Harry twice to clear all this stuff from the storeroom, to flatten the cartons and bundle them with straightened-out packing paper. Books were being printed on made over paper now, little books that would go mainly to the boys overseas, ones they could stuff in their pockets to read when they got the chance. His store, like the rest in Coshocton, didn't wrap anything now, and bagged only if absolutely necessary. Folks took to bringing their own.

Pulling in a deep breath of outside air, George admitted Harry's slowness wasn't the cause of his mood. He wasn't sure whether he wanted Holly Melborne gone early, or hoped she'd stay late, dawdling until the others left. It had only been twice, but doing it with her was what taking dope must be like—an ache in the blood and hurt in the bones when the supply ran out.

Elizabeth—his wife never acted like Holly, never used deft hands and direct woman hunger the way Holly did. So slim and strong, slicky under him and grinding, dipping, arching, taking him deep inside her young, hot tightness. She bit him and raked him with her nails and blew dirty words into his ear. She fondled and heaved and—

If he wasn't uncrating or tallying or making out bills or arranging stock, the live shadow of her hung right behind him, teasing and tempting. He went hard because his inflamed mind took him back over every wild moment spent locked into her writhing body, repeating and enlarging upon every blazing second until he needed to hit something or—or—

He wouldn't beg; he wouldn't ask her straight out to stay late. Holly would know exactly what he meant. He was old enough to be her father and then some, but not according to her. You're *good*, she'd pant; you're so damned good, Daddy. Ooh—you can fuck a girl crazy—ooh—stick it deep, Daddy —stick it hard—

Elizabeth never said anything like that, and if *he* said it, she'd think he'd lost his mind. She didn't wiggle or wrap long, sleek legs around him and set her heels behind his knees. And never had she climbed on top; *never, never* would Elizabeth lift herself to hands and knees to swing silken buttocks, beckoning him to mount her the way a bull tops a cow.

George put one hand over the front of his pants and backed up, shutting the alley door. He bumped into a barrel and leaped aside as if he'd been seared. He was jumpy at home too, but when Elizabeth said something, he blamed it on the war news. That was enough to make any thinking man nervous: Bataan, Corregidor, Wake Island, Japs victorious everywhere— except, thank God, for the big naval battle off Midway Island. That stopped the slant eyed bastards and made Hawaii safe.

A son-in-law dead, two sons overseas, his oldest daughter gone from home, and now the services were taking women, WAACs and WAVEs and Women Marines. If things got any worse, would they start drafting women? The Russians did; there'd been newspaper pictures of a Russian woman, a sniper, who'd killed twenty-two Germans—a young, kind of nice-looking woman too.

Did she screw between snipings? George walked up and down again, checked his fly, found a clipboard, and put a pencil behind one ear. Then he went into the store where old lady Blackwell was haggling over lightbulbs, expecting a reduction because she was buying several.

A lightning check of the store told him Holly Melborne was gone; frowning, he moved in to help Annie, who was trying to explain shortages to the old lady.

He said, "Look, Mrs. Blackwell—take the bulbs or not. You're lucky to get them. Annie, help those men over there."

"Well, I never!" Mrs. Blackwell said. "You'd think a storekeeper *your* age would've learned how to treat a customer. I'm a mind to go clear down to Johnson's Hardware, if this is how—"

Putting his back to her, George said as he put the bulbs back in their slots, "It's a nice day for walking. Maybe Irv Johnson will remind you there's a war on, and maybe he won't *have* any lightbulbs."

At the register, Betsy giggled, and for a second he smiled back. Then he felt bad about old lady Blackwell; she was probably buying for Steve Canfield, and Steve would give her hell. He started to call her back, but a couple of men blocked him, asking about sockets and a pipe cutter. The store stayed open twenty minutes late, and he was still edgy when he saw his help out and pulled the cracked green shade on the heavy old doors. If business kept up like this, if the war went on for four, five more years, he could have the best hardware store in the county. Irv Johnson was so old he creaked and had nobody to leave the business to.

Then George felt guilty for thinking that way; he'd like it fine if the war ended tomorrow, so long as America and the Allies won. He checked around, as he always did at closing time, putting out all but one light, straightening the merchandise. He knew he was delaying, not wanting to go home, to be close to Elizabeth. There was a war picture on at the Roxy, *A Yank on the Burma Road*; maybe Elizabeth would see it with him. She probably wouldn't; war news bothered her, and radio dramas were worse, all those shooting and bombing sound effects. She always imagined the twins in that kind of action.

The alley door—he'd forgotten to bar it. George went by the register, but didn't get to open the storeroom door; Holly Melborne did. She said, "I took care of the alley door for you. Comin' in the back ain't such a bad idea, right?"

"It—it's a good idea." George stood nervously beneath the night bulb over the cash register. "I—you look very pretty, Holly."

"My new dress, the one you paid for. It's real neat; shows off my figure real good."

"You bought it here in town?"

She popped chewing gum. "Sure; if the Bon Ton woman got nosey about how I could buy a thirty dollar dress on two bits an hour, I had a story all ready. But she never asked; too glad to make the sale."

George said, "Next time—" and hesitated. "If you buy anything expensive again, maybe you should go to Canton or Akron."

Holly worked gum around her mouth. "I don't care; Akron's got big stores. But I'd need a ride, or have to take the bus."

"Yes," George said, "yes." She had the trick of always standing a little too close, so her body heat radiated, and the musk of her reached into a man's throat. He glanced at the big front window, where somebody was passing. If somebody got curious and started gossip—

But she was an employee, and lots of businesses stayed open late these days, catching the war plant trade as workers came off shift from the tire plants and Butera's. A dozen other parts industries had sprung up like mushrooms after a spring rain.

Holly said, "How'd you like to do it right here? All day I keep lookin' at that rubber mat and thinkin' how everybody'd fall over if they even had the teeniest idea that you and me—" She laughed, balancing wadded pink gum on her pinker tongue. "Then I look at the mat again and have a hard time not to bust out laughing; I mean, I can just *see* 'em runnin' and hollerin', if they saw you puttin' it to me right there. Customers'd have to step over us, or wait till we got through. Yes'm—extension cord? Have to wait'll I get my panties on. Yessir—half inch pipe? Have to see the boss about that; he's the one puttin' up his own pipe, but *that's* sure'n hell more than a half inch."

"Holly—" he began, and had to laugh with her, because if he took even a half serious look at her wild dreams, he'd be too damned scared even to think.

She moved against him, slipping one hand behind to caress his buttock, the other stroking his rising penis. "Oh I know, Daddy. Preachers and deacons and other folks that don't screw, they'd run me outa town. That don't matter right now; feel my nipples, touch my pussy. See how hot I am?"

Resisting, he hung back when she pulled him down, but not for long. It was safer below counter level, and he thought of putting out the night light, but that might cause trouble. Too many people, including the night watchman, old man Enslee, would notice the completely dark store and think it was being burglarized.

He hadn't gotten his pants all the way off when she'd hung the new dress over the counter and her slip across it. It surprised him that she wasn't wearing bra or panties; she'd returned to the store all ready to screw. When he started to mount her, George got another jolt. She didn't want it that way; not at first.

Her heavy, scented hair poured over his thigh as she pushed him into a kneeling position. "Holly, no! You don't know —you don't want—"

"Shut up," she commanded, her breath spraying over his glans, "Hush, Daddy, and just enjoy it. After, I'm goin' to teach you something you can do to *me*."

Shocked, he took hold of her head, meaning to pull her off him, to stop this perverted thing she was doing. But she held on, and all George Parker could do was hold on and caress the tumbled beauty of her hair. She was so loving and so young, so wonderfully, beautifully young.

Out Chestnut Street and across the Muskingum River, where barges used to drift south to markets, lashed end to end and piled high with manufactured goods, Elizabeth Parker waited supper for her husband in a strangely empty house. Scooter was upstairs, reading, probably. The child was the readingest Elizabeth had ever known, more so than Randall, and he'd been a real bookworm.

She went out on the porch, letting the screen door shut easy behind her, and looked off to where the canalmen used to pass long ago. That was back before railroads came to take away the business and glamor of the Ohio River and the Erie canal. She remembered her grandma telling stories of canal boatmen, whole families sometimes living on board, their barges floating houses. Oh, those canalmen, Grandma said—hooting and hollering and acting up so that half the boys in the county just couldn't wait to grow up and beg a job traveling a barge.

It was past dark, and a few fireflies still dared the coming of fall, their greenglow taillights going on and off. Once, Delaware Indians had walked right here, Elizabeth thought, perhaps hunting across the space of her front yard, stalking deer for their women and papooses. Then the white men came, pushing them back and back until they shriveled up and disappeared. The tribes fought among themselves before that—Mound Builders, Delawares, Moravians—then fought the whites, and the whites took up arms against each other: colonists against British, blue against gray, and Elizabeth's new husband off to camp to train for war against the Germans. It was only God's grace he never had to face those spiked helmets and sawtooth bayonets.

War after war, and her twin sons gone to this one, perhaps never to return. That bronze honor roll down at city hall listing the dead already, leaving space for those yet to die. Elizabeth supposed America had no choice, this war thrust upon her. But mothers were mothers.

She looked up Chestnut, but the car lights she saw weren't on George's truck. Air suddenly cool upon her, she turned back into the house. Listening, she heard Scooter moving about upstairs. Louise wasn't home and hadn't called. George would *have* to take that girl in hand, discipline her somehow.

She was too big for a willow switch, although the Lord knew it was exactly what she needed—a bobby soxer so sassy and bold. Elizabeth hated the term, and hated that skinny, greasy haired singer the teen-age girls squealed and swooned over. Swooned, indeed; she'd like to slap them awake, and that Sinatra too, affecting young, impressionable girls that way.

Great-grandma's tall Seth Thomas chimed the half hour, and the kitchen sent forth savory smells of fresh baked bread and oniony stew. Elizabeth laid her fingertips along the old clock's dark, smooth wood and glanced down at its brass chains and weights. It wasn't easy, cutting back on her recipes, cooking for three most times. They didn't see Joyce much these days, since she got her own apartment. Foolishment, Elizabeth called it, wasting rent money when she could stay home. Oriana wrote quick, nothing postcards from Detroit and called once a week, but that wasn't having her here. Thank God she hadn't taken Scooter along.

"Grammy?" Scooter said from the landing. "When's Grampa coming? I'm hungry."

"Wash up," Elizabeth said, "and we'll eat now. I guess he's at some defense meeting or other." And to herself: He could have called; he's getting as thoughtless as little Louise.

Ladling stew into thick white bowls, she set them at their usual places, but after she cut and buttered bread, the table looked lonesome, spread out that way. She moved Scooter's bowl up close to her own. Before the girl came down, Elizabeth went into the parlor and turned on the radio. The house didn't seem quite so empty, until the music played "We Three" and got to the part about *"My echo, my shadow, and me."*

On State Road 23, going south to Marion, the big Packard purred, a heavy car riding easy as could be, so Louise Parker didn't feel the bumps. When Roger Barton went fast into a curve, the car didn't sway like a light Studebaker, either.

"Apple Blossom Time," Roger sang along with the radio, *"I'll be with you in Apple blossom time . . . I'll be with you . . ."*

Louise said, "I still think you're dippy. You don't have to go to war, but you want to."

"Hey, baby," Roger said, "I'm looking to afterward."

"You already got a big afterward, Rog—the tire plant, your daddy such a big shot—jeepers. Not like me; babies and housecleaning and all that crap."

He clicked off the radio. "You never even asked why we're going to Marion."

"A party, I guess. I'd just as soon it was only you and me, though."

Roger laughed. "It's a party, all right. Oh, boy, is it ever."

"I have to be home early. They're startin' to yell if I come in after midnight."

He laughed again, felt for the pint of whiskey, and held it so she could screw off the cap. Roger took a big swig and offered it to her; Louise sipped and recapped the bottle of Four Roses.

"You won't be going home all night, baby."

She sat up. "The hell you say! Look here, buster, my old man will just about kill me."

"Not if you're legally emancipated."

She stared at his profile, nowhere near as good looking as Deke, and the eyeglasses made him kind of a drip, but he could always get his daddy's Packard and she liked that. He was another college guy and she liked the way he spent money. High school boys were such goons.

"I thought Lincoln emancipated colored people," she said. "and I'm not colored."

It seemed Roger couldn't stop laughing, and she elbowed a warning when the car slid out of a curve. He said then, "If you're married, you automatically become an adult, and your parents can't do anything to you."

"Married?" Louise said to the road ahead, to the sprinkle of town lights coming up.

He fondled her knee. "Sure, why not? Hey, everybody knows you used to be Deke Deacon's girl, but that's over and *I* know you're not a tramp. You didn't give in to me for a month, and even then I had to get you a little drunk."

And more than a little crazy, she thought. Married!

Roger slowed the Packard. "This guy in Marion, this justice of the peace, he owes my dad a favor. I already called him and acted like it was something Dad wants real bad. He's waiting to marry us. Mr. and Mr. Roger Barton—how's that?"

"But you're going in the service, and—"

Hand around her shoulder, he pulled her close, cupping a breast. They were in the city limits, and Roger turned the Packard right, onto gravel. He said, "Baby, you don't have a thing to worry about. Besides the allotment you'll get, my dad's good for anything else you need or want. Once the marriage is a fact, he'll accept it."

"He don't even know me, Rog."

He pulled the car over and stopped it before a cottage with its porch light on. "He will, and'll probably push you into college, so you'll get the right polish—as he puts it—for a Barton family hostess. Hell, when he pays your way, why not?"

Louise looked at the porch light. "I still don't see why you have to go overseas. You can get all kinds of deferments."

"Politics, baby. Right after the war, a combat veteran will have the jump on his opponents. I mean to keep after a law degree and go for the state legislature first, then governor or Congress."

She trembled the dash lighter to her cigarette. "How come me?"

He teased her nipple, fingered the firm globe of her breast. "Because you're the hottest piece to ever come down the pike, and you really know how to make a guy happy. I mean, going down and all the stuff you do—it's terrific. And you're smart, baby, really smart. You won't let anybody stick it to me because you go where I do, out on your ass or right to the top. You'll look great on the platform when I speak, and you'll be an asset with the—well, the labor class, and help me build a political base in the county."

She was dizzy. Too many images popped in and out of her head. Louise Parker—Louise *Barton*, one of those high-society women; maybe the governor's wife. Jesus—college and everything.

"Ready, baby?" Roger asked.

"Yeah. I wish you'd told me before, so I would of worn something sharp."

Reaching across her, he swung the car door open. "Just remember you're eighteen, when the guy asks. He may not even ask, but if he does."

Louise made him wait on the porch until she put on fresh lipstick and tried to do something with her hair. She'd never really pictured her own marriage, but there'd been some vague scene of a veil, white dress, and flowers all over, Mom sniffling and Dad giving her away. Something like that, or like the quickie at home when Randy had married that goony woman. She knew Randy had better sense, so Martha must have been knocked up. Jeepers, she had really looked like a whore.

Impatiently, Roger said, "Ready now?"

"Ready," she said. The man answered his doorbell so quick he must have been waiting ever since the Packard drew up in front of the house.

As Roger said, the guy owed Mr. Big shot Barton a favor and was eager to please. Probably a lot of others in Coshocton County were eager to please, as well.

Mrs. Roger Barton. The name had a nice ring.

chapter 23

Fanatic Japanese Imperial Marines attempted another desperate "banzai" attack on soldiers of the
U.S. Americal Division last night. Led by
sword waving officers, the Japs poured through a
small gap in defense lines and overran a company
command post before being beaten back. . . .

—The South Pacific, September 9, 1942 (AP)

He rolled away from her on the sweated bed, leaving her
feeling used upon tangled sheets. It had been quick and brutal,
surprising Joyce more than actually hurting her, but she would
wear bruises and scratches for days.

Before, Franco had never made love that was meant to
punish instead of please. He'd always been strong, but tender;
powerful, masterful upon occasion, but always gentle. Before,
she was constantly amazed at his deftness, his ability to
transport her to heights of dizzying gratification. This time she
hadn't come once. This time he was making hate, not love.

The bathroom door slammed in the dark and Joyce clicked
on the bed lamp. She touched her nipples and mound and
throat; they were all sore. She might have to wear a scarf for
days.

Coming naked through the bedroom, he didn't look at her.

She got into her robe and followed. He was at the small bar, two drinks ahead before she climbed a stool.

"I'll mix one," she said. "If I drank them straight and quick like that, I'd wake up Monday afternoon."

"Grow up on *vino* and pasta, and you can hold liquor." He poured another. "The old bastard; the stupid, old-country wop. In front of you, the office girls, he slapped me around like I was a little kid—*figlio Butana*—son of a bitch. It's all over the plant, what he did, how he treated me."

It was worse because he wasn't yelling, because his voice was so flat, that voice that could be rich and throaty or light and teasing. When that voice murmured love words against her throat or hotly to her ear, it was exotic music.

"Frankie, he's just so—old, I guess. I bet all the girls are talking about how wonderful you are, because you didn't hurt him. They all worship you, anyhow."

Frowning at his glass, Franco propped both elbows on the bar top. Usually he took off the gold chain and religious medal before coming to bed, but now it winked upon the dark curling of his bare chest. Whenever she saw that, it bothered her a little; not the church thing, but a man wearing a kind of necklace. It was like Franco was fruity, and that sure as *hell* wasn't so.

"He doesn't come in again," he said. "He's lucky I don't squeeze him out of his stock, the crazy old fool. Well, he doesn't get a dime from the other outfits; I saw to that." Tossing down his drink, he frowned. Joyce didn't like his frown, the way it altered the hawklike beauty of his face. He went on: "*Marone!* Like I didn't get humiliated all my life, he's got to do *this*. He wouldn't give me time to play football, when I could have been the best. Not big and dumb like your old man, but smart and tricky in the backfield, hard to catch. Fixa' da shoe, fixa' da boot, someday you amount to something. *Madre mia!*"

When he slapped the bar top, Joyce rescued her cocktail and drank some. "That's all behind you, Frankie. Look how much you accomplished in just a couple of years. Hundreds of Coshocton people owe you their jobs, and the whole country owes you for so much production in so little time, and all the ideas you have for streamlining machinery."

"And look how he embarrassed me in front of my employees. Maybe the girls admire my restraint, but the men—yeah, the guys—laughing their asses off."

"Frankie," she said, soft and loving, "it doesn't matter. It's over and done with. You haven't lost anyone's respect. I can swear to that."

He straightened, eyes a touch red, medal gleaming against his chest. Saint Somebody. It would wear better on a woman. "Yeah," he said. "Okay, I guess you're right. He's still mad at me for not painting any Sistine Chapels and wasting the nickels and dimes he saved to send me to Italy. Like he hasn't been paid back a thousand times."

When he came around the bar, Joyce snuggled her cheek into his chest of silken hair, the man smell of him. Arms around his waist, she pressed close, lifting her pelvis and slowly revolving her hips. For the first time, it didn't work. He was upset, not thinking of sex; she had no right to push it on him. She loved him so much, so damned much. . . .

Oriana Parker Canfield felt much the same way when she watched David's train out of sight, but the emotion was mixed with such sadness she may not have recognized it. At least not beyond today, she thought; for all she felt for him, for all the love he'd given her, she was second place in his life. She couldn't compete with a war, although she'd tried. He still meant to volunteer for combat.

Walking through the station with its next-train travelers filling benches and leaning against walls, Oriana was glad—in a way—that she wouldn't be forced to fight mobs like this to spend a few weeks or months with her husband. Husband in ODs or marine green or navy blue, it didn't matter. They were all going somewhere, and for many it would be a one way trip.

On the sidewalk, she watched civilians argue over a taxi just vacated by a young mother with two children, one holding on by a reluctant hand, the other in arms, crying. Cheap suitcases stood at her feet as she looked dazedly about. Oriana took a step forward, but a redcap came from somewhere to help. She stared after them, knowing how miserably crowded, smelly, and noisy trains were. She'd seen David aboard his, and watched him step around kids sleeping exhausted in the aisle, past GIs and sailors sitting on seat arms, to find floor room where he could stand awhile and squat awhile. She would always remember him smiling.

She'd waited with him, crowd-jammed against iron gates while the engine *chuffed* and *chonged* cars into place. Station speakers then intoned: *Servicemen first, please; service personnel first.* Conductors held the gates, and when the uniforms and wives or girls were passed, speakers called the next category: service wives and children. Not all of them were service wives, but it didn't matter; men in uniform gave up seats to any woman. Some were women traveling afar for the first time.

Like me, she thought; Detroit wasn't that far from Coshocton in miles, but it was so big and different. Small town friendliness was missing, and the pace was hectic. She walked slowly back to the hotel room she'd shared with David Shepsel. She stood awhile in the echoes of his soap and shaving odors before smoothing the imprint of his head from the pillow.

Would there be other Davids in her life? Possibly, but she was no V-girl or canteen hostess. She had been Oriana the child, the bride, Oriana the wife and mother; now she was the widow Oriana. She had the chance to be herself, whatever she'd find when she sloughed off her other skins.

When her bags were stored in the pickup's bed and the bellman tipped, the doorman said, No, ma'am; ain't heard nothin' but bad about Willow Run, 'less it's the money they make out there. Whole heap of folks and no place to stay; hear tell they're rentin' one bed to three men on different shifts for two bits each. Sheets don't never get cold—nor changed much, neither.

She thanked him and checked traffic carefully before pulling away. She'd heard rumors before about how some Willow Run workers lived in packing cases and trailer slums springing up everywhere, but things couldn't be that bad. How did everyone manage? If it was all that difficult, she could always rig a kind of tent over the truck bed and sleep there, get a little oil stove —but what about baths and bathrooms?

Somehow she would make out, because she had to. She'd have to be beaten to her knees before she'd return to Coshocton to stay. For one thing, Steve Canfield waited; she didn't want to see his ugly face and the wet grin that would mark her defeat. Scooter—well, her daughter had to wait until after the war. Oriana would see her every chance she got, call and write often.

She kept the truck rolling. There were tanks to be made, big guns and shells; something she worked on would kill a Jap. All the Japs in the world wouldn't balance out Clay, wouldn't give Scooter back her daddy. But Oriana wasn't being logical; she wanted vengeance.

When she got to the converted Ford plant, she discovered it didn't make tanks or bullets, but airplanes. Sure they wanted her, the personnel man said, and experience didn't count. She would be taught on the job: riveting, welding, machinist, anything. He couldn't figure out how come more than thirty thousand—yeah, thirty *thousand* people—showed up about the same time, and no place ready for them. But they turned out planes, bigod; yes, they did. And the government was building housing units for single men and women, kind of like dormitories, yes ma'am; question is, when'll they be done?

That night, Oriana slept in the truck bed on a pile of her clothes, under her raincoat, sweater wrapped against the cold, wearing two pairs of socks. After a greasy breakfast in a busy diner, she went room hunting again and lucked out.

There was a house with four little trailers parked in the yard; flapping clotheslines; grimy kids scrambling; toys, broken and unbroken; scraps of paper blowing; overfilled garbage cans. By the time Oriana reached the house steps, she was ready to turn back, but a flashily dressed woman bounced onto the porch and blinked down at her.

Oriana started to ask if a room was available, but the woman held out a hand that flashed rings and bright nail polish. "Wait—yeah, I feel it. Oh, yeah, hon—I *feel* it. You lookin' for a room?"

Oriana thumbed at the mess in the yard. "Why else?"

"Good, great! I can just *feel* you'n me are goin' to be good friends."

"Are you the owner?"

The woman laughed, showing gold in her teeth. "*Me*? Hell, no. I'd burn this damned rat trap for the insurance, and I hope she's listening." Louder, she added, "The old bat!"

Open spike heel shoes showing rare nylons, pale blue slacks that showed generous curves, a light, equally tight blue sweater that displayed melon breasts. Her patent leather purse matched her hair and lips: glaring red.

"Honey," she said, "I always play my hunches, because a fortune teller said I was kind of psychic. Course, she coulda said *physic*, 'cause I'm awful good at bullshit, too. Anyhow, I was just goin' to look for a roomie, because"—looking over her shoulder at the house—"because the *old bat* added ten dollars a week garbage collection, since she can't *legally raise the rent!*"

All Oriana did was stand and stare; a radio blared from one trailer and a baby squalled in another. The woman came farther down the steps and held out her hand. "I'm Noreen Douglas; not really, but that's another story. Anyhow, you look like I can live with you. Now if you can live with me and my big mouth—"

"Anything," Oriana said, shaking hands. "I've called and walked and driven so damned much—"

Noreen pointed. "You got a truck! How about that? More'n more my lucky day. Hey, you goddamn kids! Get the hell off that truck! Lemme give you a hand with your stuff. You on at Willow Run? Yeah, I figured; like who ain't, huh? That ten bucks a week—wanna pay it? That's splittin' rent"—yelling back at the house—"*raised* rent!—down the middle. Good; I got a hot plate and alarm clock—you oughta see how hard it is to find them damn things—and a couch that opens to a bed. Hey, this all you got? Well, you'll take your half the closet by the time you buy coveralls and such—ain't got any yet, have you? Good, you can start work in some of my old stuff."

Stunned into silence by Noreen's machine gun delivery, Oriana followed with one suitcase, and when they were halfway to the second floor, a frowsy woman stuck her gray, flared head out a first-floor door and said, "Nothin' in your lease about *two* to a room, *Miz Douglas*—permanent like, that is—not like all them men you drag in."

Noreen leaned over the banister. "You wanna go to the Housing Commission with that? Or how'd you like to meet me out in the yard? I just might be able to forget your physical deformity."

The landlady stared up through thick glasses. "I ain't that old, *Miz* Douglas, that I can't take your measure."

Noreen put down Oriana's suitcase. "Wasn't talkin' about

age, *Miz* McCarthy; I said *physical* deformity: the fact that you got a asshole at both ends."

Her laugh rang loud and long, and Oriana had to chuckle with it. Inside the room, Noreen Douglas flopped across the bed, still laughing. "Put it anywhere for now, hon. Jesus! You see the look on the old bag's face? I been savin' that one for a month. Took me about that long to say *phys-ical de-formity* right. Whooie! That one was worth payin' for."

Oriana looked about the room: one double bed, bedraggled couch, a sink obviously added recently and hastily—it leaked; a small table, two straight chairs, a hotplate beside the sink, a gas heater; no curtains at the window, only a shade; a chest of drawers, a trunk.

"No bath, hon. That's down the hall, and if you time it right, hot water. Four more on this floor, married couples, and—you believe this?—the Smotkins work different shifts: good morning, baby; good night, baby. How long's *that* marriage goin' to last? You an old maid or divorced? Oh hell, I don't even know your name yet."

"Oriana Canfield; my husband was killed on Guadalcanal."

"Oh hon, I'm sorry. I didn't mean nothin'. My mouth drives off and leaves my brain parked."

"That's okay," Oriana said. "I'm here to get back at the Japs for him."

Noreen sat up and crossed her legs to swing one foot. "Don't know where the hell my ex is, and don't care. You got any kids? Just one for me too; one too damned many. If my ex is in the service, he's sending allotments to the kid, I guess. If he ain't, his family's takin' care of Lazlo anyhow."

"Lazlo?"

"Yeah, ain't that some name to hang on a kid? I never had no say in marryin' my husband, and no say in namin' my kid. Real old country Polacks, that's us. My name used to be Natasha Dubrowski, but I changed that soon as I left Cicero —that's a town lays up tight to Chicago; only Polacks and guineas can tell when you leave one town and cross into the other. You ain't Italian, are you? Didn't think so, but you ever notice how guineas and Polacks always live in the same neighborhood and get along pretty good?"

Oriana said she'd never been out of Coshocton County, Ohio before. Noreen got up and started a pot of coffee. "Ain't no world traveler myself; but one day I'm goin' everywhere. Soon's this war's over, I'll be the travelingest Polack you ever saw. I mean I'll go *everywhere*, find me a man to pay the way, and take off like a big-assed bird."

Unpacking, Oriana thought of David, going first to camp, then back to England. She thought of her brothers, travelers themselves now. She said, "I never thought to leave town; we —my husband had a farm and my dad owns a hardware store. One brother left for college, but it seemed everybody else got born, grew up and got married, had kids, and died. Over and over. I loved my husband and daughter, but it always seemed there ought to be something more."

Noreen slid the coffepot quickly off the burner and its odor filled the room. "Know what you mean. You'll find more at Willow Run, all right—hard work and good money and all the overtime you want. All the guys you want too. You want to get rich, make 'em learn you welding. I damned near burned down a shop, so they made me a riveter. Here, you have some coffee, then I'll tell you how to get along in the shop. You know, I think you'n me, we're goin' to be real good friends."

Out in the world on her own, Oriana thought that was good, because she'd probably need a lot of help at first. "I think so too," she said.

chapter 24

The excess loin (lumbar) and pelvic (sacral) fat
shall be trimmed from the inside of the full loin by
placing the full loin on a flat surface, with no other
support to change its position, meat side down, and
removing all fat which extends above a flat plane
parallel with the flat surface supporting the full loin
and on a level with the full length of the protruding
edge of the lumbar section of the shin bone. . . .

—Office of Price Administration, wholesale beef
  regulation

George Parker desperately wanted out, but did he dare shake
his cage? Even a zoo-born lion had something regal about its
confined stalking, but George felt like an overfed white rat
puffing on a squeaky treadmill. He had to get off before it sped
up and mangled him; maybe it would anyhow.

He could commiserate with dope fiends, fools who used
heroin or smoked marijuana. If they were doomed, sick to the
depths of burned out souls, what of the bigger fool? Holly
Melborne was a narcotic as powerful as anything a needle
carried, and somehow he had to clean her from his blood.

She was no Delilah, and he certainly no Samson, although
he was just as blinded by his own folly. The biblical reference

bothered him, and he couldn't shake the vision of the temple crashing down. If only Elizabeth and the kids wouldn't be hurt; if he could face the town after the dust cleared. There goes old George, they'd say; a grandfather, for chrissake, screwing an underage girl . . . yeah, the church deacon . . . no kid's safe, seems like . . . our young men dying in jungles and on the ocean, and their girls aren't safe at home . . .

How could a rational man gamble everything he'd worked for, and bump the pot with his future? Because sex had never been so crazy for him; because no woman—schoolgirl, dammit!—had ever done all those tricks for him, making him feel, act, *be* the most important guy in the world.

Schoolgirl? Holly was technically that; in reality she was Eve and Salome—*maybe* Delilah. There was the Bible again.

Featherdusting over half-bare tables and along counters spotted by empty bins, he saw, truly saw, for the first time in months, what war caused shortages were doing to his store. It hadn't seemed important; some government office or the other would straighten things out after a while.

He'd taken a sidewise look at his business a month or so back, and found that almost everything he needed was either back ordered or diverted to the military and defense plants. As soon as the Axis was beaten, the hardware business would be better than ever. Scarce goods would be pumped back into a civilian market eager and able to buy. Until then, he was hurting.

The state of his business was a perfect excuse to fire Holly and be done with the girl. But he'd dropped Betsy instead, and when he passed her on the street, she still looked hurt, even though she made more money at the tire plant. Harry rode his bicycle off to Butera's factory, and Parker Hardware made no more deliveries. There's a war on, he told the few complainers, or didn't you know?

Why had he doubled Holly's pay, upping it by the amount Betsy would have drawn? George knew damned well why: so she wouldn't go work somewhere else. He covered that in the books, but come tax time, Elizabeth might wonder. Elizabeth always did the taxes, but this year maybe he'd get a CPA and tell Elizabeth some government agency required it. What was one more lie?

A customer came in, said hello to George, and picked up

some rubber washers. He kidded with Holly awhile, and George knew a quick stab of jealousy. Stupid, so damned stupid, when in his heart he wanted the girl gone forever, didn't he?

If it came to handling the store alone, he could do that, or have Elizabeth come in. Before the kids started coming, she'd helped in the store, and between times when she could. He felt guilty even thinking of his wife when he was so conscious of Holly's scent, that special musk that rose through her perfume, her animal heat and animal grace.

Sex had never been like that with Elizabeth, or with the whores he'd once had. Doing it with Holly was like nothing else he'd known—wild and impetuous, making him young again, strong and daring. Once she made him do it on the floor behind the counter, made their coupling fierce and pounding and quick. The climax came just as a customer walked in, jingling the warning bell.

He'd scrambled erect, tucking in his shirt and hiding his unzipped pants by leaning against the counter. Canning jars over there, he told Mrs. Wytcherlie; better lay in all the sealing rings you can, too; don't know when we'll get any more. That damned Holly; she lay there with her skirt hiked and her fluffy mound glistening, laughing silently as he stood over her to make change.

All she had to do was run her softwarm hand into his shirt and caress his chest, or lift tiptoe for a kiss, tilting her pelvis up against his crotch with slow and seductive movements. It made him crazy, for a girl so young and beautiful to *start* something; good girls never did. All the years of marriage to Elizabeth, and never once had she begun their lovemaking; it was always him starting the foreplay. And she never gave a sign that she was ready, but only lay there passively until he let go inside her. Doing it was like a duty with Elizabeth, he thought. With Holly, it was a mania.

Behind him she said, "Gettin' late, hon. Want to lock up and come to the storeroom with me?"

George swallowed; if she so much as drew her fingernails across the nape of his neck, he'd be lost. "Not today, Holly. I was—well, I've been thinking of maybe closing the store or just running it half days. My wife could come in, and I can do war work."

She used her nails on the back of his neck, but hard and hurtful. "I like it here, hon. I mean, I can come in late and leave early like I want. And I got you."

She turned him by the shoulders and dropped one hand to cup his genitals.

"Damn!" George said, jumping back and glancing at the store window. "What if somebody saw that?"

"Like your wife, maybe?" She reached again, and took a firm grip. Wincing, George tried to pull back from the window. Holly shut down harder.

"Dammit, girl!"

Her smile was redwarm and damp, the end of her tongue flicking her lips. "I *really* like it here, hon. Don't you go forgettin' that."

When she released him, his balls ached. He heard the warning, the hint of blackmail. George remembered being a kid on his grandfather's farm, that time he got tangled in a prickly bush. The harder he pulled, the deeper the thorns stabbed him. When he tried to twist away, he found a hundred sharp needles had tiny hooks to hold him. All he could do then was scream for help, and he was still crying when his grandfather found him.

Could a grown man cry and be rescued?

"I'd pay your way to Detroit, Chicago—even out west. I hear California is great; plenty of aircraft jobs too."

"Honey," she said, "I got all I want right here. Don't even *think* about gettin' rid of me."

When she turned to take her seat behind the register, George left the store for coffee and a doughnut. He sat clear down the counter and tried to remember when this place had been Italian. Whoever the people were, they hadn't lasted long. The new folks had repainted and the door now had Kit Kat Kafe spelled out in gold leaf. The place smelled of new oilcloth and perked coffee and last night's beer. Factory workers came here a lot as each shift ended, beering it up and eating sandwiches.

They were making sixty cents an hour to start, with all the overtime they wanted. There was talk about that kind of pay going up. All that money, and nothing much to buy with it, save pitchers of beer and new, raw whiskey.

Postmaster Alexander said he had permanent writer's cramp from making out so many money orders; what the hillbillies didn't spend to get drunk, they sent home. Funny named towns in Kentucky, West Virginia, and Tennessee, Alexander said; by rights, all that money ought to stay where it was made, in Coshocton.

The country people stayed to themselves in little clumps, touchy and wary. Southerners they were, up from the Appalachian and Blue Ridge mountains, come north to help win the war, strangers in a strange land. Their young men were long gone in uniform, and a goodly part of the middle aged too; those who'd come to the war plants were graying or crippled.

They looked alike: lean men with weathered faces, wearing patched gallus overalls and clodhopper shoes. They got drunk on Saturdays, and nobody in Coshocton had ever seen their kind of street fighting, *white* men going at each other with pocket knives. Their deadly fury was more frightening because it was so silent, and they'd stand there cutting, neither man taking a backward step, until somebody fell over. Doc Shaw was kept busy stitching up winners and losers alike, and sometimes one of them died. Then the hill folks closed ranks, impassive and hard eyed. The sheriff never made an arrest stick; there were never any witnesses.

Doc Shaw said they were different because they'd been so cut off from the rest of society, on their isolated mountain farms. They'd always hunted, fished, made whiskey, and grubbed at their hardscrabble land, independent as a hog on ice. Doc Shaw laughed and said he was learning a lot of sayings like that one.

George just wished he had more to sell them. They'd buy most anything to ship home for their womenfolk; it took him a while to realize that not one had brought along a woman, and longer to realize that none of their houses back home had electricity. They'd turn an ordinary bed lamp over and over in brown, callused fingers, marveling at it before shaking their heads and putting it carefully back on display. One man bought a bathtub and shipped it off by rail, his friends joking him about getting spring water to fill it. But later on, three others came back and George had only one more tub to sell.

If he'd seen the war coming, maybe he'd have laid in a good stock of things like alarm clocks. But who ever thought those bucktoothed little bastards would sneak attack American ships at Pearl Harbor? Now the Office of Production Management decided what was needed for the front and what wasn't. A merchant couldn't plan a week ahead.

After that first flush of scarce item buying, George's business was beginning to feel the pinch. Maybe some shortages would ease, maybe not. He could hang on, but—

Dammit, he was a decent man. He contributed to the church and the Red Cross and freely gave time and effort to help the country; he had two sons in uniform and two daughters in defense work. He believed in God and country and loved his wife. Sure he loved Elizabeth; it was just—Holly was so—so—

Paying his check, George stepped outside and looked up the street at his own store. Dollars to doughnuts Holly was on the phone. Boys called her all the time, and at first he'd been jealous. Now he wished she'd get serious with one and get married. Would she quit work then? If only there were somebody he could talk to, explain how things were. If he were Catholic he could go to confession, but a thousand Hail Marys couldn't get Holly Melborne off his back and out of his life.

"Hi," he said to old Austin Warren. "Hello there, Austin. Pretty day, ain't it?"

"You got to be clean out'n your head," the old man said, and kept on down the street in his lopsided gait.

That was about the only time the mean old bastard was right, George thought. He was insane to be carrying on with a girl younger than two of his daughters, and if Elizabeth ever found out—

He didn't even want to imagine such a scene. He watched Austin Warren instead. A word hadn't passed between them since George wouldn't refund money on a Hoover vacuum cleaner Austin claimed was defective, five years after he bought it.

George grinned; some good came out of wanting to say something to somebody, anybody, to take his mind off Holly. Leaning along, with one hand where he carried his change purse, Austin kept looking back over that angled left shoulder, as though he were scared George might come running at him.

Good—he'd have to make it a point to say hello to the old skinflint as often as possible. It would worry hell out of him.

Misery loved company, wasn't that right? Old Austin was born miserable, and didn't love anything but money.

How about old George? What did he love—Elizabeth and his family, his place in the community—what? Not a young siren who excited him by smell and sight and touch, not a silken bitch so experienced in sexual tricks that she just about turned a man inside out; no, old George didn't *love* Holly Melborne, he was just hooked on her, and the barbs were set deep.

When he reached the store, Holly was impatient at the door. "If you'd let *me* close up once in a while—"

"Didn't mean to be so long. And I didn't know you were in such a hurry. Nobody else is closed yet."

Eyes gone sultry and heavy lidded, she looked at him. "If you're not interested in anything but this old store—"

"Dammit, girl, you can't expect me to change the whole pattern of my life just because you—"

"Now, now, honey." Her fingers slid into his shirt and she moved close. "You already changed. I mean, you thought you could only come once, and you thought goin' down on a woman was dirty or queer or somethin'."

He flinched at her touch, at her heat. "You don't *have* to be crude, Holly. With a little practice, maybe some night school, you could be almost anything—a receptionist, a model—"

Her nails dug in. "And you'd be glad to help me out, right? Night school and like that?" The noise she made was no laugh, although her lips stretched and her teeth showed. She held the wad of gum between them, then sucked it back.

"Sure you would. You been hintin' about getting rid of me, honey. But you'd miss me too much. I mean, you don't tell your old lady *fuck me, fuck me*, out loud; and nobody sucks nobody, right? I mean, that'd be *crude!*"

He moved away from her and pulled down the door shade. "Holly, I didn't mean—"

"Hell you didn't! But you can just forget about me workin' in that smelly old tire factory, or goin' to night school. I got better things to do with my nights." She snapped her gum hard.

A chill poked him low in the belly. "You're not going out with somebody else? Not—not laying some hillbilly who might be carrying some kind of disease?"

She ran her tongue over newly painted lips; some of the red

stuff stained a canine tooth. "Think about that, honey; you just put that in your pipe and smoke it. If I was to get burnt, catch clap or something—if I got knocked up, Betsy and Harry'd have a pretty good idea who did it. Never knew she was jealous, did you? Betsy ain't *crude*, but she wet her pants every time you and me stayed too long in the storeroom. And horny little Harry, always after a free feel because the boss was gettin' it."

Each of George's years came down on him, bending his back. He looked at his hands; they braced the bulbous hang of his belly: corset lacings, hernia supporters, veiny hands spotted brown by age.

"What do you want, Holly?"

"Like I told you, hon. I like it here real good—good enough to be careful, know what I mean?" When he didn't answer, she smiled, touched a hand to her hair, and walked off.

He heard every click of her high heels against concrete until their rhythm was blotted out by music from the drugstore jukebox. He recognized the tune:

". . . *I got spurs that jingle, jangle, jingle . . . as I go riding merrily along . . .*"

He supposed there was a wistful bit of cowboy in every man, but only a few tried to play out the fantasy; only a few still treasured Hoot Gibson and popcorn matinees.

". . . *and they sing oh, ain't you glad you're single . . .*"

If Elizabeth found out about Holly, he might very well be single, but there would be nothing merry about it. Maybe he could still keep his affair quiet, still make a real contribution to the war effort, if all the girl wanted was to laze through the war at his store.

If she didn't change her mind and blackmail him for more than he could afford.

chapter 25

Harry James, top of the heap trumpet man, says he doesn't only play for jitterbugs. "Like our version of 'Sleepy Lagoon,'" he said. "That's pretty and artistic. I like to blend hot and sweet. . . ."

—*Variety*, September 17, 1942

Everything smelled so nice and new, and Louise just loved that. She couldn't remember things at home ever smelling so just-unwrapped new. Mom's furniture had always been busted and rickety or trailing strings and leaking cotton. But at the Barton's house: These are antiques, child; please, do be careful, child—that antique silk brocade is priceless. Hell, old stuff was just old.

"Child, your ass," Louise said in her very own apartment where she could say whatever she wanted. "I'm your perfect little boy's *wife*—but you don't want to even think about him and me in bed, right?"

Damned right; how Mrs. Rodney Barton hated her for marrying sweet Roger, dear Roger: But you're so young, Roger dear . . . we had such plans for you . . .

Foot propped on the shiny coffee table, Louise added a touch of that new red shade to her big toenail. Yeah, plans for college and business and marrying him off to somebody of his own "class."

. . . I simply cannot understand, Roger dear . . . you could have an automatic deferment . . . the plant . . . vital to the war effort . . . at least, at the very *least*, you might have accepted a commission . . . and tying yourself down with that child . . .

Sometimes Louise suspected that Roger got married and enlisted just to get away from his mama. His daddy wasn't a bad guy, just quiet and mousey like; but that old bag—

No, it wasn't all running from Mama; Roger really dug her. He went crazy for her in bed and made so much noise, which probably drove his mama nuts—which probably had a lot to do with Louise moving out into a place of her own. Roger really, really dug her.

"Dig that," Louise said, like hepcats and jitterbugs said. She sang: *"Dig, dig, dig, well all right . . . chop, chop, chop, well all right.* Come on, all you jitterbugs; we're going to cut a rug. Call in your requests to Station—ahh—Pee Dee Kyu."

She made a face. Like hell, she'd cut a rug to Torrance's jukebox. What young Coshocton guy would date a married woman? She was so damned left out of everything: dancing and parties and the prom night she never got. A place of her own didn't make up for everything, especially with Roger gone, and she was tired of canned soup. Even peanut butter was starting to taste cardboardy, but she'd been home for dinner night before last.

Putting her foot down, Louise compared it with the other. Okay, she had her hair set, a fresh pedicure, and so what? She wasn't going anywhere until work on Monday. That was no fun, either. What she really needed was to get out of this little town and go somewhere exciting for a change, like New York or Hollywood.

She said, "Hollywood," tasting the word and finding it sweet. Hollywood and the Stage Door Canteen; the Andrews Sisters and movie stars. The USO was always saying it needed girls to make servicemen feel at home, and if she was around the Canteen, she couldn't help bumping into somebody like Clark Gable. No; he was in the Air Corps. Well, Spencer Tracy or Tyrone Power, any big star who'd see she was more than just patriotic, that she had talent and looks. Then she'd take Ginger Rogers' place with Fred Astaire, or dance with that crazy Donald O'Connor.

Fat chance; Louise Parker might have had a shot at fame, but *Mrs. Barton*? She'd be working in that dumb office until Roger came home. File clerk, phone answerer, because she couldn't type and hadn't finished school, and Mrs. Rodney Barton wouldn't have her son's wife working on the tire line like some common laborer.

Which meant she didn't get any overtime, but kept her pinkies clean. She didn't need the money, since Mr. Barton —she could never call him Daddy—paid for her apartment without Mrs. Barton knowing, and Roger's allotment came through on time every month. She had lots of clothes and shoes and enough makeup to last until she was forty—the same with perfume and cologne. Roger liked to buy things like that for her.

Louise turned on the radio to sticky Wayne King music as redblue light bounced from her ring set. She never thought she'd get a diamond that big. Maybe Deke Deacon would have bought one for her someday, but she didn't think so. He wasn't thick as Roger. When her husband got back, she'd make him get her a bigger diamond, a full carat maybe, to flash on the long trip they'd take: New York, Hollywood, maybe Hawaii. She smiled; like Sophie Tucker said, it was just as easy to love a rich guy.

If this was love; if she wasn't bored out of her mind, so bored that the fan magazines and radio didn't help much anymore. Sure, she could understand that her favorite magazines had to leave off a bunch of pages because of the paper shortage, and she could see why everybody liked "There's a Star Spangled Banner Waving Somewhere," even if it was a hillbilly song, even if it had never made "The Lucky Strike Hit Parade." But she wanted to dance and hear boogie-woogie and see the Stage Door Canteen.

Damn—why *had* Roger gone off to play war?

Across town and out West Chestnut Street, where bare trees snuggled to evergreens in tingly, early fall weather, Elizabeth Parker stood looking after the Western Union boy as he mounted his bicycle. His *Sorry, Miz Parker* echoed as the telegram shook in her hand. Which one? Oh, God—which one? She couldn't open the yellow envelope, and turned off the porch into the house. Two blue stars in the window; oh, God, oh, God!

George—where was George? She couldn't be expected to carry this burden alone. He was her husband, the boys' father —the *boys*. She refused to look down at the yellow envelope, but instead stared out the window where lawn had been cleared from the sunny side of the house and her Victory Garden put in. Golden pumpkins graced it now, and yellow winter squash; frost had touched the crabapple tree's darkened fruit with warning slashes of gold.

Not in our window, please—no Gold Star. But why else would a telegram come? Oriana had gotten the same kind when Clay was killed. When Elizabeth swallowed, her throat was achingly dry. She moved stiff legged through the house, this empty and waiting house, to the kitchen. Carefully she placed the telegram on the table and held her back to it while she made herself put the teakettle on.

She wished she smoked, wished harder that she drank—not sippy drinking, but the hard, oblivion seeking kind. After the telegram was opened, maybe. Elizabeth didn't realize how long she'd been looking down at nothing and out over half the insane world, until the kettle whistled and made her jump.

Doing everything precisely, slowly, as if habit and ritual could hold back any ugliness, she poured steaming water over the little tea strainer, then held it in the cup until the color was right. No lemon in the icebox, and she didn't like milk; there ought to be lemon. She'd pick up a couple when she went shopping tomorrow, when George took her to town in the truck.

Her first swallow of hot tea threatened to come back up. She put down the cup and, dizzy for a second, held to the tabletop. Between her hands was a dent where the oilcloth covered a scar in the wood below. Ronald had banged the table with something after one of those shouting, why-do-you-do-it arguments. Such a temper Ron had; her brother—her *dead* brother —used to get as mad, so Elizabeth supposed Ron came by it naturally.

She picked up the envelope and fumbled it around. Across the table was another nick, that one carved by Randall in an experiment. He'd wanted to see if the wood was the same on the inside.

Which boy?

Elizabeth opened the telegram, a pasted strip of gray words on creased yellow paper: *The War Department deeply regrets to inform you that your son, Private Ronald* . . .

Ronald, dear God! *Ron.*

. . . *Parker, was seriously wounded* . . .

Thank you, Lord; wounded, not dead. Not dead.

. . . *while serving his country in the European Theater of Operations. Signed, the Adjutant General, United States Army* . . .

Not dead, and nothing less mattered. A tear spilled off Elizabeth's chin and was immediately absorbed by the telegram. Rough, re-pulped paper, she thought; there's a war on.

He might be coming home. Surely they wouldn't keep a seriously wounded boy in service. She put a hand to her mouth, another to her belly; suppose he'd lost a leg, an arm? Oh, dear God, what if Ron was blind? They ought to tell a mother more than *seriously wounded*. Maybe there was some way to find out, somebody to write or call. She would send a telegram back to the adjutant general, that was it.

She went to the telephone and gave the operator the store number. "Sorry," the girl said, "that line's busy."

After three more tries, Elizabeth gave up to sit beside the phone and read the telegram again. No mistake; he was badly hurt, and now she felt slow anger creep over the first grateful relief. Nobody to ask about Ron, nobody to tell, and the store phone stayed busy ever since George had hired that cheap, flashy girl.

"I'll learn to drive," she said. "I won't be cut off this way again; I just won't."

Alone in a house once warmed by her entire family; Oriana a widow and moved to Detroit; thank God she'd left little Scooter. Joyce gone too, though not so far; involved with a pretty young man whose eyes just didn't set right. Louise married to that Barton boy; for a while, Elizabeth had thought her youngest daughter *had* to get married, but Louise wasn't showing, and that made Elizabeth a little ashamed of her suspicions.

Two boys gone off to war, and one coming home crippled.

She put the back of one hand to her mouth. Oh, Jesus, holy
Jesus, those horror stories from the other war about American
boys who got gassed and coughed out their lungs years later.
The terrible stories of soldiers shipped home in a basket
because they had no arms and legs.

If that had happened to Ron, she could take it; she knew she
could, because she was his mother and loved him. But could
Ron accept being a basket case? *Would* he?

Joyce—she could reach Joyce by phone at her office.

When Joyce hung up, she sat back to sort her feelings. She
believed what she'd told Mom about great medical care in the
army, but not the soothing words, how Ron was really okay
and all that. Nobody could know.

Getting up from her desk, she went to the coffeepot—a
privilege of the boss's private secretary—wondering that she
didn't feel more shock and pain. But it wasn't like Ron had
been killed.

Joyce stirred in sugar and cream, only half the amount she
normally used. She wasn't close to Ron; only Randy was.
She'd probably feel worse if Randy was wounded, but that was
Ron's own fault. He'd always been so wild and thoughtless,
tearing through life and not giving a damn about anybody else,
except maybe Randy.

Still, he was her brother and maybe she could find out more
about him. Franco was always talking about his Washington
connections, and it was possible one could reach overseas, as a
favor. She was coming to know about favors. If the news was
very bad, she'd keep it from Mom awhile, and kind of prepare
her bit by bit.

Franco wasn't in the office. At the last minute he'd ducked
out of facing the typing pool, still embarrassed about his father
slapping him around. She couldn't much blame him, even if
the whole office crew was on his side. Old man Butera had no
right to do that to Franco, no *right*. The old fart had done
enough to his son over the years, depriving him of school fun,
cutting him off from kids his own age, forcing him to work,
work, work, then getting mad because work was so important
to Franco.

Joyce sipped coffee and made a face at its semi-bitterness. If
Franco had gone to ballgames and school dances, she might

have married him instead of Joe. Life would have been so different for them all. Looking into her cup, Joyce wondered how she'd feel if the War Department telegram were about Joe.

Long ago, she'd stopped loving him—if she ever did. Whatever they had was pallid compared to the emotions Franco aroused. But she didn't want to see Joe badly wounded, and God forbid his being killed. If Franco asked, she'd divorce Joe in a second, but if he came home a cripple, she might be chained to him forever.

The phone buzzed again and again, and business eased Ron from the forefront of her mind. No, Mr. Franco Butera wasn't in, but on a short business trip. Of course she'd take a message —two, four, a dozen. No, *that* Mr. Butera wasn't in or expected. She'd suggest Mr. Giuseppe Butera be contacted at this number . . .

Bobbing the phone switch, Joyce reached the factory switchboard. "Ellie dear, when anybody asks for old man Butera, give them his home phone. He won't be coming in anymore. It's for the best. That awful display of senility—you've heard about it? Thank you, dear; I'll tell the boss how everyone you talk to is behind him."

And that meant about everyone in the plant, Joyce knew. Ellie Thomas thoroughly enjoyed supervising her small empire of telephone operators, and although she was a nonstop talker, she managed to hear every whisper.

Mom was so worried about Ron. The rest of the family would be too, as soon as they got the news. Tell your father, Mom said, *if* you can get him on the phone; God knows I can't.

Funny, Ron was the one Joyce would least fret about, unless to worry about his getting killed on the highway, or killing somebody else in a barroom brawl and going to jail for the rest of his life. She picked up her empty coffee cup, but decided against a refill. If Franco were lying in some army hospital, she'd find *some* way to be with him.

How to go about getting overseas? Not in a tacky women's service uniform. Maybe through the Red Cross or as a civilian pilot. Joyce grinned; she'd have to learn to fly first.

How did Ron get hurt in the European Theater of Operations? As far as anyone knew, no American soldiers were fighting over there; not yet. She'd read about U.S. Air Corps flyers based in Ireland and England, but no ground troops. Ron was an infantryman. Air raid, she thought; Hitler's planes were always bombing London—*blitzing* it; RKO newsreels showed people sleeping in subways, and huge fires blazing on the streets, building walls crashing down. It would be like Ron not to take cover when the air raid warning sounded.

She reached the hardware store on the second try, and the girl said, "Yeah? Parker Hardware."

Joyce said, "My—Mr. Parker, please."

"Ain't here."

"Can you reach him? This is his daughter and it's important." She didn't know what Daddy could do, except hold Mom's hand, maybe that was enough.

"Uh-uh; don't know where he went. He's been hangin' around that I-talian restaurant and leavin' me to close up." The voice carried a whine.

"Thanks," Joyce said. Help was hard to get and business slow since civilian production had been severely cut back, especially metals, and that left a hardware merchant high and dry. The Controlled Materials branch of the War Production Board even had people turning in crumpled toothpaste and shaving cream tubes, when they wanted to buy more.

Daddy ought to shut down. No, better if he stayed open on a shoestring and went to work in one of the plants. Franco would give him a good job here, something that paid well and wouldn't work him hard. For certain, he'd have to fire that girl. She sounded like Mortimer Snerd, and probably wasn't as bright as that weird looking dummy Edgar Bergen sometimes used.

So many people called; so many papers needed Franco's attention, his go-ahead. Twice, mill foremen slammed out of the office because he wasn't there, and a long distance caller jumped all over Joyce, as if it were her fault. She realized how indispensable Franco was; the plant couldn't run smoothly if he was gone a few hours, and would shut down completely if he walked away.

That wasn't good for the country, she thought. He should appoint a vice president, someone to take over in an emergency and carry some of the daily work load. He was so busy trying to juggle other companies he'd become involved with, desperately trying to produce things the country badly needed, despite the trouble with his father. Other people were jealous of Franco's success—petty, envious men who whispered that he was greedy and arrogant, that he was ruthless in business dealings.

Joyce lifted her chin, ready to defend him against all comers. He stood head and shoulders above the old fuddies in this town, thinking ahead, thinking modern. Franco Butera walked among them like a tiger, disdaining the jackals that snapped at his heels. He'd continue to grow, to extend his influence far beyond Coshocton, perhaps to Columbus, maybe even farther—to Washington itself.

She was a little afraid of that, Joyce admitted. If he became governor, he couldn't be involved with a married woman. The newspapers would cut him to pieces, for his name and religion —even if he didn't practice it—were difficulties enough. How many old fuddies, how many farmers, would vote for a Catholic Italian?

Maybe she'd be secretly glad if the obstacles of birth and church were too much. She would still be able to reach out and touch him then.

The phone rang, her father on the line. "Joyce, why in hell didn't you get hold of me? Your mother's been going crazy—"

"I—it's been hectic around here, so busy that—"

"Nobody's *that* busy. I heard about your brother from the Western Union kid, Terry something. I'm home now."

Joyce gnawed her lip. "I tried to reach you. That girl said you weren't around. Didn't she tell you?"

"She closed shop before I got back. Damn it, Joyce, you have a family, responsibilities."

"Sorry, Daddy. Have you called Louise and Oriana?"

"Louise got my message at work. The number Oriana sent —some woman answered and slammed the receiver before I could explain."

"Her landlady," Joyce said. "She has a bitchy landlady. I'll get through to her this evening. It's—it's not like anybody can *do* anything, Daddy."

"Yes," he said, sounding old and tired. "Your mother—we just want the family to know."

Joyce said, "I'll be home as soon as I can."

She didn't make it that night, because Franco called and said to meet him at the apartment right away, that he needed her. When she phoned home to explain, Mom said all right, dear, all right.

But it wasn't all right.

chapter 26

Meeting in an extraordinary session, the Russian
Politburo today renewed demands for a second
front. "Our allies must do something to relieve us,"
a spokesman said, "something beyond a few planes
and tanks. Russia cannot go on fighting the war by
herself. . . ."

—Moscow, September 22, 1942 (Reuters)

He kept trembling. It was funny how long he shook all over,
like one of his grandpa's farm horses when it was badly
spooked. Randy wasn't actually scared, just shaken and
embarrassed, and that was plenty.

The officer of the day nodded at the two guards. "Take her
on out of here and see her on the bus."

"You—you messenger of Satan," Martha hissed. "I have the
right to visit my husband, the God-given *right*."

Thick necked and red faced, the lieutenant said, "Not less'n
God signs a pass, you don't. Miss, go along easy or I'll have to
turn you over to civilian cops. You don't want that."

"Martha," Randy said. "Please—"

"Your fault, all your fault! You'll pay for what you've done
to me, Randall Parker—as God is my witness, you will pay!"

He put out a shaky hand, but suddenly she whirled and

stamped from the orderly room; the abashed sentries followed. The OD looked at Randy, at the company CQ. "That better be it, dammit. I got more to do than herd some fuckin' draftee's shook up woman."

"I had no idea she was coming," Randy said, "and she's hysterical, I guess. I couldn't stop her yelling, any more than you could."

"Ain't *my* old lady," the OD said, hitching up the pistol belt that strained around his gut. "But your *ass* is mine, boy, does she come around again."

"Yessir," Randy said, saluting because it was expected.

When the man was gone, the heavy smell of Martha's perfume lingered in the orderly room, overripe and cloying. "Jesus, Parker," the charge of quarters said, "I couldn't do nothin' else. All that hollerin'—"

"That's okay," Randy said, and didn't stop trembling until he had four beers in town. Indiantown Gap was a funny POE. The highway ran right through the middle of camp, and there were no manned gates. You could walk out of the port of embarkation anytime you wanted, because it wasn't really a port, but a shipping center many miles from open water.

He felt shamed and sick, and was glad to see the first platoon medic in a bar. Rich Shriver was well into a happy drunk and Randy needed something, someone, to help him out of this black mood. He tongued the little cut Martha had slapped inside his mouth and sat down with the guy he knew slightly, mainly because they were pill rollers attached to the same heavy weapons company. There was another with the mortars-and-.50s platoon, but Randy didn't know how long such surplus would last. Usually no more than one medic was assigned a company.

Shriver was happy to see him, also glad to be off post for a little while, and his celebration got louder and happier. No cause for the pair of MPs to lean on him, though, not because one lousy button was open. Maybe it was the beer, or frustration at Martha; maybe Shriver reminded him a little of Ron, always in trouble. Whatever, Randy unloaded on the nearest MP, tripped the other under a table, and hauled ass up the street with Shriver in tow. They became friends, and it was good to have a buddy three days later at Pier 19 in New York.

Like so many tagged and numbered insects, they sat and

stood in a confused column, inching their way through the cavernous, echoing warehouse. When they off-loaded the ferry that brought them across the harbor, Randy saw the next slip over, where the blackened liner *Normandie* tilted into bottom mud, the great sweep of her false bow accusing. She had fled Nazi occupation with her Free French crew, to refit as an Allied troopship. Sparks from a welder sank her at the dock. Accidental fire, censored newspapers said. Sabotage, ran the whispers.

Next to her rode the mighty *Queen Mary*, biggest ship in the world and the cause of her competitor's false bow. Beyond was an empty slip where the *Queen Elizabeth* berthed when she was this side of the ocean, and somewhere along the busy, noisy waterfront lay the U.S.S. *United States*. No more bon voyage parties for these huge travelers; no music and confetti and bright lights; they too had been drafted.

Randy couldn't smell the sea, but only paint—fresh gray over the *Mary*'s great whale belly, OD on his new-style helmet, on entrenching shovels and pick mattocks, covering boxes and bayonet scabbards. It was ironic that the army spent so much time and effort polishing everything that would take a shine—clear down to tiny brass eyelets in web belts—then painted over them when war came. He sighed when the line caterpillared again, and struggled forward with his barracks bags. They were ballooned blue mushrooms tagged A and B, and although emptied of almost everything personal, they were as heavy as sin. Marth's idea of sin, not his; how she could twist things.

"One-one-three," called the exec. "Parker!"

"Randall," he said, "Tee-four."

"Go!" the CO said, checking off his boarding list, and Randy sweated along a low gangplank across greasy, lapping water and into the bowels of the ship. Just ahead, Rich Shriver said *kee-rist*! and stumbled along the passageway. It angled, cornered, and Randy caught other odors through the paint: cooking grease, vegetables, diesel oil.

Two Englishmen in funny looking sailor suits trotted by, and up ahead, the first sergeant of D Company thumbed the first platoon and Shriver one way, Randy's platoon another. "Medic," the first sergeant said, "you're in with company headquarters, top bunk."

Five of them in narrow wooden bunks walling a stateroom meant for one tourist, third calss, and the top kick took up room for two. A bags and B bags, weapons and helmets, full field packs; a tiny latrine but no porthole this far down; the top and supply sergeants, company clerk, and company mechanic. It was stuffy and sweaty, with only a small ventilation fan laboring, and when the ship's whistle shuddered the bulkheads around them, Randy flinched.

"Pullin' out," the first sergeant said.

"And we don't get to wave good-bye to New York."

Sergeant Schneider looked at Randy. "Ain't that a fuckin' shame."

When he discovered the sleeping system—twelve hours on deck, twelve hours below—Randy opted to remain on deck around the clock. He stood at the rail with Shriver and belched the taste of sausages that looked great but contained a lot of sawdust, breakfast eggs that had been faintly green.

"Kee-rist," Shriver said. "They oughta boil the resin from the sawdust first. Better'n mutton stew, anyhow, all that goddamn ground up bone and a sometimey piece of wool."

Randy grinned. "That's not wool; it's underarm hair."

"Shit." Shriver spat. "Thanks. Good thing I lost everything first day out."

"We have the world's longest chow lines and eat just twice a day, but I'd rather be on the *Queen Mary* than a regular troopship. We'll make it to England in four, five days, not ten or twelve. We're on the fastest ship afloat."

Grunting, Shriver said, "Yeah, but where's our destroyer escort? We got a million miles of ocean crawlin' with U-boats."

"She's too fast for convoy."

"Can't outrun torpedoes. Kee-rist, when that fantail gun opened up for practice, I thought we had it for shit sure."

Randy turned and pointed at the sundeck. "About a thousand BARs up there—a *thousand*, Rich. If dive bombers find us off the coast of England, there'll be some surprised Nazis and Messerschmitts scattered all over."

"And Focke-Wulfs and Stukas. I had to attend them damned aircraft identification lectures too. You want to see this GI shit himself? Just let *one* airplane—any kind of fuckin' airplane —fly over this tub. Seventeen thousand guys on board, and how many make it if a bomb or torpedo nails us? Look at them lifeboats—bet you officers ride them. Them open-ass rafts piled on deck—they're for us, *if* they float off the sinking tub like they're supposed to. Then there's sharks; our asses be hangin' off in the water for bait."

"I don't know if sharks are this far north, this time of year."

"Fuckin' shark don't know nothin', either." Shriver chuckled. "I'll pop him with a morphine syrette, drop a bottle of APCs down his throat, and paint his ass purple with potassium permanganate. Teach him to fuck with a combat medic. Come on; let's get outa this wind."

Randy laughed. "Nothing can kill a hardhead like you. You're like my brother, always with your tail in a crack, but always saving it. He's immortal; walks away from car wrecks and torn up bars and pissed off boyfriends. Old Ron's somewhere in England, and if I get lucky, I'll see him soon."

"I wasn't hardheaded until MPs started hittin' me with sticks," Shriver said. "Your brother a dogface?"

"First Division."

"Kee-rist. He's dumber'n you. That outfit's damn near all regular army. A draftee must have a rough time protectin' his ruby red ass."

"Only wrote once," Randy said as they hunched on deck beneath a lifeboat, where the gigantic amidships stack helped cut the chill Atlantic wind.

Ron wouldn't bitch, but he'd sure resent authority and rebel against chickenshit. It was a wonder he'd gotten overseas without making the guardhouse. So long as he took care of himself; Randy's stomach flexed and he tasted salt back in his throat when he tried to imagine his brother killed in action. He'd done his damnedest to hold back thinking of that; he couldn't picture life without Ron. But Ron would be okay; he was immortal.

"Must have been great, vacationing on this ship before the war," he said, facing aft and pulling his neck deeper into the field jacket collar. The swimming pool had been filled with water and leggy girls, not GI cots, and passageways had shown evening gowns at night, instead of a never ending chow line. The bright, open dining room had served real food, and the decks hadn't stunk of vomit and grease and wet, olive drab wool.

"Rich folks sail this barge in peacetime," Shriver said, pulling a blanket around his shoulders. "You rich, Parker?"

Randy laughed and Shriver said, "Me neither; bet you and me, we're the only guys in this man's army wasn't makin' at least a hundred a week before the draft. Never run into so many rich men still smokin' Bull Durham, but I'd say this ocean voyage is the first for all of us. So long as I get a round trip ticket."

"Like I said, nothing can kill you, buddy."

Shriver moved his feet so an English sailor could pick his way along the deck. "Less'n I take a shot like you hit that big MP. You throw a mean punch, Parker. Did you fight pro?"

"Jesus, no. That's the first time I ever hit anybody, and probably the last."

"Shit," his friend said.

Deck chill and the dank cold of iron plates eased through the folded blanket they sat on. Randy lifted himself to sit on his Mae West, the celebrated orange life jacket that was said to be visible for miles in gray and choppy seas. He hoped never to use it for more than a seat and pillow, for Shriver was right: Few men would make lifeboats and rafts, and German U-boats often machine gunned survivors.

Aft, beyond the squirm of stocking-capped troops, on past the fantail boundary and its wake of bubbled ocean, lay all Randy was familiar with, home and family, and he knew a fleeting ache for them. Mom and Dad had been worried about Ron a long time, and now fear for Randy's safety was added. He was glad his other siblings were sisters, and thought of them as the *Queen Mary* slid into a patch of fog: little Louise, Joyce, Oriana—what were they doing?

Oriana Parker came tired from the shop after twelve long hours; her eyes smarted and her face was baked; there was nagging pain between her shoulders. She felt good, though. The crew was ahead of schedule, and she'd showed them a woman could weld as good as any man. Her seams would hold; she didn't doubt that. Maybe she wasn't as pretty with her work as old time welders, but it was solid. The planes would roll and the welding would hold, and that was what counted. She wanted every B-24 to be perfect, for David Shepsel might fly one, even though he was a fighter pilot.

She was getting used to grime, and to carrying a dozen little burns, but she'd never block out the noise of Willow Run, the constant clangor that echoed in her head long after her shift. Oriana pulled off her scarf and shook down her hair to work the tip of a little finger into each ear. It didn't help, any more than the plugs she sometimes wore. She sat in her truck cab with the door open, and smoked while waiting for Noreen Douglas. Noreen bitched about putting in so much overtime, but she stayed and worked. Most women did, if only to prove they could carry their weight. Slowly, men were beginning to accept them.

If only they'd keep their hands to themselves. Some guys thought women war workers were only in the plant to play grab ass. Just about everybody was away from home and lonely, and Oriana could understand. Understanding hadn't stopped her from slapping the man who offered her money.

At times she wished she could be like Noreen, out raising hell with this man or that and seeming to enjoy every hectic minute. But Noreen wasn't a war widow with a child, and she hadn't found another man now doing his damnedest to get back overseas. Damn it, David had done his part and more; if he somehow got back to the skies over the English Channel, the searchlight skies over burning London, he'd be killed. She felt that in the deepest part of herself, saw it in sweated dreams —his plane smoking, whirling down out of control, his hands frantic at the canopy that would not open—

And what about her? Hadn't she given enough?

"Hey, girl—think I ran off with the leaderman?"

Oriana half smiled. "After twelve hours in there? More power to you."

Noreen went around the truck and climbed in, her lunchbox rattling. "Not that I *can't*, you understand. It's just I got a reputation to uphold, and runnin' out of steam ain't part of it. But tomorrow's Saturday, and Saturday's got a night, and —hey! You still mean to go home over Sunday?"

"Sure. I promised my little girl, and you can have the apartment to yourself." Oriana started the truck and moved it through the muddy ruts of the unfinished parking lot. So much of Willow Run was raw and unfinished, ticky-tacky. But it produced airplanes. B-24s rolled out and flew off.

Putting one hand on her arm, Noreen said, "You really don't

mind? I mean, old lady McCarthy's one thing, but if *you* don't like the idea of a guy visitin' our place—"

"I'd like my own guy in our place. I'd give a lot to have my own guy there."

"You mean your old man, the guy you were married to. I never got past seventh grade. What do you call a dead husband?"

"Gone," Oriana said, steering past a late bus disgorging the next shift. "Whenever I see a bus like that, I'm glad you shared your apartment with me. I'd be spending all my gas coupons and half my time running back and forth to Detroit. I guess I should feel guilty, hanging on to my old C stamps from the farm."

"Guilty, hell; you're talkin' guilty account of you slipped. Who's the guy you'd like in our place? Gimme his name and I'll drag him to you by the ears if he's so dumb. Look, honey, you got a right. You mourned your man and work your buns off to pay back the Japs, so you got a right. Where does it say a woman's got to die with her old man?"

Gritty eyelids threatened her with sleep. Oriana shifted position on the bench seat, rolled the window down an extra inch so the cool morning air could wash her face.

Noreen clicked on the radio. "Gee, I don't know if I wanta hear war news. We keep gettin' kicked in the ass all over the world. Them poor bastards on Corregidor—think MacArthur's goin' to get 'em out?"

"No," Oriana answered. "They call themselves 'the forgotten bastards of Bataan,' and I guess they're right. We can't get to them, can't supply them, and we might as well forget them. The Japs will overrun Corregidor soon, and we won't have to feel guilty."

"Poor bastards," Noreen sighed and lighted two cigarettes, passing one to Oriana. "But you got me off track. Who's the guy?"

"You don't know him—a flyer."

Twiddling the dial until she found music, Noreen leaned back. "Gee—I could cream every time I listen to Bob Eberly sing that. *Yours, till the stars have no glory—da-da-da* . . . A flyboy, for chrissakes; you must *like* bein' sorry. Soldiers are poison, and flyboys double. Gimme a fat, 4-F leaderman—no, a shop foreman—who won't go off to war and get shot."

Oriana was silent for awhile. On the radio, Carmen Miranda yelled "I Yi-Yi-Yi-Yi-Yi Like You Very Much," and Oriana pictured the vivacious little woman cavorting beneath a ridiculous piled-fruit hat. Music stayed happy; people stayed happy; keep our boys' morale up; don't you know there's a war on? Oh, David, David, should I feel guilty for missing you, and not Clay?

She missed Clay; she'd been married to him and had a child by him, so she missed him as a husband and father. As a lover? As she yearned for and needed David Shepsel? She could barely recall the feel of Clay's body, remember him inside her only as she might have read it in a book. But every moment with David in bed could be vividly relived.

Noreen was talking about her date, and because Oriana had heard its like before, she only half listened. It would be good to get home, even if only for a few hours, to romp with Scooter and get filled in on family news. Mom had called when Ron was wounded, but nobody had been able to find out more than the fact; no details available.

When Clay was killed, Oriana hadn't wanted to know the details. She knew Japs had done it, and the where and how wouldn't bring him back. Her stomach did a little flip when she asked herself if she would *want* Clayton Canfield returned.

"Lousy war," she said, swinging the Ford off into the trash-and kid-cluttered yard. "My God, would you believe that? Miz McCarthy's got guys working on that old shed, turning it into a room."

"Room, hell," Noreen said, swinging down from the cab. "The old bat'll turn it into a goddamn three-room apartment, with outside crapper, of course. Like the goddamn septic tank ain't already backin' up."

Muffled, the landlady's voice followed them upstairs. "If some people didn't stuff unmentionables down the toilet—"

At the landing, Noreen yelled down, "You forgot how to say Kotex, you old bat? Been so long back, you forget how to use 'em? You don't give us bigger garbage cans, I may just *mail* mine to you."

Oriana giggled into the apartment. "You know, I think you'd do it."

"Damned right, but she'd get the post office on me—and I ain't seen a mail carrier I'd *want* on me."

Oriana laughed. "Noreen, you're crazy."

"It helps, you know."

"Maybe I should think about it—doing something crazy."

Noreen flopped on the couch. "You can have the first bath. Crazy like visitin' your flyboy?"

At the bathroom door, Oriana paused. "I hadn't thought of it —not really. I mean, I can't get the time off, and my crew—"

Kicking off her shoes, Noreen said, "Can do just like they'd do if you took sick. And that's how you get off—get sick; we got sick time comin'."

"I—I don't know." Oriana shook her head. "It's like cheating, and the planes—I don't know how David would take it. I don't want him to think he owes me anything, that he has to—"

Noreen unbuttoned her work shirt and loosened the man's belt from her narrow waist. "He'll love it. If he don't, he's a jerk and not worth your time."

Putting a hand to her face, Oriana said softly, "I'll have to think about it. First I—I have to go home. He—David didn't write that he was shipping out, just that he was trying."

Noreen sat up. "Look, honey, I had it bad for this sailor. Oh, not like in the movies, I guess; Marty didn't use pretty words or talk marriage, but I could *tell*, know what I mean? He was goin' to ship and asked me to come to the Great Lakes Naval Station, kind of see him off, you know. It ain't that far, but we just started workin' double shifts, and I said next time maybe. Only there wasn't no next time. His ship's off the Solomon Islands, on the bottom of the Pacific."

Oriana held the coveralls she'd just taken off. "I didn't know, Noreen. I'm sorry."

"Don't be sorry for me; you'll be sorry for yourself, if you let your man go without lovin' him one last time. Oh, shit, I sound like a sob sister, don't I?"

Softly, Oriana said, "No. You're a smart woman, and I'm listening."

God, no—not a *last* loving time, a good-bye-for-now time. She didn't think she could handle another, greater loss.

chapter 27

"If you want to sell a housewife Jell-O, you don't tell her: Madam, it is highly probable that your son is coming home a basket case, or totally blind . . . the radio public may be made to forget that by this time the handsome fellow with the silver wings has had half his face burned off in a crash, and that Joe is drawn and skinny from malaria, and has unattractive jungle lice in his beard. . . ."

—*Hollywood Song Writer*, September 30, 1942, on war songs

He hadn't told them he was coming. He was surprised himself when the hospital said he could have thirty days' furlough, and he wasn't sure he wanted to go home. But he had to face it sooner or later, so he listened to the doctor and nurse repeating instructions for the care of his arm and said sure, he'd watch it. Tender as the damned stump was, did they think he'd bat hardball with it?

Thirty days; he stepped down from the bus and waited for the driver to unload his duffel bag. The new-issue, long OD jobs beat hell out of barracks bags, but were no easier to carry. Thirty days—what the hell would he do for a whole month?

"Lemme call somebody for you, soldier. I mean, if it's tough on you—" The driver stared at Ron's sleeve.

"I've been practicing," Ron said, and swung the bag one-handed to shoulder its sling. "Thanks anyhow." People meant well; he knew that, and was learning to hold back irritation. He only bit them in the ass if they pushed the oh-you-poor-boy shit too far.

He wasn't going far—not on Chestnut Street, anyhow. Before seeing the folks, he needed pumping up. Blinking at a bar sign he didn't remember, he lowered the duffel bag and dragged it into beery semidarkness. Climbing a stool, he propped his garrison shoes on the bag. "CC with Schlitz on the side."

"All I got's draft beer. Bottle stuff's gone two days after it comes in. Got half a bottle Canadian Club, and you're lucky."

Shaking out a cigarette and working the Zippo lighter with practiced ease, Ron said, "Where's all the booze?"

"Alcohol, sugar, any damned thing else gets the shorts. I ain't complainin', see; it's a pain in the ass scufflin' for enough stock to keep the war workers happy, but if our boys overseas need the stuff—"

"Medics use a lot," Ron said, breathing deep at the hot bite of whiskey. "Rest of the army'd as soon drink it."

The bartender leaned forward. "I never noticed—here, one on the house, soldier. You must be in the air corps, huh? I mean, ain't nobody else fightin'—except them poor bastards on Corregidor. How'd you lose your hand? Nazi plane shoot it off?"

Ron drank most of his beer, drank the free whiskey, finished the beer. "I'm not air corps. I'm a fuckin' infantryman."

"Them ribbons—you been overseas, right? So what happened to—"

"Thanks for the drink, sport. My hand? Praise the Lord and pass the ammunition—building fell on r , that's all."

Half a block down, Ron jerked his bag into a cab and gave the address. If he wanted to get drunk, it would have to be in some familiar gin mill, maybe with some of the old guys. He'd have to run a check on Mike Martin, Evan Blackwell, guys like that. They couldn't all be in the service. Hindeman—if stubborn, ornery Gunter Hindeman was alive, they could go helling around in Sandusky whorehouses.

The cab stopped. "You're one of the Parker boys," the driver said. "Didn't recognize you at first. Welcome home. That'll be sixty cents."

He stood awhile on the curb as leaves fell around him. Running point, he thought; leaves going early before the main body, and dying quick like most soldiers out as scouts. Well, he didn't have to think about that anymore. The outfit had pulled out for Scotland while he was still in the limey hospital, and only Sergeant Bickston came around to say good-bye. The last time they met, Bickston had kicked his ass good, but here he was:

"You're a lucky son of a bitch," Bickston said. "You'd be starting ten, twenty years for desertion if you weren't so fuckin' lucky."

Ron nodded at the stump with its sewn-over skin flap. "Yeah —how lucky can you get?"

Bickston said, "Brought your barracks bag and personal stuff; when you get transferred to a GI hospital, it'll go with you. The outfit's moving out. You asshole."

"There was a woman. She got blown to hell."

"Lot of women in England get blown to hell. You were a fuckin' soldier and could have been a good one. But good soldiers put the outfit first, the army first. They don't go over the hill because their woman dies. They go shoot the fuckin' krauts that blew her up."

Uncomfortable, Ron had turned on the bed; he'd never gotten use to the rustling of the wartime English mattress stuffed with straw. "Where's the outfit going?"

Bickston shrugged. "Back to Scotland for dry run landings. After that, the Second Front everybody hollers about—France, Italy, how the hell do I know? If the London air raid wardens didn't write letters and come see General Allen personally, your ass'd be out to dry. Saved a little girl, they said; great risk to your own life and all that courageous shit. Company commander wanted to put you in for the Soldier's Medal, but Terrible Terry Allen couldn't see it, since you were AWOL at the time, carried as a deserter with a book of phony passes. Everything's in your 201 file, even an explanation from the limey fireman who had to cut off your hand to save your life. You asshole."

Sighing, Ron hoisted the duffle bag and pushed up the walk.

It smelled good here—browning leaves, air smoky and crisp; down the street, house lights looked warm in twilight. God-dammit, he shouldn't feel guilty. The little girl—Jean Marie Fallinger—would have burned in that wreckage if he *hadn't* been over the hill, and he didn't owe the Big Red One and the Sixteenth "New York's Own" Infantry his fucking life.

On the porch, Ron heard music inside the house, jitterbug music on the radio, soft rattlings of his mother readying dinner. He'd written her only once, a note to say he was all right and making it just fine. She didn't know about his missing hand, and now he thought he should have waited to come home until Halloran General Hospital had his mechanical gadgets rigged. That might be harder on her, though—the hook, and a clamp he could work by rolling his shoulder, even a prosthetic hand that looked almost real, once it was screwed in. For evening wear, the shop GI said, grinning. Goes great with a tux; the hook's more for sports, like. You do any fishin'?

Ron hesitated as it grew darker, while lights came on along West Chestnut and leaves whispered down one by one. Finally he turned the doorknob and stepped inside. He could smell pork chops and his mother's salad dressing; "*Amapola,*" Helen O'Connell sang, "*pretty little poppy . . .*"

His mom's voice: "Scooter! Turn down that radio, please. And set the table."

He'd never been away. Here nothing changed; here no bombs screamed down and nobody died driving an ambulance; a child didn't cry from the rubble. Home, Private Ronald Parker—you asshole.

"Grammy!" His niece stared, balanced on her toes and ready to run. "Grammy—somebody's in the house!"

"Just me, Scooter; just Uncle Ron."

Wiping floured hands on her apron, coming steamy from the stove, Elizabeth made an abrupt stop. "Ron! Ronald, m-my baby—oh, my Lord—"

He felt hunkered down and tense against her, but she hugged him close, squeezed him hard, and remembered too late that he'd never liked being fussed over. "Ron—you didn't let us know—nobody said—"

Nothing mattered except that she could touch him again, brush back the rebel lock of golden hair, know the reality, the living breath of him. Ah, thank you, God. "You—are you hungry? Let me look at you. You've lost weight, son; we'll fix that, now that you're home again, and—"

His right hand was gone. Mother in heaven, his beautiful hand was missing. It had grown from chubby pinkies to little-boy grubbiness to slim, strong perfection. Now the uniform sleeve ended in nothing: *The War Department deeply regrets to inform you . . .*

"It's okay, Mom." He sounded so much older, and very tired. "It's all right. The doctors say I won't miss it much, after a while. When I go back, they'll fit me with all kinds of useful substitutes."

"Substitutes," Elizabeth said. "Thank God it was no worse. Nobody would tell us anything—how badly you were wounded, what happened, anything. And your note said not to come. You could have telephoned, Ron."

She watched him move, restless, across the living room, this wounded boy intent on making himself a stranger, even to her. As a baby he'd tried to hide pain from her, and he carried deep hurt within him now. "I'll call your father," she said. "He should be on his way home, but I'll call to make sure."

He'd better not stop and drink beer at that Italian place tonight, she thought; George found all kinds of excuses to go there of late, but tonight he'd just better not. Surprised that her hands were shaky, Elizabeth gave the operator the store number. Waiting through six rings, she watched her son roam the room. He looked at everything, each old picture and knickknack, as if he needed to be sure they were still there.

"Your father must be on his way home. Scooter, did you say hello to your uncle Ron? He hasn't been gone *that* long."

The girl said, "What happened to your hand?"

Elizabeth's heart turned over. "Scooter!"

Ron said, "Mom—it's a fact of life. My hand's in London, under a bombed wall. A fireman had to chop it off to pull me out before the rest of the building fell on us—on me."

"Did it hurt?"

Elizabeth pressed hands to her belly, wanting to draw the memory of that agony into her own whole body. Mothers couldn't forever divert the pain, but they tried; from the ripping birth pangs on, children were an ache. But a sweet and welcome ache, Lord, and if someone had to be crippled, why

not me? I've been here so long and he hasn't; Ron doesn't even
have a wife and maybe he won't ever, now.

"Scooter, set another plate. I—son, would you like some
coffee, or do you want to eat right away? Your father should be
here any minute, but if you're hungry—and I think there's
some elderberry wine—"

"Coffee'll be fine, Mom—but let me get it? You don't know
how good it is to do for yourself. Everybody tries to do
everything for me, and I'm not totaled out, you know. Some of
the basket cases—I'm sorry, Mom." He swung away into the
kitchen and she drew a steadying breath.

Scooter said, "He looks different. I mean, even if he had his
hand back, I almost wouldn't know him. Grammy, I'm sorry,
too. Talking about his hand, I mean. I think it bothers him,
even if he says it doesn't."

"Just—we just act natural around Ron, I guess." Elizabeth
unclasped her belly, let her arms fall. "Natural as we can,
anyway. Where *is* that man? His son home, and George
Parker's swilling beer with those—those *Italians*."

Scooter said, "If we aren't eating right off, can I turn the
radio back on? Aren't we fighting the Italians, Grammy?"

"Not these." Elizabeth tangled hands in her apron, both
hands. "Maybe we ought to be, though. That cafe woman
looks enough like Mussolini to be his sister." Not his twin. If
only Randy were here; if only they were a complete family
again. She didn't want to, but she called the cafe and asked if
George was there. No, the woman said; ain't seen him today.
Elizabeth said icy thanks and clamped the phone down hard.
Where was he, on this of all nights?

It was full night, but there were still lights in Doc Shaw's
waiting room. Outside, George fidgeted, resenting the flood of
war workers that kept Doc from coming up for air. It was
getting so his old, steady patients couldn't see him.

George moved up the sidewalk and leaned against a shed-
ding maple, pulling shadow around him. What was the old
devil going to say? He wouldn't just let it lie and treat George.
Oh, no—he'd make a big joke of it, keep rubbing it in until
nerves were raw. But as a favor to an old friend, Doc wouldn't
report it to the Board of Health. And that was why George
wasn't going to Columbus for treatment.

A woman clacked along the walk, and when she saw him, she pulled nervously aside and hurried past. George turned from the maple shelter, back to the clinic door. He felt so damned *grimy*, uncomfortable with the dampness in his shorts. Jesus—clean all his life, and turned fool at this late date. But he'd never thought of just average young girls, Coshocton girls, having a—being burned, carrying gonorrhea, dammit. Nobody thought that; clap was something whores had.

My God—the clap! He shuddered and dug nails into his palms. If he let it go, it might kill him. He wasn't sure if it worked like syphilis, but he couldn't chance it any longer. His belly knotted, and the seepage in his shorts seemed monstrous.

He might also have syphilis; his brain could be rotting away this very moment. How did you tell if you had it? Rash. A rash, that was it. And open sores—great, drippy lesions—oh, God. He'd kill himself first. Before bringing that horror home to Elizabeth, he'd kill himself.

George went inside, breath sighing out as he saw the empty waiting room. Doc's nurse wasn't at her desk, either. George felt a lot better as he opened the hall door. "Doc?"

"Back here. If you're not hurt, go home and see me tomorrow."

"It's George Parker, and I'm hurt so damned bad I may not get well."

Shirt open and tie askew, Doctor Shaw motioned George into one of his two treatment rooms. "Don't see any blood, George, and no sign of heart attack. What the hell's wrong with you? You have to take off your shirt and take up my time? I'm tired and hungry, George; if you've just got a bellyache, I'm goin' to see that you shit for a week."

George bit his lip. "I have gonorrhea."

"*You*? Lower your pants and skin 'er back. Be damned—old George Parker, pillar of the church, dippin his wick in an unholy hole."

Hands shaking, George lowered his pants and unbuttoned shorts. "It's not funny, Doc."

"Is to me. Puzzlin', too; what promiscuous lady'd stop to spread her spirochetes on old pudgy, churchgoin' George? You even *know* any promiscuous ladies? Gimme a phone number."

"Dammit, Doc! Look at this and tell me what to do."

Doc Shaw grunted. "Do? Put your pecker in your pants and

take it home. You got nothing more'n a strain. Comes from overuse of a rusty instrument."

"A *strain*? You—you mean I don't have the clap?"

"All you have is a leaky glans; your testicles got so surprised they left the valves on. That's it, you lucky old fart."

"N-no clap? But Doc, shouldn't you run a test for—for syphilis?"

"Scared shit outa' you, didn't it? I'll run a Wassermann if you want; make a buck that way. Who's the gal, George? Somebody I oughta stay away from?"

"None of your damned business, you buzzard. She—well, I won't be seeing her again. Not like that." He felt like shouting. No clap, and since that showed she wasn't dirty, then almost certainly nothing else.

"Sit down and gimme your arm. I'll get this damned tube around it and—clench your fist. That's it."

"*Ow!*"

"Never get smartass with your doctor. Didn't figure gettin' another poke out'a this dull needle until you did. Hell, I know who she is; that ass-switchin' kid works in your store—one of the Melborne litter."

"I—she—oh, hell, Doc. I never thought."

"I got this theory," Doc Shaw said. "You hear all about menopause and how it shakes up a woman, makes her feel worthless because she can't reproduce. I figure a man goes through somethin' like menopause, only he can't check his sanitary napkin. Gets worried about usin' his hammer; can he get it up for another woman if he don't with his wife? Feels fat and old and time slippin' away. Right—he don't *think*."

George pressed the cotton wad against his punctured vein. "Thanks, Doc. I feel a lot better. When'll you know on my test?"

"Monday, but none of the Melbornes ever checked out positive, busy as they are. And I don't give a shit if you feel good. Be grateful you got off easy, that the girl don't come cryin' in here for an abortion. Don't know's I'd protect your ass that way. Go on home, and soon's your faucet stops drippin', make it up to Elizabeth. You had your big fling."

Pulling on his jacket, George walked slowly through the waiting room. Doc Shaw followed, turning off light by light. George walked lighter, almost bouncy, feeling good. Just for the hell of it, he might stop at Torrance's and buy Elizabeth a box of candy. Because I wanted to, he'd tell her; no other reason. Can't a man buy his wife a present if he feels like it?

He'd have to face up to Holly Melborne, even if it meant closing the store to get rid of her. He didn't know what he'd do, if she carried tales to Elizabeth. Take his medicine, he guessed; nothing else *to* do. Maybe he could deny everything. There was only her word against his, and he might make his wife believe Holly was getting back at him for firing her. He couldn't just say, All right, I lost my head and did it with the girl. That would be like slapping Elizabeth. Five children and the long, good years, and some cheap little hussy easily turned his head, somehow made none of it count?

Close the store and make Holly take some money—not a lot, because the store really wasn't doing that good. Threaten her with—what? Being a friend of the sheriff? Not if she remembered the trouble his son Ron had. How about testimony from other men that she took money for her favors, and could he get anybody to swear? Damn, he was feeling grimy again.

At the door, Doc Shaw said, "George?"

"Yeah?"

"From your limited experience, tell me—think this kid is worth the time of an expert like me?"

George stared at the closed door while Doc Shaw laughed his way back through the clinic.

chapter 28

Bicycles: sale, shipment, and delivery frozen pending rationing. *Electrical appliances*: civilian production ceased. *Flashlights and batteries*: use of iron and steel curtailed; aluminum, rubber, chromium, nickel, tin (except in solder), and brass and copper (except in electrical fittings) banned. *Metal household furniture*: iron and steel restricted and all other metals banned. *Plumbing fixtures*: critical material use curtailed. . . .

—*Business Week*, October 12, 1942

Joyce dutifully pulled blackout curtains. With air raid wardens as thick as smells in a cow barn, there was nothing to see anyhow, only taxis and official cars driving with "brownout" lights. In three days and nights, she'd seen damned little of Washington, D.C. Oh, the Monument and the White House —from the outside; all tours were canceled for the duration —and the Lincoln Memorial; stuff like that, but there'd been no night life.

She didn't count the party at Mr. Jackson's house; that was only canned music and heavy drinking and some sweaty wrestling that pretended to be dancing. Everybody was older, fatter, and the men kept rubbing against her; nobody seemed to have heard of jitterbug or the Big Apple or even the Lambeth Walk. She wasn't so sure they knew the waltz or fox trot, either.

"Who is he?" she'd asked Frankie. "A senator or something?"

"Something. He gets people in to see other people, or finds ways around stupid regulations and stupider shortages."

She tried to be bright. "Is there a cow shortage? How about horse, or maybe we could make boots out of old footballs?"

Handing her into the taxi, he said, "The Butera Corporation is more than GI boots. We got a good shot at picking up the Norden subcontracts, and some for making airplane starters."

Putting a finger to her lips, Joyce frowned at the driver's back. Franco Butera said, "Oh, hell. If anybody wants to play spy, Coshocton's just as good as Washington."

The hackie glanced over his shoulder. "Damn right, lady. What the hell is a Coshocton?"

"But we don't have a plant ready to turn out anything so vital," she said, as they waited before an imposing door in colonial Georgetown. "The bombsight—don't we need that in a hurry?"

"The country needs everything in a hurry, and I'm in a bigger hurry to get it produced." Frankie passed his hat and coat to the butler, not waiting for Joyce. "Mr. Butera and Miss Parker."

Not Mrs. Butera, but not Mrs. Dayton, either; she supposed she should be grateful for that.

"Yes, sir," the man said, and took Joyce's fox fur wrap before quietly announcing their arrival into an eddying, smoke-swirling crowd that turned none of its faces their way.

"Don't bother your head about business," Frankie said. "Stand around, look pretty, and smile a lot."

He hadn't cared that red faced, jowly men pawed and propositioned her, that she had to grind her spike heel into one jerk's instep before he realized she meant *no*. Twice, after the party got loud-drunk and spilled over into hallways and bedrooms, she reached Frankie's side and wanted to go home. Shooing her off, he paid more attention to a crepe necked woman in a girdle and orange hair. She lost him for a while after that, and when she finally got him to the taxi, Frankie was drunker than seven hundred dollars.

Joe Dayton's expression: drunker than seven hundred dollars. After she put Frankie to bed, she lay looking up at the ceiling and thought about her husband. She could do that now, lie beside another man and think about Joe. His V-Mail notes came sporadically: It was okay where he was and say hi to the gang. Nothing personal, but no reason to expect it. He enjoyed being with a team again, she could tell. He might even turn into a star player, once more the hero.

How would she feel if Joe was killed on some weird little island nobody ever heard of? Depressed, certainly; she didn't imagine any woman could share herself with a man for years and not feel blue over his death. But she wouldn't truly mourn, and wondered how many other women felt exactly the same. Even women who cared more for their men, if the war lasted a long time, would find the images fading as years passed, as they found other men. A lot of servicemen would come home to missing wives.

"And maybe," she whispered to the hotel ceiling before dizzying into sleep, "your conscience is nagging, and you're trying to cover up."

A hangover didn't sit well upon Frankie next day. He fussed over papers and got on the phone several times; he drank black coffee with a splash of brandy and didn't say much to Joyce.

Keeping the radio low, she listened to "One Man's Family," not really interested in those familiar problems. When the "Gangbusters" siren shrilled up into tommygunning, she turned off the floor model Sparton. It was a big, classy model with the new green light eye that showed if you were right on the station.

Frankie said, "Jesus, these bastards are getting greedy as old country *paisans*, but I'll play their game. When the fireworks are over, they'll be out and I'll still be in."

She went to the little corner bar. It made her feel very rich, a private bar in the hotel suite, and she wondered how many exotic people had rested elbows on its polished wooden top. A turbaned emir, she thought, who tossed black pearls around as signs of his favor; maybe a romantic and mustachioed Spanish nobleman who'd escaped Franco to languish in exile here. Who else? Presidents and kings and mice who looked at queens.

"Did that woman corner you last night?" she asked.

He looked up from the briefcases he was rummaging. "What woman?"

"Miss Turkeyneck of 1929. Does she have to hide that flaming orange hair from blackout wardens?"

"Oh—Tippi."

"Tippi? What the hell kind of cute name is that?"

"Bring the brandy over here. I was nice to Tippi so she stays on my side with Mark. That's her husband, Mr. Jackson, the guy who gets people in to see important people. Remember Jackson, the guy I came to Washington to do business with?"

She put the brandy at his elbow on the room desk. "Okay, okay. I—oh hell, Frankie, those jerks feeling me up and all—"

"You're all grown up. You can handle yourself."

Back at the bar, she made a too-early, defiant highball. "You wouldn't care if one dragged me into a bedroom?"

Frankie made a face. "Damned coffee's cold. Get another pot from room service."

"Dammit," Joyce said, "would you care?"

Black eyes stabbed up at her. "*Basta!* Enough, woman. You expect me to punch some D.C. bigshot to protect your virtue? Like I said, baby, you're a big girl."

She flared at him: "Old enough to catch the train back by myself!"

"If you want," he said, and the suite turned silent around her, strange with its private bar and green eye radio.

"Frankie," she husked. "Oh, Frankie—don't be angry with me. I guess I'm jealous of everybody and everything that steals your time from me. It's so confusing, one change rolled over by another and another, and I'm helpless to stop any moment in place."

He said, "Change—everybody claims to want it and everybody's scared shitless of it. You think Coshocton'll be anything like before the war? You think it all goes back to Protestant football and Torrance's sodas? Will *you* be the same, your husband dead or alive? And the broads in my factory, the other plants—they go back to diapers and mixing color into margarine and yes-siring their old man because what the hell can they do if he leaves them? Not after making money the first time in their lives, not after they got the chance to look around and find their old man's not so much, anyhow. The young get first lick at the cream on top of the bottle, a big

swallow of free, fat, and sassy; good money and good
screwing and doing something *important*, jobs most of the
world needs done. Change? Damned right, and only old
bastards and gutless broads don't see it and want it."

Going to him, she stroked his hair and leaned down her
breasts to his head. He liked her doing that. She said, "I'm not
gutless, Frankie; I'm not old. And I love you."

"Yeah," he said. "How about that coffee?

Louise Parker was trembly inside, because the way Danny
talked, the way he kept whispering those awful, exciting things
in her ear, he might be a little crazy. But she just *had* to find
out, and if she was real careful, nobody'd ever know.

He was far from home and on his way overseas to fight, and
so good looking. Right there in the bus station, she'd told him
he ought to be a movie star when the war was over, he was so
handsome.

"Handsome Danny Orr," he smiled, all tanned face and
gorgeous teeth. "I'll give Robert Taylor a run for his job
—maybe Richard Greene."

"You could," she said, meaning it. He had the same wavy
black hair and sparkling eyes, even that cute dimple. But that
wasn't what got him a ticket to her apartment; it was something
else, something downright shocking.

That's what Mom would call the things Danny said: *shocking!* Then she'd call the police. Guys got locked up for talking
like that to women, and Louise might have screamed or
slapped him or something, only she was too stunned.

He didn't seem a bit nervous, standing in her neat apartment
like he belonged there. "Nice," Danny said, "real, real nice.
Your husband must be 4-F with a great job."

Wishing she had something besides a bottle of red wine,
Louise said, "I pay my own way, and—and I don't have a
husband." She didn't exactly know why she lied, only that she
didn't want to scare him off, and she was so damned tired of
sitting home or going to Mom's for dinner.

He was so handsome, and the things he said—

"I only got wine," she said, and he said that was fine, he
liked it. Louise watched him take off his blouse with the single
stripe and shooting medal on it, and it was kind of natural for a
man to be standing in her living room, the first there.

She turned on the radio, and about then he came up behind her and put his arms around her. "All you did was blink when I said I wanted to go down on you."

"Jeepers! I nearly fell off my chair, and I nearly slapped you, and—do guys really do that? My—boyfriend said it was okay for a girl to do it to a guy, but the other way around is dirty."

He was hard against her butt, and his hands cupped her breasts from behind, his warm breath tickly down her neck. He said, "He's crazy. I love doing it."

Turning her, Danny kissed her gently, easy, sweetsoft tongue caressing instead of demanding, and his knowing hands roamed her. Louise trembled a little, kind of cold-hot, and it was sort of like the first time with Deke, in that tacky tourist cabin. Only now she knew it was a bunch of bullshit and wasn't scared. What she promised to do was probably more of the same, but she wanted to know, had to know.

The little pink night light plugged down beside her bed was enough, and romantic. Louise came from the bathroom with the gadget placed and saw him stretched bare ass on top of the covers, not a bit embarrassed. He was pretty all over, his thing shaped as right as the rest of him, rising from a nest of tightly curled hair. She wondered if Robert Taylor's cock hair was so black.

He made her claw the sheets and hammer the mattress with her heels. Danny was good and in no hurry; she wiggled and gasped and went through the motions expected of her, but she was getting excited at the way he teased. Over one boob and down her ribs, mouth trailing wet fire; down, down to her flexing belly, so his breath blew into her pubic hair. Then back up, seesawing her body, licking and nipping and fondling.

When he plunged his face between her thighs and his mouth ate her up, Louise thought she'd gone crazy. She clamped him in her legs and pulled his hair and called him every sweet-dirty name she knew, and some she made up. God, he was beautiful. The world was beautiful, crazy, lovely—

"*Ahhh!*" she cried, and cresting, "*ahhh!*" again, and for some bullshit reason she was crying and couldn't stop. When he slid up and over her, when he entered her, she drifted in another place, a land all warm moonlight and softness, tendrils of honeyed fire sparkling softly along her veins. The air was perfumed and she tasted the man sweat of him against her lips as he went off. Dimly, she knew he wasn't wearing a rubber, because she felt the geysering.

Two days later, she married Daniel Orr in a little jerkwater town on the outskirts of Louisville, Kentucky. The justice of the peace was sweaty and boozy and stared at her crotch while he rubbed the twenty bucks Danny gave him. She was still dazed when Danny sold his army railroad and meal tickets in St. Louis, but still certain of what she wanted, and that was Danny himself.

He drove the big Packard more carefully than Roger had, and she had a hard time keeping her hands off him. She wanted to do anything for him, everything: comb his hair, brush his uniform, whatever gave her an excuse to touch him. Danny had changed the world for her, so how could she help loving him? He made her come.

Roger—she sat back against the seat and let the whole Roger thing come back into her head. Okay, so it wasn't exactly his car, but his daddy's. She wasn't *stealing* it, because Mr. Barton had given her a key and said she could drive it anytime she wanted. Its big C sticker would get them gas clear to California. As for being married to Roger—well, she couldn't let that matter. She was really, truly in love for the first time. She just wouldn't say anything about Roger until he came back from overseas and she'd tell him she wanted a divorce.

She could kind of sit on everything and not let Danny know, or anybody else, until it was all straightened out. The car's back seat and trunk were stuffed with her things and Danny's army bag; she had her savings and the money from Roger's allotment checks in her purse, and she'd left a note for the Bartons, and called her mom for tears and yelling.

Coshocton and kid stuff were behind her, and Hollywood lay ahead. If Mr. Barton didn't do something stupid like calling the cops about his car and getting them stopped on the road, Louise Orr would soon be in golden California. Out there, people lay around in bathing suits and ate oranges right off the trees, and movie studios waited.

"I might catch hell for driving instead of catching that train," Danny said. "Might confuse 'em if I get there before I'm supposed to, and with this big old car—hell, I might not even lose my stripe. Don't care if I do."

Stroking his thigh, Louise leaned her head on his shoulder.

"It doesn't matter. I'll get a job in a defense plant out there; I'm real experienced. We'll make out just fine."

He blew down her blouse neck, making her shiver. "We surprised everybody, didn't we? I wish I could've met your folks, but like you said, we only had time for ourselves. My mother's too far away, in Massachusetts, and—I just wish it could've been a real wedding for you, white dress, orange blossoms, and everything."

Snuggled to Danny, feeling the vibration of his deep voice through his chest and khaki shirt, she listened drowsily to him as he told of his mill town on the Merrimack, of blazing fall colors and springtime apple blossoms. He didn't like the mill, but it paid okay; someday he'd have a little garage of his own. He was good with motors, Danny said, good with tools and his hands.

Louise thought briefly of Joe Dayton, of how miserable her sister Joyce was in her marriage. *Had been*, she corrected; Joyce was having a high old time with a gorgeous boyfriend while Joe was in the Pacific. Danny's garage would be different because Danny was. Man, she'd never leave Danny for another guy, even if he stayed overseas for years. He was too special and all she wanted was to make him happy.

And come again and again and again. Every time, it was as if she halfway expected it not to happen. Now that she knew how it was, being cheated would about kill her. No more great, golden light . . . thunderflash of sharp joy and pain mixed . . . the lifting out of herself . . .

She tried to make it happen when he just screwed her, but it was like being with Deke or Roger, just getting to the edge maybe, then the gray drop into disappointment. But Louise never let her new husband know; she was damned good at pretending, and it made him feel good. She hoped it was as wild and terrific for him, and knew a twinge of guilt if it wasn't. How *could* it be as good for Danny, or any man?

All her life she'd dreamed of traveling, and found a little lift of excitement whenever they crossed the border of a new state. Louise didn't know exactly what she expected—different trees or grass, or people who looked different on shiny postcards —but there was never such change. Kansas was boring, flat, and ugly, and the Colorado mountains kind of spooky, Utah worse, and it was getting chilly.

They had fun in Reno—she could have stayed a fevered forever in the thrill of silver cartwheels on green felt and money machines, but they lost twenty-two dollars as it was, and Danny worried about making it to San Francisco on time. If Mr. Barton had notified the cops about his Packard, they hadn't caught up. Anyhow, she meant to give it back to him when she drove home for the divorce. He probably hadn't even told his wife, and dear, bitchy mother-in-law would be ecstatic over Louise running off.

Ecstatic—that was a good word she'd learned from Danny. He might be a mill worker, but he was no dummy and he read a lot. When he drove them through Sacramento before stopping for hamburgers and malts to go, Louise thought about not going to college, as Roger and his dad wanted her to. It would have been okay, but it meant finishing Coshocton High first, and she'd have felt kind of dumb there, a married woman and all. Probably old man Halburton wouldn't have let her come back anyhow; he was a mean old principal who'd give extra periods if he caught you jitterbugging during lunch hour.

All behind her, she thought. She was in California and a new, wonderful life. It was going to be just great.

chapter 29

More than 100 Luftwaffe planes took part in a raid
on the capital last night, dropping an estimated 450
tons of bombs. This total is considerably down
from most nights during the "blitz" and the Battle
of Britain. Nazi propaganda broadcasts monitored
here claimed that 97 Spitfires were shot down. . .

—London, October 26, 1942 (AP)

She felt more a part of him, waiting just beyond the gate in her
pickup, one of several women waiting for their men. Now they
waited for them to come down out of the sky, or just from
barracks; before long, most would be marking time not on
watches, but on calendars, and David and his heroes would be
far away. Some would never return.

Not David—please, God, not David. He had done so much
already, and she needed him to look forward to. Oriana turned
the ignition key so she could use the dashboard lighter, and
nursed a cigarette. How much of her determination for defense
work had to do with avenging her husband's death, and now,
how much with David's safety? If she helped hurry out more
planes welded and riveted strongly, perfectly, maybe other
men would use them to end the war before he got back to it.

Part of it had been getting away from Coshocton and her father-in-law, part a blind running from shock piled upon pain. And after learning her job, after weeks and months of gritty, sweaty work behind her torch, Oriana felt what other plant workers did: a stubborn, angry determination to get it done faster and better, to produce more and more. It was only right they put in twelve to sixteen hour days; America's fighting men had no coffee breaks or holidays, and didn't draw overtime pay. They were laying their lives on the line for every American's right to freedom; every American should in turn stay on the production line.

Two men laughed through the gate, casually returning the guard's salute. One was David, so Oriana sat up and stubbed out her cigarette, heart quickening as she patted her hair. She could pick David from any crowd, day or night. He carried a glow that homed in upon her, so that she warmed her hands at it and hugged it to her soul.

At the window he said, "Hi, this is my wingman, Ace Burrows."

Dark and slim, the man gave Oriana his hand. "It's Asa, but I get called worse."

She laughed. "I'll bet. What's a wingman do, Ace?"

David said, "Keep bogies off my Asa."

"Unkind," Burrows said. "Pip-pip, Major—Oriana."

" 'Pip-pip? I can understand," she said as David climbed into the cab, "but 'major'?"

"Celebration due." He kissed her mouth. "In the RAF, I'd get to wear two pips and a crown; here, just an oak leaf."

She moved the truck out on the highway, heading for a glow beginning to lighten a darkening sky, aimed for the crowded hotel where so many desperate good-byes were said. "A promotion, a wingman. You're going back. Damn you, David Shepsel, you're going back."

He touched her arm. "We've gone through this, Oriana."

"That doesn't make it more palatable. When?"

Warm upon her forearm, his hand caressed her. "Soon. I can't say any more."

"Sure. I might be a German spy."

He was quiet and his hand stopped moving to drift down and rest upon her thigh. She wanted to close her eyes and know his hands, their nails and knuckles, skin and pores, each fine hair.

"I'm commanding a flight; the whole wing is going together. That's better than as replacements. We're used to each other —friends."

Oriana compressed her lips and peered through the windshield, her foot heavier upon the accelerator. "The situation is nasty in Europe," she muttered. "You might even say desperate. Half trained kids shipping out."

"There wasn't much time, but they're pretty good."

She swung the truck around a dawdling car. "Nazi pilots are damned good, right? *Damned* good."

"Darling—"

"So tonight we celebrate. Christ—I never thought I'd be living *Wings*. Did you see that old movie? Of course you did; you're a flyer. Champagne glasses hurled into the fireplace; 'Here's to the next man to die.' My God."

He took away his hand to light cigarettes for them both. Angrily, she drew and spat smoke as he said, "It's not like that anymore. It's not a game, no longer a—a joust. People get blown apart and burned and drowned and there's no chivalry to it. My guys want to give me a promotion party; they like and respect me that much, and it's one remaining tradition. We can leave early."

Pulling the Ford into the hotel parking lot, she shut it off and pulled the key. "I'm a pain in the ass because I love you."

"I know."

"Oh, damn, how soon is 'soon'? You can't fly those little fighters all the way to Europe."

David turned on the seat. "Unplug your spy radio and I'll tell you we hopscotch east, gassing up at airfields along the way. Our planes get left at the port for shipment while we pack into a B-17. Good thing we're not a bomber wing; it'd take a fleet to get that overseas."

It was dark and she could barely see his face. "Off to war in a Flying Fortress," she said. "Maybe one of *my* Boeings from Willow Run. Somehow I feel guilty about that. I should have stuck with my first idea and made tanks."

"Instead, you made us. Wait, now! Us made us; better?"

She leaned to kiss him, not daring to linger. "Much. Okay, we wet down the new major's oak leaves. Isn't that what they say, wet 'em down?"

"Water 'em," David agreed and reached for her, but she slid

from the cab. He got out on the other side. "Water the gold leaves properly, they turn silver: Lieutenant Colonel Shepsel; how about that?"

She walked around the truck, joining him but not touching him as they passed into the hotel entrance. She couldn't handle that just now, and certainly not up in the room. She said, "I can't understand ranks. I mean, why does silver outrank gold? Second Lieutenant gold bar, first lieutenant silver; and the oak leaves—and why does a major outrank a lieutenant, but a lieutenant general is higher than a major general?"

David was a step ahead as they climbed the stairs. Two couples bounced down, laughing past, and Oriana resented the enlisted men and their wives. This was a fighter pilot training base, and these men were probably permanent cadre; they wouldn't be going overseas now.

Unlocking their room, David said, "No rule says the army has to make sense. Armies never do, I suppose."

Quickly she went to the bath. "I'll get ready first." Peeling out of her clothes, she heard him turn on the radio, heard Harry James's clear, mournful horn, Helen Forrest's sultry, polished tones: *"I don't want to walk without you, baby . . . walk without my arms about you, baby . . ."*

Men and their lousy wars.

Randy Parker turned over on the lower bunk. It was damp and chill, the very walls of Tidworth Barracks impregnated with ancient cold, ancient fear. He'd have felt better about the coming move if he could have found Ron, but that outfit was gone. To Scotland, said the whispers, and sure as hell, off from there to the Second Front. But nobody knew for sure; just latrine rumors.

Mail from home was all screwed up too, so Randy didn't know what was going on anywhere. The only thing coming through on time—and that must be accidental—was pay. It was in English funny money: pounds and ten-shilling notes and silver shillings, florins, tenpence, thrupenny bits, pence—confusing if you tried to keep it balanced with how much each coin was worth in "real money." The crap and poker games got big, because everybody looked at the pound note—worth four dollars and twenty cents—as a buck. Hell, it had "one" on it, didn't it?

The little towns on each side of the huge barracks area were jam-packed, and you were lucky to get a drink at overflowing bars. There'd been British servicewomen here, rumor said, but they'd been shipped in a hurry. Good thing, Randy thought; the ATS girls would have been overrun, too.

Women—guys went on pass to London and came back rattling on about women; free lays or whores, the limey girls were great. Randy didn't know; he still had the bad taste of Martha in his mouth, the acid sweat of her deep under his skin, where scrubbing couldn't reach. She made sex something brutal and grimy, made it guilty.

"Sundays are hell, aren't they?" The guy sat on the edge of Randy's bunk, offering a Phillip Morris. "Everybody's off to somewhere, getting drunk and screwing girls and fighting. We had three guys brought in by the MPs last weekend."

Randy took the cigarette, accepted a light. "Our platoon had four; one is up for court-martial. He punched a limey officer."

"Oh, gee," Mac said; Mac-something, who'd joined the outfit just as it shipped out. "That's too bad. But then, maybe he'll miss the invasion and live through the war."

Sitting up, Randy blew unfamiliar smoke. "He might do ten years in prison."

Mac tilted his head and drew on his cigarette; he was a slim and fine boned man a year or so older than Randy. "Still—but why aren't *you* in town? If you haven't seen Salisbury Cathedral—"

"After that, what? I saw Big Ben and Buckingham Palace—"

"Piccadilly Circus whores?"

Randy coughed. "I passed. Too much like drinking whiskey from a glass a dozen GIs used just a minute before."

Mac's eyes glistened. "Yes—oh, exactly. I knew it; I just *knew* you were my kind of person. I mean—sensitive and intelligent. Look, if you're tired of being lonesome and blue, I know this little place—"

"Where everybody drinks from the same glass, if they can get it refilled."

"No, no, nothing like that. It's a private club, in Andover, but GIs don't know about it. There's good food—just duck or fish, but well prepared—and some good wines put by before the bombings—"

Randy took another drag. "No drunk GIs crawling all over? Real food and wine?"

"And a piano in tune. Do you play?"

Randy shook his head. "But I'd enjoy hearing any *other* kind of music. Who'd think you could miss a radio so much?"

Mac bounced up. "Exactly; oh, exactly! Come on, Parker —it is Parker, isn't it? I'm *still* not used to calling everybody by their last names. It's so cold and—and institutionalized. I suppose it was inevitable that everyone in the army would tag me Mac, but I'm Lester—Les—Macready."

"Randy Parker, U.S. 1355—practicing in case I'm captured. Yes, sir, Herr; name, rank, and serial number only, Sir Herr. But if you'd *really* like to know the military secrets of my unit, and please put down that bayonet, there's a super bedpan that works like this—"

Randy suddenly felt elated anticipating. There was the whole day and night, and he had plenty of money. Jesus, to be semi-private for a change, to eat and get quietly soused like a human being, hear something besides hillbilly music. He could sink his worries about Ron, and waterlog that last sticky, scarlet image of Martha for awhile. He pulled on his overcoat, set his cunt cap at an jaunty angle. "Let's go, Les."

The guy hadn't been kidding. A short ride in the near empty bus and they were in Andover, walking the quaint, narrow streets to a door and skinny window in the corner of a low office building. The polished brass plate said *The Bounders.* Up the block, GIs and Tommies boiled out of a pub, yelling and clubbing each other.

"Oh, Lord," Macready breathed. "Inside, quick." He used a key and urged Randy through the oaken doorway into a dimly lighted hall. Beyond waited a big sitting room, its windows properly curtained for blackout, a baby grand in one corner, a coal fire winking cheery welcome from its grate. Two men sat reading in wingback easy chairs of cared for leather; another leaned at a small bar, talking to the barman; there was a rack of magazines and newspapers, and the floor was deep pile carpeted. Through an alcove, Randy could see a small dining room.

"Damn," Randy said in awe, "it's beautiful. It's quiet and warm and the only word is beautiful."

"I knew you'd appreciate it," Macready said. "This club has kept me sane. I—I don't know what I'll do when we ship out."

Randy headed for the bar. "You'll make out. Somehow, we always do."

"I suppose. Oh, Jacob—this is my friend Randy. And do meet Nickie, who does marvelous things with alcohol. What would you like, Randy?"

"Beats me. I'm still in shock. I'll have whatever you drink."

"Singapore Slings, then. They're sinfully sweet, but I like them."

Jacob was a meaty, jowled man with thin hair; his business suit looked rumpled. He said, "I hoped you'd come today, Les. Would you do something from Brahms or Chopin?"

"Feeling soft and sentimental, Jake? If you'll excuse me a minute, Randy?"

Macready could play. Randy didn't know longhair music, but he knew that what was happening at the keyboard was excellent: soaring, wheeling notes sliding one into another, ringing suddenly clear and individual—tripping, beckoning—a call denied, a sublime loneliness, honeyed and low, murmuring off into dim and dimmer echoes.

Jacob's eyes were wet. He said, "That bitch can really, really play. My God, that he should be a private soldier. If he should be killed, if he should ever have a hand injured—"

"Bitch" evidently meant "son of a bitch," Randy thought; limey slang was confusing. Like "knock you up tomorrow" meant only "see you then." He was surprised to see the bottom of his glass, surprised that the pink stuff went down so smoothly. When he put it down, Nickie the barman refilled it.

Macready was playing something else, beginning quietly along a garden path where trees sang whispers and the wind was counterpoint. Excitement rose note by note, interwoven with pleading, and from a forest-deep lair, something hungered. It was not a hunger to be fed potatoes and beans, but a darkling ache of the flesh, a need of the blood. *For* blood?

The music crashed denial, thundered no, damn you all, *no*! And it changed, planing gently down a scale like an old, curved stairway whose railings were polished by generations of caring hands. And at the bottom, ever so softly at the base, came the pleading again. This time it was muted and filled with unshed tears.

Beside Randy, Jacob said through his teeth, "May your arse blister in hell, you bloody whore!"

Nickie pushed another full glass at Randy. "Now, laddie—"

But Jacob was already across the room at a shambling run. The door slammed as the music stopped. When Macready came over, Randy said, "What the hell was that?"

"My own variation on an old theme. Did you like it?"

Randy drank. "If I was alone in the barracks, I'd have sat and cried. Why did it make Jacob so mad?"

"Did it? Oh, I see he's gone. Music affects people differently—doesn't it, Nickie?"

"Music is as it does, says I."

"Nickie is a realist. Are you hungry, Randy? It seems a shame to take the edge off these Slings, but—"

Stringy duck was softened by an exotic sauce, and the yams were good, peas creamed. Do the English call English peas American peas? Randy wasn't sure he asked that, but he knew the wine kept coming, cool and sharp or cool and mellow; and brandied fruit; and just brandy in a big goblet like Robert Taylor swirled in the movies. Randy didn't try it, because his lips were numb and his hands kind of clumsy.

He didn't remember how they got to the room, either. But there they were, and the bed was fluffy. He could sink into it so far the damned army would never find him again, never make him sleep on straw matresses or the cold, cold ground. Massa's in de cold, cold ground and so is your GI ass, soldier. And if you don't like it, you can bitch to Jesus because the chaplain's on furlough; or save time and blow it out your stacking swivel.

"W-what?" he said, and Macready—Les—said, "Never mind, never mind."

Randy wasn't all *that* drunk. The room kind of swayed and his tongue was thick, his ears ringing like telephones in an empty room, but he wasn't all *that* damned drunk. When Les Macready slid naked in beside him, Randy knew what was going on, or had an idea at least. And past that first jolt, he didn't want to stop it.

The bed was soft and the bed was dark. Far off, the piano was making music—not the way it had called and cried for Les Macready, but music nonetheless. That was as it should be.

chapter 30

It goes down in the books as the Battle of the Santa Cruz Islands, a fight once again dominated by air action on both sides. The Japanese fleet aircraft carrier *Shokaku* was badly damaged and limped from the scene under cover of smoke; the light carrier *Zuiho* also took bombs but managed to escape. American pilots and antiaircraft gunners claim 70 Zeroes shot down. . . .

—Somewhere in the South Pacific, October 26, 1942 (UP)

Elizabeth knotted her hands, wanting ever so much to strike him. She shuddered in a deep breath and fought against her eyes misting over. For an agonizing moment, she wanted to hit him as hard as she could, and keep hitting him until he broke into sorry little pieces.

Surprisingly, her voice was controlled. "Not once since we were married, not once since I first saw you, have I ever called you a real name, George Parker. Plenty of times I have been mad enough, but words thrown in anger can never be called back, or their hurt forgotten. But now—now I call you a son of a bitch—a son of a bitch! And I don't want to take it back."

"Elizabeth, I—"

"And a dirty *bastard*, and a—a—" She couldn't think of anything else and wished she had more words to beat him with.

He held out both hands. "You're yelling. Scooter's home, and Ron—"

"Did you think of them when you got involved with that cheap little slut? Did you consider your family at all? My God, I thought I knew you. *Let* them hear; let them know what kind of man you are."

He dropped his hands and she watched him go to the sideboard where he kept the whiskey. The bottle rattled against glass and he spilled some on her carpet. All the years she'd put up with that thing, handed down by his mother. No stain could hurt that old rag, but whiskey would give him indigestion and she was glad.

George said, "I tried to do something about it, dammit; I tried. But if I'd paid her what she wanted, if she just went on blackmailing me forever—"

Elizabeth again heard the whorish voice in her ears, the sneering, cutting words. Her husband and one of those raggedy Melbornes—George Parker doing it to a girl younger than most of his daughters. Oh, God, the shock and sickness of it, the pain centering deep in her stomach.

"Your reputation," she said. "Your position with the church. *Your* damned image around town."

"Only in part. I worried more about you, Elizabeth."

"I see." Marching to the sideboard, careful not to brush him, she took a defiant drink right from the neck of the bottle, then battled to hold back a cough. "When you tired of your conquest, you worried about me. Did you think of—of *disease*? Those scruffy Melbornes, that promiscuous girl—"

He turned his head, and she exulted that he couldn't look her in the eye. Oh, how she wanted to hurt him back. He said, "I checked in with Doc Shaw."

"Do *I* have to face Francis Shaw too? Let him examine my —examine me for a loathsome infection that'll rot my brain? And Scooter—she kisses your cheek—"

"You don't get it like that." After another drink he made a face and returned the bottle, pushing it closer to Elizabeth. He wanted her drunk, she thought, wanted her maudlin and crying so she'd forgive him. No chance. "You're not infected, Elizabeth. Even if I was, *you* couldn't be. It's been months."

"Don't you *dare* try and blame me, George Parker! I never refused you, never; I always did my duty."

"Duty," he said. "You never made it fun, Elizabeth."

"Fun? *Fun*?" She snatched off her glasses and wiped angrily at her eyes. "I'm a good woman and the mother of your children, not some strumpet, a disease-ridden hussy. I have been a good wife, a—"

"I don't know what I expected," he said, walking away from her to stand with hands behind his back and stare out the dining room window. "What the *hell* I expected. I wanted to tell you before she did. I felt dirty and guilty, and I didn't know what to do because she has me in a corner. The store isn't doing much and I don't feel right being out of the war effort and—dammit, I just didn't know what to do. Maybe I needed to purge myself so I could be me again, or because I thought you might somehow be able to help me, that you'd *want* to. The store —our security—the kids—she's so young and there might be something illegal; if the *Tribune* gets hold of this, and the church deacons—"

She said to his back, "You should have thought of all that before you lusted after—"

"Oh, for Christ's sake, Elizabeth!" He whirled upon her. "You sound like Bible school, and if I did everything I *should have* all my life, things would be a hell of a lot different now." Red-faced, he stamped toward her and she thought: *He wouldn't dare!*

But he only poured another drink, and she knew he'd be up half the night with a bellyache. When he blinked at her, she noticed how tired he looked. He said, "I never wanted to take over the goddamn store. I wanted to stay out on Grandpa's farm and work the land, but nobody asked what *I* wanted. Certainly not Pa; if *he* liked running a hardware store, bigod I should too. When he died, I kept on with it because Grandpa's land was gone and I *should have* kept the store going—for you and the kids and folks who needed credit and suppliers who gave me credit and because I should have. But dammit, I never *wanted* to!"

"Hush," she said. "They'll hear you. And stop drinking that stuff; you know what it does to your stomach and blood pressure."

George lifted a hand, but she moved back. He said, "I'm so goddamned sorry."

"I know. Go wash up and I'll start supper. Afterward, you can teach me how to drive."

His eyebrows shot up. "*Drive*? What the hell does driving have to do with—"

"And you'll have to teach me fast, because I have things to do. Don't worry; maybe you don't know it, but I'm a fast learner."

"Elizabeth, I don't know what—"

"After supper, George. Then we can decide what to do about the store. No—I've already decided that, and what to do about—her."

It was more fun finding an apartment with Danny, Louise thought, better than doing it alone with lots more money to spend. It wasn't exactly an apartment—more like a room with a kitchen crammed in one corner and a bathroom down the hall. If she hadn't saved so much from her salary at the plant —gee, so far away, the Coshocton tire factory—they couldn't afford it, anyhow. If things got really tough, she could always sell her diamond ring and the wedding band she kept hidden in Kotex boxes.

She went right to work as a file clerk in the Monterey Bank, and Mr. Patterson told her she'd soon move up to cashier. Because Danny's basic training was way behind him and he was already a PFC, he got off a lot. Not every night, the way she'd like, because he pulled guard or went out on pretend-combat maneuvers along Fort Ord's rolling and foggy sand dunes.

Making love stayed wonderful with him; he was so good at making her come, teasing and caressing and going down on her. Sometimes she'd get mad at everybody else, especially Deke and Roger, for wasting all that time for her. They were so dumb and selfish, thinking about themselves instead of her, cheating her out of coming. *Orgasms*, Danny said, and she rolled the word around inside her mouth like she rolled Danny's penis, smiling at everyone who passed her file cabinets. *Orgasm*—she wondered if they'd smile back if they knew what she was pretending.

Danny was so handsome her heart swelled each time she saw him come leaping up the stairs. She reveled in his tenderness, his thoughtful way of doing things, the time and care he took showing her how to really read. She was sorry about screwing off so much in school, and tried to make it up now, carrying a book with her to open on her lunch hour, to read on the bus that climbed Blueberry Hill and let her off only about six blocks from the rooming house.

Only one guy at work, a smartmouth 4-F not even ashamed that he wasn't in uniform, tried to fool around with her. He quit after she wound up and punched him low down in the belly, trying for his crotch. He laid off work that afternoon, suddenly real sick, and Louise almost laughed out loud when Mr. Patterson said yes, he looked kind of pale, all right.

Soldiers and the few coast guard guys around Monterey made passes at her and wolf whistled a lot, but that was okay, as long as she didn't take them up on it. Twice, Danny brought his sergeant home for supper, an older guy almost thirty. Sergeant Oscar Yancey had a cute way of talking, kind of like Scarlett O'Hara in that movie. He complimented her on her cooking, and bragged on Danny. She ate it up, because she did pretty good on the little gas stove after she looked up how to bake cornbread and some other Southern dishes. Louise was grateful to Mom for making her stay in the kitchen sometimes. It was good for Danny's sergeant to like him, Danny said, and sure enough, two months later he came home wearing two stripes: Corporal Daniel Orr, by golly.

"Gee," she said, "I wish Mom could see how all her kitchen instruction worked out. I used to *hate* it when she made me cook, but she said girls ought to learn early, so they could make good meals for their husbands."

He pulled her onto his lap. "Sounds like a great lady. I wish I could meet her before we—"

"Before we what?" she asked when he stopped. "*What*, Danny? You're not—the regiment ain't—isn't—shipping out?"

"Hey, baby." He stroked her hair. "I'm a soldier, remember; and there's a war on. The outfit'll go pretty soon, I think. Not tomorrow, but latrine rumors say a week or two. When we get put on alert, it'll be certain."

She gripped her arms hard. "On alert. You won't be able to come home."

"Nobody will; all passes and leaves canceled. Hey, baby —it's not *yet*, and besides, we've really been lucky so far. You finding a job and us getting this place and Sergeant Yancey giving me so much off time—"

She tried to chase away fear. "He likes you on account of —because—you're such a good soldier. I hope he'll t-take care of you over—overseas."

Danny cuddled her closer, being kind and understanding for her. God, how she loved him. He said, "I can take care of myself. Yancey's cadre; he won't go. Not this time, anyhow."

Pulling back, she dug in fingers and shook him. "You know more than you're telling me! Dammit, I feel it, *know* it. How can you go fight and the sergeant—"

"Now, now," he murmured, easing her into his arms in such a way so that when he stood up, she sort of fitted along the warm length of him. "Now, now," like a daddy soothing a kid when she skinned both knees, petting and stroking so the hurting world went away and it was warm, safe, and perfect here.

She didn't help him with her clothes when he lay her gently on their bed. Sometimes he liked to do every bit of it himself, and she could easily tell when. Eyes closed, breathing deep and slow, Louise gave herself up to his lovemaking. She only cried out once, when she was brought to orgasm with every tiny hair, every inch of pinkdamp skin singing.

Only afterward did she lie awake as he slept peacefully, and allow herself to think of Danny going overseas. In natural and scary order, other realities came marching. Old man Barton hadn't turned her in to the cops for taking the Packard, so that was one jump cleared; he'd probably written her off, at his wife's urging. But she shouldn't drive the car back.

Oh Lord, the old bat had no doubt dipped her pen in acid and written it all to Roger. She'd *love* telling her darling son that his trashy wife had stolen the car and run off, nobody knew where. I *did* tell you so, dear Roger . . . not our kind at all, and we're well rid of her, darling . . .

Maybe they were, but how did Louise explain to her own family? She clamped teeth onto her lower lip; she'd written Dad at the store, but she hadn't told him she was married again, only how she hoped he'd understand she *had* to get out of Coshocton. She'd just about come out and told him the Bartons were too much to be married into, and possibly he'd understand. Mom had been really hurt when she took off without a word, but how could you explain Danny to somebody like Mom, always so safe and sure in her own marriage?

Mom couldn't know what it was in sex, to balance always on the very edge and never take that dizzying plunge into selflessness. She couldn't imagine what it was like, having real love made to you. Louise chewed her lip again, uneasy even thinking about her mother and sex. It wasn't right, somehow.

Later, she told herself; everything would be worked out after. When Danny was shipped out—she reached to touch him —she could go home for a while, see about the divorce, maybe even work in a defense plant there until Danny came back. No, that would never work. She was her own woman now, and could do just fine by herself, thank you.

There wouldn't be any leftovers to speak of, but nothing was stopping her from keeping this room and remaining with the bank. Besides, when Danny returned, she'd be right here on the West Coast, waiting for him. If she knew when and where, she could meet the ship, so there wouldn't be one more unnecessary second separating them.

Damn, she missed him already and he wasn't even gone. Louise moved closer to him, snuggling in the cool night air, breathing the man smell of him, Danny's special scent, and feeling his hard, warm back, the satiny finish of his skin. He always felt so smooth and tingly, his chest hairless, with cute little nipples. Not much hair on his slender legs, either, but plenty around his thing. Beautiful, beautiful thing.

When he suddenly turned over and trapped her in his arms, Louise giggled in surprise. "You! I thought you were asleep."

"Awake is better, even though I was dreaming of you."

"Really? Really and truly? Not about Ginger Rogers?"

He kissed her. "Ginger's cute, but you're cuter. Besides, you're right here."

"Danny—ooh, stop it! Danny, how can you—we—oh, Danny—"

It was always so warm and natural, no nice and huggy. She never felt dirty with him, never had to bury her shame. In every way, Danny Orr was her husband, not Roger Barton. Certainly not the guy who broke her in, Deke Deacon. Everybody else seemed such kids, greedy and fumbling.

"Oh, Jesus," she breathed. "Oh, my God—Danny, Danny! I wonder—I wonder if you know how much I really love you, *love you!*"

His voice was muffled by her flesh, her heaving flesh, but she heard every word clearly: "Of course I do—just as much as I love you, darling."

Don't, she prayed, *oh, please don't take him away from me . . . I'll do anything you say . . . I'll be good and go back to church . . . even go home . . . just don't take him away from me.*

chapter 31

Racketeers bound and tortured a woman service-station operator today when she refused to buy counterfeit "C" gas ration coupons. When the hoodlums left, they burned all her legitimate coupons and robbed the cash register. . . .

—Newark, New Jersey, October 27, 1942 (INS)

Joyce Parker Dayton applied liquid makeup to the side of her throat and watched it dry in the mirror. Touching the spot, she winced. Franco was getting rougher, and it didn't seem like lovemaking anymore. She didn't want to think what it might be like.

Turning, she critically inspected her throat. It was slightly darker there, but no one would notice. She made a last minute check of the apartment, put on her new coat, took her newer purse, and left, clicking the door, stopping to rattle the knob. Christ, this wasn't Main Street and she didn't live in anybody's hardware store. When she climbed into the slightly used Desoto, she thought maybe she didn't really live anywhere. She slept here; sometimes they made love—no, sex—here; sometimes. The apartment on the edge of town, almost out in Tuscarawas County, wasn't home and never would be.

Gunning the car away, Joyce said to the cold outside wind,

"Home sure as *hell* isn't where you hang your hat, or bra; it's not where the heart is. Where can it be? Damned if I know."

Breakfast coffee taste lingered in her throat, even though she overlaid it with cigarette smoke, and coughed. Lately she seemed to be coughing a lot; maybe she'd switch from Spuds to something milder. She'd never liked menthol anyway, and only smoked the brand because Franco did.

A stoplight halted the car on Walnut, and she ran a gloved hand over its maroon and leather dashboard. It was beautiful and supposed to be hers, but he'd never given her the title and she suspected it was in his name. Did he ever let go of anything? Drawing hard on the cigarette, Joyce drove off on the green light.

Franco-Frankie—Mr. Butera, would loose her quickly enough. She didn't want to think so, but the fear was there. She was scared to resist him too much, to deny him anything he wanted for long. There'd been a certain finality in his tone when he wanted her to be nice to Matt Gruning, and when she looked into his eyes, what she saw there knotted icy panic into her stomach.

How could a man send the woman he loved—*said* he loved —to the bed of another man? Joyce tooled the DeSoto through light traffic, aiming for the Butera plant parking lot. How could she let Franco degrade her so? Where were her guts?

Gone, she admitted; she couldn't imagine a future without Franco Butera. Where would she go—back to that cruddy house, to her folks, her lawful wedded husband, where? Oh, she could find another job, but another man like Franco—there weren't any. Even turning mean around the edges, or at times ignoring her completely, he was still more romantic than anyone she knew. Maybe no more than Matt Gruning, but so much stronger.

Parking the car, she climbed out and looked up at the third floor corner office, then down at the empty space reserved for the sparkling new convertible Packard that Frankie had somehow gotten delivered. It wasn't there, so she sighed and walked into the building, hearing the growing rumble of machinery and smelling the always present odor of leather, feeling the leap of the factory.

After the first few minutes, it hadn't been all that difficult to be nice to Matt Gruning. So damned square he has corners on

his head, Franco said; damned fool's trying to do it all fair and
honest, trying to make sense out of a hundred screwed up
government regulations.

Then how can *I* reach him, she'd asked, and Frankie said,
How else? He couldn't keep his eyes off you all night; I mean,
his tongue was hanging out, baby.

You don't mean—? she asked, and he said, Why the hell
not? It's not like you'll *mean* it, baby. *Cara mia*, you can
really help me here. If he turns loose the stuff I need for the
synthetic tire company, and I get priority on some more
strategic materials—well, all I can say is nobody else in the
whole world can do this for me; *nobody*. It can make me a big
man, Joyce, bigger than anybody dreams—even you. Do it for
me, *cara mia*—for *us*.

Climbing the stairs because the elevator was up and she
wanted time to think, Joyce still couldn't quite figure how he
talked her into doing it. Maybe she'd known he'd just walk
away from her if she didn't—walk away forever. She couldn't
stand that.

So she seduced Matt Gruning in a Washington hotel that had
probably seen plenty of seductions. It wasn't hard, because
deep down she knew it was as Franco said: Matt was enthralled
by her.

He was tall and silvery, a quiet and dignified man who
carried himself erect. He had a wonderful shy smile and was in
his early forties. An old line Democrat, he'd been a Roose-
veltian from the first, and the administration had at last
rewarded him with a top spot on the Strategic Materials Board.
Matt Gruning worked hard at his job, and rarely went home to
upstate New York and his family. Part of that was dedication
to his job and country, part a wife he could no longer stand, but
children he adored.

"Joyce," he said when she stood before him in the negligee
bought especially for the moment. "Joyce—you are so beautiful you *hurt*."

Trembly, some of her feeling like a frightened new bride
and some like a new whore, she hurried him into bed, anxious
to get it over, still wondering how to ask him for something in
return, for her payoff. Didn't whores get their money first?

But Matt wouldn't hurry, although he was desperately
eager, and she thought he'd long been without affection,

without the warmth of a woman who cared. *She* didn't care, and she was a liar and thief for making him think so.

His hands were gentle and his kisses sweet, boyish. Despite herself, Joyce was aroused—just a little at first, just the betrayal of lifting nipples, the quickening of her breath, a laxness in her tensed body. And when she finally responded, Joyce told herself that it was only an act, that she was doing it for Franco, that it didn't *mean* anything, as he said.

She'd been a terrific actress, because she came twice with Matt the first time around, and twice more after she showed him how to go down on her. He'd never done that before, but he loved it. Maybe he loved her, too; he said so over and over —against her breasts, into the damp gasping of her mouth, into her surging mound.

"Good morning, Mrs. Dayton," Peggy said, and the greeting was echoed by Dotty, Kate, and the new kid. Joyce smiled and nodded into her own office, where fresh perked coffee perfumed the air. She glanced into Franco's private office; he hadn't come in yet. She knew that, but looked again anyway, and tidied his desk before helping herself to coffee.

Before she finished the first cup, the phone started ringing and didn't stop for almost an hour. All around her she felt the factory, its heartbeat of machinery, its breath of new leather and the musical rattle of combat boot buckles. The plant was alive, not only with the men and women who fed and catered to it, but with its own blood pulse. She could almost understand Franco's need for the place, and didn't want to recall the hurt in old man Butera's eyes when he lost it. But it really had never belonged to the old man; *his* shop was a hole in the wall, a dingy room divided by a counter Franco had to work behind. Franco had made *this* plant—*Franco*—just as he'd put together the other defense units: the tire factory, the ironworks, other places Joyce wasn't sure of, using one as security against another, and borrowing against government contracts, forthcoming or not.

But he shouldn't have hired the greasy little man with the movie camera. She'd already gotten what Franco wanted from Matt Gruning's office, priorities left and right for just about everything, because Matt couldn't deny her whatever she wanted. Franco didn't need that filthy damned film that showed it all, that dirtied every movement she'd made with Matt in that bed. It was like one of those obscene movies from Mexico, but much, much worse, because the greasy little man was a good cameraman. When Franco ran the film for her in another Washington hotel, Joyce ran to throw up.

She certainly was in no mood to make love to him afterward, but he didn't ask. It could almost have been called rape, and he didn't mind that she lay stiff and unresponding —that time. Whenever he got angry with her, Franco ran the damned film and made her watch. Pretty good, he'd say; you go after that guy's cock like you really mean it, the way you go after mine. Ol' Matt Gruning really ought to see this; it'd give him a *real* hard on.

You didn't have to take it, she said. And Franco said, Hell I didn't; I always keep an ace in the hole, baby, always. What if he gets tired of screwing you? It happens, right? Then I got this to make him sit up and take notice. You really enjoyed it, didn't you, baby?

Loved it, she yelled; I loved it, you son of a bitch! But he didn't care; Franco didn't care.

He swung through the office, curly hair gleaming, cheeks pink over olive from crisp October wind, teeth whiter than white. She wondered where he'd been since he left home—left the apartment while she was showering. "Hi, baby."

"Good morning. Here's the phone list. Mr. Jones was insistent, and there were two calls from some man who just wanted to know if you were in; I think it was the same man."

"No importante," he grinned. "Gruning didn't call, did he?"

She bit her lip and stared him into his own office. Glaring at her typewriter, she wasn't aware of other machines going quiet in the typing pool. When she looked up at a shadow, she flinched. Giuseppe Butera stood before her desk.

"My son," he said.

"Mr. Butera, I can't—I—the gate guards—how did you—?"

Two men were behind him—big, solid men with darkly shaven cheeks and flat eyes. They wore business suits and black ties, and hadn't removed wide brimmed hats. Joyce glanced over her shoulder at Franco's desk; he had his back turned, looking out the window while he talked on the phone.

"I see," Giuseppe Butera said, and when he started around her desk, she got up to stop him, to signal Franco, to buzz a guard, something.

One of the men put a big hand on her shoulder and pressed her back into her chair. Old man Butera didn't go into his son's office, but stood at the door and said, "Franco," then, louder: "Franco!"

Frankie spun, face going dark as he whipped to the door. "Damn it, I *told* you—"

Giuseppe Butera held up a callused hand. "One time only; you get out and give me back my factory?"

Franco lifted his own fist. "You crazy old fart—if you don't get the hell outa here, I'm going to forget you're a crazy old man and kick your ass! Get out, get out!"

Giuseppe Butera shuffled back and shook his head. "I'ma sorry; I'ma true sorry, but a son cannot say to his papa—go, I take your shoe shop from you. I'ma sorry."

When the old man moved back through the steno pool, Franco saw the others. One of them shut the outer door; the other snapped Joyce's phone line like dry spaghetti, and squeezed the communications box until it splintered in his massive hand.

"Jesus," Franco breathed, his cheeks paling. She watched him wet his lips with his tongue. He caught himself and straightened, shoulders back. "What're you guys, hired muscle? I'll double what the old man's giving you—triple it. And better yet, I'll forget you were ever here. That'll save your asses from the law, from the Feds, even. This is a national defense plant, and you don't know what the hell you're getting into with me."

"Hey," Gold Tooth said. "Hey now, *paisan*, you hear this *figlio putana*? This son of a bitch pushes out his own papa, then he says to us how we don't know from shit. You think we don't know, *paisan*?"

Franco took a quick step toward them, hands coming up. "Look, you—"

Joyce would have screamed, but the other man anticipated it and closed that giant hand around her neck. He looked down into her eyes and shook his head.

Gold Tooth hit Franco along the side of the head with something short and black. When Franco pawed out and tried to stagger back, the man followed, hitting Franco's arms, his ribs. Franco went to his knees and the big man kicked him in the belly, very hard. Franco fell over on one side and retched.

Holding Joyce's throat, one man said, "That's a good girl.
You can't help him nohow."

God, she thought, it must hurt to be dragged by your hair
like that. Franco's eyes were rolling, and there was yellow
stuff on his chin. He choked it out: "*M-mafiosi*—oh, God, how
could he—who does *he* know—money, you guys, money—I
swear I'll give you more than you've ever seen—Christ, the
Black Hand—Sicily—"

Gold Tooth hit him twice, very fast, holding his hair in one
hand as Franco's head rocked and blood flew. "Cocksucker,"
the man said. "Cocksucker that throws out his old man; only a
cute son of a bitch like you, he don't know nothin' about honor
and friendship, huh? Money, you know—only money."

Joyce winced when the man backhanded Franco and she
heard his nose break, when Franco tried to scream and it was
muffled by his blood. "Your old man, he gave the Don a hand
when he needed it, away back in Sicily. You understand
Sicily, you son of a bitch? There, guys got balls, and they
don't fuck over their papas. There, a man pays what he owes,
and the Don, he owed your papa. You're lucky; you're a real
lucky cocksucker. Your old man said don't break your arms
and legs this time. The Don, he goes along, *this time*. You fuck
around Giuseppe Butera again, the Don, he takes it personal,
you understand? You don't get lucky again, because he gives
the word to kill your ungrateful ass, *after* we break your arms
and legs and maybe make you swallow a couple handfuls of
broken glass."

He hit Franco again, and said sharply, "You got that?"

"Y-yes," Franco groaned, "Oh, my God, yes."

Gold Tooth let go his hair and Franco slid down the wall to
cup blood in one hand and stare dully at it. "Today," Gold
Tooth said. "You haul it outa here today. If we come back and
find you anywhere on the fuckin' grounds, you ain't gonna like
it. It you try anything—anything at all—to grab this plant
again, you sleep with the fishes. You understand?"

"I understand," Franco mumbled.

The other man freed Joyce's neck and put a sausage finger to
his lips. Wide-eyed, she only stared and rubbed her throat.
They went out and closed the door behind them, but it was long
minutes before their presence faded and Franco stirred against
the wall.

She went to him, kneeling to take him in her arms. He slapped her. "Get away from me, you bitch."

"Frankie—Franco—I—it doesn't matter, darling. You couldn't do anything, couldn't—oh, God, you're all over blood—couldn't even defend yourself when he hit you with that—that thing."

"Blackjack," he muttered, hand at his ruined mouth. "Goddamn *mafioso* with a blackjack. Oh, shit—oh, goddamn—the old man and some old-country Don. Who the hell could foresee that? He never said; the sneaky old bastard never said. The plant—oh, my god, my plant—he took it. I—I hurt, Joyce. I hurt like a son of a bitch, but don't—don't look at me. I don't want anybody—you—to see me like this. Don't *help* me, goddammit!"

She forced herself to look away, to fist her hands in her lap. "You—can they really make you give up the plant? The police—"

"You heard them, *stupido*!" She heard him pant in his struggle to climb the wall. "*Mafiosi*—I can't get over it. I think he broke a rib, and my nose—you're fuckin' right they can make me give it up. If I don't, they'll put me on the bottom of Lake Michigan."

The door rattled and Joyce flinched. He said, "Block that thing. Tell 'em—say anything you have to, but don't let anybody in."

"I won't," she promised. "Oh, I won't." And at the door, she made herself sound angry. "If Mr. Butera needs anything, *I'll* call you. Oh, Dotty—if you don't mind, we—I had an accident with the phone and intercom so if you'll contact someone in housekeeping—"

Leaning against the door, she shivered. There was a spray of blood along the wall where Franco had crawled up. Christ, in this day and time, men like those animals—feral and deadly, come to hurt, to kill, if necessary. They would have killed her, too; that giant holding her neck in his hand, his opaque eyes—

Hurrying into the back, she found Franco at the sink, bathing his poor face. Helplessly, Joyce put out her hands, then drew them back. He didn't want to be helped, to be touched. His pride was hurt because she'd seen that monster beat him. As if that mattered; as if anything counted except Franco's well being.

She said quietly, "The tire factory and ironworks—you'll make them bigger than this plant can ever, ever be. Your father —*nobody* can manage it the way you do. He—it will go broke, or somebody from the government—"

"*Basta!*" he said, wheeling his battered face to her, so that she gasped at his nose twisted to one side, the hanging tooth. "Enough, bitch! Clean out my desk, the safe. Get the safe first; you know the combination."

"N-now? What'll I tell everybody—the foreman, the girls, people in the shop—"

"Nothing, dammit! Tell 'em nothing. Just clean out this office while I'm on the phone. Didn't you *hear* that bastard? They mean it; they'll *kill* me if I'm not gone when they come back."

Joyce hesitated, her stomach queasy, her mind jumping this way and that. He was so *frightened*; she found it difficult to see Franco Butera as frightened. He'd always been so strong; he was strong now.

"Move!" he snarled, towel to his face as he brushed past her. "They didn't rip out my phone, so I can call—*move*, Joyce! Are you—will you desert me now?"

She took a long breath. "No, Frankie. I won't leave you now. I won't ever leave you."

chapter 32

In a massive attack, American soldiers swept
ashore in Morocco and Algeria at 1:00 A.M. this
morning, a combat landing that opened the Second
Front. French and Foreign Legion troops put up
spirited resistance in spots, acting under orders
from Vichy France. In other areas, fighting was
light, and American casualties minor. . . .

—Somewhere in North Africa, November 8, 1942 (AP)

Mostly, Randy was conscious of the cold. It was worse than
England's constant dampness, because there you could usually
find a warm spot. In these wet and windy mountains, no place
was friendly, and blankets had been soaked through days ago.

Huddled over an unheated can of meat and vegetable hash,
he spooned the congealed grease and shivered while chill water
dripped from his helmet. They hadn't shaved in a week, and
hadn't taken off shoes for longer than that. He held out the can
of rations to the man huddled beside him in a wide hole
laboriously chipped out of the mountainside. "Want the rest of
this?"

"Christ, no. Even the goddamn A-rabs quit eatin' this shit."

Morosely, Randy chewed his hard cereal cake, wetting one

rim enough so he could worry a bite loose and soak it more in his cheek. "Good you came over anyhow, Shriver."

"Thought you might have a fire, that's why. Ain't them krauts ever gonna move? Ever since we took this valley from the wops, we been expectin' krauts to come in. Screw 'em; let's you'n me pack up and go the hell home."

Randy chuckled. His medic buddy from G Company could always make things better. "Don't you wish we could?" He looked across the pass, high in Tunisia's mountains. "I'll never bitch about anything again, if I ever get home. If this damned war doesn't go on and on, forever."

Shriver had a cigarette going, cupped in one grimy hand so the glow couldn't be seen; he handed it to Randy, who took two deep, hidden drags and passed it back. "Know what you mean," Shriver said. "Man don't know when he has it good. When we come bustin' in on the landings, that oughta been it for us. We played hero once, goddammit; they oughta send in somebody else. Wasn't no hell of a lot of us left nohow, but I guess they mean to use up the survivors so we won't keep tellin' how they fucked it up."

Randy didn't want to think about it again, but that panicky night came pushing in, and the dampness of his ODs became the deadly ocean wet of Oran Bay. The tiny, onetime coast guard boats hauling a special force of the 6th Armored Infantry from Scotland had done their job, smashed through the guard chain, and barreled into the harbor itself. The damned things had played fishing cork all the weary way, hanging to the rim of the huge invasion convoy, bouncing and leaping and beating the hell out of seasick troops trapped scared in the cockleshells.

Think of the honor, the captain said: You'll be the first troops into the town; the rangers won't get any farther than Arzew, but *you'll* take the surrender of French troops in Oran.

Honor, shit; surrender, more shit. The French battleship *Jean Bart* and assorted destroyers along the docks blew the cockleshells out of the water. Cold water, so fucking cold, and the long quay offering refuge, offering life—if it weren't for the machine guns strung along it. The choppy water jumped with vicious little white geysers as Foreign Legion gunners zeroed in on struggling, drowning GIs.

What was left of assault companies of the 6th Armored was

taken prisoner that still dark morning of November 8. Shaken, sickened by the senseless carnage they'd blundered into, Randy and Shriver and a handful of others sat guarded and somehow guilty until American tanks roared into the city two days later. Then their Arab guards and French officers took off, but not before grinning and trying to shake hands. Randy had never wanted to kill anybody before, but he was already sick of killing and of the hate beginning to grow in him. The French hadn't *had* to fight, goddammit. They could have given up their bullshit and welcomed the GIs, like G-2 said. Right away they'd been armed with U.S. equipment and sent north to fight Rommel's Afrika Korps. They didn't *have* to butcher GIs first, the bastards. *Liberté, Egalité, Fraternité* . . . bullshit.

"Well," Shriver said, "guess I'll be gettin' back to my own company. Ain't no *big* hole like this, but it's home. Some asshole'll be sproutin' a fever blister or wantin' a magic pill for the GI shits." He snuffed his cigarette, hunched deeper into his raincoat, and said, "Take care, Parker."

"Yeah," Randy said. "You too."

The 88's flat scream tailed its explosion. Shriver was down outside the hole, but as Randy climbed out, the man leaped up and zigzagged full speed down the ridge. There was no more time to watch; other 88 shells landed in the company area, whipping around shards of rock and hissing steel.

"Medic—medic!"

Oh Christ, casualties. Aid kits banging his thighs, Randy ran toward the cries and flinched at the keening sibilance of incoming mortars. The krauts were up to something, maybe mounting an attack.

He found Swanson outside his hole, femur smashed and bleeding heavily. Pouring sulfanilamide into the thigh wound, he applied pressure and got a pad on, then inserted the morphine syrette.

"Medic! Goddammit—*medic!*"

"Don't leave me," Swanson said. Dirt from a mortar explosion sprayed them both. Randy said, "Crawl for my hole; you can make it."

Bronkowsky stopped one in the chest. He cursed steadily as Randy dusted the redblue hole and got it wrapped as tight as he could. Air still whistled in and out. "Shut up and press down on the bandage; crawl for my hole. It's better protected."

His own medical practice; oh, goody. Small arms and automatic weapons fire crackled around him, and pieces of Tunisian real estate kept blowing in Randy's face. Medic! Medic!

He had to drag the third guy back, resting for breath every few yards. Sergeant Taferelli had taken shrapnel right through his helmet, and Randy damned near vomited at the sight of splintered white bone and gray oozings. Somehow he got it all covered and hauled the big, pale man back to his improvised aid station.

Whap!!

Ears ringing, Randy spat dirt and fought for air. Close one; near miss. Inches from his nose, a line of bullets speared the ground. Taferelli! Where was—there, he had him; one more pull and one more and—suddenly he rolled into his expanded hole, scraping his cheek as Taferelli fell heavily atop him.

"Dammit, you guys help—"

Three others in the hole besides them; Randy didn't know where Fawcett came from, hardly recognized him. The corporal cradled an arm that tried to flop the wrong way. "Make some room for the sergeant," Randy said. "Dig that side deeper. Wait a minute, Fawcett. You got a hole in that arm, too?"

"Damned if I know. It's kind of numb. Is it supposed to be that numb?"

"Let's see—"

He worked steadily, deftly, but not mechanically; Randy was conscious of each inch of bruised skin, every touch of torn flesh. He knew the ragged metal that slashed the air and ripped at the rim of his aid station. He felt the cold and fear and smelled the mud, the blood pain, the acrid smoke. These were his guys, his patients; they were already out of action; why couldn't the krauts let them be?

"Parker—watch it!—son of a bitch!—"

The carbine singed his ear with its blast. Swanson thumbed out the empty clip, fumbled for a full one. "Jesus, oh, Jesus —they're all over the fuckin' hill! Get us outa here, medic. Come on, *get us outa here!*"

"I can't," Randy said, staring at the upper torso of a dead German, half in, half out of the hole. A machine pistol dangled from limp fingers of a dirty hand.

It was funny to be thinking of her hands, here. Maybe when the mind couldn't absorb any more fear and shock, it pulled back to good memories, Randy thought. His fingers were busy plugging new holes in Taferelli's shoulder. Wanda's hands were the softest he ever knew, so clean and small and delicate, but they knew every tingling place on a man's body. Maybe they even caressed the mind; it felt like that.

"I had this girl in Oran," he said across to Bronkowsky. "I was the luckiest bastard in the First Armored Division, First Infantry, too. While the rest of you guys were lining up at whorehouses, I had this French girl."

Bronkowsky stared. "What the *fuck* are you talkin' about?"

It was so beautiful with her, all it was supposed to be. It wasn't that way with Martha, who made everything dirty and bitchy, who made him feel there had to be something better, even if that had to be with another man.

But Wanda, every French word sensuous off her tongue, that busy, knowing tongue that could reach all the way into his soul; Wanda, who moaned to him of wonders he made her feel, of his strength and vitality—ah, Wanda!

The aid station rocked again, all the world teetering crazily in thunderspouts of steel and dust and smoke.

She was more than loveliness there in Oran, more than cleanliness and romance. She was assurance, proof of his *rightness*, and with her he had learned an important lesson —that by making a woman happy, he made himself happy —and loved.

BLAMMM!

He spit wet dirt and tried to hold on to Wanda, to the silken feel of her body and the gripping of long slim legs, tried to keep the cushioning of her breasts against him. She was the first woman he ever loved, the first woman who loved *him*.

He couldn't hear through the roaring in his ears, and they kept trying to throw him off the earth.

Love, Randy thought; he spoke of love and beauty and a great passion. Who'd ever have thought high school French would come in so handy? She was trim and sleek and so pretty, with dark, questing eyes and hair like windblown night. Wanda Leblanc, accidently met, so fortunately recognized, for she was just as lonely, just as seeking.

Rapraprapppp!!

"Fuckin' Schmeisser," Swanson said. "They won't shoot no medic, will they? They won't shoot no wounded?"

Wanda had a husband somewhere in Spain, if he was alive. She hadn't heard in nearly two years. She was soft and so very clean, and he found he could make her laugh, push back the shadow in her eyes. She laughed at his schoolboy French, and learned English phrases quicker than he could believe.

Three days after Oran fell, she led him to her room on the Rue de Revolution, just past the Arab quarters, where rent was still cheap. She worked for the coastal railway, and sometimes went out of town, to Relizane or all the way to Algiers. He didn't care what she did; she could whore or spy for the krauts; Randy didn't care. Not after she gave him the wide, clean bed and her glowing self in it.

"Oh, God, oh, God, oh, God."

Randy stared. How could Taferelli talk, with that great hole in his head?

"They're gonna kill us all," Bronkowsky said. "Maybe if I hide this weapon—"

A grenade arced into the aid station, a potato masher spinning end over end. Randy caught up its wooden handle and pitched it back over the rim of the hole. The explosion kicked dirt back over them.

"Oh, God," moaned Taferelli, "oh, God."

Wanda gave all herself to him those two marvelous days and nights. She was beautiful and generous and real, taking him into her hotsweet flesh gladly, joyfully. He loved her then, for all she gave and let him give. He loved her mouth, tasting of geraniums, her pointed little nipples redbrown and erectile, her belly smooth, her curlyfluff mound, and there was manhood in the enchanted depths of her cunt, strong manhood, sure and undeniable.

"My other arm!" Fawcett screamed. "The cocksuckers blew off my other arm!"

Blood everywhere; smoke and dirt and so damned much pain nobody could make it go away, not even God. Where was He, anyway?

"Oh, God, oh, God—"

You're being paged.

"Son of a motherfuckin' bitch—"

So is somebody else.

Rapraprappp! Rapraprappp!

The German plunged over the rim of the hole, machine pistol firing a wild burst. Randy jumped up and kicked him in the head, so that the man's helmet flew off. The German came to one knee, Schmeisser wobbling and head lolling.

"No!" Randy's scream tore his throat. "No! They're wounded . . . my patients . . . no, you bastard!"

And he took the entrenching tool stuck in the mud wall of his aid station and damned near cut off the kraut's head with it. They were all over the place then, firing and grabbing, and Randy stood among them, swinging and clubbing, swinging and clubbing. The gory little shovel rose and fell, slashed and circled. Something hit him on the forehead and he lost his own helmet. Something else crashed into his hip and he went down, but only for a moment.

Then he was back up, mauling and tearing. He couldn't see for the blood, couldn't breathe for the smoke or hear for the yelling, the guns. His arms were so tired, so very tired, and he kept falling over guys. Where the hell did they all come from? Medic, medic!

"Here," he grated, tasting salty fluid in his mouth. "Here I am, but I'm—only—a—medic . . . I'm not—not God!"

And finally his arms gave out and his hip locked or something, and Randy fell into the swirling red haze that had been pulling at him forever.

There was dirt in his mouth, gritty along his teeth. He tried to push it out with his tongue, but couldn't. It might be muddy shit, bloody shit. Oh, God, oh, God—

He couldn't feel his legs, his lower belly. He was numb, and getting stiffer. Why was it so goddamn quiet? Hey, medic, is it supposed to be so numb? Hey, medic, medic—what the hell do I know?

Wanda Leblanc I love you. I'm not queer and you proved it. I love you, Wanda, but where are you now? Where am I? *Am* I, *am* I?

One ear was blank, jammed into mud, and the other was dimming. Randy heard somebody; the voice was familiar but he was unable to pinpoint it: "Jesus, Lieutenant—wouldja look at that? I mean, we got here as fast as we could, after them fuckin' krauts hit, but—Jesus, what a mess."

Another voice, farther away; Lieutenant Somebody, slipping farther away: "Is anybody alive?"

"Couple of 'em, I guess. Parker set up his aid station here and—"

"Is *he* alive?"

"Can't say. But look at all the dead krauts. Looks like he beat 'em to death with a shovel. A fuckin' *shovel*, Lieutenant."

Randy stopped listening.

chapter 33

Seventeen year old Elvira Tayloe has been arrested
by federal agents and charged with defrauding the
government. Hostess in a local nightclub, she
married six sailors shipping out from the naval base
here. This "Allotment Annie," who drew $50 per
month from each of her "husbands," was uncovered
when two of them met by chance in an English pub
and compared photographs. . . .

—Norfolk, Virginia, November 14, 1942 (UP)

Her mouth was gummy and her head throbbed. One opened
eye caused her to flinch at the light. Carefully, Louise sat up
and pressed knuckles against her temples.

He slept on his back, mouth open and snoring—Jimmy,
Johnny, whoever. His snore was harsh and irritating, not like
Danny's soft breathing. Oh, Christ—Danny.

Out of bed, she barely made it to the toilet. Only yellow
stuff burned its way up and out. She sat awhile on the seat, chin
in hand. How long this time—a week, two? Not that time
mattered, or anything else. It just helped some if she knew
where she was.

After bathing her face, she found a toothbrush she didn't
remember and used it, then pulled a wet comb through her

hair. Back at the hotel bed she didn't remember either, she stared down at Jimmy-Johnny. He'd turned over and gone quiet, and wasn't bad looking—a little old, maybe.

Her eyes searched the room and found the pint on the dresser, nearly full. The ice bowl held water beside smeared glasses and a Coke gone flat. She choked down a big swallow of Four Roses and chased it quick with the Coke. It stayed down and she lit a cigarette from a crumpled pack of Chesterfields. If her stomach didn't rebel, in a few minutes she'd have another drink and it would all get better. Not good, but better than this miserable, lonely fucking world had a right to be.

Sitting on the room's only chair, she watched him wake with a hard on and stumble into the bathroom. At least he closed the door. Louise took that other drink before he came out and started another smoke, feeling closer to human.

She was wishing for another Coke, a cold one, when he came smiling out. "Morning, darling. Good morning, Mrs. Noskoff."

That was his name—Noskoff. Billy Noskoff, from somewhere in Pennsylvania. *Somewhere in Pennsylvania*, like the newspapers were always saying *somewhere in North Africa*, or *somewhere in the South Pacific* . . .

Mrs. Noskoff?

"Ah, Billy—"

He was beside her, bending to kiss her cheek, cradling her head against his ribcage. He was still hard. "Kinda early to be hitting that bottle, ain't it, baby? Oh, what the hell. It's a celebration, right? Our honeymoon. Hot damn—the guys'll never believe ol' Noskoff finally got hooked, and to the prettiest, hottest girl in the country. Hot damn."

"Hooked?" Desperately, Louise tried to bring the immediate past into sharper focus. She didn't even remember meeting Billy, only being with him here and there—Carmel beach, Alvarado Street, even that hillbilly joint in Seaside.

"Just an expression, like. Everybody says a guy gets hooked when he gets married. It don't mean nothing. Hot damn—I'm real glad you married me."

When, where? You had to wait three days in Monterey County after the blood tests. Would the army do it quicker? Had a GI chaplain—oh, God, she had to cut down on her drinking. Louise saw his blouse draped across the foot of the bed: sergeant's stripes, Fort Ord's training command patch, the same Danny had worn.

Grabbing the bottle, she said, "Here's to us, then—and we'd better get some Cokes and ice." She blamed her tears on the whiskey. You couldn't cry for anything else, all you could do was hate.

"In a little," Billy Noskoff breathed. "Ain't no big hurry, right?" His hands stroked her hair and she felt the pulse of his cock along her cheek. Shit—first thing in the morning.

She snatched herself up and away. "No big hurry for *anything*, right? You going to get me some Coke and ice or not?"

Startled, he dropped his hands to cover his crotch and took a backward step. "Why—I—sure, baby, if that's what my little wife wants, that's what she gets."

The son of a bitch owed her, she thought. He had no right to booze it up, to dance and laugh and strut around in his uniform. The fucking army had no right to stay alive, and the goddamn country owed her too. Ten thousand insurance dollars? What the hell was that? It wouldn't pay for one softly curled hair on his head; his poor, poor head.

"Goddamn right; hot damn right," Louise Parker-Barton-Orr-Noskoff said. "I goddamn well deserve everything I can get."

George Parker felt uncomfortable in his own store. Elizabeth had changed things all around, and it looked different, woman-ish, not like a hardware store ought to. No puffy curtains at the window or anything like that, but feminine, although he couldn't put a finger on the cause.

Besides, although Elizabeth was talking to him again, it wasn't about anything consequential. Like Ron; something was bad wrong with their son, more than his lost hand, but she wouldn't discuss that. If he tried to say something about Ron sleeping all day and drinking away the night, she went quiet and stared at him. He knew then that she hadn't forgiven him for the thing with Holly Melborne. Maybe she never would, but, by God, that oughtn't interfere with them doing something about their boy's life before he threw away the rest of it.

"I—well, I came to tell you I'm going on the night shift," he said. "They need workers around the clock, if we're going to win this war, and—well, it's not like we're losing each other's company."

Elizabeth's hands were resting upon the counter next to the register. She'd moved a stool behind there, where he always stood, waiting customers. "All right," she said. "I'll leave lunch out, as always. Now you'll want coffee too, so I'll bring home a thermos."

Behind him the entry bell tinked, so he moved to one side and said quickly, "Is that all, dammit?"

"Is what all?" Elizabeth looked beyond him. "Ron—how nice."

George looked at the boy. Ron hadn't changed that hook, and there wasn't all that cause to wear it instead of the false hand. It was as if he were flaunting his handicap, blaming everybody else for it.

"Hi." Ron's eyes were red and he hadn't shaved. "Just thought I'd drop by and see how you're doing, Mom. Need any help around here?"

George said, "Help? With shortages of everything, and—"

"That's thoughtful of you, son." Elizabeth came quickly from behind the counter, hands outstretched. "I sure do. The stockroom is such a mess, and if you could lend me some muscle—"

What the hell was she doing, trying to make a liar out of him? George opened his mouth, but she warned him with one of those looks. This time he barely heard the bell clatter in the slamback of the door.

"Look here," Holly Melborne said to the three men with her, "they're most all together. Now ain't that cute?"

Elizabeth put her hands on her hips. "I told you, you don't work here anymore, and I won't have you as a customer, so just get on out."

The girl looked hard at George, and he felt his face heating up. She said, "These here're my brothers, *Mister* Parker. Don't matter which is which, 'cause they're all of the same mind. They don't want their baby sister pushed around."

Ron said then, in the lazy, arrogant way that rubbed people wrong, "Pushed *around*, Holly? Don't you mean *over*, like in push*over*?"

One of the Melbornes started forward, but Holly put a hand

on his arm and said, "Not now, Buster. First this old bastard and his old woman got to do right by me. They got to pay me good for what he did to me."

George swallowed. "I offered you money once, but you wanted—"

"Oh," she smiled. "Oh, *Mister* Parker, that price has gone way up. What's it worth to a big churchman, so everybody don't know he got a young girl pregnant?"

George heard his wife draw a sharp, pained breath. He shook his head. "You—you could have come to me on the quiet, Holly. I—I'll do my duty, pay for my sins. There was no reason for you to hurt my—Mrs. Parker, and my son."

There was triumph in her voice. "Five thousand dollars I want. Enough to get out of this crummy town before anybody else finds out and my reputation gets ruined."

"Reputation?" Ron laughed.

George said, "Boy, dammit! Don't antagonize her."

And Elizabeth said, almost whispering, "We don't have that kind of money."

Holly giggled and nudged her closest brother. "Expected you'd say that, big store owners and all. But you're goin' to get it up, borrow or beg it, I don't give a damn. Just get it up damn quick. *Mrs*. Parker—you were so righteous, stompin' in here to fire me and all. Don't it do me good to see you squirm? You still teach Sunday school, *Mrs*. Parker?"

"That's enough," George said. "I—I'll get in touch, but that's enough now. Get out of here."

"Shit," Buster Melborne said. "Baby sister can talk long's she wants, anywheres she wants."

Maybe he didn't really mean to; maybe the stricken look on Elizabeth's face forced it. George swung a fist into Buster's leering face, and the grimy man hit him back, hard. Surprisingly, George didn't go down, even if he tasted a split lip.

Then Ron was among them, swift and silent, frightening in his mute savagery and fluid expertise. George kind of fell forward and held on to Buster while Ron beat down the other two, his shiny hook blurring. It was so fast, George was struggling to get in another punch when Buster grunted and slid down.

"I guess you could've handled him yourself," Ron said, "but it's quicker this way." He spun to Holly, who shrank back against the near empty electric wares case. "Look, girl—find another town and another sucker. You get nothing here but trouble."

His hook gestured at the two men lying flat, one pushing up to sit with blood running down his face. "Next time I'll stick this thing through their guts. *You*, pregnant? If you weren't sterile, you'd already be dragging a convoy of little bastards. Hell, you've been screwing since you were twelve."

She moistened full lips. "Ron Parker, if you think—"

"I think you're going to leave town right away. Or I come hunting these no good bums." Buster wavered up and Ron dropped him with the good hand. George barely saw the punch. "Right, Buster?"

"Godsakes, Holly," Buster mumbled. "You never said *he*—"

"Okay!" she flared. "Okay, you bastards. Quick enough when you thought you could make some money, but run into a little trouble—"

Another Melborne sat up and looked around in a daze. He saw Ron and began crawling for the door. Holly said, "I was leavin' anyway. Knocked up by this old fart? Hell, he don't have the juice for it."

When they were gone, George didn't look directly at Elizabeth. Even though there'd been no blackmail, this made everything worse, ripped the scab right off the wound. He put a handkerchief to his mouth.

Ron said, "You did all right."

"I *did* need help with Buster."

"No you didn't. You were choking him good."

"That right?"

Elizabeth slapped the countertop. "Oh, for goodness' sake! You two act like—like I don't know what! As if violence fixes everything, as if—oh, go to *hell*!"

George stared as she swept out of the store, and Ron said, "First time Mom ever cursed."

"Not quite," George said. "She had some words for me, earlier."

"Yeah. Bad cut?"

George shook his head. "You hurt?"

"Those bums? Nah." They were quiet a moment, then Ron said, "All that war work you were doing; who's got it now?"

"You mean the scrap metal drives, the grease collecting, War Stamps, things like that? Nobody, I guess. It's more important to work in the defense plant. *I* feel better about it, anyway."

Ron moved to the register counter and rested a hip against it. "Think I'll have a shot at it. Don't feel up to working in a plant just yet. Never did, you know, and with this—" he cupped the steel hook with his good hand. "It'll be outside work where I can talk to people. Maybe I can still give guys like Randy a hand." He grinned. "Not this one, though."

George smiled back. This boy—no, this young man—was straightening up. "You're not—disgusted with your old man for—for—you know?"

Ron laughed. "*Me*, of all guys? Hell, no, Dad."

"Thanks, son. I—well, thanks for not judging me."

His boy's face was still. "And thanks for not still judging me."

David Shepsel fought the controls as his Thunderbolt skidded across flak torn sky. As the horizon wheeled past, he saw flame and smoke where a B-17 bomber had gone in, saw himself cooking like that if he couldn't kick his plane out of the sickening spin.

Then the canopy stuck, and he struggled with that, hammering the damned thing with gloved fists as fatal seconds ticked past, each flinging him faster and harder toward the earth. Smoke poured into the cockpit and David tried to pray, but the words got mixed with curses at the canopy.

Blessedly then, he was whirling in the air, spinning free and safe, thank you God safe, as he found the ripcord handle. The chute purled up, up above him, the most beautiful sight ever, its ballooning *pop!* the music of life.

Penduluming down, David tried to steer away from French farmhouses, working the shroudlines as he'd been taught. But the wind was ignorant and carried him where it willed. There —far across the hedgerows, came a wink of redwhite light that had to be his P-47 crashing. His, or another casualty of an unlucky mission. Straining around over one shoulder, he could barely make out the target and its tenting of drifting flak puffs. Between it and him, dark plumes marked the pyres of American bombers downed by antiaircraft fire or German fighters. The Messerschmitt 109s and 110s had slashed down out of the sun, just as a flight of Focke-Wulfs lifted from a camouflaged airport below. There had been too many of them.

Dead trees clawed jagged tops up at David, and he twisted desperately, sawed frantically at his lines as the chute spilled air. Then he was beyond that danger and into another, slamming into hard green things that snatched his air and raked his face. Spiraling down through cracking branches, he was jerked upward—hung helpless on some high limb.

No! It snapped and let him plunge for the ground. He just got his knees bent when he hit, and starshells burst behind his eyes. Hurry—ticktick—hurry; follow Standard Operating Procedure—ticktick—hit the release button, roll out of the harness. Hurry, hurry; if you can hide the chute, do it quick. Find cover, bury yourself in the bushes, under leaves, anywhere. Hurry; if you last the day, maybe you can make it to a farmhouse under cover of night. Most of the French will help a downed pilot escape. Ticktick . . . ticktick.

He couldn't rip the parachute free; it was hooked on a stub of a branch like a gigantic signpost. David gripped his .45 as he scuttled into the hedgerows of Normandy, thick and thorny brush that stabbed and barricaded him. Burrowing, panting, he worked himself deeper into the ancient, tangled growth. When he stopped for breath, he tried to figure his position from his emergency compass: somewhere in France on the return leg of an ill-fated mission. Some B-17s got through and unloaded on a German factory; maybe a few would return to England, but most were scattered across France, with their fighter cover.

Listening hard, shielded by chill and greendark shadows, David heard a far off plane, the wind, a cow lowing. Crouched low in a pocket of brush, he allowed himself a cigarette and wasn't surprised to find his hands shaking. He hadn't even seen the kraut who shot him down; too busy banging away at another Luftwaffer, and caught with his attention down. Damn! Not as I *do*, young and inexperienced flight, but as your commander *says*.

And what do you say now, trapped on the ground like some crippled bird awaiting the cat? They were coming, the Nazi soldiers; they always came quickly for pilots who might have new information, coming to kill or cage flyers for the duration.

Prisoner of war. David sucked on his cigarette and waved

away its smoke. He carried no more than regulations said: AGO card; pay book; wallet with pictures, but no addresses; dogtags.

Dogtags that identified him by name, number, and *religion*. He'd been proud of that big J stamped in the metal, a Jew fighting back. David Shepsel standing tall, not ashamed of his name: David Shepsel, Jew.

They'd kill him for it. First they would torture and degrade him, drag him through German streets for pure Aryans to spit on, castrate him so no possibility of Jewish sperm could infect an Aryan maiden. And when they tired of their baiting, their animal sport, SS troops or Gestapo executioners would hang David Shepsel, Jew, to a tree as an example to any underground survivors of the faith.

Lighting another cigarette from the butt of the first, David went through his wallet and found no contraband, no letter from Oriana that Nazi agents could use to pressure her, nothing remotely secret; nothing else with his name on it. He tore the Adjutant General's Office identity card into bits and stuffed them far down into the ground. His paybook followed, and David was careful to spread covering dirt. He held his dogtags for a moment, his six-pointed star, still warm from his skin, then buried them in another spot, buried them deep.

. . . Papa, oh, Papa—I understand now. I know why you changed your name. I'm doing the same thing, and I don't face anything like what you did to get us out of Russia. The first threat, the first idea that being a Jew might get me killed, and I cave in, I hide my Star of David with my faith. Forgive me, Papa . . .

He heard the guns first, as they fired short bursts into clumps too thick for penetration. Then he heard the dogs; they made eager, whining, snuffling noises as they darted along this row or that. David saw them flash by, their brownblack, torpedo shaped bodies all muscle and fang. His .45 was sweaty in his hand.

A German yelled, answered by another. A machine pistol ripped the far end of David's hedgerow. A dog stopped, pointed ears erect and white teeth showing.

"Hey!" David shouted. "Hey, you guys! Here I am, but

take it easy—American, okay? American *soldaten*! I—I give up."

The dog growled. Slowly, carefully, David stood up, pistol on the ground at his feet, hands reached high over his head. The German was squat and thick, and the twin metal lightnings of the elite *Schutzstaffel* winked at his collar. He stared at David over his lifted machine pistol.

chapter 34

The tragic Coconut Grove nightclub fire, which
claimed so many revelers from Boston College and
Holy Cross is rumored to have been started deliberately. This publication sees it as a Jewish plot
against Irish Catholics, and accuses owner Barnett
Welansky, a Jew. . . . .

—*Social Justice*, a tract prepared by Father Cough-
lin, November 22, 1942

Somewhere in North Africa, Jan. 31, 1943 (INS):
A column of Nazi armor, backed by Stuka dive bombers,
pounded American troops in Tunisia today. Despite heavy
losses, Americans clung to the high ground until forced to
evacuate by overwhelming odds. Commanding officers said
the winter defense line will soon be straightened. . . .

Samuel Shepherd looked from the newspaper to the telegram
beside his cash register. There was news and there was news,
and there were ways of writing it so it didn't sound too bad.
Then there was the telegram; the Adjutant General had no way
of making that good. *The War Department deeply regrets to*
inform you . . . But it didn't say *dead.* Definitely, it did not
say *dead*; it said *missing in action*. So there was a chance
David was alive; a prisoner maybe, but alive. Could be he

wasn't even wounded, much less crippled. David was a good pilot, a fine pilot with all that experience.

How long before a man knew whether his son was dead or alive? Missing in action; what did that mean—disappeared, sunk in the water, what? How could a whole airplane disappear?

He blinked and took off his glasses, then put them back on to stare at Mrs. Parker. She was saying, ". . . so sorry, Mr. Shepherd. The news gets out right away, of course. I came by to tell you that everybody is praying with you."

"So? That's nice, Mrs. Parker. I—does your daughter know? The one in Detroit?"

She frowned. "Oriana? Why should she know anything about—"

"*Nu*, they wouldn't tell her, only me. My David and your Oriana—he wrote about her, Mrs. Parker."

"Oriana never said. Were they—are they—serious? Oh—we wouldn't know, of course. Oh, Lord, first Clay—her husband, Clay—and now David. She should come home."

"Yes, children should be at home."

"Why," Mrs. Parker said, "she wouldn't even recognize the name if she sees it on casualty lists. A misprint: Shep*sel*, they said, instead of Shep*herd*. Everybody here knows who it is, of course, but—"

"No misprint," Sam said. "It's his name, my name. We are Jews, Mrs. Parker. David wasn't ashamed, and changed his name back for the army."

"Well," she said, "I think that's very brave."

"Yes," he said. "Excuse me, please." He walked around her to reach the storeroom, his ladder, and a can of paint. She was on the sidewalk when he came out into the icy wind, and he felt her watch him climb.

It wasn't neat, and he was no sign painter, only a yardgoods merchant, only a tired, frightened old man with cold hands. But when he painted over SHEPHERD and squeezed in SHEPSEL, nobody could be mistaken: SHEPSEL & SON.

When he stood down and looked up at his sign, Mrs. Parker clapped. Two women passing looked at them like they were *meshuggah*, but Samuel Shepsel didn't mind; he was proud, a new feeling.

Elizabeth unlocked and entered her own store, flushed by cold and excitement. She'd never understood why Jews might think they would be persecuted here, of all places, but perhaps there were some prejudiced folks around. Especially, she thought, among those hillbillies come up from the Southern mountains. Still, Mr. Shep*sel* had done a brave thing, what with his son shot down and all.

She knew how he felt, receiving that awful telegram. There should be a better way of wording it; the message was practically the same for killed, missing, or wounded. In all cases it was a shock.

Her own sons—but now one was safely home, and without guilt she thanked God for that, while she prayed for the other's well being. No day or night passed that she didn't breathe a few words for Randy—and for Ron to get over his horrible loss.

She hadn't prayed over George, not one bit. Her heart was hard there, because it was every bit his fault. Maybe the Lord could excuse George Parker for what he had done, but she couldn't. At least, she amended as she took a deep look into her soul, at least not now.

She turned on the store radio, for everybody listened to the news these days. It wasn't all that good. There'd been all that excitement when the Second Front opened, although Josef Stalin didn't call it that. At first there was only jubilation, for the army found little resistance, and surely, as President Roosevelt said, this would cause the Axis powers to reconsider their aggression.

Then things slowed down as the Germans counterattacked in Tunisia. Randy's few letters home had only complained of the cold, and even if it seemed odd that wild and jungled Africa should be cold, she immediately sent him thick socks and gloves and a wool scarf. Elizabeth hoped with all her heart that nothing would happen to Randy, that he'd somehow be sent home soon. But not like Ron, dear God, not like Ron.

Turning from dreary thoughts, she opened a catalog. If the store was to be kept profitable, she had to find things to sell. So much was considered vital war material, and she didn't resent things going to the boys in service. Still, there had to be ways around shortages, local folks who could build, say, sinks and tubs out of scrap not needed for defense. Old man Rensett could make creditable beds and chairs, for instance, and wood wasn't in short supply.

It was like working those crossword puzzles in *Ranch Romances*; you simply had to figure what made sense to fill the spaces. Elizabeth could see herself a year from now, two years, though the war shouldn't last that long. She could have the store expanded into furniture, knock out that east wall, put in more lights. It was an interesting game, and she was finding she was good at it.

She couldn't just sit and wait; she had to do something now. Sam Shepherd—Shepsel—waited for news of his missing son; if things were serious, Oriana would have to wait too. But Elizabeth had to *do* something. Working on the store would keep her from dwelling on the rupture of her marriage.

Oriana; she had to let her daughter know about David. That was something else that couldn't be held back. Elizabeth brought out her address book and looked up the phone number.

That was when the Western Union boy walked in, carrying another telegram.

George Parker stood back from his machine and wiped sweat from his face. His back ached and his arms were weary, but he'd never felt better. He was showing them that determination meant more than age, that he could work double shifts as well as any kid.

By now used to the stink of synthetic rubber, he pictured the tires—*his* tires—on a jeep or a command car roaring for the front. The other wing of the plant turned out bigger stuff for deuce-and-a-half trucks, for the front ends of halftracks. It was a good feeling, to be doing something directly for the boys. Making guns or planes or tanks would be better, but that would mean leaving home, and he wasn't ready for that.

And the money—George glanced up at the wall clock—he felt guilty, making so much money per hour. But everyone else was doing it, and the harder and longer people worked, the quicker the war would be won. He was saving every nickel, putting it all into War Bonds. After the war, the kids would be well off even if the store went bankrupt, with Elizabeth running it into the ground.

Let her; when his War Bonds matured, he could start up

again, and maybe she'd learn her lesson and go back to the kitchen. It was all right for women to work in war plants because the country needed them, what with men gone to fight. But when Hitler, Mussolini, and Tojo were whipped, *good* workers would come back.

Even Ron; it was good to see the boy taking hold. The kid was really fighting for the country in another way; Tuscarawas County had never been combed so thoroughly for scrap and tires and whatever else the nation needed. Ron had Boy Scouts and 4-H youngsters working for him, selling as many War Stamps as they picked up pots and pans. He showed fine aptitude for organization, and folks were starting to forget what a hellion he'd been, remembering only that he was now a wounded hero still doing his part.

Oriana, Joyce—even if the whispers about her and that man were true—Randy overseas; all his children were doing their best for the war effort. Only little Louise—he shook his head and concentrated upon his machine; the girl had gone bad, or crazy. The last time old man Barton had talked to him, it was to inform him that Roger had filed for divorce. As if George gave a damn. He'd rather have the kid home. He could hope for that much.

A hand tapped his shoulder; George turned to look into his foreman's face.

At the train station, Steve Canfield picked up the new generator for his truck, and a boxful of spare parts for other vehicles, impossible for most people to get. It was good to be next to somebody as important as the Butera boy. Through his jobs on the city council and draft board, his positions as Defense Coordinator and such, he could pass on tidbits of information to Frank Butera. The boy always reciprocated, like the time he loaned five thousand dollars, interest free, so Steve could pick up those tax lots near the Lafayette County line. All Steve had to do was trade one to Butera and the debt was paid; he was home free with a valuable piece of property. There'd been other deals since, and Canfield was well on his way to becoming a wealthy man. Nothing like Butera, but rich enough. Smart enough, too; he meant to keep a good hold on the boy's coattails, because if anybody in Coshocton was going places, it was Frank Butera.

Too bad Joyce Parker was hanging around him, but maybe that could be fixed, or used. Steve wasn't about to forget what her sister had done to him. That bitch would pay, if it took the rest of his life and all his money, she'd pay. She would come crawling to him, those big tits hanging down and her fine ass swinging, and she'd beg him—*beg* him—to take her, to please fuck her.

One way or another, war or peace, Steve Canfield would see to that.

Joyce struggled to get her new desk in place. The steel company office wasn't bright and open like the new shoe factory, but she could make it passable. The trouble was, Franco didn't help and brushed off her requests. She hardly saw him now, usually in passing or when he stumbled into bed.

He worked so hard, so *hard* since his father had those animals attack him. She still thought he should have called the police, used his legal rights, do anything but just take his defeat. You don't know what the hell you're talking about, so just shut up, he said.

And she did, determined to show him she could work as hard, as efficiently as he could. He needed her for more than a romp in bed, dammit, and from now on she would show him how much.

The phone rang; it was her mother.

Ron Parker sniffed the winter air for something indefinable. Something ought to be there, but he didn't know what. He was restless again, but not quite in the old way. He worked hard and said excuse my hand so others wouldn't feel too uncomfortable about it, and ran around the county so much he ought to fall dead tired into bed at night. But he didn't, and Randy was on his mind.

Flinging himself into his father's old truck, he rattled on past the Upper Basin and over the dirt road to Route 76, turning left at the edge of Lake Park. Before, when something nameless made him this edgy, he'd go for a bar and trouble. Now he just wanted to get home. Randy, combat medic with the First Armored; Christ, that was the only job rougher than an infantryman's. Medics had to answer the call, get out there where the bullets were whipping and patch up the wounded, or try to haul them back. Front line infantry looked down on every other branch of service, but damned well respected combat medics.

Ron frowned into the windshield as he turned right again, onto 16. What the hell did he know about combat, except what he'd been told? Big, bad Ron Parker, terror of the ginmills, but when the chips were down, where was he? Over the hill, drunk and hurting while his outfit got ready for the invasion of North Africa.

"Shit," he said to his non-combat lost hand, his war hero wound, and goosed the old truck for home. He'd swap places with Randy if he could. Randy never wanted to fight, even though he wasn't all that serious about his new religious convictions. That wild eyed bitch wife had brought on all that crap, but still, Randy didn't belong in war's bloody messes. Not that he'd back off; his brother would never do that. Randy was just a lot more sensitive than your average Joe. If he claimed to be a conscientious objector, that was what he meant.

Pulling into the yard, Ron saw lights in the house, though it wasn't dark yet. Pushed by dark foreboding, he set the handbrake and left the truck while it squealed to a stop.

Franco Butera kept moving while he waited. He was like the country itself, plunging on because it must, waiting with bated breath to see if its soldiers held up in Tunisia, in the South Pacific, if its planes held up against the Luftwaffe and the Emperor's Zeroes, if the merchant marine could outlast sinkings by wolfpacks of U-boats.

But his waiting was secure, because Franco *knew*. Time and the war were on his side, and if the Axis gained a few more big wins, so much the better. The country needed everything he produced, and paid handsomely for it. All he must do is not slow down, to get all that cost-plus-ten-percent he could, reach high and spread wide. When the waiting was over, he would be the biggest man in Tuscarawas County, if not in Ohio.

What the hell did one lousy shoe factory mean? He called the steel company shop, but his private line was busy.

Giuseppe Butera waited too. Not only for the war to be won, but for the return of his only son.

And Mary Joann—Scooter—Canfield was impatient for spring vacation. After Christmas was the longest time of the year, and she hadn't seen her mom for almost three weeks. Okay, so she was needed to make airplanes, like Daddy had to fight in the war, but it was like losing both of them.

Downstairs, she stopped as her Grandma burst through the door. It wasn't like Grammy to run.

Oriana drove straight for Coshocton, still in coveralls. Her mother got through at the plant because it was an emergency, and Oriana left immediately. To do what? Comfort Sam Shepherd, let him comfort her? Nobody dispensed that kind of ease.

Mom would hold her and cry. Crying wasn't enough; neither was screaming. Oriana had already tried that, screaming into the windshield with all her furious strength, but it didn't find David and bring him back.

Pushing the truck, she ignored speed limits and made for home anyhow. David wouldn't fly the next plane she welded, so it didn't matter that she was off the line. He might not fly again. But he wasn't dead; she wouldn't allow herself to think *dead*. Not for David; not ever for David.

It was dusk when she rolled into the front yard and climbed wearily from the GMC. Wind caught her jacket as she trudged up the walk toward lights and family where she could warm her hands, if not her soul.

Everybody must be home; a lot of people passed across the windows.

"Telegram," Elizabeth said. "I got the telegram first, then the phone started ringing, and it was Washington, D.C. I couldn't believe it—Washington, D.C."

George said, "For God's sake, Elizabeth. All the foreman said was emergency, my son—and I didn't know which one until I saw Ron—"

"Dad," Ron said, "Oriana's here."

"What's all this?" she asked. "Gathering of the clan, what? Oh, God, not—not Randy too?"

"No, no!" Elizabeth waved the telegram. "Not like that. It's Randy, all right—but good news, wonderful news! Your brother's coming home. He—he was wounded, but he'll be all right and he's coming home!"

Softly, Ron said, "To receive the Congressional Medal of Honor from the President himself. Randy Parker and the Medal of Honor. I told you; I told everybody about Randy, but nobody listened."

"President Roosevelt," George said.

And Joyce: "My brother, decorated by the President."

"That's great," Oriana said. "That's just great."

Then she began to cry.

Bestselling Books for Today's Reader — From Jove!